MURDER MOST MOZART

Frank was panting now, his hands rising to claw at the unbearable constriction in his chest, in his throat. But he turned to stumble through the piles of clothes and books, the half-emptied duffel, the stray coffee cup, toward the cabin's screen door. He didn't want to die alone.

He swayed and grabbed at the door lintel, his heart careening, his vision beginning to dim. From his swollen mouth came a strangled sound, something between a sob and a groan. Who had he thought would hear him anyway, and what good if they did?

Someone had wanted him to die. Someone so fearful of the Truth that they would kill to deny it. Faces swam before him, and conversations. Then one came into focus and he felt an overwhelming need to bear witness. He had to tell someone, anyone, but he could no longer speak. If only he had a pencil!

Almost detached now, he felt himself sinking to the floor. His hand was pressing against something hard and flat. It was the score of *Così fan tutte*. He stared at it, the letters on its cardboard cover wavering in and out of focus. In a final flash of clarity, they came together and he saw what they were telling him. Just before his hand went slack, he pressed with his thumbnail on the cover, forming a crude *X* across the name: Amadeus.

DEATH OF A BARITONE

KAREN STURGES

BANTAM BOOKS
NEW YORK TORONTO LONDON SYDNEY AUCKLAND

DEATH OF A BARITONE

A Bantam Book

Grateful acknowledgment to reprint the following excerpts from *Così fan tutte* by W. A. Mozart, text by Lorenzo da Ponte, English translation by Ruth and Thomas Martin. Copyright © 1951 (renewed) by G. Schirmer, Inc. (ASCAP). International copyright secured. All rights reserved. Reprinted by permission.

ISBN 0-7394-0702-3

FOR BILL

... ALWAYS

ACKNOWLEDGMENTS

There's nothing like writing a novel for discovering how much you don't know. The following people were generous with their time and expertise in answering my many questions, and I acknowledge them with gratitude:

Adrienne Auerswald for making sure I didn't commit any major musical gaffes; Donald Chrisman for advising on medical facts; and for further invaluable assistance, Giovanna Bellesia, Ange DiBenedetto, Dorothy King, Kenneth Pease, Sharon Rust, Ellen Schleicher, Thomas Scott, and Paul Serio. If I've gotten anything wrong, it was in spite of their efforts.

For their support and encouragement, my thanks go to my husband, William Sturges, my children, Nathan Hood and Morgan Lindley, and my brother, Jay Duke; to Marijane Meaker and the Ashawagh Hall Writers' Workshop; to Deborah Hecht and Julia Aldrich; and to Anne Eliot Crompton, author and lifelong friend, for her patience and her sage advice.

Thanks to my wonderful agent, Ruth Kagle, and my discriminating editor, Stephanie Kip.

And thanks, lastly, to happy summer memories of the Seagle Colony in Schroon Lake, New York, which, of course, resembles the Varovna Colony only in its most delightful aspects.

THE VAROVNA OPERA COLONY
presents

COSÌ FAN TUTTE

—⟳—

Music by WOLFGANG AMADEUS MOZART
Libretto by LORENZO DA PONTE
English translation by RUTH AND THOMAS MARTIN

Cast of Characters

FIORDILIGI	Amanda St. James
Sisters, living in Naples	
DORABELLA	Rita Michaels
FERRANDO *Officer, betrothed to Dorabella*	Stefan Kowalski
GUGLIELMO *Officer, betrothed to Fiordiligi*	Chris Fox
DESPINA *Chambermaid to the Ladies*	Jennifer Allen
DON ALFONSO *An old Philosopher*	Jason Lee Jones

Soldiers, Servants, Wedding Guests:

students of the Anna Varovna Opera Colony

Music Director and Pianist	Laurence Peterson
Stage Director and Designer	Theodore Morse
Costume Coordinator	Gerta Hofstetter
Box Office	Phoebe Mullins

This production of COSÌ FAN TUTTE *is dedicated to
the memory of our dear friend and gifted colleague* FRANK PALERMO

PREVIEW

I cannot utter a whisper,
I cannot draw a breath.

Così fan tutte, act 1, scene 15

TUESDAY, JUNE 19

BECAUSE HE WAS STUDYING SO INTENTLY, HE MISSED THE SIG-
nificance of the first telltale symptoms. Not that it would
have made a difference. From the moment the white pill
had slid with such innocuous ease off the back of his
tongue and down to the moist and industrious cavity of
his stomach, he had been as good as dead.

He sat propped on the narrow bed (unmade—ah
well, he'd get to it later), his back against the white-
painted headboard, knees bent to support the vocal score
of *Così fan tutte*. Size 12 Reeboks were planted half on the
sheet, half on the rumpled blue spread. The fingers of
one hand pressed themselves to his forehead, from time
to time combing back abstractedly through a mass of
curling dark hair. The other hand thumped out a rhythm
against his thigh. "*Dum*-dum *Dum*-di-dum, *Dum Dum,*
Dum di-di," he muttered. "No, dammit—di-di dum di-
di—shoot, I won't have it by rehearsal, that's for sure."

It was a cardinal fault with him—procrastination.
One he'd confessed often enough to the other Children of Truth. "We understand, Frank," they'd said, "we
know you're fighting it, we know you'll win in the end."
And then, in a soft chorus: "The Truth shall set you free."

Now, in the absence of fellow Children and the sure knowledge that his fellow singers would take a far less tolerant attitude, Frank acknowledged to himself the truth of his failure, forgave himself, and looked around for a pencil. He'd have to carry the score onstage one more time, but at least he'd mark this place in the first-act finale that kept tripping him up. He patted futilely at his chest—oh, right, he was wearing a tank top, no pockets—did a quick visual sweep of the room, and sighed. Jeez, what a mess, he'd really have to clean up, finish unpacking. He'd do it tonight—no, tonight was for memorizing the rest of *Così*. Tomorrow night, then. Tomorrow night for sure. Now if I were a pencil . . . He swung his legs off the bed.

And froze.

Because he knew at once what was happening— what must be happening, impossible though it might seem. The sense of unease that he'd attributed to his distress over not knowing the music had grown to a heart-racing agitation. His body prickled and his face was hot. In only moments, he knew, his throat would begin to close. Jesus, he thought, I'm going to die.

He was nine years old and perched on the doctor's examining table, fighting back tears brought on by the sting of a needle plunged into his buttock. Beyond the doctor's white-coated back he could see his mother's face. She smiled at Frank while the doctor explained to her that the shot should start taking effect right away and he'd be giving her a prescription for more penicillin by mouth. As the doctor talked on, Frank began to feel funny—all hot and itchy and his heart was bumping and it felt like the inside of his mouth was swelling up. He saw his mother's expression change to concern, then horror, saw the doctor whirl around. "Christ!" the doctor said, and Frank knew something real bad was happening because doctors didn't talk like that, at least not in front of children.

Now he really wanted to cry but he couldn't, he could hardly even breathe. His mother was crying, though, and holding him, and the doctor was at the door yelling "Never in! Never in!" (only later they told him it was "epinephrine"). There was a trundling of wheels and someone forced a plastic cup over his nose and mouth. The cup was gassy and smelled of rubber and he fought, terrified, to push away the smothering thing. Then a nurse, huge in white, loomed over him, holding another needle. The doctor grabbed Frank's upper arm with both hands, squeezing hard as the nurse pushed the needle home. Soon he was sobbing freely in his mother's arms.

How much of the detail of this scene Frank remembered and how much was the accumulation of his mother's repeated recitations ("Oh my poor baby, I tell you, bright red spots all over him and his little tongue swollen like a balloon") he could never be sure. But the physical sensations, the terror, he had never forgotten.

Now he pushed himself off the bed, his sudden momentum sending the score of *Così fan tutte* skittering across the floor. No! It couldn't be happening! There was some other explanation, some temporary allergic reaction that would run its course, that he'd soon be talking about, laughing about as he made his excuses for being late: "Jesus, for a minute there I thought . . ." Ridiculous! He was far too young, too talented . . . too *good-looking* to die.

Immediately, he felt ashamed. He was not a vain man. He accepted that his looks were an asset to his career, knew that women found him attractive. But he was not a womanizer. Actually he had more genuine women friends than most men he knew. Because he was a nice guy, a sympathetic guy, a guy both sexes felt comfortable with, confided in. *A guy God would not let die at twenty-five.*

Skirting a pile of dirty laundry, he crossed unsteadily to the white-framed mirror over the dresser, seeking its familiar reassurance of health and normalcy. But there, cruelly, his reflection only confirmed what his gut already knew: The flushed face, the angry red dots spreading where his tank top left his arms and upper chest bare—the symptoms were unmistakable. There was a throbbing in his ears and he could feel the soft tissues of his mouth starting to swell.

Somehow, for the second time in his life, he had been given penicillin.

I'm going to die, he thought again. Right now, right here, while Amanda and Theo and Larry and the rest are waiting for me down at the barn. I'm going to die.

It was a simple statement of fact. "Ten minutes," the doctor had said as he instructed Frank's mother in the mechanics of injection, "he's got to have it within ten minutes. If it ever happens again." And until he left home his mother had kept the hypodermic syringe and the supply of epinephrine within close reach and even insisted, to Frank's embarrassment, that he carry a kit with him whenever he left the house.

But it never had happened again. Stings from bees, hornets, and wasps had come and gone, inoculations, an aspirin he'd swallowed in an unwary moment. It seemed clear that penicillin alone was the enemy, and penicillin was easy enough to avoid. Over the years since Frank had left home, the hypodermic kit had been abandoned.

Ten minutes. Less now, much less, maybe three, four. Time, if he chose, to make it halfway to the barn, halfway to Anna's House. And to what purpose? In the mirror, stricken eyes stared back at him from the face of this man—this dying man—and he wondered at his own calmness. Already he seemed to have left his body, to be observing the man called Frank with curious detachment.

Through the noise in his ears, he heard another sound, labored, rasping. It was his own breathing, he realized, and he was back in his body with a jolt. Now the panic struck, the rage. Along with his heart, his mind raced, his thoughts leaping with astounding clarity, searching, looking for the truth. He was going to die. But why? Why him? Why now?

He began to tremble violently. The prickling sensation had intensified to a fire and the effort to breathe was making his chest hurt. He grasped the edge of the dresser to steady himself and his gaze fell on the row of vitamin jars ranged soldierlike beneath the mirror. The jars from which not twenty minutes ago he'd selected and swallowed his morning doses. Impossible. It could never happen—not by accident. And if not by accident . . . So easy for someone who wished him ill to substitute a look-alike pill, an alien substance. So ridiculously easy to know what that substance should be, God knows he hadn't made a secret of it, they all knew. All his friends . . .

He reached to grope among the jars and then in a gesture of fury and impotence swept them to the floor. What did it matter which had been the source of the fatal pill? Someone had poisoned him. Done it on purpose. Someone had wanted him to die.

And it was *unfair*—so unfair! As if he would ever deliberately hurt anyone! As if he'd ever wanted anything but to help, to share the Light and the Truth. To show the Way to Heaven on earth. All he'd ever had, he thought (typically with no sense of irony), were the best of intentions. Dear God, let me live, he prayed. I can explain. If I've hurt anyone I can make it up. *I still have so much to do!*

A memory swam into his consciousness—his own voice, a Schubert lied. *"Ich kann nicht mehr singen, mein Herz ist zu voll—"* Heinzberg interrupting, his pudgy face moist with earnestness: "The beautiful sound, Frank, it iss not enough. 'I can sing no more, my heart iss too full.' This man, Frank, he iss in pain. It must come from here," pounding his own ample chest, *"auf dem herz.* From the heart, Frank."

German had never come easily to him . . . *Die Schöne*

Müllerin . . . Dichterliebe . . . he had worked so hard! And now that he knew, really understood, he would truly sing no more and it was all too late.

He was panting now, his hands rising to claw at the unbearable constriction in his chest, in his throat. But he turned to stumble through the piles of clothes and books, the half-emptied duffle, the stray coffee cup, toward the cabin's screen door. He had to tell someone, anyone. He didn't want to die alone.

He swayed and grabbed at the door lintel, his heart careening, his vision beginning to dim. From his swollen mouth came a strangled sound, something between a sob and a groan. Who had he thought would hear him anyway, and what good if they did?

Someone had wanted him to die. Someone so fearful of the Truth that they would kill to deny it. Faces swam before him, and conversations. Then one came into focus and he felt a great burst of sorrow and then an overwhelming need to bear witness. If only he had a pencil!

Almost detached now, he felt himself sinking to the floor. There was a stench in his nostrils and an immense pain at his heart. His hand was pressing against something hard and flat. It was the score of *Così fan tutte*. He stared at it, the letters on its cardboard cover wavering in and out of focus.

In a final flash of clarity, they came together and he saw what they were telling him. Just before his hand went slack, he pressed with his thumbnail on the cover, forming a crude *X* across the name: Amadeus.

As *Newsday* would duly, if inaccurately, report the following day, Frank Palermo, "rising young tenor," had died suddenly at the Varovna Opera Colony of anaphylactic shock under "puzzling circumstances."

Since he would never again rise in his own defense, it would be left to others to point out to *Newsday* that Frank Palermo had been, in fact, a baritone.

1

Now at last you are acting
like a woman of the world.

act 2, scene 10

TWO DAYS EARLIER

"Mrs. Schmitter?" I said. "I need to make a phone call and I can't seem to find the telephone."

I stood in the doorway of my landlady's kitchen, regarding her with an expression designed to convey friendly confusion. Despite the assurances of Robert Schmitter the Third, this was not, I feared, going to work out.

Mrs. Schmitter, sitting—huddled, rather—at the far side of her kitchen table, did not look happy. In fact, she looked besieged. The language of her round little body, swathed in a wraparound lavender print housedress and surmounted by a round little face totally outfitted with buttons—button eyes, button nose, button mouth—was not hard to read: it said: *Get me out of this!*

"Um . . ." she ventured, "telephone? Little Bobby didn't say . . . The phone bill, you know . . . I really don't . . ."

"But, Mrs. Schmitter, I'm sure you remember. . . . I mean, your grandson told me you were concerned and I did put down a pretty good deposit against the phone bill. He explained that, didn't he?"

The buttons drew together, as Mrs. Schmitter gave

every impression of trying to remember whether, indeed, Little Bobby had relayed this information and, if so, whether she should believe it.

"To be perfectly honest, Mrs. Mullins," he'd said to me, "my grandmother is . . . well, getting along in years. And like many old people, she gets hipped on a certain idea and can seem—heh, heh—downright unreasonable. Not that she isn't real pleased—excited, even—about having a lodger. Oh my no, she's just tickled to death. It's just that some friend of hers fed her stories about summer guests running up big phone bills and then disappearing. All exaggerated, of course. And I'll be honest with you, if I can tell her you've paid in advance . . ."

I wondered idly now why I'd believed for a moment any word out of the mouth of Robert Three. The open, cherubic face, the warm, steadfast gaze, the terribly sincere handclasp—God knows I'd encountered enough of those to be on my guard. I'd even formulated a rule to keep a minimum distance of one yard from anyone who protested his honesty more than once in any given conversation. During this one, Robert the Third had already done it four times.

The wondering was idle because I knew the answer. I needed a place to stay during The Season in the impossibly pricey Long Island Hamptons. And I'd immediately fallen in love with Mrs. Schmitter's upstairs back bedroom.

It must have seemed a fine and logical idea to Little Bobby and—who knew?—even to his grandmother at first. She herself, it seemed, still living alone in the old house, seldom climbed the stairs anymore and had sometime since turned the downstairs back parlor into her bedroom. And it certainly wasn't as if they were giving it away, "affordable" in the lexicon of the Hamptons being a sort of self-contained oxymoron.

It was evident, though, that the reality of land-ladyship was causing Mrs. Schmitter considerable distress. What, I wondered, had Little Bobby told her about me? "A recent widow," I imagined him saying, "Phoebe Mullins is her name. Has to support herself now, poor woman. She's got a secretarial job out here for the summer and needs someplace reasonable to stay." Which, to be fair, was about as much as I'd told him. A general air of respectability on my part and four weeks' rent in advance, not to mention the phone deposit, had sealed the agreement.

But I could imagine that the person now standing in Mrs. Schmitter's kitchen doorway making demands on her telephone might not be at all the person conjured up for her by the comfortable words *widow* and *secretary* and *reasonable*. I could imagine that in her eyes this rather too-skinny woman with the bony face and overexuberant black hair might better fit the image of the East Hampton artistic element, and goodness only knew what they might get up to. Dressed like it too, in those wrinkled blue pants, that red paisley shirt with the cuffs rolled back, those canvas shoes.

Oh, Mrs. Schmitter, I longed to cry, *don't judge by appearances. I'm forty-eight, Mrs. Schmitter, I'm on my own for the first time, and I'm scared.*

Instead, I smiled as warmly as I knew how and said, "It must be hard all of a sudden having a stranger in the house. I do understand. But really, Mrs. Schmitter, I'm not a bad person and I hope we can be friends." I watched her expression become minimally less wary before adding, "And I do need to use the phone."

Mrs. Schmitter cleared her throat and attempted a stern gaze somewhere to the right of my right ear. "Would that be a long-distance call?" she inquired huskily.

"No," I said, "just local. To the place where I'll be working." We'd deal with long distance, I decided, when the question arose.

"Oh. Well, then, I guess . . . sure, go ahead." There was relief in her tone now, and a hint of self-congratulation as if for having taken her stand in the face of the foe. She even went so far as to smile at me and nod encouragingly toward the door.

I sighed. We had come full circle. "But, Mrs. Schmitter," I said, "I can't *find* the phone."

She frowned, then her face cleared. "The phone! Yes, of course. Just let me see now . . ." She hopped off her chair and maneuvered herself around the table and past me to the hallway beyond.

As I followed, I noticed that her legs, properly encased in sensible grey hose even on this warm June morning, were so slender as to look dangerously fragile beneath that butterball body. The black oxfords on her tiny feet must, I thought, have been bought in the children's department. If I hadn't faced coping with her vagaries for the rest of the summer, I might have found it all quite endearing.

The hall was dim and carpeted with a runner whose blue, rose, and green flowers had muddied with time into a mottled mauve. The walls were wainscoted in walnut. Above the wainscoting, faded sepia prints in dark frames—London Bridge, The Stag at Bay, Notre Dame Cathedral—blended self-effacingly into their background of equally faded wallpaper.

There were not many houses like this left in East Hampton, where each senior citizen's death provided yet another desirable property to be snapped up, painted white, and furnished in wicker, dhurrie, and Laura Ashley. It reminded me of my grandmother's house in Massachusetts—down to the combined odors of lemon polish, lavender, and very old dust. On first seeing it, and the big, backyard-facing upstairs bedroom with its four-poster, mahogany wardrobe, and flowery wallpaper, I'd had a sense of safety, almost of homecoming.

Too bad, I thought, that Robert Three had neglected

to mention that his grandmother had a screw loose. Or had he—God forbid!—hit on the lodger idea as a means of providing the old lady with a keeper? One who was paying for the privilege at that. What had I gotten myself into? Was it, perhaps, I who needed a keeper?

"Now, I *believe*," Mrs. Schmitter was saying, as she stood just inside the door of the living room, surveying it with an earnest and vaguely apologetic air, "I *believe* I put it away because, you know, it has such a *very* loud ring and I didn't . . . Ah!" She pointed to a cord that snaked behind the overstuffed sofa, disappeared under the rug, and emerged at the base of a top-heavy oak credenza. "Now I remember." She stooped to open a cupboard door at the base of the credenza and triumphantly produced a beige telephone with a rotary dial.

If she hadn't first had to remove a concealing stack of books, the gesture would have been a good deal more convincing.

And after all, what I got was an answering machine. A youthful female voice informed me that I'd reached the Varovna Vocal Colony but unfortunately, etc. Succumbing to the fear, which frequently overcame me on these occasions, of committing something really stupid to tape, I hung up in the middle of instructions about waiting for the beep.

Fifteen minutes later I tried again and was rewarded by the same voice, live this time, though sounding somewhat breathless. Or was the breathlessness my projection, from finding myself suddenly overcome by an extreme case of nerves? I confirmed with the voice, which belonged to a Jenny Allen, that I would arrive at the Varovna Colony to begin my duties at ten the following morning, and got off the phone fast. Mrs. Schmitter, I thought, *would* be pleased.

After hanging up I sat for a moment, waiting for my heart to stop racing, my palms to dry. For God's sake,

Phoebe, I scolded, it's only a job! Then, rallying, I reflected that maybe I had some excuse. At the age of forty-eight, I, Phoebe Mullins, liberally if haphazardly educated, world-traveled, semifluent in three languages besides my own and with enough of several more to request room service, decline further autographs, order a cab, and explain that "My husband needs an Alka-Seltzer," was about to tackle the first paid employment of my adult life. Humiliating, but there it was. And if I played it cool enough, perhaps no one would guess.

2

What commotion! What excitement!
And why all this confusion?

act 1, scene 2

MONDAY, JUNE 18

THE ROUTE TO THE VAROVNA VOCAL COLONY AND OPERA
Workshop led northward from East Hampton village
through woods—lots of woods. Nice woods, as Papa
Hemingway might have put it, nice and big and full of
trees. A lifelong city dweller, that was about as specific
as I was prepared to get. Pressed, I might have ventured
such technical terms as "scrub pine," "oak," and "beech."
And in the thick undergrowth I thought I recognized the
deep, shiny greenery of holly bushes among the ferns.

Mostly, though, I kept my eyes on the road, as befit-
ted one who had achieved legal driving status a scant
two weeks previously. My little red secondhand Toyota
hummed obediently along. Through the open windows
the warm and brackeny forest smell drifted pleasantly. I
still couldn't believe I was here instead of where I'd been
five days ago—sitting in a New York West End Avenue
apartment, packed and ready, with sublet tenants set to
appear at any moment, and no place to go.

Because the job had fallen through. The job for
which I'd learned to drive a car and plumbed the mysteries of WordPerfect. The Vermont summer camp for

adults, which had promised, in return for long hours and a meager salary, "a fun-filled atmosphere of good health and good fellowship." Instead, due to one of the owners turning out to have a wee drug problem, the camp had gone bankrupt and I was up the appropriately named creek.

The call from an old friend and colleague of my husband's had come like a literal answer to prayer. Did I recollect former Met Opera star Anna Varovna? Did I know that she still ran a summer program for singers on the East End of Long Island? Her longtime summer secretary/assistant had failed her at the last minute. "Heard the word *computer* and phoned in her resignation." Would I be interested in the job?

Had I been prone to superstition, I'd have thought it all too good to be true. But in any case the timetable gave me no room to brood. Madame Varovna was already ensconced in East Hampton. She was evidently prepared to take, sight unseen, the recommendation of the old friend. I drove out from New York on the Long Island Expressway, arriving on the East End white knuckled but alive, spent roughly a week's salary on one night in a motel, found Little Bobby and his grandmother . . . and here I was.

And what, I wondered as I drove, would Anna Varovna be like now? I'd seen her only once, years ago, in *Cavalleria*. How small she is! I'd thought then; Where does the voice come from? On recordings the sound had been impressive—rich and seamless, evoking the stereotypical image of a formidably padded and more or less stationary diva. On the stage of the old Met the voice had been the same, but the image . . . I could see her still, dark, intense, restless, hear her promising to adore Turiddu despite beatings and insults: *"Battimi, insultami, te amo e perdono!"* Some object lesson for an impressionable teenager! I cringed now, thinking how I'd lapped it all up, how I'd cried. How I'd known that this, *this,* was true love. But I'd never forgotten Varovna.

How far was this place, anyway? A sign on the right, they'd said, you can't miss it.

I began reviewing what little I knew of Anna Varovna's story, well documented in past issues of *Opera News* and program notes from the old Met. How she was the daughter of Russian expatriots living in Paris; how, during the German occupation in World War II, she and her family had risked their lives by aiding the Resistance; how she'd been discovered after the war, singing Russian folk songs in a Left Bank club, by Gregory Dmitri, an artists' manager fifteen years her senior, who had subsequently married her; how she'd been groomed by him for a vocal career, and finally again been "discovered" by Rudolf Bing, while appearing with a provincial French opera company, and brought to the Met in Bing's third season as general manager.

And now Varovna would be, what—seventy? Would she be very grande-dame-ish? Would she accept Phoebe Mullins as a professional working woman who knew what she was about? Or would she bore right through my masquerade with those intense Santuzza eyes? I thought of the four weeks' rent in advance (not to mention the phone deposit). In a way, it had been a gauntlet thrown down to myself. No hedging now, no turning back, no failing to make this work.

I rounded a bend and there on a small post was a painted sign, black on white: THE VAROVNA COLONY, and an arrow. Well, that was unpretentious enough—a good omen, I thought. I swung the Toyota to the right onto a dirt road and into the woods.

Fifty yards on, a curving driveway on the left led off to a grey-shingled house just visible through the trees. But "Go until you see the water," I'd been told, and another fifty yards brought me abruptly out of the dappled shade into the sunny open. Straight ahead, sheltered bay waters shimmered achingly blue.

I slowed, then stopped altogether, partly in acknowledgment of the startling beauty of the place, partly because I wasn't sure which way to go. I could follow the fork to the left, which led past a string of small white cabins and on to a rambling two-story white house partially surrounded by hedges. Or I could go straight, where the road sloped down and a large barn-like structure on the right looked a good bet for being the theater.

As I pondered, a square figure wearing dark green shorts, sneakers with no socks, and a black T-shirt emerged from the end cabin, spotted the car, and came hurrying toward it. I had time to notice that the figure was female, with lead-grey hair hacked carelessly into a Dutch bob. I also had time to be thankful that I'd opted, after much inner debate, for the simplicity of a denim skirt, pale yellow jersey, and navy espadrilles. Casual was evidently the tone at the Varovna Colony.

A fleeting question as to whether this might be Anna Varovna herself was dispelled as the woman approached. The face that presented itself at my car window was not soulful and dark eyed but round and flat, the eyes light and protuberant.

The person regarded me warily; an anxious frown creased her forehead. "Yah? Could I help you?"

"Hi," I said, "I'm Phoebe Mullins. I'm supposed to be meeting a Jenny Allen but I'm not exactly—"

"Oh. Sure," the woman said, her face clearing. "Jenny iss down at the theater. They rehearse, you know. It iss the brown building there, looks like a barn." She gestured in the relevant direction, nodded several times, and started to turn away.

I stuck my hand through the window. "Thanks," I said.

The woman looked momentarily taken aback, then

grabbed my hand and shook it vigorously. "Ach, no problem. Ass the young people say." She grinned suddenly and nodded a few more times. "Gerta Hofstetter," she said. She turned and moved back toward the cabins. It took me a moment to realize that this last had been a form of introduction.

The reason why the Varovna Theater resembled a barn, I deduced cleverly after I'd crossed a raised stone patio and walked in through the main entrance, was that at some time in its history it *had been* a barn. The massive stone fireplace in the left wall had undoubtedly been a later addition. But the loft area stretching the width of the building above and behind me, and the rough-hewn beams supporting the central roof, had an unmistakable authenticity.

I had time only to note this much, and that there was a bunch of people huddled around the stage area at the far end of the space, when one of the group disengaged herself and came hurrying up the aisle.

"Ms. Mullins? Jenny Allen. I'm sorry I wasn't— Did you have any trouble finding us?"

Jenny Allen was very young, very pretty. She was wearing jeans, a plaid shirt with tails tied at the midriff, and leather sandals. Her fairish hair was held back from her face with a band, Alice-in-Wonderland fashion. She seemed nervous. I was beginning to wonder what it was about me.

"Please," I said, "my name is Phoebe, and no, your directions were perfect. When I drove in, someone named Gerta told me I'd find you here. Gerta Hofstetter? Did I get that right?"

"Oh, yeah," Jenny Allen said. "Gerta is Anna's housekeeper, sort of. Friend. Companion. Probably dresser, once. They've been together forever." She stopped, seemingly at a loss, glanced at the stage and then back to me. "Look, why don't you sit here," she said, pointing to where the rows of seating began, "and watch the rest of the rehearsal. We're doing *Così fan tutte*. Do you know it?"

I nodded. Was a knowledge of Mozart opera, then, a job requirement?

"Great. Anyway, Anna thought you might like to watch the rehearsal and then afterwards . . ."

"Jenny?" a male voice called out. "You coming?"

"Okay, okay, I'll be right there." She gave me an apologetic shrug. "So . . . afterwards I'll show you around a little and then it'll be lunchtime and you can meet Anna."

"Fine," I said. "I'll just—" but Jenny Allen was already walking away toward the stage.

I was aware of some curious glances, a muttered "Who's that?" and Jenny's answering, "The new secretary, don't you remember?" Then a muffled, "Oh shit, yeah." It seemed that this, for the present, was to be the extent of the pleasantries. At the very least, I thought, it relieved me of the necessity to be polite.

The man seated at the grand piano directly below the stage caught my eye, smiled, then grimaced and shook his head. I nodded back. He had an ugly, interesting face and I wondered for a moment if I didn't know it from somewhere.

Another male type, lanky and balding, unfolded himself from a front-row seat and came up the aisle toward me. He was strikingly attired in lime-green golfing pants and a shirt striped vertically in yellow and blue. His face was round and smooth, like a child's, under wispy fair hair. Behind thick lenses, light brown eyes gave the impression of not quite working in concert. "Theo Morse," he said as we shook hands. (At least "Morse" was my interpretation, since what he actually said was "Mo-wuss.") "Welcome to the Colony. Jus' remember now, this is an early rehearsal."

He went back to his post and called out, "All right, y'all, we'll go from the beginnin' of the first-act finale

and try runnin' it. Anythin' you're not sure of, fake it."
He folded up into his seat again until only a straw-
colored tuft was visible over its back.

Feeling a need to be unobtrusive, I moved over and
sat down at the far left end of the back row. This was
not, to say the least, what I had expected. Did it indicate
mere informality, or something less attractive? Was it a
test of some kind? In any case, since this was where I'd
be spending a lot of my life during the next two months,
I thought I might as well start taking in my surroundings.

The fifteen or so rows of seats on each side of the
center aisle looked like—and probably were—relics of a
vintage movie house. Their plum-colored plush was
faded and in many places threadbare, wooden arms dark
with age and the pressure of generations of sweaty
palms. In spite of the open windows on both sides, the
smell of last winter's mildew was strong.

The stage, too, was unprepossessing, hung with
drapery of a rusty black and lit with a couple of bare
bulbs. Though the minimal lighting, I realized, was a
function of rehearsal economics, still it was obviously
opera on a shoestring. I couldn't imagine that Anna
Varovna would lend her name to anything mediocre.
Nevertheless, I thought with some misgiving, *Così* . . .
Mozart . . . hardly an enterprise for amateurs.

They began. Less than two minutes into the first-act
finale of *Così fan tutte*, I was smiling. The amenities might
have been primitive, but the music was choice. I stopped
wondering what I was supposed to be doing there and
gave myself up to the pleasure of six attractive and well-
trained voices blending in a Mozartian ensemble.

They were singing in English—the clever Ruth and
Thomas Martin version—which, no matter how you
might feel about opera in English, is a big help in following the typically convoluted plot. At the moment, the
two lovers of the sisters Dorabella and Fiordiligi, having
pretended to march away to war, were back in disguise,

each wooing the other's girlfriend to settle a bet with Don Alfonso, the resident cynic, about the faithfulness of women. Alfonso was in on the deception, the lady's maid, Despina—if I remembered right—was not. But it hardly mattered. Tenor and baritone declaimed and moaned and pretended to die. Soprano and mezzo dithered in thirds. Basso and soubrette burbled and chirped respectively. I was delighted, charmed, and, as far as any little breaches in etiquette were concerned, thoroughly disarmed.

Who were these people, anyway? I began to study the six singers more closely, bringing into play my well-honed associative system. It was a method I'd developed in the days when I served as hostess for my father, the pianist, and later for my husband, the conductor, for keeping straight the slew of names and faces I was expected to recognize and acknowledge. Then, of course, I was expected to convey the information to the clueless artist of the moment, thus averting the music world's equivalent of an Incident. It wasn't easy.

The technique had served me well. Happily, the only time I'd slipped up, to speak of, was in addressing an artists' representative I'd privately dubbed The Frog Prince as "Mr. Frog." Fortunately he hadn't been listening, being too occupied in searching past my shoulder for somebody—anybody—really important.

Fiordiligi, for instance—the tall soprano with a mass of frizzy pale hair wrapped Grecian-style in a trailing length of white chiffon. She was a cross, I decided, between a blond Little Orphan Annie and the White Queen. A certain air of dishevelment, accentuated by a filmy white blouse buttoned up crooked and with a lot of floppy collar and sleeve, decided in favor of the White Queen. All her features seemed exaggerated—large, heavy-lidded eyes, wide mouth, long, sloping nose. Up close, I thought, the effect was probably formidable; onstage it was arresting.

The other sister, the mezzo, was half a foot shorter than the White Queen. She was stocky, high cheek-boned, and dark, with straight hair in a thick braid down her back. Although she was playing the softer, more sentimental sister, I'd have bet it was against type. She had intensity and a certain earthiness in contrast to the White Queen's rather prissy cool. Keep it simple, make her the Red Queen. Both she and the White Queen were wearing grubby, floor-length, costume-trunk petticoats and carrying stick fans.

Now the two of them were fluttering over the baritone and tenor, who lay prone, having ostensibly attempted suicide with poison. At least the tenor lay prone. The baritone was propped awkwardly on one elbow, the only cast member using a score. He was dressed in jeans, sneakers, and a white short-sleeved polo shirt. Dark curls tumbled fetchingly over a handsome forehead—an easy Rudolf Valentino. I'd noticed the others frequently resorting to pushing or hauling him into position as the action proceeded. Not very bright? I wondered. Or just underprepared?

And there was Jenny Allen as the lady's maid, Despina, reentering disguised as a doctor. She'd thrown a piece of dark material around her shoulders and carried an enormous prop magnet with which she pretended to bring the two suicides back to life. Although she appeared younger than the rest of the company, she was more than holding her own onstage. Her light voice was round and perfectly focused, her acting assured and quite funny. Alice in Wonderland? Perhaps.

Don Alfonso, meanwhile, wove among the other characters with the fluidity of a Baryshnikov, stage-managing his little drama. He was a compact black man wearing loose-fitting dark slacks and a black sweatshirt. Had to have been a dancer at some time, I thought, and experienced the familiar twinge of envy and regret. His English was Jamaican accented, giving an added fillip to the character. I had the impression he was holding back vocally. Every now and then he turned aside to smother a dry cough.

The tenor was eluding me. He was of medium height and would probably in not too many years cross the line from plump to obese. He moved, however, with unexpected grace, and the arms in the navy T-shirt were well muscled. Still, *bland* was the word that came to mind—bland fair features, bland light tenor voice. It made it difficult to pin . . . Weren't they taking this awfully fast?

At this point the scene was further enlivened by a bit of extraoperatic drama.

It started with the Red Queen tossing her fan. It hit the stage-right proscenium arch and fell to the floor with a clatter. One by one the other singers broke off raggedly. The pianist followed suit. The Red Queen strode to the lip of the stage, hands on hips, and announced into the silence, "Listen, Theo, if this is the tempo you're planning to take, just forget me and hire fuckin' Donald Duck."

From the front row, a long arm extended ceilingward, palm out in a placatory gesture. "Relax, darlin'," said Director Morse. "Of course it was too fast. I don't know what got into y'all but I just wanted to see . . . Larry, what happened?" He turned to the man at the piano.

"Damned if I know," Larry the Piano Man said. "I was just trying to keep up."

Valentino wiped his nose with the handkerchief into which he'd been honking surreptitiously during this exchange. "Listen, people," he said. "I really apologize. It was probably my fault. I'm still shaky in some spots but I promise I'll have it—"

"Don't be silly, Frank," interposed the White Queen. She took his arm protectively. "It's not your fault. We know you've been pressed for time."

Valentino's liquid Italian eyes regarded her gratefully. "Well, and my sinuses, you know—this humidity . . ."

"Oh yes," the Red Queen said, "we *do* know your sinuses, Frank. They're *old* friends."

"Old and dear," murmured Baryshnikov, just loudly enough to be audible to everyone. "Quite Members of the Company." He directed his gaze up to the flies and executed a small soft-shoe tattoo.

"Well, *really*," the White Queen said, "if we're going to behave like *children* . . ."

"Aw, come on, guys," Valentino said. He smiled his handsome smile, his arms spread in a "let us reason together" gesture. "I think we all know that the truth of the matter . . ."

If his intention had been to smooth the choppy waters, he'd miscalculated badly. There were two distinct and simultaneous snorting sounds and the Red Queen exploded anew.

"*Truth!* Christ, Frank! We've all had it right up to the ass with your friggin' *truth!*"

"*People,*" Jenny Allen said with emphasis.

There was a sudden silence and then a group stare in my direction, which immediately tried to pretend it had been no such thing.

Hey, I thought, don't mind me. If you didn't want a witness to your little family quarrels you shouldn't have invited me in.

Before the general embarrassment could become too pronounced, Director Morse said calmly, "Simmer down, y'all. Now as long as we're stopped, let's take it back to the same place and go section by section. We'll break at twelve-thirty, back here at, say, two-fifteen. Any problems with that?"

No one admitted to any problems, and the rehearsal resumed.

Why on earth, I wondered, were these people so tense?

3

Please tell me all about it!

act 1, scene 9

"LUNCH WILL BE IN ABOUT HALF AN HOUR," JENNY ALLEN said. "D'you want to walk around some?"

In rehearsal, Jenny had been quick and confident. Now she seemed nervous again, her eyes unable to focus for more than a moment on any object, including me. Twice, in the course of leaving the theater, she'd dropped her vocal score. Why, I wondered, had Anna Varovna designated this particular young woman to be my greeter and guide?

Down on the narrow strip of sand bordering the bay, a short pier jutted out over the water. On either side, a small tethered boat rocked gently. It looked soothing. "Could we go down there?" I said, pointing. "I've been in East Hampton two whole days without setting foot on a beach."

Rehearsal over, the company had dissipated with speed. Only the Jamaican Baryshnikov had lingered at the theater with Director Morse and the Piano Man, all three huddled over the keyboard in earnest discussion.

The still–Nameless Tenor headed up the road toward the cabins. The White Queen floated away in the opposite direction, toward the beach, where a second string of cabins extended off to the right.

The Red Queen strode across the grass in the direction of the big white house. I was interested to see Valentino emerge from the theater, take a look around, and then set off purposefully after her.

"Explain the geography to me," I said as I and my uneasy escort made our way to the beach. "The big white house, for instance—what goes on there?"

"Oh, well, that's more or less the central gathering place," Jenny said. She seemed relieved by the direct question. "It's where we all eat, and the office is there— your office, now. And there are guest rooms upstairs. It's called Anna's House because when Anna and Gregory— her husband, Gregory Dmitri—first bought the property, back in the fifties, they lived there. Now Anna lives in the studio she built up in the woods. But the big house is still called Anna's House. Confusing, I guess, but we never think about it. I mean," with a sideward glance, "it's better than calling it the Big House."

Okay, she did have a sense of humor—a quality to be encouraged. I laughed appreciatively. "Indeed. And what about all those little white cabins?"

"The place used to be a summer camp for kids," she explained. "Boys' cabins up there by the woods, girls' down here on the beach. I suppose they just never bothered taking them down, and then when Anna started having more and more students come out for the summer, they came in handy."

"I passed another house on the way in. Is that part of the property too?"

"Oh yeah. In the old days Anna and Gregory used to let friends build places—the property's more than twenty acres—but I think now she's bought them all up."

"Twenty acres in the Hamptons!" I observed. "Mr. Dmitri must have had second sight. In the fifties they probably got it for a song. Did you ever meet him? Anna's husband?"

Jenny shook her head. "No, he died . . . let's see . . . eight years ago. Before I started coming here. He was a lot older than Anna."

From her tone I gathered that the dead-and-gone Mr. Dmitri held no interest for Jenny. Okay.

"You were telling me about the houses."

"Right. Well, besides Anna's private studio there's a place they call The Octagon because it's—well, for obvious reasons. And the house you passed is where Theo and Rita are staying."

"Rita?"

"The mezzo, Rita Michaels. She and Theo are married, you know. Well, no, probably you don't." She broke off. "I'm not doing this very well, am I? All these people and names all at once—you must be totally confused."

"No, no," I said. "I'm doing just fine. Here, why don't we sit on the dock and you can fill me in on who everyone is. I won't remember it all, but at least it'll give me a head start."

I led the way the twenty feet or so to the end of the pier. The sun was now almost directly overhead, but its heat was relieved by an offshore breeze that ruffled the water and caused the two boats—one a small outboard, the other a rowboat with flaking green paint—to thunk companionably against the pilings. A faint odor of gasoline mixed with the other marine smells of salt, seaweed, and sun-baked wood.

I sat down on the warm boards, knees drawn up, back against one of the pilings. After a short hesitation, Jenny Allen dropped down opposite me and sat cross-legged. She'd removed her Alice in Wonderland band, so her shoulder-length hair fell forward. Every so often she reached up and brushed it away from her face.

It was indeed, I thought, a very pretty face—wide-set grey eyes, straight nose, chin just soft enough to escape being pointy. But it wasn't a happy one. At the moment it wore the uncertain expression of an unprepared student braced for the next question. Was there a concerted effort afoot to make me feel like an ogre?

"So Rita Michaels," my Red Queen, I had figured out, "and Theo Morse are married. Mr. Morse, I gather, is your stage director."

"Yes, and Rita teaches voice and coaches languages. During the rest of the year they both have jobs at a college in Virginia."

"Then they're both part of the staff."

"Well, we all are, in a way. That is, most of us still take lessons with Anna, but the actual students—the paying ones—won't be here for another few days."

"Okay, then maybe you could run the staff down for me. The tall blond soprano, for instance. Does she teach too?"

"Yes. Amanda St. James. Besides here, she teaches part-time at Barnard and does quite a lot of professional singing, oratorios and so on. Same for Jason Lee Jones, the Don Alfonso. Except he teaches privately, mostly coaches repertoire. He used to be a dancer too, did a lot of Broadway shows."

Ah—Baryshnikov, I thought smugly. I said, "And the good-looking baritone? With the—um—sinus condition?"

"Oh. Frank Palermo." She wasn't sharing my amusement. "Yes, he'll be . . . as far as I know, he'll be teaching this summer. He's been in Germany on some kind of grant." She stopped, then went on rather hurriedly: "And then there's Larry Peterson, who does a lot of the vocal coaching—he was playing the piano today. He's a composer, too, he's had things commissioned. Let's see— oh, Stefan Kowalski, the tenor. He teaches music at a high school on Long Island. And here he does all kinds of stuff—plays for lessons, helps build the sets, runs errands for Anna. He's an EMT too. You know, the ones who go out with the ambulances. Oh, and he lifts weights."

So, I'd underestimated the Nameless Tenor. "This is really very helpful," I said. "I'm glad Madame Varovna thought of easing me into the setup this way. Or was it your idea?"

Jenny Allen looked gratified and even offered a small smile. "Oh no, it was Anna's. She thought . . . well, you know, that you should get the flavor of the place before . . ."

I wondered whether she was thinking what I was—that perhaps I'd gotten rather more flavor than the thoughtful Anna had intended.

"And what about you?" I asked.

"Oh, me." Jenny's eyes shifted sideways and then down. Her right index finger picked absently at a splinter on the worn decking. "I don't teach or anything like that. I'm . . . Anna hired me to sew costumes, help out in the office and the kitchen, things like that. She knew I couldn't pay and would want to feel I was earning my keep. Essentially, I guess, I'm to do whatever jobs are left over."

"Like shepherding around the new secretary?"

Jenny looked up, colored, and then produced her first genuine smile of our acquaintance. Her bottom teeth were slightly crooked. "You're nice," she said.

I was surprised and unexpectedly moved. I even had a brief impulse to confide something of the insecurities that had made her simple statement so reassuring to me. Then I reflected that the last thing this very young and seemingly troubled woman needed was a dose of unsolicited midlife angst. So I simply said, "Thank you."

"Actually," she said, "I'm awfully glad you're here. I've been filling in for the last few days since Georgiana—that was Anna's assistant before—pooped out on us. I can't type worth a damn, but I'll help you any way I can."

I expressed the appropriate gratitude. This, I supposed, was the logical place to pursue the question of what my job here actually entailed. Instead I reverted to the subject that had aroused my more immediate curiosity.

"So, have you all known each other before, you staff members? You don't give the impression of being recent acquaintances."

"Oh no. Everyone here has been coming to the Colony off and on for years. Some of us, like me, started out as students. In fact, except for me, everyone who's here now was here last summer too."

"Oh? And what were you doing last summer?"

Jenny did not respond immediately. Then she said, "I was sick."

If I had been glancing away at that moment, I would have missed the bitter little twist of the lips that added ten years to Jenny Allen's face. It was gone in a flash, but I made a quick decision to drop the subject. Besides, I'd had enough experience of closed artistic communities to know that whatever Jenny's story was, I was sure to hear it sooner or later.

"I'm sorry," I said. "You must be glad to be back. It's a beautiful place."

Jenny nodded but made no other reply.

I'd been sitting facing the bay. Now I got to my feet and took a good look around.

In the transparent air the colors of the landscape— the pale ribbon of beach, the bright green of the grass, the deeper green of the hedges, the spanking white of Anna's House, even the patchy grey of the wooden dock—glowed like poster paint. Across the spangled water another shoreline—Shelter Island, I thought— stretched hazily, without sign of life or motion. Two seagulls hovered above us, then curved down and landed on the ripples to bob like a pair of floating toys in a giant bathtub.

I shook my head. " 'Beautiful place' doesn't quite do it. It's unreal. All this and Mozart too. It seems a lot like heaven."

"Yes," Jenny Allen said. "It can be. That is . . ." She had remained seated, staring out over the water. Now she tilted her head up abruptly as if she'd arrived at some decision. "I want to say . . . I wouldn't want you to think . . . that rehearsal, you know, people losing their temper and sniping at each other. It's not the way we really are. I mean we really are—have been—good friends."

"I did wonder about the tension level," I said, careful to keep my tone free of any unbecoming eagerness. "Any particular reason?"

Jenny wrinkled her forehead. "Well, yeah. It started when Frank arrived. He came a few days after the rest of us. Up to then everything was fine."

"Frank . . . ah, yes, the handsome baritone. That's surprising. I thought he seemed quite good-natured. But he came bearing seeds of discord?"

"Well, you see, that's just the thing." Jenny gazed up at me earnestly, grey eyes wide and perplexed. "Frank's the last person you'd expect to make people uncomfortable. He's an old Colonyite, been a student of Anna's for years, one of those types who's everybody's friend. But since he arrived this time, he's managed to put an awful lot of backs up. It seems to have to do with some sort of cult he's gotten involved with."

"Does this cult have a name?" I asked.

"The Children of Truth."

"Oh dear," I said.

"You've heard of them?"

"No, but . . . 'the Children of Truth'—it has an ominous ring. Whose truth, I wonder?"

"I don't know, I haven't talked to Frank much. Anyway, I guess he thinks he's found the shortcut to heaven and he's bound to let everyone else in on it." She shrugged. "Shoot, he's probably just annoying everyone to death and I'm making too much of it."

Having a profound respect for the destructive potential of religious fanaticism, I was not at all sure. A phrase from my childhood came suddenly to mind—a proverb, among the many trotted out by my Portuguese nanny from a seemingly endless supply: "Truth is the most horrible joke of all."

Then I thought, Come on, Phoebe, aren't we getting just a tad operatic?

I said, "You're probably right. This . . . enthusiasm of Frank's will likely cool down eventually. Especially when he finds he's not making any headway with his friends."

Jenny looked relieved. "I just mentioned it because . . . well, I didn't want you to start off with the wrong impression of us."

A loud ringing of what sounded like a ship's bell came from the direction of Anna's House.

Jenny jumped up. "That's the first bell for lunch. Come on. There'll be just time for me to introduce you to Anna."

Can't wait to hand off the responsibility, I thought. And why not? She obviously had other things on her mind. So did they all, it seemed. Was it really because of Valentino and his Children of Truth?

In any case, I reminded myself, it was no concern of mine.

4

How explain it? What to say?

act 1, scene 2

THE ROOM THAT JENNY AND I ENTERED—THE "CENTRAL gathering place" of her description—was brushed warmly with the unfakable patina that comes only from years of congenial occupation. Long and low-ceilinged, it stretched thirty feet across the front of Anna's House. Directly opposite the front door was a fireplace of grey fieldstone, its sooty interior enlivened by a spray of dried flowers, grasses, and cattails haphazardly arranged in a tarnished brass pot. To the right, through a pair of french doors, was a glimpse of red floor tiles and a couple of long tables surrounded by wooden folding chairs. A doorless opening just to the right of the fireplace gave onto a corridor, from beyond which came sounds of clattering crockery. A cooking aroma involving onions drifted from the same direction. At the far left end of the room, a big bay window looked across the lawn to the theater. In the shelter of the bay, a semicircular seating arrangement was upholstered in worn red corduroy.

The rest of the seating consisted of several wicker pieces with floral-patterned cretonne cushions in now-faded greens and golds and, facing the fireplace, a huge overstuffed brown velour sofa with a brightly striped afghan thrown over its massive back. Flower-bespattered rugs, colors muted and textures thinned by the years, lay about the age-darkened plank flooring; the white plaster walls were hung with a haphazard assembly of framed group photos and posters announcing past Colony opera productions. To the left of the fireplace stood an old-fashioned upright piano, piled high with scores and dog-eared sheet music.

Everything was clean, everything was casual, everything was comfortably shabby. I liked it a lot.

Again, though, the human atmosphere left something to be desired. My first impression on entering was that most if not all of the company was assembled. My second was that some sort of discussion or activity had ceased abruptly with my arrival. While part of me continued to be intrigued, another part was working up a considerable testiness at being reacted to like the bad fairy at the christening.

Before I had a chance to expand on this feeling, Jenny hustled me across the room to where an erect figure with silver hair and deep-set eyes stood in front of the bay window.

In three-inch platform sandals, Anna Varovna's eye level was still below mine at five-foot-five. But her lack of stature was more than compensated for by a powerful aura of self-possession. Even in a simple wraparound dress of brown linen, she exuded an elegance that supported the discreet touches of gold jewelry at throat and ears. In contrast with the silvery hair, still abundant, which she wore pulled back in a classic knot, the remarkable eyes appeared almost black.

"Anna," Jenny said, rather breathlessly due to the healthy clip of our journey up from the beach, "this is Phoebe Mullins."

Anna Varovna extended her hand. Her grasp was firm. "My darling," she said in a voice unexpectedly deep and a touch husky, "is wonderful to meet you. Already you begin to know us, yes? Already you see that at Varovna Colony is one happy family."

The look that accompanied this pronouncement was at once so warm, so intelligent, and carried such an undercurrent of amusement, that my incipient ill feelings expired without a flutter. The legendary Varovna charm had not been exaggerated. Yes, I was being conned, but hey . . .

I smiled, shook the warm, small hand in return, and said, "Madame Varovna, you're right, of course. I'm delighted to be here."

I would have bet that Anna Varovna was habitually a two-handed shaker. At the moment, though, her other hand was occupied in resting firmly on the forearm of the Red Queen, who stood beside her looking flushed and a little ashamed.

"But you must call me Anna, my darling, as everyone does. And have you met our so wonderful mezzo, Rita Michaels?"

The Red Queen nodded amicably enough in my direction. "Not formally," she said, "but I'm sure Ms. Mullins doesn't feel like a stranger."

I was spared the necessity of replying by the second pealing of the bell and a subsequent mass movement toward the french doors.

The two outside walls of the dining area were fitted with continuous casement windows, most of which were open. Terra-cotta tile flooring and white-painted siding on the two remaining walls further indicated that the room had been created from what once was a porch.

Two other doors gave access to the main part of the house, and from one of these emerged a person I hadn't seen before, a slight and mousy woman wrapped in a huge blue-and-white-checked apron. She deposited a basket of rolls on each table and scuttled back the way she'd come, passing Gerta Hofstetter on the way. Gerta was carrying a tureen between mitted hands and calling out, "Take care! Iss hot, very hot!" She had changed for lunch, I noted, to the extent of substituting black polyester slacks for the green shorts.

Valentino, following after with a similar tureen and a concentrated expression, almost collided with the group consisting of me, Anna, and the Red Queen. "Oops!" he said cheerfully. Then, with a playful glance at the Red Queen: "Better not hang around Rita carrying hot soup!"

The Red Queen glowered, and Anna smoothly propelled her forward to one of the two long tables, herself taking the chair at the head of the other. "Now," she said, "Phoebe is sitting here next to me and Jenny here, right and left, you see, and Frank, you are putting the soup down, so, in front of me, and then you are playing Papa." She indicated the chair at the opposite end of the table. The White Queen and the Piano Man took the remaining two places at Anna's table, while Rita the Red Queen presided at the other with her husband, Director Morse, Stefan the previously Nameless Tenor, Baryshnikov, and Gerta Hofstetter. If Anna had not actually shoved us into our seats with a firm hand on each shoulder, the effect was much the same.

On each table were three large bowls containing salads—chicken, pasta, and garden—as well as the baskets of rolls, a plate of butter, and metal pitchers of ice tea, water, and milk. The soup that Anna was ladling from the tureen was a thick and aromatic split pea.

"Heavens! Do you eat this well all summer?" I inquired, slathering butter on a roll, which was crusty and actually hot.

"Perhaps with twenty or so more mouths to feed the rolls will not always be so warm," Anna replied, smiling and passing soup bowls with equal aplomb. "But singers, you know, they are like athletes. They are being always hungry."

"I didn't realize," I said, "that the school itself—is that what you call it?—hadn't actually started yet. When do the students arrive?"

"The first bunch will be coming in next Sunday," Larry the Piano Man said. "Actually, there's a good deal of coming and going throughout the summer, but most people stay at least over the course of one major production. After *Così* it's *Bohème* and then *The Bartered Bride*."

"And will the staff be performing in those as well?"

"Oh no," the White Queen said. Her voice had that habitual-teacher tone, which I charitably assumed to be unconscious, that announces you've just asked a stupid question. "Those will be cast from among the students. That is, after all, what they come here for. Of course, they're all *quite* good. But Anna feels that having the staff do the first production gets the season off to a quick, professional start, don't you know. And of course we *do* love working together." She encompassed the table with a head gesture that sent the white chiffon scarf fluttering perilously close to her soup bowl.

There was an inadequately muffled sound of dissent from the other table.

"Frank," Anna said, "I am sure you have much to tell about your wonderful year abroad. We are all wanting to hear."

Valentino looked up from his plate as if surprised at being called on. "Oh—sure—well," he began. "Um . . . it was all terrific. Particularly Professor Heinzberg in Berlin. I coached lieder with him for two months, all of the Dichterliebe and a lot of Wolf. Marvelous man, just marvelous." He waved his fork expressively. "It was he who put me in touch with the Children, you know, and that was . . ." He checked himself, and shot an apologetic glance at Anna. "Okay, sorry, I know—forbidden subject. Let's see now . . . and then there was Paris." He hesitated, then said, "Funny thing, Anna, I ran across an old friend of yours from Resistance days—man named LeClair. Georges LeClair. He said you'd remember him."

I had been hoping to learn more about this period of Anna's life, and turned to her expectantly. What I saw jolted me. Anna Varovna's eyes, meeting Frank's across the length of the table, were opaque and staring, black as mud in her bleached face. Except for a tightening of muscle around the jaw, her features might have been set in granite.

There was a crashing sound, and Gerta Hofstetter rose awkwardly out of her chair at the next table. A shattered glass lay on the red tiles at her feet.

"Ach, how I am clumsy," she muttered, sponging with a paper napkin at the rivulets of liquid further darkening the black slacks. "No, no, Rita, I make the mess, I will clean it up." She waved away the Red Queen and strode heavily off in the direction of the kitchen.

"LeClair," Anna said slowly. "No, I do not recall your Monsieur LeClair, Frank. But then those were not so happy days, my darlings. For some, perhaps—they remember only drama, only excitement. Agony they have forgotten. But many of us—we do not want to dwell on those days."

She turned to me. "So. Phoebe. This afternoon I show you office, yes? I show you what needs to be done, is all very simple. For you it will be—how do they say?— like soup off a duck's back."

"I must say, I am curious," I said. "I'm grateful to have the job, and I only hope I can do it well. You're taking a good deal on faith in hiring me, I think."

Anna looked at me kindly and gave an infinitesimal shake of the head. "I am mostly careful woman, Phoebe. I do not, in my life, make many mistakes. And about you I am not worried whatsoever."

I thought I saw her eyes turn briefly again to Frank at the opposite end of the table. Then she asked a question about costuming for the opera and the conversation turned to theatrical matters.

Whatever the import of Frank's bombshell—and I was certain that's what it had been—there was no sign of it now, except for the silent witness of the food remaining untouched on Anna's plate.

5

If ever my candor should weaken or falter . . .

act 1, scene 2

NO ONE LINGERED AT THE LUNCH TABLES.

Anna Varovna, after pressing my hand and urging me to feel "mostly at home," said she would meet me in the office in an hour. She then left the dining room by a side door, accompanied by Gerta Hofstetter. They walked away toward the woods in back of the house—the direction, I supposed, of Anna's private dwelling/studio.

Several of the others smiled at me and made polite noises before taking themselves off. Only the Piano Man hesitated, as if wanting to say more, but he was hurried away by the Jamaican Baryshnikov with an apologetic flap of the hand and murmurs of "Just enough time . . . the new John Duke song reissues . . ."

Nobody, I realized, standing alone in the main room, had told me where the hell the office *was*.

I wandered over to the bay window and stared across the expanse of green to the theater—or rather its roof, since the slope of the land set the onetime barn considerably lower than Anna's House. Wonderful, I thought, how the concerns with which I'd started the day—could I do the job? would I like the job? what *was*

the job?—had become secondary to my curiosity about
this quirky group of people and what on earth they were
in such a twit about.

On the face of it, the general unease did seem directly traceable to Frank, the handsome baritone. But I
found the idea hard to credit—to me he seemed the opposite of threatening. In fact, in spite of his stereotypical
Italianate good looks, I began to think "Valentino" had
been a misnomer. No smoldering sexuality there, no invitation to danger. Rather a kind of goofy charm and almost an excess of goodwill—hardly the stuff of villainy.
I couldn't imagine him deliberately inflicting harm on
anyone. It was all, as Anna would have put it, mostly
intriguing.

I turned back to the room and began to browse
among the photos on the walls.

They were not hung in any observable order. A
group photo marked in white ink VAROVNA COLONY, 1965
was beside another dated 1979, and next to that was a
sepia-toned full-length shot of Anna herself as Aida, presumably sometime in the fifties.

I searched for familiar faces and soon spotted
Valentino as a rather callow Don Giovanni being berated
by Amanda St. James (the White Queen) as Donna
Elvira. The Don, I thought, didn't stand a chance. And
there was the Red Queen, Rita Michaels, a good many
years younger and pounds lighter, as Carmen. And Frank
again, this time with Stefan the Tenor as the "Gondo-
liers," with . . . yes, there in the chorus a surely not more
than teenage Jenny Allen.

Larry the Piano Man appeared over and over, both as
accompanist and in group photos as far back as 1978.
The characteristic slouch of his thin shoulders and the
long, homely face with its somewhat sardonic expression seemed hardly to change over the years. Again, I
had the strong feeling I'd seen him somewhere else.

I paused to study a typical Colony group picture

hanging on the strip of wall to the right of the front door. As in the others I had seen, thirty or so people posed in three rows in front of the theater. Those in front sat on the grass, those in back stood on the broad patio steps. Many of the faces were familiar: Anna in the center, sitting in a lawn chair; Gerta Hofstetter at her shoulder, Jenny cross-legged on the grass in front of her; Frank, Stefan, Larry—all of the current crew. Everyone smiled into the camera.

Except for one. At one end of the second row a slender figure with a thatch of tight, light curls stood slightly apart, head tilted, eyes slid to the side. His attitude gave the impression that he was listening to something only he could hear. He looked, I thought, like a creature from the woods that had been corralled on this bright summer day to take part in an uncongenial ritual: at any moment he might bolt from the scene. Paradoxically, he thus became the focus of the picture, the one to whom the eye was inevitably drawn.

I looked for the date in white ink at the bottom of the photo. Two summers ago. I wondered who he was, this faun with the slippery eyes, and whether he would be returning.

But enough, I told myself, of idle speculation. There's supposed to be an office somewhere in this building and I bet I can find it.

The corridor leading toward the back of the house brought me first to another hallway on the left, which ended in yet another outside door. Off this hallway, a wide inner door opened into the kitchen.

I glanced in. The Mouse in the oversized apron was standing at a big, old-fashioned galvanized sink, washing pots while Jenny Allen stacked plates and glasses into a dishwasher of only slightly more recent vintage. They both looked startled at my appearance in the doorway. Really, I thought crossly, this has to stop.

"I'm looking for the office," I said. "But first," with a

friendly smile to the Mouse, "I don't think we've met. I'm Phoebe Mullins."

"Oh, I'm sorry," Jenny said. "Phoebe, this is Sarah Kirk. She—uh—cooks and everything."

Sarah Kirk nodded, mumbled something I didn't catch, and turned back to her pots. They were heavy pots, I noticed, serious iron cookware, but the Mouse, despite her wispy appearance, handled them with dispatch.

"That was a wonderful lunch," I said.

The Mouse gave me a sidelong glance that could equally have conveyed either umbrage or acknowledgment, and muttered something that might have been "Thanks."

Oh well, I'd tried.

Jenny raised her eyebrows at me and shrugged expressively. "The office is down the corridor on the right," she said. "Sorry I can't show you around it, but I've got to finish here and then get to rehearsal."

I assured her I understood, and went on my way.

The office turned out to be a smallish room in a state of apparent disorder that I hoped would turn out to be deceptive. Surely there was some logic behind the tipsy stacks of paper, pamphlets, brochures, and scrapbooks, not to mention a bulletin board where memos swarmed over one another three deep.

The room was furnished with an old-fashioned oak kneehole desk, a swivel chair, and three or four other chairs of assorted design. On the desk were a telephone with answering machine, a venerable Selectric typewriter, several overflowing and undifferentiated In and Out baskets, and a number of cracked and handle-less coffee mugs holding pens, pencils, scissors, markers, paper clips, and so on. Atop one of the In (or possibly Out) baskets a bowling trophy with a marble base was acting as a paperweight—incongruous enough in this setting to be, I judged, someone's idea of whimsy. Jutting back from one side to form an *L* with the desk was an auxiliary surface that held a computer and printer. Behind the desk, on a shelf that ran under two big, curtainless windows, was a copy machine.

The three inside walls were nearly invisible behind bookshelves, file cabinets, and the aforementioned bulletin board, which was a good four feet square. What wall space could be seen was painted white. A well-worn oriental rug covered the floor.

All in all, I felt a good deal relieved. If the place had been a model of neatness and efficiency, I would have been intimidated. Messiness I could deal with; it spoke of a certain insouciance toward matters of business that I'd always found to be healthy and not, in the long run, any serious obstacle to getting things done.

I went behind the desk to take a closer look at the computer. It was an IBM clone, brand new. Scotch-taped to the desk just to the left of the keyboard was a handwritten note: "The computer man's name is JERRY. He's on retainer. <u>Use him</u>," followed by a local phone number. One of the few details about the job I'd managed to glean was that I would be responsible for ushering the Varovna Colony (kicking and screaming, by the look of the office) into the Information Age. Since my knowledge of computers was limited to a single word-processing program, I anticipated the development over the summer of a close and meaningful relationship with JERRY. I hoped he'd be kind.

All of which reminded me that my very own Word-Perfect floppies were at that moment sitting over by the theater in my car in the sun and very possibly melting. A glance at my watch told me I still had forty minutes before my appointment with Anna. I scooted back down the corridor and out the front door. From there I had the option of striking out directly across the treeless expanse of rough lawn or taking the slightly longer, considerably shadier route that led past the boys' cabins. It was hot, I had plenty of time. I took the path.

I had reached the midway point in the string of cottages, when I was brought up short by a voice carrying clearly from the cabin at the far end. "You just don't get it, do you, Frank?" The voice belonged, I was pretty sure, to Stefan the Tenor. "I'm not asking, I'm telling you—fucking lay off!"

I hesitated. Should I make a discreet retreat? On the other hand, was it my fault if these people insisted on spilling their private affairs at top volume? Was that what came of a constant immersion in opera? I continued on.

An answering murmur in a placating tone evoked an even higher decibel rate.

"Shove it, Frank! God, you've been so brainwashed by those sniveling Truth freaks you can't think straight anymore. You're fucking crazy, Frank, you know that? And on top of everything else you've gotten it wrong, it's not what you think. So listen up, I'm spelling it out for you. You don't want to end up with a bloody nose, you keep it the hell out of my business!"

The screen door of the end cabin exploded outward and Stefan Kowalski charged through, his pudgy face flushed to a sunset pink. When he caught sight of me he halted abruptly on the small stoop. Then he shrugged, ran down the steps, and without a backward look strode off in the opposite direction.

The screen door opened again and Frank Palermo stepped out. He made a halfhearted gesture in Stefan's direction as if to call him back, but instead brought his hand up and ran it heavily through his dark hair. By this time I had come even with the foot of the little stoop.

"Ah well," he said, acknowledging my presence with no indication of embarrassment, "better to let him cool down." He smiled indulgently and shook his head. "Stefan has quite a temper. Says all kinds of stuff he doesn't really mean."

I, on the other hand, thought I had seldom heard more sincerity in a man's voice and was feeling embarrassed enough for the two of us. I nodded wordlessly and was about to walk on, when Frank said, "Would you like to come in? Take a look at the cabin?"

There was a tone to the question that told me he could really use the company. Besides, this was the first gratuitous gesture of hospitality I'd yet received. I assured myself that WordPerfect could hold out for ten more minutes and climbed the three wooden steps to Frank's cabin.

It was a room about twenty feet square, furnished with a single bed, a dresser, a small table and straight chair, and a wicker basket chair, all painted either blue or white. Braided rag rugs were scattered on the pine floorboards. Window openings in three of the yellow-painted walls were protected by heavily patched screening. At the back of the cabin a doorless opening gave access to a narrow screened-in passageway.

The bed was unmade. A footlocker, two suitcases, and a knapsack sat on the floor in various stages of overflow. A jumble of clothes and books covered all the furniture with the exception of the dresser: On its peeling blue surface was an orderly array of a dozen or more vitamin bottles, along with an atomizer or two, tissues, Band-Aid tins, boxes of herbal teas, several plastic bottles of spring water, and a cup from the top of a Thermos.

Frank looked around distractedly, as if just waking to the fact that he'd invited a relative stranger into a scene of considerable personal squalor. He hurriedly removed a pile of shirts from the basket chair, dumped them on the bed, and invited me to sit.

"Sorry for the mess," he said. "As you can see, I'm

still moving in—" He checked himself, snapped his fingers in a there-I-go-again gesture, and produced a disarming grin. He had very white teeth, large and even. "Not true. The truth is, the place won't look much different for the rest of the summer. I am simply not a neat person."

I had the impression that congratulations were being called for. Instead, I opted for some honesty of my own. "Well, at least it's big," I said. "Roomy, I mean. I was picturing some sort of dormitory arrangement."

"When it was a kids' camp there would've been wall-to-wall cots— Oh jeez! I almost forgot." He wove a path to the dresser and began opening jars and shaking pills onto his palm. "Vitamins," he explained over his shoulder. "Sorry, but if I get off schedule . . ." He poured water into the cup, tossed down the handful of capsules in quick, successive gulps, then turned back to me. "You're probably thinking I'm some sort of health nut."

"Well no, actually I—"

"But I don't overdose on this stuff," waving a hand at the bureau. "I'm real careful about what I put into my body, believe me. When I was a kid I almost died from a reaction to penicillin. I mean really. If I hadn't been in the doctor's office . . . But a singer has to keep healthy, you know, and I'm in pretty good shape. A little back trouble. And my sinuses now and then, I have to fight that. The dripping, you know, when that gunk starts to coat the vocal cords . . . but hey, you don't want to hear about that."

Too true, I thought but did not say.

"Anyway," he went on, "about the cabins. For now there's just me here and Stefan in the cabin on the other end. When the season begins there'll be five or six other guys in three of the cabins in between, and we keep one for a utility room—ironing board, hot plate. Telephone. Not that we're supposed to use it, the phone, I mean. Incoming calls and emergencies only, and ours isn't even working, mice got to the wires. That passageway connects the rooms along the back. Needless to say, we all get to know each other pretty well."

It was too good an opening to miss. "I gather that those of you here now go back a number of years. That you're pretty old friends."

"Oh sure." For a moment the dogged optimism of Frank's expression lapsed and he allowed himself to look almost gloomy. "Unfortunately, at the moment . . . well, I guess you've noticed. There's been a certain amount of misunderstanding. If I could just get them to listen to me without jumping to conclusions. I mean, if my old friends won't try to see . . ." He had wandered over the screen door and stood peering out, drumming his fingers lightly against the frame.

"But, hey!" He turned around, good humor again overspreading his handsome features. "It'll all work out. Everything does with faith, you know. I still forget that sometimes."

Time was passing, my floppies were calling. I had a job to do. It was no good—curiosity won out. "This experience of yours," I ventured, "a conversion, could you call it? Happened in Germany?"

Frank's eyebrows rose. "You want to know about the Children of Truth?"

"If you'd rather not—"

"No! God no, there's nothing I'd rather talk about. It's just that I haven't had many invitations in the last few days—more the reverse, if you know what I mean. Oh sure, I get carried away, but when you've found something like this you can't keep it to yourself." He leaned back against the door frame, his dark eyes shining. "The joy, Phoebe! The freedom! You can't help yourself, you want everyone to share it. You see," the resonant voice became husky with intensity, "I've found the Way!"

"Ah," I said.

It seemed to be enough.

"Found the Way and found the Truth." He began pacing the floor among the islands of clutter. "Right there in Germany. There I was, plugging away, trying to get ahead, impress the right people, beat out the next guy. And feeling more and more that there was something— you know—wrong with it all. Something missing. And then the man I was coaching with, Heinzberg, asked me to go with him to some kind of religious meeting. And I thought, What the hell? And I went."

He stopped in front of the basket chair and fixed his eyes earnestly on mine. "And that's where I found the answer, Phoebe. That's where I looked on the face of God and heard His Word: 'Ye shall know the truth and the truth shall make you free.' John eight, thirty-two. That's it, Phoebe. It's as simple as that."

Some response seemed called for. "Well . . . yes, I see," I ventured, "as far as it goes. But, if you'll forgive me, as a life philosophy it seems pretty general."

"Not at all," Frank said. "With the Children, you see, it's very specific."

He tipped a pile of books off the seat of the straight chair, swung it around, and straddled it. "We tell the truth—always! Now think about that, Phoebe, think what it means. No more lying, no more cheating, no more cover-ups, no more secrets. Among the Children we've freed ourselves from all that. Total honesty. It works, Phoebe. I've never felt so close to a group of people in my life."

"By total honesty," I said, "you literally mean . . ."

"Total. Honesty. Hard concept to grasp, isn't it?" He smiled kindly. "Okay. Example. Small thing. You're late for a lunch date. Because, frankly, you forgot about it. No, 'Gee, I overslept,' or, 'The car wouldn't start,' or, 'My mother called just as I was leaving.' Just, 'Hey, I forgot. I'm really sorry.' See how clean, how simple?"

I nodded doubtfully. Actually, I thought I would have settled for the one about the car.

"Or take the two of us," he went on, "we've just met, right? But I can come right out and say, Phoebe, you're a hell of an attractive woman. I mean for an older woman—forty-seven, forty-eight, am I right? And you're nice. Simpatica, you know? I could tell right away. I know we'll be good friends. Now isn't that better than being all formal and polite?"

To say that I was left speechless doesn't quite do justice to my feelings of the moment. Apparently Frank took my silence for agreement, because he plunged happily on.

"Or take something more serious." He leaned forward against the chair back, his expression appropriately solemn. "You're a married woman who's been having an affair and now you find you're pregnant. Do you make it worse by hiding it from your husband as long as possible? No, you go to him, tell the truth, clear the air, and start fresh. Of course," he went on more slowly, as if thinking it through, "if you were a Child of Truth you wouldn't have had the affair in the first place. You'd have said to your husband, 'Look, I don't find you sexually attractive anymore,' or whatever, and taken it from there. I mean, if husbands and wives can't have total honesty, who can?"

I gave an inward shudder. No need to ask if there was a Mrs. Frank Palermo.

Fortunately, that question, too, had been rhetorical. "And think what it will mean to the world as the movement grows. Ninety percent of what's wrong in the world comes from countries trying to hide things from each other. Billions of dollars spent, thousands of people slaughtered because of suspicion and misunderstanding. Take away the secrecy, bring in Truth, and you have the basis for understanding. Peace and love for the world!

Plato knew it: 'Truth is the start of every good thing.'
Shakespeare too: 'Tell truth and shame the devil.' "

He broke off and looked at me anxiously. "Do you
see, Phoebe? Am I making this clear?"

The light had certainly dawned about what it was
that had Frank's friends in a sweat. I, however, was no
Child of Truth. "Oh yes," I said. "It's . . . fascinating. I—
um—hadn't gathered this was a world movement."

Frank laughed easily. "Oh hardly—yet. To para-
phrase the song, 'Let there be Truth on earth and let it begin with me.' Our job now is to recruit by example. To
show people the happiness they'll gain by throwing off
the shackles of deceit."

"Uh-huh." I paused, struck by another bit of illumi-
nation. "Am I right in supposing that part of the recruit-
ment process lies in telling people to come clean about
matters they'd rather keep to themselves?"

" 'Encouraging' them, Phoebe, encouraging. Convincing them it's the Better Way. Hey, we don't go
around spilling other people's secrets—they have to do it
themselves to Learn the Way and Earn the Joy. It's a common misunderstanding."

"I can see that. How people might be made uneasy, I
mean."

"But they shouldn't be, Phoebe, that's what I'm saying. That's what the Bible says: Galatians four, sixteen:
'Am I therefore become your enemy, because I tell you
the truth?' "

"But suppose," I persisted, "you knew something
about another person which you considered to be morally
reprehensible. Even illegal. What would your position be
then, as a Child of Truth?"

Frank hesitated and directed his gaze momentarily
out the cabin's back window. "That might be difficult,"
he said finally. "It's a grey area."

He brought his eyes back to mine, hesitated again,

and then said, "Funny you should bring that up. Because as it happens I'm having a bit of a problem making a decision about—"

"Frank? You in here?"

For some minutes I'd been aware of increasing sounds of activity outside. Passing snatches of conversation, a shout or two, the slapping sound of a screen door swinging shut, a soprano voice vocalizing up the scale in liquid roulades.

Then there was the clatter of someone mounting the steps and Amanda St. James's frizzy blond head peered around the screen door. "Rehearsal's about to start, Frank. They'll be waiting for you."

By the time Frank had located his score under the pile of shirts on the bed, searched in vain for a pencil and ended up borrowing one from me, the three of us were hurrying down the road to the theater, and the chance for Frank to air his "bit of a problem" was long gone.

6

From morning to midnight
you work, you slave, do your best . . .

act 1, scene 8

"So you see, my darling," Anna Varovna said, "is easy,
but perhaps a little bit interesting too for you, yes?"

"To tell the truth," I said, "I'm finding it somewhat
overwhelming. Quite a bit more complicated, I mean,
than I'd anticipated."

As in: *What?* You expect me to do *what?*

Anna dismissed my concern with a smile and wave
of the tiny hand that I'd begun to envision equipped
with a cat-o'-nine-tails. Whatever the distress she had
suffered at Frank's hands during lunch, there was no evidence of it now. I found myself hoping, ignobly, that
while it lasted it had been severe. "You are mostly intelligent woman, Phoebe," she said. "In a few days you will
feel happy here like oyster. You will see. I am not worried whatsoever."

With that, a final smile, and an encouraging squeeze
of my shoulder, she took herself off.

I sat in the swivel chair, staring at a pad full of notes
written in ever-more-hectic scrawl:

"Correspondence . . . applications . . . filing syst . . .
chcking accnt #1 .. chkng acc #2 . . . kitch expend. (see
Sarah Kirk) . . . payrl . . . tckts . . . prgrms . . . publ releses . . .

newsltr..." I squinted at something that looked like "ink pen set." Ah yes, internal phone system. "Colny #, ext. fone locatns (t b usd *nly* w spcl permissn), Anna's pers. num, Theo & Rita's #, Octagon Hse #, how to swtch clls... phn bil brkdn..."

The salary that had seemed so generous at first flush I could now see was going to be well and truly earned.

Which discovery, in the light of the past half hour spent with Madame Legree, came as no surprise. If nothing else, I had gained a respect for my employer quite apart from artistic considerations. Anna Varovna might talk like a fugitive from a bus-and-truck tour of *Ninotchka*, but her grasp on the principles of capitalism was firm.

I was startled to learn how much cash aspiring singers—or in many cases their parents—were prepared to fork over for the privilege of studying with a re-nowned former diva of the Met. Also the relative modesty of the stipends received by the artistic staff. Also the level of scrutiny directed by that soulful portrayer of Butterfly and Mimi toward matters ranging from the wattage of light bulbs in the cabins to the weekly consumption of coffee beans. Also the depth of the scholarship fund, thanks to a list of (I consulted my notes) Benefactors, Patrons, Sponsors, and Contributors, all of whose names were required to appear in every program with excruciating attention paid to correct spelling and preferred modes of address.

Also (to be fair) the cost of maintaining a prime piece of East Hampton waterfront property.

I sighed, cleared a space on the desk, and began to get organized.

It must have been half an hour or so later when the Mouse appeared in the doorway, bearing a small tray with a mug of coffee, cream and sugar, and a plate of gingersnaps.

"Anna said to bring you this," she announced

abruptly, as if to ward off any suspicion that the thought-fulness had been her own.

"How nice!" I said. "Just what I needed." I got up from my knees in front of a file drawer where I'd been trying to get a handle on my predecessor's extremely idiosyncratic filing system and pushed aside an In box to make room on the desk. "You can put it right here."

The Mouse sidled over, deposited her tray, and darted a glance around the room. "Looks better," she said.

I felt a swell of gratification. Surely, coming from the Mouse, this was a major commendation. "Thanks," I said.

"That other one," the Mouse observed, "she was a real bitch. Bring the dishes back when you're finished," and she left. Before, I surmised, she could be tempted into any further demonstrations of goodwill.

For the rest of the afternoon I sorted, stacked, filed, and labeled. The resultant lessening of the apparent chaos might not have been striking to the casual eye, but at least now the chaos was mine. I also made lists, installed WordPerfect into the computer, and browsed briefly in the typically obtuse instruction book that ac-companied some software to be used in designing the programs and newsletters. I abandoned the book and penciled in at the top of my to-do-tomorrow list: "Call JERRY."

"I was wondering," the Piano Man said from the doorway, "if I could take you out to dinner."

I looked up, confused, then down at my watch. It was five-thirty. Slowly my conscious mind registered the dinnertime smells drifting down the hallway, and the murmur of voices. "Good Lord," I said. "Quittin' time!"

Larry Peterson grinned. "Rough day in the cotton fields? You do look as if you could use a drink and a good meal. Away from here, I mean. How about it?"

I considered. I had been planning, sensibly, to go home, cook up something basic in Mrs. Schmitter's kitchen, and go to bed early. On the other hand, a rather intriguing man, not quite a stranger and demonstrably on my wavelength, was asking me to dine in the Hamptons. "I'd like that," I said.

Jenny Allen put her head around the door. "Hi! Is everything okay? I would have come over right after rehearsal but Anna said you'd rather not have anybody butt in while you were finding your way around."

Oh Anna did, did she? Well . . . yeah, she'd been right. Outlining the job and then leaving me alone to get on with it had been the best approach she could have chosen. "Yes," I said, "I think everything's pretty much okay."

I let myself in at Mrs. Schmitter's front door and had almost made it to the stairs when I heard my landlady call my name from the living room. I sighed and backtracked to the door at the left of the small entryway.

"Yes, Mrs. Schmitter?"

Doris Schmitter was sitting in front of the television in an oversized brown leather recliner that loomed so far above her head that she seemed in danger of sudden ingestion. On a tray at her elbow stood a teapot, a small water pitcher, two cups, and a plate of crackers and cheese. She was still wearing the lavender print housedress of that morning but there was something different about her that I couldn't quite . . . Was it in her face? Of course. She was smiling, that must have been it.

"I was hoping you'd have a cup of tea with me," she said. "You must be exhausted, out all day."

"I'd love to another time, Mrs. Schmitter. But as it happens I'm being picked up in an hour to go to dinner and I really need a bath."

Mrs. Schmitter cocked her head. "Ah! A date! Well, enjoy yourself, my dear." She turned back to the TV screen and released the Mute button on the remote. "I want to buy a vowel," The TV said. A roar of applause followed me up the stairs.

A "date"? I thought, as I watched the water creep up the sides of the big claw-footed tub. Was that what it was? I'd been a wife for twenty-five years, a widow for barely one. "Date" was an alien concept. What were the new rules? Should I offer to go Dutch? What did I know about the Piano Man? Was he married? Was he gay? Did it matter?

What should I wear?

In the end I settled for a full black skirt, ruby red silk shirt, and high-heeled, strappy sandals. I added a pair of dangly earrings and some gold beads and studied the result in the big mirror over the dresser.

My hair, curly and damp from the steamy tub, which had also tamed some of its regrettable tendency to frizz, clung here and there rather winningly, I thought, around my face. The half hour with Jenny on the dock had given my cheeks a touch of color that needed only slight cosmetic enhancement. My eyes, which are close to black and set wide (and which I'd so often been told were my "best feature" as to wonder where that left the rest of me), stared back from the mirror, narrowed, appraising. If only my face were plumper. And my neck. Well, and my chest, come to that. If only those smudges under my eyes would disappear. And those lines at their corners. If only, you mean (I told myself acidly) you weren't, as good old Frank had so acutely put it, forty-eight.

As for my other questions, I had arrived, in the course of my preparations, at the following answers: (1) Screw the rules; (2) it was his idea, let him pay; and (3) no, it didn't matter.

7

And what about our dinner?

act 1, scene 12

"I DON'T KNOW HOW TO SAY THIS WITHOUT SOUNDING LIKE something out of a dime novel," Larry Peterson said (actually, I've never read a dime novel, have you?) "but here it is: I know who you are."

I laughed. I was enjoying myself. The Old Mill was a soothing bastion of quiet pseudo-colonial elegance. Our table for two was roomy and swathed in white. In its center a fat little candle glowed prettily. Whether the food would be worth the prices I'd tried to ignore on the menu was still to be discovered. I'd had one martini, which, tired as I was (had it only been that morning . . . ?) had been enough to produce a near-nirvanic state of relaxation.

Larry was wearing a silvery grey suit, white shirt, and pale blue tie. His eyes, under their half-mast lids, matched the tie. His mouth, with its somewhat pendulous lower lip, was slightly off-center, and although it seldom smiled outright, it was, I had found, extraordinarily expressive. I wondered whether there was a masculine equivalent for *jolie-laide*?

"At least you didn't tell," I said. "I *am* trying to—what's the catchword?—establish my own identity?"

"Yes. I'm enlightened enough to assume you wouldn't choose to be introduced generally as the daughter of famous pianist Yannis Angelopoulos and the wife of famous conductor Mischa Mullins. Widow, I should say, I suppose. A sad word. I'm sorry."

"It is, isn't it? Better than *relict*, though. And it's all right. It's been a year, I can talk about it."

"Then tell me, if you don't mind, why 'Mischa'? A nickname, I know, but everyone seemed to use it and I've never understood. . . ."

"Mama was Russian," I explained. "If she'd had her way it would have been 'Mikhail Rostov' all the way. But Papa was Irish and even more of a terror than she was and he put his foot down. Ah, here are our salads. No, actually mine is the vinaigrette."

The waiter, a young, collegiate Apollo who had not introduced himself by name (score one for the management), actually blushed as he switched the plates. He gave me a sheepish smile. I smiled back. He blushed deeper. Hey, this was fun!

I turned back to Larry. The expressive mouth, I noticed, was twitching.

"Anyway, Mick suspected early on that a conductor named Michael Mullins might be more of a novelty than just one more Russian. My husband had an excellent instinct for promotion."

Larry Peterson's eyebrows had shot up. " 'Mick'?"

"Oh, he was very, very Irish. Of course I only called him Mick in private. Or in front of his mother if I really wanted to get to her."

"You have a wicked streak one wouldn't suspect, Phoebe Mullins."

"Very mild, I'm afraid, and all very sub rosa. My prep-school roommate called me 'the closet witch.' "

"And what did your husband call you?"

" 'Fee.' " Suddenly I wanted very much not to talk about Mick. "My father called me 'Hebe.' In fact, that's what he wanted to name me, but my mother wouldn't have it. She had a sense of irony, you see, and my father didn't."

"Irony?"

" 'Hebe'? Cup-bearer to the Gods? It wasn't a role she wanted for me, God knows she'd played it enough herself. But then she died."

"How old were you?"

"Seventeen. I barely made it through high school and then it was off with Dad. Foreign travel. Exotic company. Holding his head while he barfed before every performance—oh, sorry, not table talk." I shot an apologetic glance across the white linen. "You must be a witch yourself," I said, "or warlock, whatever. You've gotten me talking about things I haven't . . ."

"Then this will be my last—I promise—nosy question. Why are you doing this?—working for Anna, I mean."

I waited while the Bashful Apollo managed to get our entrees right the first time—lemon chicken for me, fillet of beef for Larry. He then poured the wine, spilling only a negligible drop or two, and retired triumphant.

We sampled the food and pronounced it good. After a few minutes devoted to pleasurable consumption, I said, "The answer to your question is a two-parter, and I don't mind telling you. (A) I need the money. It's one of those boring stories where when you hear it you always think, How could they have been so naive? The trusted financial manager with, in our case, a gambling problem. Who certainly didn't expect Mick to die of a heart attack at fifty-five. Symphony conductors, after all, are supposed to live forever. So—money gone, investments evaporated, insurance lapsed, you name it. Fortunately I had a small cushion of my own from my dad's estate, but it's not much. And (B) I need the self-respect. I'm forty-eight years old and I've never held a paying job."

I looked at Larry over my wineglass, then raised it in

salute. "So there you have it, Larry Peterson. I have told all—or at least as much as I intend to for now."

"I'm flattered," he said. "Truly. I've been prying and you've been extremely generous. What can I do in return?"

I had been admiring the deftness of Larry Peterson's hands—long, bony hands, neatly manicured. They manipulated knife and fork, salt shaker and wineglass with the same quick, nervous precision with which they moved over the piano keys. His manner of speaking too was quick, the voice rather light, on the edge of breathlessness. *Where* had I heard it before?

"You can tell me, for starters, where I know you from. We have met, haven't we?"

"Yes, but I'm astonished you should remember. It was ten years ago. In Baltimore."

I shook my head.

"At a reception by the Baltimore Symphony for the finalists in a competition for young composers—well, relatively young. Your husband was doing a guest-conductor stint, so he got stuck with being gracious and flattering to all of us—seven, I think there were. I didn't win, by the way, although the orchestra did play my piece once or twice later on. Not, of course, with Mischa Mullins conducting."

I bet not, I thought. I could hear Mick now, as on many similar occasions: "A party? Sure. Free booze and spread a bit of the old charm? Congratulate the winner on his unique contribution to world music? No problem. Just so long as I don't have to conduct the bloody thing."

I said, "No . . . Well, my husband, as I'm sure you recall, wasn't known for his championship of contemporary music. In fact, for him the day the music died was in 1949 with Richard Strauss. But yes, if you were there, that must be where I remember you from. Did we talk to each other?"

"Briefly." Larry Peterson rested his elbows on the

table, made a steeple of his long fingers, and stared at me over them. "Actually, I was more intimidated by you than by the maestro. You had something of a reputation, you know."

"I . . . what?"

"Oh yes. Some mention of iron hands and velvet gloves. Fierce protectiveness, the power behind the career, and so on. You were wearing white and looking very Greek. I thought you were quite fascinating."

"Good Lord!" I exclaimed, genuinely astonished. "But it wasn't like that at all! You've got to be teasing me!"

The Piano Man spread his hands. "Would I dare?" he said. "But in any case, I've answered your first question. Are there more?"

I was silent for a moment, overcome by this portrait of a woman who, as far as I was concerned, had never existed. Had I really given that impression? Laughable, if so, but still . . . No, I'd have to think about that one later.

Larry, now . . . My years of on-the-job training in diplomacy and the social graces dictated an inquiry into his interests, his achievements: *Tell me about your composing, Mr. Peterson. You've been awarded several grants, I understand. That must be very* . . .

"I had an interesting and rather weird conversation with Frank Palermo," I said.

"Ah," Larry said, "I can imagine." His mouth twisted to one side, clearly conveying his estimate of the joys of conversation with Frank.

"I rather liked him," I said, "in spite of this new (I gather) bee in his bonnet. Which I couldn't help noticing isn't very popular. What's his story?"

We had both by this time declined the dessert cart and progressed to coffee. Larry slouched comfortably, one arm thrown over the back of his chair. With the other hand, he circled a spoon slowly in his cup of decaf.

"In some ways, Frank has more talent than any of them. In the sheer beauty of the instrument, I mean, and he's deeply musical—once he gets something learned. The consensus is that Frank could very well be looking at a major career."

"But?"

"Well . . . at the risk of sounding harsh . . . you've heard the one about the tenor who was so stupid even the other tenors noticed?"

I hadn't, and it took me a moment to regain my composure.

"Change that to 'baritone' and apply it to Frank. Oh I know," he said, forestalling me, "he's a really nice guy, well meaning and all that. I've known him a long time, and I'm fond of Frank. But face, it, Phoebe, he's a grown man and he's got no sense! He's like an adolescent, one short-lived enthusiasm after another. One year it's the meaning of names," he gave a short, humorless laugh, "turns out 'Laurence' means 'covered with laurels.' The next it's astrology. Badgering everyone for their exact time of birth and telling them not to take a trip on Tuesday because Leo's in the House of the Sun or whatever. Then it was graphology, everyone had to provide handwriting samples and listen to Frank analyze their character. All essentially harmless, if occasionally tiresome. But this thing—the Children of Truth, for Gawd's sake! I only hope he gets over it before he creates any more drama."

Since that had been essentially my reaction, I could hardly argue the point. "Have you talked to him much yourself?" I asked.

"Hardly at all," Larry Peterson said in a tone that made it clear he'd prefer to lay the subject of Frank Palermo to rest.

I allowed myself to wonder in passing whether Frank had gotten under Larry's skin in any specific and personal way. Then I said, "Tell me about Jenny."

"Ah, Jenny. All right. Where to start?"

"Perhaps at the end? I get the impression that something has happened recently to throw her into a pretty fragile state. It makes it difficult to know how to talk to her."

"Either you're extraordinarily perceptive or I haven't been paying attention," Larry said, "because I thought she was doing well, considering. To put it as briefly as possible, two years ago a friend of hers—a very close friend—died in, well, in horrible circumstances. They were sharing an apartment in New York. One evening Jenny went out and Charlie—Charlie Judd was his name—fell asleep with a lighted cigarette in his hand. The entire apartment was gutted. Jenny arrived home just as the firemen were removing his body."

"My God!"

"Indeed. And for some reason she managed to blame herself. I don't know the whole story. You might ask Frank, he was close to them both. But the upshot was a total nervous breakdown, mental collapse, whatever the term is these days. She spent the better part of a year in some hospital in Vermont."

"When did she come out?"

"Several months ago. All at once, there she was back in New York, working at a record store in the Village, living at the Y, and studying with Anna again."

I thought of Jenny as I'd seen her that morning, nervous and ill at ease. Then onstage, skilled and confident. Then again awkward and almost childlike in her desire to please. Then that momentary expression of bitterness—good God, no wonder! Poor Jenny!

Larry Peterson said, as if continuing a train of thought, "It was hard on all of us—Charlie's death. We all knew him. He spent a summer at the Colony. That's where he and Jenny met."

"He was a singer?"

"No, a pianist. And a composer. Actually, he was a

student of mine at Manhattan School of Music. I wangled the job for him at the Colony—wanted to get him out of the city, give him time and space to work on his composing. He made his living playing in piano bars and clubs, he was a wizard at the piano, could play anything. Improvise too. He'd take off on some theme and work it out so perfectly nobody'd believe he was making it up on the spot. Oh, Charlie was immensely talented."

I waited, then said, "Do I hear another 'but' coming on?"

Larry glanced at the ceiling and rubbed his jaw. "How to put it . . . he was eccentric. Squirrely, you might even say, but eccentric will do. Secretive to the point of paranoia. His student compositions were, well, better than good, but after his student days, though we all knew he was writing stuff, he wouldn't show it to anyone, wouldn't even make copies. Said he wasn't ready, it wasn't good enough yet. And when he . . . died, his work went with him. All burned in the fire. A real tragedy."

"And Jenny was in love with him."

"Oh, yes. Oh, yes. And not the only one, I might add. Charlie had charm. Lots and lots of charm."

He fell silent.

I drew a deep breath and let it out slowly. "Well, thanks for filling me in."

Suddenly, I felt exhausted. It had been a long day. Enough was enough.

When the Bashful Apollo presented the bill, unhesitatingly, to Larry, I remained true to my decision and let him pay it.

8

How I hate to break the news!

act 1, scene 2

TUESDAY, JUNE 19

DIRECTOR MORSE SAID, "WHAT'S KEEPIN' FRANK?"

He had been leaning over the pit piano, using it as a desk. Now he straightened and surveyed the theater through his thick horn-rimmed glasses, his head moving deliberately on its long neck. Today he was wearing shirt and slacks of contrasting tartans. One long leg was wrapped around the other as he stood, giving him the look of a studious plaid flamingo.

Since the rehearsal had been called for 10:00 and it was now all of 10:03, I concluded that while he might seem casual, the director ran a tight ship.

I had stopped by the theater on my way to Anna's House, bearing mail I'd collected that morning from the Colony post office box in East Hampton. The noon mail run, usually made by Stefan the Tenor, had somehow been skipped the day before. Because he'd been too busy chewing out Frank? I wondered.

Jenny said, "I think I saw Frank heading for his cabin right after breakfast."

I was still holding Frank's mail—the latest issue of *Prevention* magazine and two letters, one with a French postmark. I was about to offer to stop by the end cabin

on my way to Anna's House unless, as seemed more
likely, I met him on the road, when Amanda St. James
said, "Maybe he's forgotten the time. I'll go see."

I thought Theo Morse was about to object, but by
that time the White Queen was halfway to the door. He
shrugged and turned back to his clipboard.

Today the chiffon scarf wrapping Amanda's wiry
curls was a pale sea green. She was wearing a gauzy
blouse of the same shade and floppy, cream-colored
pants. As she went out the door and into a stiffish
breeze, the scarf and the wide pant legs fluttered in
her wake.

As I stood by the front row of seats, hesitating over
whether to wait for Frank or hand over his mail to someone else, the Jamaican Baryshnikov ambled over to me
and offered his hand.

"Jason Lee Jones," he said. "I have this uncomfortable feeling that we haven't been properly introduced.
Phoebe, isn't it? Well, Phoebe, what's your opinion of all
this so far?" His left hand encompassed the barn and its
occupants. "Think you can put up with us?"

Jason Lee was older than I'd first judged. Also
smaller, only an inch or so taller than I. His dark, smooth
face was boyish, with a short, flat nose and very round
eyes. But the expression in those eyes was shrewd, the
close-cropped hair sprinkled with grey, the hand I shook
papery with wrinkles and heavily veined.

Why, I wondered, was he choosing this particular
moment to be charming? If he'd wanted to be cordial, he
could have done so yesterday at lunch.

"Put up with you? Oh, I think so," I said. "And if I
can't there's always the music. I was really impressed by
the rehearsal yesterday."

"Ah, diplomatic of you to say so," Jason Lee said
with an expression so ingenuous that it had to be a
challenge.

Okay.

"Beyond that," I said, "I sort of have the feeling I've wandered into a production of *Six Characters in Search of an Author* and it's fascinating but no one's given me a program."

Jason Lee threw back his head and howled with laughter. The sound drew several curious glances, and it occurred to me that the barn had become unnaturally quiet. Later, I wondered whether I had conjured up after the fact an atmosphere of tense anticipation among the group clustered around the front of the stage. Or was it only from one, so powerful that it infected us all like a miasma?

In any case the scream, when it came, had an electrifying effect.

With a choreographic precision that in other circumstances would have been comic, every head jerked up and around in the direction taken by the White Queen.

Larry Peterson's hands had been resting on the lyre of the piano as he leaned forward, talking to Theo Morse. They slipped and hit the keys with a discordant crash.

Several people exclaimed some variation of "Good God, what was that?" Stefan Kowalski automatically wisecracked, "About a D-sharp," and immediately looked chagrined. Whatever the cause, there could be no doubt that the scream had been genuinely anguished.

And now it was being repeated, in a rhythmic pattern that indicated full-blown hysteria.

I found myself in the midst of a convulsive mass movement up the aisle and out the front door of the theater. From there, the boys' cabins were clearly visible. So was Amanda St. James, staggering along the path that led from the cabins to the road. Her hands were clasped to her head. Her mouth, from which the screams continued to emanate, was stretched into a perfect O.

For a moment the scene froze before me: the string of cabins, starkly white in the glare of the sunshine, the woods dark behind them, the lone figure with its pale, fluttering garments and attitude of woe. It was unreal: a publicity shoot from a rehearsal for the third act of *Lucia*. Any minute someone was going to yell, "Cut! Run it again from the top."

But then Theo Morse was pushing unceremoniously past me. His long legs windmilled up the slope. Stefan Kowalski, running with surprising speed considering his bulk, quickly joined him, with Jason Lee Jones and Larry Peterson only a short way back.

Then I was running too. Behind me I heard Jenny's voice, high-pitched and tense, say, "Oh my God, something terrible's happened, hasn't it? Something's happened to Frank!"

She caught up with me and took hold of my arm. Her hand was like a chunk of ice.

Rita, on Jenny's other side, said, panting, "Maybe it's not as bad as . . . You know how Amanda is."

Under the barrage of those continued screams, neither of us replied.

Theo reached Amanda at the end of the path, where it joined the road. He took her by the shoulders and gave her a shake. She sagged against him, half turned, and pointed a shaking arm at Frank's cabin. Theo looked back in our direction. He motioned urgently to Rita, thrust Amanda toward her, and ran on. I saw him take the steps in a single leap and disappear through Frank's door, with Stefan on his heels.

Amanda sank to her knees. She had stopped screaming and now was crying in harsh, gulping sobs. Rita crouched beside her and held her tightly, rocking her and making soothing sounds. Larry had stopped too, and stood by the two women breathing hard and mopping his forehead with a white handkerchief. His face had lost its coolly ironic expression. He looked bewildered and, I thought, frightened.

I would have stopped as well, but Jenny, still gripping my arm, continued to pull me along the path. Rita caught my eye. "For God's sake, don't let Jenny go in there!"

No fear, I thought, as long as she's hanging on to me. My dread of what might be waiting in Frank's cabin was deep. I found it inconceivable that a grown woman could be reduced to Amanda's state by anything less then genuine horror.

I pulled Jenny to a halt just short of the steps. She turned to stare at me. Her face was white and stunned.

"They'll let us know what's happened," I said. I put an arm around her shoulders. "You'd better sit down. You look . . ."

I felt her stiffen, and followed her gaze. Theo Morse had reappeared at the door. From behind him, Stefan Kowalski pushed roughly past, leaned over the banister, and vomited onto the grass below. Theo's face too, was white tinged with green. He sat down abruptly on the top step.

"Frank's dead," he said. "It looks like—like he's been poisoned or somethin'."

Beside me, Jenny gasped. She turned and buried her face against my shoulder.

"It's anaphylactic shock," Stefan Kowalski said. He leaned against the cabin wall and wiped his sleeve across his mouth. "I mean, that's what it looks like. I've seen it before. But then, it wasn't anyone I knew." He drew a shaky breath. "It's an allergic reaction. He must have taken some penicillin by accident. That's what he was allergic to, wasn't it?"

"Accident!" Amanda St. James struggled to her feet and advanced on the group by the cabin, followed by Rita and Larry. The green chiffon had come loose and been used, by the look of it, to wipe vomit from her lips and the front of the sea-green blouse. Her hair stood out from her head like an angry halo. "Frank would never take penicillin by *accident*! He isn't stupid, you know, in spite of what some of you like to think!"

"A bee sting, then," Larry Peterson offered. "Maybe he'd become sensitized—"

"Bullshit!" Amanda said. The word, issuing from her ordinarily prissy lips, was shocking. "Frank's been stung plenty of times. The only thing he's allergic to is penicillin and everyone here knows that. And the only way he'd take any was if he was tricked into it!"

"Amanda, love!" Jason Lee expostulated. He went over to her and placed a gentle hand on her shoulder. "Don't say things like that, don't make things worse than they are. You can't possibly think—"

"Don't 'Amanda, love' me!" She threw off Jason's hand and turned on him fiercely. "And yes, I can possibly think. If it comes to that, what were you and Frank talking about Sunday night in the kitchen? I saw you come out of there looking like you could spit nails!"

Jason Lee stepped back, shaking his head. Amanda swiveled to face the group on the path. Her body swayed slightly, her voice rose higher and higher. "Somebody tricked him! Somebody did it on purpose! Which one of you did it? Which one of you . . ."

"Amanda, my darling, that is enough!" Anna Varovna, who had come up behind the group, made her way through it and went directly to the White Queen.

"They've killed him!" Amanda shrieked. "They've—"

With no hesitation, Anna Varovna raised her hand and delivered a stinging slap to Amanda's cheek. Amanda gasped. For a moment she stared at Anna, then she fell weeping onto the smaller woman's shoulder.

Anna staggered but remained upright. "Ah! There, there, Amanda," she said. She smoothed the wild hair for a moment or two. Then she gently detached herself and turned toward the cabin.

Theo said, "Anna! Don't!" but she shook her head, mounted the steps, and went in the door.

Jenny wept silently against my chest, her body rigid and trembling.

When Anna Varovna reappeared, her face was ashen and her lips pressed into a thin line. Her eyes glistened, but her voice was firm. "We must all be strong, my darlings. Poor, poor Frank. He is surely with *le bon Dieu.*"

She grasped Theo's shoulder as if to steady herself. Stefan moved over to put his arm around her. She gave him a grateful look, but her posture remained upright, her voice clear and firm. "Whatever has happened, my darlings, a young man has suddenly died. Now is no question what to do. Go please, Stefan, and call police. And all of you come away. Is best we wait for them together."

The waiting turned into a very long morning followed by an interminable afternoon.

The big main room at Anna's House, yesterday so warm and accommodating, now seemed crowded and claustrophobic as ten people struggled in their various ways to come to terms with the enormity of sudden, violent death. That the death had been violent was clear. None of the four who had actually witnessed its aftermath—Amanda St. James, Theo Morse, Stefan Kowalski, and Anna Varovna—volunteered to the rest of us a single detail of what they had seen. At one point I observed Rita murmur to Theo what appeared to be a query. He shook his head and again started to turn green.

Eventually, when the second wave of police had descended, there was an eleventh person—a uniformed cop who stood by the doorway to the dining room, rocking on his heels from time to time and determinedly directing his gaze just above our heads. But that was after the police had decided, as they put it, that there were some "puzzling features" to Frank's death. They would appreciate all of us staying where we were until they could get around to interviewing each of us separately.

From the first moments of our trooping into Anna's House, I was aware once more of a closing of ranks, manifested in oblique glances, sentences broken off, and a general avoidance of my vicinity. This time I couldn't really blame them. I was patently the outsider—unknown and unwelcome—at a family tragedy. How could I possibly empathize with, understand, share in their emotions?

But although it might have seemed presumptuous to say it to these people, I felt a terrible sadness that Frank was dead. I had liked him. He'd been warm and genuine, and I'd sensed that this present aberration of his had a good chance of passing away. I hoped against hope that his death would turn out, after all, to have been accidental.

Oddly enough, this point, which I assumed, after Amanda's dramatics, must be central to everyone's thoughts, was not discussed—at least not in my hearing. Even before the advent of the watch cop, the question of whether Frank had died by accident or by design was, like the elephant in the living room, elaborately ignored.

At first, there had been a good deal of bustling and agitation. Stefan had returned quickly from making his call to announce that the East Hampton Town Police were on their way. Gerta Hofstetter, assisted by Rita Michaels, had lugged in and set up a mammoth coffeemaker, along with cups, milk, cream, and sugar. Anna had added a bottle of brandy. While we awaited the arrival of the law, people variously paced, fidgeted, rattled coffee cups, and spoke in undertones. Nobody spoke to Amanda.

Amanda's sobs had subsided to hiccups and then stopped. Somewhere along the way she'd managed to wash her face and pull her hair back with a rubber band into a thick, frizzy ponytail. The soiled blouse had been replaced with a T-shirt bearing the logo of a local Public Radio station over a picture of Beethoven (looking, I couldn't help thinking, suitably glum). She had been the first to receive a medicinal dose from Anna's brandy bottle and was probably looking better than the rest of us. All that screaming, after all, had to have been therapeutic. She sat straight backed in a small armchair in the far corner of the room and stared at the coffee cup in her lap. If she still believed that one of her colleagues was a murderer, at least for now she was keeping it to herself.

Jason Lee Jones, on the other hand, looked terrible. He had flopped into a wicker chaise not far from the bay window where I was sitting, and lay there with his eyes closed. His dark brown skin seemed to have acquired a kind of grey frosting and the sockets of his eyes a new prominence. When Gerta Hofstetter brought him a cup of coffee, he looked up momentarily and waved her away. She gave the coffee to me, instead. It was sweet and heavily laced with brandy and I was grateful for it.

When the town cop arrived, Anna and Stefan went to show him Frank's cabin. Because the cabins were hidden from view by the tall hedges on that side of the house, the rest of us could only wait in restless impatience.

Amanda, addressing her colleagues for the first time since her outburst on the path, said fretfully, "I must say, I *don't* see why we all have to be corralled in here like children."

"I agree," Rita said. She turned to her husband, who sat beside her on the sofa. "Theo, couldn't we just . . ."

"It iss what Anna wants," Gerta said, in a tone that announced the question was settled. But I noticed that her hand shook as she poured yet another generous dollop of brandy into her cup. Also that she moved constantly about the room, straightening cushions, moving small objects and then moving them back again, unable to settle anywhere for more than a few seconds.

"The young policeman tells us to stay here," Anna said on her return. "He sends for, I believe, detectives." With a sympathetic half-smile, she added, "Is very young, this policeman. I think he very much wants to pass to somebody else the responsibility."

"Puked all over the place," Stefan Kowalski said with understandable satisfaction. "And now he's stringing that yellow tape around the cabin and the path. It's unreal. I have to keep reminding myself it's Frank in there and not a scene from a movie."

"My darlings," Anna said, "listen to me. We all know is *mostly* absurd that any one of us would on purpose harm poor Frank. The policemen will find that has happened some terrible accident. Meanwhile, when they ask you, you only must tell the truth."

Nervous nods all 'round. No opinions offered.

Anna's gaze lingered for a moment on Amanda. Then she turned to Gerta. "My darling, perhaps you and Stefan be so good as to make sandwiches. Is possible we are here for some time."

Rita said, "Where's Sarah Kirk?"

It had been niggling at me that someone was missing. Where, indeed, *was* the Mouse?

"She hass phoned this morning, early," Gerta said, "She iss not feeling well. But she iss sure she will be back tomorrow." To Anna, she said, "I will see what iss in the kitchen. Come, Stefan."

Amanda sniffed. "Probably hungover," she said, "or her husband is and she's busy holding his head. They all drink, you know, these locals."

Really, I thought crossly, did the woman work at being unlikable or did it come naturally?

As if he'd heard me, Jason Lee on the wicker chaise opened one eye. "*Chère* Amanda," he murmured. "Always to be counted on for the appropriate offensive remark."

"Oh, well," Amanda retorted, "I don't pretend to be p.c. like the rest of you."

"What you don't get, Amanda dear," Rita said, "is

the difference between political incorrectness and pure fucking insensitivity."

"My darlings! Please!" Anna Varovna's voice was uncharacteristically sharp, but there had been a telltale catch in it as well.

Rita jumped up from the sofa, went to Anna where she stood by the mantel, and put her arms around her. "Oh, shit!" she said contritely. "Oh, Anna, I'm sorry. We're all sorry. This is so awful for you. For all of us, of course, but especially . . . Oh, hell, you know what I mean." She drew Anna back with her to the sofa.

Larry Peterson had been standing by the piano, idly riffling through the piles of music on its lid. He turned, caught my eye, shook his head ruefully, and turned back. Remembering last night's camaraderie, it didn't, to me, seem adequate.

Amanda St. James, after adding a murmured apology to Rita's, had leaned back in the armchair. Her hands still clutched the coffee cup in her lap. Her eyes stared blankly at the ceiling.

On the big sofa in front of the fireplace, Rita, Theo, and Anna sat close together, occasionally exchanging a few murmured sentences.

Only Jenny, emerging from the powder room in the hall, searched me out and came to sit beside me on the window seat. She was still pale but seemed fairly composed. "Thank you for taking care of me out there," she said.

I couldn't remember having done much of anything and said so, but she said, "Oh yes, you did. I was so scared." She took my hand and squeezed it.

Shortly thereafter she picked up a magazine and curled up with it in a corner of the window seat. Whether or not she was reading it, I couldn't tell.

It reminded me, though, of Frank's mail—the magazine and the two letters. They had been my responsibility. To whom, I wondered, should I turn them

over now? I seemed to recall stuffing them into the side
pocket of my shoulder bag, but when I looked, only the
magazine was there. I checked my immediate vicinity
and quickly spotted the letters on the floor near the window seat, half-hidden under a small set of shelves.

But when I went to retrieve them, there was only
one envelope. The other one, the one with the French
postmark, was nowhere to be seen.

9

Who would force unwished attentions
on us now amid our woe?

act 1, scene 11

"MY NAME IS LIEUTENANT SAUL FREED. I'M WITH SUFFOLK
County Homicide."

The speaker stood in front of the fireplace, facing an
audience not disposed to be welcoming. We had been
waiting together in that room for almost two hours.

At his announcement there was a spate of protests.
He raised a placatory hand. "I know, I know. Believe me,
we are not jumping to conclusions. We don't know yet
what happened to Mr. Palermo. But until we have a better idea, this is the routine. After all, we wouldn't want
to miss anything by making assumptions."

No one rushed to agree with him. He sighed and
rubbed his forehead with thumb and forefinger. "Well,
anyway . . . I happened to be in East Hampton, so they
sent me along."

The lieutenant's voice had a mournful quality that
might or might not have been habitual. In any case, I got
the impression that he was no more thrilled with his
presence there than we were.

He was medium tall, medium thin, with a posture
that managed both to be erect and to suggest that a
heavy weight was pressing on his shoulders. He had sad

eyes, a snub nose, and a neat, downturning salt-and-pepper mustache. His clothing—grey cotton slacks and a blue-and-white-checked, short-sleeved shirt—suggested he had been summoned to this present duty from more pleasurable pursuits.

The appearance of the woman who had followed him into the room suggested that she'd been summoned from a Gauguin landscape and absurdly crammed into a pair of tan twill slacks and matching blazer. She was tall—only an inch or two shorter than the lieutenant. Her full mouth was pink without the aid of makeup, liquid eyes tilted above alpine cheekbones. A cloud of smoke-black hair was held back with a shell-pink plastic hoop. Matching earrings perched on either side of her face like pink butterflies.

Her entrance had occasioned an involuntary chorus of male throat noises. Stefan Kowalski's jaw dropped, and though after a moment he did think to close his mouth, his gaze remained fixed and slightly stunned.

Rita Michaels, I saw, had also observed Stefan's reaction. Interestingly, she looked annoyed.

The lieutenant introduced the Island Princess as Detective Delgado.

He then rubbed his forehead again and consulted a notebook he'd pulled from his pants pocket. Madame Varovna, he said, pronouncing the name with care, had made the Colony office available for interviews. He would see us there one at a time. He knew we must all be anxious to have the circumstances of our colleague's death cleared up. He appreciated our cooperation.

Amanda St. James, presumably due to her role as discoverer of the body, was the first to be summoned. She rose and left the room with what, if I'd been disposed to be unkind, I would have described as an overdone *tragédienne* air. I noticed that she gripped a crumpled handkerchief in one hand, though she hadn't so much as blown her nose for the last hour and a half.

Just what was—had been—Amanda's relation to Frank? Had there been, as they say, "something"? She had certainly set herself up as his champion, but in the brief time I'd had to observe, I'd seen nothing on Frank's side to indicate a romantic attachment. Which didn't mean it wasn't possible. I put Amanda's age in the middle thirties—arguably, to Frank, not yet too far gone in decrepitude. Ah well, it wasn't a question I could very well bring up at the moment.

Even though, as the morning had worn on, I'd felt a slight thawing of attitude toward my presence. Gerta and the multitalented Stefan had produced a raft of tuna salad, ham, and cheese sandwiches and a big pot of chicken noodle soup, which they'd set up for self-service on the dining porch. The watch cop, who had taken up his post sometime into the second hour of our incarceration, eyed each of us as we went in search of food as if he expected, even hoped, that someone would make a break for it. I was grateful to him. As an even newer stranger and common adversary, he had to some degree relieved me of the role.

After Amanda's exit, Rita got up, stretched, and strolled to the piano. She pulled a volume from one of the stacks on the piano's top and sat down at the keyboard. Today she was wearing her thick, dark hair unbraided and gathered at the nape with a black bow. It rippled down her back almost to the rim of the piano stool, lending her stocky body an unaccustomed air of youth and vulnerability.

She flipped through the pages, stopping here and there to play a few bars and hum under her breath. The book was a collection of German lieder. I couldn't make out the name of the composer.

She broke off, rotated the stool to face me at the window, and said, "Do you play, Phoebe?"

Taken by surprise, I said, "No, I'm afraid I didn't inherit—that is, no, I don't play."

"Didn't inherit Papa's talent? No need to be coy, Phoebe. Not all singers are as ignorant of the wider musical world as certain instrumentalists would have you believe." She grimaced at Larry Peterson and turned back to the keyboard. "In any case, I'm glad to hear it. What this world needs is fewer frigging musicians and more intelligent listeners."

At the moment, rather than intelligent I was feeling rather foolish. I had indeed, I realized, on some level absorbed Mick's dictum that established "singers" and "musicians" as distinct categories. "Not their fault," he would explain magnanimously. "Poor bastards discover in their late teens, twenties even, that they have this freak combination of vocal cords and body cavities. No education, no background, no taste. Can't even read music. Can't count, some of 'em, for God's sake." It had been one of his favorite riffs.

Rita had begun to play, and to sing at half-voice, one of the songs in the book. Even in this muted performance, the song was meltingly beautiful. Since German is a language where my powers are limited to *"Wo ist das W.C., bitte?"* and the like, I couldn't guess at its meaning.

She completed the song and the brief, tender piano postlude. Her hands dropped to her lap and she seemed, for a moment or two, to be studying them.

"How perfectly wonderful," I said, "What was that?"

"Schumann," Rita said. *"Frauenliebe und Leben.* A Woman's Love and Life.' First song in the cycle."

"Rita does the whole cycle beautifully," Theo Morse said, from the couch. "It's perfect for her. But she won't sing it anymore."

"Gorgeous, but massively antifeminist," Stefan observed. He leaned against the wall near the dining-porch entrance, wolfing down yet another sandwich. Making up, I supposed, for the breakfast he'd lost outside Frank's cabin. It occurred to me to wonder that Stefan, (the EMT, presumably inured to the uglinesses of physical trauma,) had been the only one besides Amanda to exhibit that particular reaction.

Rita's head came up and she swung around on the stool. Her eyes were wet. Ignoring Stefan, she said to me, "I don't sing it anymore, Phoebe, because the poems are the most god-awful, self-abasing drivel—written by a man, of course—about what a woman is *supposed* to feel. The gist being, 'Oh, this man I love is a god and how incredible that he should stoop to marry poor unworthy me!' Then in the last song he dies and her life is over. *'Ich bin nicht lebend mehr!'* I ask you!"

"Well, yeah, it does seem rather—"

"Not to mention the little number about the joys of pregnancy." Rita was on a roll now, tears gone, eyes glittering as if from some long-pent emotion. "About which I'd love to set the bastard straight."

"You have children?" I said.

"Three," Rita said. "Each one representing the failure of yet another foolproof contraceptive device. Foam baby, pill baby, IUD baby. I'm a goddamn medical miracle, I am."

"Don't let Rita fool you," Theo said to me. "She's crazy about the kids."

Rita turned on him. "Of course I am, Theo, you idiot! They're beautiful kids, I'd die if anything happened to those kids! That's not the point. The point is—" She brought herself up abruptly. The steam seemed to leave her. "Ah, hell, I don't know what the point is." She turned back to the piano and began again to turn the pages of the songbook.

"You are perhaps right, Rita," Anna observed. "We should no longer allow these men to tell us what we are feeling." She had been sitting quietly on the couch and spoke as if the discussion were still centered on Schumann's song cycle. Evidently Rita's public sharing of highly personal information was habitual enough to be unworthy of note. "But *Frauenliebe*—such beautiful music, my darlings."

"She should haff heard Lotte Lehmann," Gerta Hofstetter growled from the hall doorway. She and Jenny had been given special dispensation, under the eye of another uniformed cop, to clean up the lunch things in the kitchen. "Lehmann—now there wass a voice!"

At the piano, Rita's shoulders rose and fell expressively, but she offered no further comment.

Later, after Rita had been summoned for her interview, I picked up the Schumann songbook from the piano. I wanted to know what that first song of the Frauenliebe cycle was about—the one that Rita had sung all the way through, the one that had made her cry. The English translation began, "Since first I saw him/I think myself blind/wherever I look/I see only him," and went on in the same infatuated vein for another ten or twelve lines.

What, I wondered, was the connection? Was it her husband Rita was weeping over? Stefan Kowalski? Frank? Or was she just feeling generally overwrought, which, God knew, would hardly be surprising.

All in all, I felt no wiser than before.

I was the last one to be called.

Each interviewee in turn had been excused, as it were, from custody. Either by choice or by police direction, none returned to our waiting room. By the time my turn came, I had had almost two more hours to sit and stew over what had happened, what was happening, what might happen. Not to mention what I knew and didn't know, what I might be asked, what I should say.

It was all very well for Anna to say, "You only must tell the truth." What the hell was the truth? Unlike poor Frank, I was very much aware of the chasm that could exist between truth and perception. What right did I have to make judgments about the behavior of people I hardly knew? Where exactly was the line between telling the truth and tattling?

Why was I working myself into a state about a matter that, please God, might turn out to have nothing to do with evil intent or with any member of the Varovna Colony?

Because, I answered myself, you don't believe that. You don't believe in massive coincidence. You do believe in the promptings of your gut. You believe that someone at the Varovna Colony deliberately killed Frank Palermo.

No, I don't.

Yes, you do.

10

I must talk, I have no choice . . .

act 1, scene 2

LIEUTENANT FREED HAD CHOSEN TO SIT NOT BEHIND THE desk (*my* desk, I thought jealously) but in front of it on a Naugahyde-upholstered chair with wooden arms. The Gauguin Princess nestled discreetly on a metal folding chair in the corner to his right.

The chair they had selected for their interviewees was a chintz-covered number, cushiony and with plump little arms, that looked as if it belonged in a boudoir. It hadn't been in the office yesterday; they must have brought it down from one of the rooms upstairs. Was this a thoughtful gesture or a ploy? Perhaps stereotypically, I didn't believe the police went in much for thoughtful gestures.

The lieutenant rose and held out his hand. "Saul Freed," he said. "Sorry you had to wait so long." He gestured to his partner. "Claire Delgado."

The Gauguin Princess looked up from her notepad. "Gladdameetcha," she said. The voice was pure Long Island, the once-over from the liquid eyes direct and shrewd.

Lieutenant Freed motioned me to the boudoir chair, waited until I was seated, and then sat himself. I was disarmed, as always be any display of old-fashioned gallantry. In my peripheral vision, I saw the Princess roll her eyes.

The lieutenant sat with left ankle resting on right knee. A pencil in his right hand tapped absently at a closely written, steno-type notebook propped on his leg. He was wearing white socks and blue Keds.

"I left you until the last," he said, "because I gather you're the only one here who wasn't an old friend of the dec—of Mr. Palermo."

I nodded. "I never met any of them until yesterday. I've just started working here. As I'm sure you've been told."

He nodded in his turn. "Uh-huh. And how did you happen to start working here?"

I gave him the short version: husband dead, needed a job, heard about this one through a friend, it seemed to be something I could do.

"You have a musical background?"

I explained, somewhat grudgingly, about Mick and my father. What, I wondered with some annoyance, did my personal circumstances have to do with Frank's death?

The lieutenant nodded again, with an air that implied my answers had somehow given him satisfaction. He flicked with a finger at the pages of the notebook. "What I was hoping was that you could maybe give us an outsider's impression. Things you might have noticed, a . . . perhaps a more objective viewpoint."

I swallowed. "I'm really kind of uncomfortable with this. I mean, I hardly know these people. I might get things completely wrong."

"Well, yeah. I can understand how you feel. So let's say we give you credit for being observant but not infallible. And you give us credit for being able eventually to mosey on through to the truth."

I felt myself flush, which made me mad. Come on, Mullins, I told myself, you're perfectly capable of deciding what or what not to tell. Aloud I said, "Well, okay, I'll do what I can. What kind of thing did you want to know?"

He flipped over a page of the notepad, wrote something at the top, then underlined it twice. "I understand you had a conversation with Mr. Palermo yesterday. Where was that?"

"In his cabin."

"Ah. Could you describe what the cabin—his room—looked like at that time?"

I thought back. "Clothes all over the place. Duffle bags. Books. Coffee cups. Bed unmade. It was a mess. Except for the top of the bureau. That was military-neat."

"And what was on the bureau?"

"All his jars of vitamins and things. All lined up. And some bottles of spring water, and a cup."

"How did you know they were vitamins?"

"I could see they were. Besides, he told me. Actually, he took some while I was there, tossed them down like—" Suddenly I felt sick. "Oh God, was that what . . . ?"

The lieutenant ignored my question. "You were not, I take it, one of the people who entered the cabin today?"

"No. I didn't. I mean, why would I?"

"Be glad you didn't. Mr Palermo's death was not a pleasant one."

From her corner, the Princess made a graphically descriptive sound in corroboration.

The lieutenant's mouth twisted. Whether in annoyance or amusement, I couldn't tell. "Getting back to the bureau. When you left the cabin yesterday, it was as you described—'military-neat'?"

"Yes. Why?"

He made his characteristic forehead-rubbing gesture. "Because when we—that is, when the East Hampton police first arrived—the bureau top was bare. Everything on it appeared to have been swept to the floor on one side. Suggesting, if the four people who did enter the room are telling the truth, that Mr. Palermo knew, or suspected, the source of the substance that killed him."

"Mad as shit and knocked the stuff off," the Princess observed, illustrating with a sweep of her arm.

Lieutenant Freed raised a cautionary hand. "Possibly. Possibly."

The image of Frank realizing what was happening to him and striking out in frustration and despair was horrible. I felt tears spring to my eyes and saw the lieutenant's puzzled look. I scrabbled in my bag for a Kleenex. "I know I only met him yesterday," I said rather testily, "but I liked him. I think he had a good heart. I hate to think of—if he knew what was happening, why didn't he try to get help?"

"According to the medical examiner, by the time he realized what was going on it would have been too late. And he would've known that. Corroborated by the fact that everyone I've spoken to so far has quoted me the story about when he was a kid and almost died from a penicillin reaction."

"Oh yeah," I said. "He even told me."

The Princess's head jerked up. The lieutenant looked thoughtful.

He made some more squiggles on his notepad and flipped the page. I noticed that he could write without looking. "So," he said, "what else did you and Mr. Palermo talk about?"

"There was this—I guess you could call it a cult he'd recently joined. The Children of Truth. I asked him about that."

"And?"

"I thought it sounded . . . in a word, nutty. Everybody telling the unvarnished truth to everybody all the time?"

Saul Freed actually smiled. It was a nice smile that included the corners of his eyes. "To a cop, that sounds a little like heaven."

I smiled back. "Sure, but you know what I mean. The way Frank talked, it was the kind of rigid dogma that doesn't allow for common sense or courtesy or regard for other people's privacy. I thought it showed him to be pretty naive. And I thought it made clear why a number of his friends seemed to be seriously irritated with him."

"Ahhh," the lieutenant said. He settled back slightly in his chair. "Perhaps you could enlarge on that."

Oh, perfect. So much for my precious discretion.

I gestured toward his notebook. "Well, surely the others have mentioned this Children of Truth business. I mean, they must know more about it than I do."

He gave a slow nod and began riffling pages. He stopped at one and read: " 'Frank was always getting some sort of bee in his bonnet. None of us took it seriously.' " More riffling. " 'Frank Palermo was one of the sweetest people. He couldn't possibly be a threat to anyone.' " Another page. " 'We were *friends*. All of us. This cult business was just silly. We knew he'd get over it.' "

He looked up. "Interestingly, several people came up with some version of 'Pay no attention to Amanda, she tends to overdramatize.' But the lady herself—the tall blonde, Ms. St. James?—was not at all helpful. Pretty much gave us to understand that we were incapable of understanding her or Mr. Palermo or the artistic temperament. Didn't choose to share any thoughts she might or might not have had."

In the corner, the Princess's rosy lips silently but unmistakably articulated the word *bitch*.

"However," he went on, "a couple of people did mention incidents that were—well, suggestive. So if you could just add any observations of your own . . ."

Obviously, he wasn't going to tell me what "incidents" had been mentioned or by whom. I might as well get it over with.

As accurately as possible, I described the scene on the path following the discovery of Frank's body. I emphasized that Amanda was obviously hysterical. I said I had noticed some tension—okay, perhaps even amounting to ill will—at the morning rehearsal the day before. After a brief hesitation, I told about overhearing Stefan's confrontation with Frank in his cabin.

From the way the lieutenant nodded, I deduced that he'd already heard about that. Must have been from Stefan himself, I thought, in anticipation of what *I* might say. And Lieutenant Sneaky hadn't told me, waiting to see if I'd come up with it on my own. God, I hated this—him—the whole incredible mess.

When I fell silent, he said, "There was mention of an incident at lunch yesterday. When Mr. Palermo made a remark about meeting a friend of Madame Varovna's in Paris. It seemed to upset her. You were there, I believe. Did you happen to notice?"

"Good Lord!" I burst out. "You're talking about Anna Varovna! You're suggesting she might be involved in—in the death of one of her pupils over some—" I broke off. "You really do think Frank was murdered, don't you?" I said.

The lieutenant gave me a considering look. Then he leaned back in his chair. "What I think is this. Here's a young guy, talented, doing well, they tell me, in his profession. Only big health scare he's had in his life that we know of is this allergy to penicillin. No problem—just stay away from penicillin.

"And here's the M.E., who says, Don't quote me, blah blah blah, we won't know for sure until the autopsy, but it sure looks like this guy died from anaphylactic shock. Which turns out to mean an allergic reaction. So if penicillin is what he was allergic to, says the M.E., more than likely that's what did it.

"And here's a bunch of people who all knew the victim real well, and knew about the allergy. And when I talk to these people, every last one of them, in my opinion, is fudging and backpedaling and in general protesting too much.

"Add to that fact that there are no locks on the doors in those cabins and, what with everyone being such good friends, it seems anyone could wander in and out of just about anywhere without causing comment. Also, the evening of the day that Mr. Palermo arrived—last Thursday, I believe, almost a week after everyone else—the whole bunch of 'em gathered in his room for what was described by the ones who bothered to mention it as 'an impromptu get-together.' So everyone knew exactly how available those pill bottles were.

"Now, not a one of these people is suggesting the possibility of suicide. And if they had, no one could convince me he'd choose that way of doing it.

"Accident? Penicillin isn't exactly your common or garden-variety substance. Not likely to get sprinkled on your eggs, say, by mistake. And we know that Mr. Palermo wouldn't go near the stuff or have any in his possession.

"An isolated case of product tampering that happened to end up in the hands of the one person out of a hundred with that kind of allergy? Too big a coincidence for me.

"So yes, Ms. Mullins, to answer your question. Yes, on the whole, I think Frank Palermo was murdered."

There was a knock at the door. It was opened by a man in plainclothes I hadn't seen before. "Lieutenant? Sorry to interrupt, but I think you should see this."

"Excuse me," the lieutenant said. He went out, closing the door behind him.

The Princess stood up, stretched, gave her body a loosening shake that would have reduced Stefan Kowalski to tears, and arranged herself again on the metal chair. She looked at me kindly.

"Hey," she said, "don't take it so hard. The lieutenant's the best. And I'm not so bad either, or he wouldn't put up with me, ya know? No one's gonna get hurt that doesn't deserve it. Trust me."

She gave me a smile and then, for good measure, a wink and an A-Okay finger sign. I was diverted enough to have the urge to ask how she'd ever ended up in Homicide.

Before I could act on the impulse, however, Lieutenant Freed reappeared. In one hand he held a booklike object encased in a plastic bag. His expression was gloomy.

He handed the object to the Princess. "I was afraid of this," he said. "I hate this kind of case."

The Princess held up the bag, turning it this way and that, squinting at whatever was inside. "Jeez!" she said. "You think he did this? A friggin' clue?" She cocked her head up at the lieutenant, her brow creased. "What the hell, 'Amadeus'? Like in the movie?"

The lieutenant's shrug was eloquent. Though his back was to me, I could sense the long-suffering roll of the eyes.

The Princess lifted the bag again, and through the plastic I caught a glimpse of the familiar orange and brown cover of the *Così fan tutte* score. Frank's? Well, who else's, dummy! But . . . *Amadeus*? What were they talking about? It seemed they had forgotten I was there. Maybe if I kept very still . . .

The lieutenant retrieved the plastic-wrapped score from the Princess and turned around. "Oh, um . . . Ms. Mullins. Thank you. Unless there's anything more you can think of . . ."

"No, nothing." As the lieutenant continued to frown

down at the cover of *Così fan tutte*, I assumed I'd been dismissed. As anxious as I'd been a short time ago to put this interview behind me, I now found myself gripped by a powerful curiosity about the new development. However, I got up out of the boudoir chair and started for the door.

As I reached it, I heard the lieutenant heave a sigh and mutter, "If he wanted to leave a message, why the hell didn't he just write it down?"

Well, *I* knew that. I turned. "It was because he didn't have a pencil."

Lieutenant Freed raised his head. He seemed surprised to find me still in the room. "You know this? That he didn't have a pencil?"

I explained about Frank's borrowing mine the day of our conversation. "And I'm pretty sure he'd borrowed somebody's that morning at the rehearsal. I got the feeling it was part of his persona—you know, 'That crazy Frank, never has his own pencil.' Well, you saw his room—" I broke off, remembering. "And there was something . . . before the pencil business, before Amanda came to the door. I was trying to pin him down about the rules in this Truth business. Supposing you knew something about a person behaving unethically or even illegally, would you feel compelled to make it public—that sort of thing. And he started to say, as near as I can remember, that at the moment he was facing that sort of decision. And then we were interrupted."

The lieutenant sat down in the chair I'd just vacated and stared at me as I stood by the door. His expression was bemused. "He told you all this? You'd just met?"

"Well, I'd asked. I think it was a relief, being able to talk about this experience that was so important to him. Nobody else wanted to hear about it anymore."

"And you asked because . . ."

I shrugged. "I was curious."

"Ahh," the lieutenant said.

He exchanged a glance with the Princess. Then, still sitting, he held the package in his hand out to me. "Mind taking a look at this?"

Feeling a slight shiver of what might have been either excitement or revulsion, I walked over to the chair, took hold of the book in its plastic casing, and studied the cover. Superimposed on a color photo in golds and browns of sweeping tiers of boxes at the Metropolitan Opera House, an orange medallion carried three rows of lettering: G. Schirmer Opera Score Editions; Wolfgang Amadeus Mozart; COSI FAN TUTTE. Puzzled and disappointed, I shook my head. "I don't see anything."

"Tip it toward the light," the lieutenant said, gesturing at the window.

I did so. And yes, there it was, an unmistakable and deliberate *X* over the word *Amadeus*, pressed into the soft cardboard as if with a pointed stick. Or a fingernail. I pictured Frank, frantic, in extremis, once again without a damn pencil, making this last desperate effort to communicate what had happened to him. Hastily, I thrust the book back into the lieutenant's hands. "Yes, I see, but—"

"Mean anything to you? Amadeus?"

"Other than Mozart's middle name?" I shook my head. "Actually, the word means 'Beloved of God.' Nobody I've met here so far springs to mind."

The Princess snorted delightedly.

"I just thought," the lieutenant persisted, "you being familiar with the world of classical music and all . . . there might be something, some special significance the sergeant here and I are missing."

"Yeah," the Princess chimed in, "like it could be a code or something. That only other opera types know about."

I smiled in spite of myself. "No, really, nothing like that. And in any case, what makes you think the *X* has anything to do with Frank's . . . death. Where was the score found?"

The lieutenant hesitated, then said, "It was under the . . . it was under him. Actually, one hand was still clutching it. In the circumstances, it's hard to believe there's no connection."

I found suddenly that I wanted nothing more to do with any of this. It was all too sad and awful. These are not my people, I told myself, not my problem. I don't want to think about them. I just want to be somewhere else.

I said, bluntly, "Can I go now?"

The lieutenant sighed again heavily, and stood up. "You're sure there's nothing more you can tell us?"

"No," firmly. "Nothing at all."

"Well, if anything does occur to you, or, say, you should should discover any . . . uh . . . interesting facts about the people here . . ." He regarded me consideringly. "Because, Ms. Mullins, it seems that you not only have an inquiring mind, but you're a person people find it easy to talk to."

"*I* would," the Princess said. "Spill my guts, prob'ly. You got that kinda face, ya know? Warm, and you don't feel like you're gonna be shocked if it turns out maybe you're not Mother Teresa."

Oh, right, I thought. I am really about to encourage people to confide in me and then rat them out to the police.

I looked the lieutenant in the eye. "Of course," I said.

The lieutenant nodded sadly.

I got out of there.

11

What a shameless imposition
on good faith and true devotion . . .

act 1, scene 16

I TURNED LEFT IN THE HALLWAY AND HEADED FOR THE FRONT
door of Anna's House. My workspace had been preempted, God knew where everyone had scattered to,
and basically I needed in a big way to get outdoors. To
reassure myself that the sun was still following its
accustomed course, the birds singing, the water being
blue, all that stuff.

It was a belated version of the reaction I'd had when
they came to tell me that Mick had collapsed and died in
the middle of a rehearsal. A panicky response to the unreality, the *unacceptability* of an event so vast it seems as if
the whole world must have swerved at the same time
into another zone where nothing can be counted on to
be the same.

If I could just get into my car, alone, and drive
through the woods until—

"My darling. I have been waiting for you."

Anna Varovna rose from the sofa. I had been barrel-
ing by, my eyes on the door, my mind occupied as described, and she startled the bejeesus out of me.

She sat back down and gestured for me to join her.

"We are all, perhaps, on the edge," she said kindly. "It is to be understood."

I sat, wondering what on earth she wanted now, and why it couldn't wait. Was she going to load me up with yet more tasks? Was she going to warn me against talking to the police about matters that were none of my business?

"I want," Anna Varovna said, "for you to find out who has done this terrible thing."

"You what?"

"I want for you to discover who has murdered poor Frank."

"What?"

"To listen to people," she elaborated patiently. "To be mostly observant. To understand what is reason behind this so dreadful act."

"But, Anna, the police—"

"We cannot expect, my darling, that these policemen—no, not even the clever Lieutenant Freed—will be able to discover secrets of the heart. Who here will be telling such things to strangers? No, even innocent ones, they hide, they cover up, they create confusion."

"Well, possibly, but, Anna—"

"Oh, maybe police get lucky. Maybe they find, like they say, burning gun. Then all is quickly over. But I do not believe. I believe they must find reason, they must know *why* before knowing who is responsible."

"Anna," I said, "please. Wait. Even supposing the police are as incapable as you say—and I *don't* suppose any such thing—I'm a stranger here too. What makes you think people will talk to me? And you—why should you trust me with something like this? You hardly know me."

"My darling," Anna said, managing to look injured and complacent at the same time, "I am old, yes, but I am not stupid. Do you imagine I hire without sight someone to work at my Colony unless I have asked many questions? Just because I am retired, I am not sticking my head in a bucket. I know many people, I have friends. I find out, my darling, just who is this Phoebe Mullins."

"Oh . . . uh—" I said.

"I learn, for instance, about young girl who accompanies her famous papa around the world making sure that he behaves himself. Or if not that he is at least discreet. And then of woman who does the same for husband even more famous. I learn too that this woman has more friends than, perhaps, she knows, who are happy to tell Varovna, 'Yes, this Phoebe Mullins is good person, wise person, person to trust.' So you see, I am not swatting in the dark."

My amazement—even chagrin—at having been the object of such a thoroughgoing inquiry was overridden by a second realization that had finally caught up with me. "Then you think . . . you really believe . . . that Frank was actually . . ."

"Ah! We do not want to believe, do we, that a thing so ugly, so bad, could happen to this nice young man, this man we know." The dark eyes that had been earnestly fixed on mine abruptly shifted their focus to some inward place. "But such things do happen, yes. The human heart is mostly capable of great cruelty when it fears . . . or even when it loves."

Varovna heaved a sigh, gave her head a brisk shake, and again turned her attention to me. "So yes, my darling, I do believe that Frank was murdered. And now I must be, you see, mostly crass. I must say, How do I protect my Colony, my pupils, my summer season? Even, my dear Phoebe, where do I find at such short notice another baritone for *Così fan tutte*? And I say to myself, For sake of everybody this terrible question of who has killed Frank must quickly have an answer. And then I think, This Phoebe Mullins, she is clever, she knows people. She will help me."

Beyond Anna's shoulder, the big bay window was admitting a brilliant flood of East End midafternoon sunlight. The room itself felt overheated and my head was swimming from a combination of bedazzlement, weariness, and bizarre-incident overload. I made what I sincerely hoped was my last effort of the day to think clearly. Out of the approximately one hundred and three reasons I knew were out there as to why Anna was asking the impossible, I grabbed two.

"Look, Anna," I began.

"Sorry to interrupt, ladies—no, don't stop, we're just leaving." Lieutenant Freed, with the Princess in his wake, was making the crossing from the hallway to the front door. Having reached that harbor, he did a Columbo-like check and half-turned. "There'll be a couple of men still here, looking around—trash cans and so on."

Anna nodded an acknowledgment. "Of course, Lieutenant."

"Well then. I'll probably be seeing you tomorrow."

His mournful eyes rested on mine for a moment, speculatively, I thought, and one eyebrow twitched.

The Princess grinned. *"Ciao,"* she threw over her shoulder as she followed her boss out the door.

I turned immediately back to Anna, fearful of a derailment of my already rackety train of thought.

"For one thing," I said, "I *have* a job—the one you hired me to do. That's already more than any one person should be expected to handle. I couldn't possibly do that and play detective too, even if—"

"But, my darling, I do not ask of you the impossible. I make sure you have help in your work. I ask only that you listen, that you ask here and there questions, that you think about what you are being told."

"Yes, but—"

"You have only to sit there in your office, I guarantee people will come. And they will talk to you. Because you are easy person to talk to, Phoebe. Believe me, my darling."

I was far from accepting this assessment, but there

seemed little point in debating it. And since my second point had been just this unlikelihood of anyone telling me anything, I was left momentarily speechless. Anna was leaning toward me, her hand placed gently but persuasively on my arm, her eyes full of sincerity. Was I being bamboozled? Did I have a chance?

"Well, if you think . . . I'll do what I can, but I certainly can't promise . . ."

Anna pressed my arm. "Thank you, Phoebe."

I would have risen but she still held me. "Is one other thing."

Good God, the woman was insatiable!

"I have noticed the little Jenny has taken to you. That she trusts you." She hesitated. "You know, perhaps, what has happened to her?"

I nodded.

"I am mostly sorry that she should have now to go through such trauma. I thought, you see, that I did favor to bring her here this summer and now . . . ah well. But I think she will need some special friend. I just mention it, you see."

She squeezed my arm and released it. "And now, my darling, we go together and figure out what you will say when press begins to call."

My brain being in a truly weakened condition, it took me a moment to register her meaning. Then my first reaction was: Oh shit, of course—the newspapers, the TV. "Mysterious Death at Former Met Diva's Summer Hideaway." My second was: What do you mean, what *I* will say? My third was resignation.

Even so, there was still one question I had to put. "Anna, why do you find it so easy—or at least not so hard—to believe that Frank was murdered?"

"Ah!" she said, and paused, as if considering her answer carefully. "Frank, you see . . . Frank was one of those people who is danger to himself and others because he thinks he knows people—human psychology, you understand—whereas truly about people he is very stupid. Such a person is like a bull in a glass house— mostly in danger of causing breakage."

I'd have to mull that one over. But in the meantime I had another question (all right, I lied): "Do you have any idea who could have feared—or hated—Frank enough to do that to him?"

"No," Anna said. "No idea, my darling."

I, on the other hand, had many ideas. They racketed in my head, confused, jumbled, half-formed—inchoate, I suppose, would be the word if it were a word I ever actually used. By the time I was making the left turn onto Mile Hill Road by the modest Varovna Colony sign, I'd already given up the attempt to clear my mind of the lot of them.

So, then . . . What had happened today? What did I think about it? What did I *know* about it?

A fragment swam to the surface: ". . . Looking around. Trash cans and so on . . ." Looking for what? Of course! A pill bottle. If penicillin had indeed been introduced into one of Frank's vitamin bottles by someone at the Colony, it must have come from somewhere. From one of those little amber cylinders with the typed prescription label. Indestructible plastic, the policeman's friend. If I were going to get rid of a pill bottle . . . I thought of acres of underbrush, not to mention square miles of bay. Good luck to them.

". . . A bull in a glass house." I permitted myself the smile I'd suppressed in the face of Anna's sincerity. But hadn't Frank struck me more or less exactly like that, and on, Lord knew, far shorter acquaintance? There'd been that example he'd given about the lunch date. And another . . . something about an affair? Shoot, why hadn't I been paying more attention. "Take away the secrecy . . . peace and love for the world" . . . dear God, poor Frank! And then, ". . . a bit of a problem making a decision . . ."

A decision about *what*, Frank? And what the hell does "Amadeus" signify? If anything. And why didn't you ever carry a pencil?

I found myself actually beating my hands against the steering wheel. Being such a recent driver, I'd only experienced the gesture vicariously through the movies. As a gesture, it felt good, but didn't clarify anything.

And finally: Who could have done it?

More images: Anna's stony face at the lunch table, the crash of Gerta's water glass. Stefan Kowalski bursting, red faced, through Frank's screen door. The Red Queen's fan hitting the stage proscenium. Amanda in hysterics, shrieking at Jason Lee, "What were you and Frank talking about . . ." and, "Somebody did it on purpose!"

Then suddenly, as if a few alien frames had been inserted into an ongoing film, Anna's voice: ". . . this woman has more friends than, perhaps, she knows. . . ."

At the time, the words had slipped past me, subsumed in my amazement at the idea of being investigated. Now, remembered, they gave me a feeling of . . . well, warmth. Pleasure. I thought back to the time of Mick's death, of how quick I'd been to lump every offer of help, every evidence of friendship, into the same category. Friends of Mick. Admirers of Mick. Pitiers of Phoebe. (Poor old Phoebe. Lived for her father and then her husband. No skills, no talents, no life of her own. Whatever will she do now?) How quick I'd been to cut and run, pull no strings, ask no favors. And now it seemed there were folks out there who had assured Anna that I was . . . what was it? . . . a good person, a wise person, a person to trust.

A person, even, who might be recruited to befriend "the little Jenny," facing the second violent death of her young life. Because I suspected that this—the providing of a protector of sorts for her most vulnerable staff member—had been Anna's primary purpose in waylaying me. It had to be. "Discover who has murdered poor Frank" indeed! Absurd on the face of it!

And yet . . . hadn't the lieutenant urged on me something uncomfortably similar? Was it possible that I could in some way . . . in between, of course, fielding calls from the media, readying the books for the accountant, ordering the tickets, putting together the program for *Così fan tutte*—the program—that mysterious publishing software . . . JERRY, I never got to call JERRY . . . perhaps if I . . . but on the other hand . . .

I was right the first time. For the state of my thinking, *inchoate* was precisely the word.

"That you, Mrs. Mullins?"

"Yes, Mrs. Schmitter." Again, I hadn't made it past the living-room door. I looked in. There sat my landlady in her huge recliner, her little legs sticking out before her like a doll's. She was holding a teacup, and was just replacing the water pitcher on the table beside her.

"My dear," she said, "what a terrible thing to have happened, you must be so upset." Her expression was solemn, but her eyes were bright with anticipation.

How could she already know? Then I remembered that East Hampton is, after all, a village, with a typical village grapevine beside whose efficiency the modem and the fax fade to insignificance.

"My friend Edith's grandson is with the village police," Mrs. Schmitter said, in unconscious corroboration, "and he told her that they think . . . oh, Mrs. Mullins, is it really *murder*?" The look on her button face under its corona of wispy white pleaded with me to say "yes."

There was no getting out of it. Anyway, why be cruel? "Tell you what, Mrs. Schmitter. I picked up a sandwich and some salad at the deli. Let me go put them on a plate and I'll come and eat in here with you and tell you what I know."

Mrs. Schmitter was a considerate hostess, insisting

that I have my supper before trying to talk—"You look starved, poor thing, and worn out too"—making small talk and sipping from her teacup. I couldn't get over the difference in her behavior. Only that morning she'd gasped at coming upon me in the kitchen, innocently pouring out my orange juice. I'd had to remind her who I was, at which she'd flushed and apologized and practically run from the room.

Now she listened with every appearance of perfect comprehension, from time to time asking sensible questions. When I'd finished telling her what I knew—or as much of it as would shortly be common knowledge—she nodded thoughtfully. "It'll be about love," she said. "There'll be passion at the back of it, mark my words."

For a moment her eyes, which were a faded blue, seemed to dim over, and a puzzled expression crossed her face. Then she perked up and turned to me. "What am I thinking of," she cried, "I haven't offered you a drink!"

"Oh no thanks, I really—"

"Tea or gin?" she said brightly. "Myself, I always find a little drinkie in the evening most relaxing. Although I'd prefer," she added with a confidential air, "that you wouldn't mention it to Little Bobby. The children think they know everything, you know? And they're wrong about so much."

As I prepared to fall into bed, exhausted in every way and now somewhat drunk as well on lukewarm gin straight up, a tune teased at the corners of my mind and wouldn't let go. A spiky, staccato-y tune: "dah, dah, dah, dah, dah, dah, *daaa*." Oh, of course. "Things Are Seldom What They Seem." *Pinafore*, second act. "Skim milk masquerades as cream." Yes, that was it. Well, *duh*, I said to the bedpost, figure *that* one out, Ms. Freud.

But I fell asleep with the tune nagging at my consciousness, and I guess at my unconscious as well, be-

cause it was still chattering away when I woke in the
morning:

Black sheep dwell in ev'ry fold,
All that glitters is not gold . . .
Yes, I know,
That is so.

12

We cannot alter what has already happened.

act 2, scene 13

WEDNESDAY, JUNE 20

". . . A TRULY VALUED COLLEAGUE. AND A LONGTIME FRIEND
of all the staff here. Oh yes, mostly—uh—enormously
talented. Yes, it is a real tragedy. No, I can't tell you anything more than what the police have already . . . Yes, we
believe they will find that Mr. Palermo's death resulted
from a tragic accident.

"Not at all. Goodbye."

Jenny raised her head from the file cabinet where I
had set her to work culling material on the Colony's history. (If I was turning into a Varovna spokesperson, I'd
decided, I should begin to learn whereof I spoke.)

"You're awfully good at that," she said.

Yes, I thought, only a little surprised, I bloody well
am. Assuming the voice of authority. Being civil to the
importunate and irritating. Fudging facts. Shoot, lying
with a straight face—all skills acquired in the course of
three decades spent keeping an artist, his public, and a
slew of prima donna performers of both sexes on terms
of mutual admiration. Or, on the side of the artist, at
least of grudging tolerance.

In fact, I'd gotten up that morning with a sense of
confidence that was quite heady and certainly new. Be-

yond the horror of Frank's death hung the emerging image of Phoebe Mullins as a person of unsung capabilities. Lieutenant Freed thought so. Anna Varovna thought so. Larry Peterson had said I was . . . what was it? . . . intimidating! Wow! It might even be true.

Although it wouldn't do, whispered the remembered strictures of my childhood, to get a swelled head, to get above yourself. . . .

Fuck off! I said to the whispers.

Lightning did not strike.

Thus emboldened, I gave myself an extra pat on the back for one wise decision—to live on my own, away from the Colony. Anna had initially offered, along with the job, room and board—for, naturally, a suitable reduction in salary. But my instinct had been for a certain preservation of autonomy.

And my instinct had been good, I reflected as I drove through a light drizzle along the now-familiar route to work. Despite the greater cost, despite the vagaries of my landlady. Because the physical distancing, minor as it might be, was proving invaluable in keeping a healthy perspective. Why, even now, I told myself, yesterday's events had evolved in my mind into a strange and sad story about people I hardly knew. All I had to do was show up, put in my eight hours, and leave.

This figment lasted as long as it took to reach and drive by Frank's cabin, still fenced around with bright yellow plastic tape. Under the pale grey sky, the tape glowed like some horribly inappropriate celebratory bunting. My stomach flipped, and once again the strange and sad story claimed me as a participant.

Even supposing I had survived that hurdle, the sight of Anna Varovna's face as it appeared at my office door a few minutes later would have done me in. Despite skillful makeup, it was drawn and weary—for the first time since I had met her, the face of a seventy-year-old woman.

As promised, she had assigned me extra office help

in the shape of Jenny Allen. There were several messages on the answering machine that she had left for me to deal with. Sarah Kirk (the Mouse) was still laid up—some sort of virulent stomach bug. Stefan and Gerta would be doing kitchen duty. They would bring me the receipts for any food purchases.

Anna herself had just now been on the separate phone line from her own house, talking with members of Frank's family. "I have called yesterday to break the news. But now, of course, they are wanting details, answers. Answers which I do not have."

I realized I hadn't given a thought to Frank's family, or even to whether he had a family, so strong was the feeling of the Colony itself being family. I asked where they lived.

"Mama and Papa in Brooklyn. Is also two brothers and four sisters, all married, all living not far. They are, of course, mostly devastated."

She shook her head. Briefly, her small shoulders slumped. Then, as Jenny Allen came through the door, she pulled herself upright. "So, you see, here is your assistant." She smiled at Jenny and turned to me. "If young man is calling named Chris Fox, you may put him through to phone at my house—so, with button, you remember? Otherwise, I leave all to you. Is big comfort, Phoebe, that you are here."

Sure, I thought as she disappeared into the hallway, just call me the Designated Buffer. Then I recalled, with some shame, that it was not I who had had to break the news to Frank's mama.

Now I said to Jenny, "By the way, do you know who this Chris Fox might be?"

"Oh, yeah," Jenny said. "He's a singer. A baritone. Anna probably wants him to replace Frank in *Così*."

The casual tone of her reply was somehow chilling. The feeling must have registered on my face, because she colored and said, "I guess it sounds heartless. But this first production of the season is really important to Anna. Well, to all of us, really. For me, it's the first major part I've done here, and it'd be awful if . . . I mean, of course it's more awful what happened to poor Frank, but . . . it still doesn't seem real, you know?"

Nice going, Phoebe, I told myself. You're supposed to be lending support, not ladling out guilt.

"No, it doesn't," I agreed. "And of course the show must go on." I stopped short of a fatuous "Frank would have wanted it that way." Besides, forget Frank, talk about something else. "Speaking of which, I can't believe Despina is your first big role. From the rehearsal I saw, you seem like a pro."

Jenny looked immensely pleased. "I've had smaller parts, and I've always loved it—the stage. From the time I was little and started doing plays in school, I've been happier there than anywhere. Finding out I could sing was just kind of a bonus. Being onstage . . . well, it's better than real life, you know?"

This was said with such matter-of-factness that I was temporarily stumped for a reply.

"Oh, look," Jenny said. She pulled a snapshot out of the file folder in which she'd been rummaging. "What's this doing here? The folder's labeled '1986,' but this must be from last year. Theo and Rita and the kids. Aren't they cute?"

She handed me the photo.

The family sat in the green rowboat by the dock. Theo, skinny and white in bathing trunks and looking truly denuded without his glasses, held one oar. Beside him, both hands planted on the other oar, sat a little girl of six or seven with long, fair braids. In the stern, facing them, Rita's plump bare arms encircled a child on either side, boys of maybe two and four. All five had their heads turned to the camera and appeared to be laughing, as if at some irresistible joke by the photographer.

Remembering Rita's emotion yesterday as she sat at the piano, her apparent ambivalence toward motherhood, the photo was almost unbearably poignant. I propped it on the desk against the bowling trophy and studied it. "A happy family," I said.

"Rita's a wonderful mother," Jenny said. "Theo too—father, that is. But Rita, she's fantastic with those kids."

"Where are the children now?"

"Visiting Grandma—Rita's mother—up the island. They'll come for the summer once *Così* is over and the students are here. There are plenty of baby-sitters then."

"Will your parents be coming to see you in the opera?" I said.

"No," Jenny said shortly. Then, as if feeling some sort of explanation was called for, "We don't get along."

Jeez, I thought, why doesn't somebody *tell* me these things?

"The thing is," Jenny began, but was interrupted by a knock on the open door.

It was Jason Lee Jones. I thought he was about to come in, but he checked himself when he saw Jenny, who was kneeling on the floor by the file drawer.

"Ah, busy, I see! Well, then, I won't—unless there's some way I can help?" His round eyes flickered over the cluttered surfaces of the room. I thought he looked better than he had yesterday, though there was still an ashy quality to his chocolate skin.

"I'll need an updated short bio," I said, "as soon as possible. For the program. And I'd appreciate your passing the word along to the others."

"Surely, surely," Jason Lee said. He made a flourishing motion with one arm. "Thirty-five years of *fascinating* experience neatly reduced to one pithy paragraph."

He advanced a few steps into the room. "I don't suppose," he said with studied casualness, "that you've heard anything more from that—um—rather dishy lieutenant? Any new developments?"

"Not a thing."

"Ah. Well, there were a number of boys in blue searching the grounds late yesterday, rummaging in trash cans and so on. I wondered if they were planning to do the same to our personal spaces."

"I've no idea. But I think they'd have to get a warrant."

"True," he said. "True. Not that I've anything to hide, it's just an uncomfortable thought."

He drifted toward the door again, hesitated, then turned to Jenny. "Doing all right, are you, Jenny?"

"Yes," she said. "Fine."

After Jason Lee had left, she sat back on her heels and gave a little grunt of exasperation. "I wish they wouldn't do that," she said. "All of them, you know? Tiptoeing around, keeping an eye on Jenny, afraid she's going to lose it again."

"I can understand how you feel," I said.

"Because I really am okay," she went on. "Actually, I'm the only person here who has a piece of paper saying in writing that I'm okay. Sane, mentally fit, whatever."

"I'll bet you are," I said. I wasn't going to risk any more observations based on my very sketchy knowledge of Jenny Allen's history. Besides, she seemed not to need any prompting from me.

She was still sitting back, head slightly tilted, a thoughtful expression on her face. "Maybe I'm not being quite fair," she said, "because they really don't understand. . . . I mean, I've never talked about . . ." She shifted her gaze to me. "Could I tell you something, Phoebe?"

I thought of my list of the many many tasks I was being paid to accomplish. Then I thought of the unlisted one that, apparently, took priority with Anna. I hoped she would remember.

"Of course," I said.

Jenny got up from the floor. She seemed about to sit in the boudoir chair, which no one had yet removed to its proper home (another item for my list). Instead, she thrust her hands into her jeans pockets, wandered to the door, and leaned back against its frame. The day was considerably cooler than the last two had been, and she was wearing a rose-colored sweatshirt and sneakers with socks. Again her fair hair was held away from her face with a simple fabric band.

"What they don't understand . . . what I've never told . . . they think my blaming myself for Charlie's death was just some totally neurotic, unreasonable reaction. They don't know about the quarrel."

She had, I noted, with the typical self-absorption of the young, assumed I knew the basics of her story.

I took my cue. "Quarrel?"

"I couldn't bear to tell them, it seemed so . . . We never quarreled, you see, Charlie and I. We didn't need to. I loved Charlie so much." Her voice started to catch, but she hurried determinedly on. "I guess everybody says it, but, Phoebe, I don't see how anybody could ever love anybody the way I . . . It's so hard to explain. I was perfectly happy. For the first time in my life. Perfectly."

She wasn't looking at me now, but stared past me at the window. The drizzle had hardened into a steady rain. A fitful wind occasionally blew the drops pattering against the panes. But I didn't think it was the rain she was seeing.

Outlined by the tight-stretched fabric of her jeans pockets, her hands balled into fists. Her shoulders hunched forward.

"Then that night, after dinner, Charlie came out all of a sudden with this totally off-the-wall idea that he was ruining my life. That he was keeping me from getting on with my career, from meeting other guys. Guys, he meant, who'd want to get married. Shit, Phoebe, I knew he'd never marry me. Charlie was . . . he wasn't like other people, he was . . . outside the rules, you know? And I didn't *care*! I just wanted to be with him, to take care of him. I loved him!"

The tension in her voice was palpable now, the words spilling out faster. "And now here he was saying he thought we should split up! Jesus, I was so *scared*. And I yelled at him. I said, Who's been putting stuff like this into your head? and he said, Why, didn't I think he was capable of thinking of my welfare all on his own? And then I accused him of having somebody else, of wanting to get rid of me. And I was really screaming by now, and crying, and I didn't know what to do or what to say. How to keep him from doing this terrible thing. So I just grabbed up my coat and ran out the door."

She stopped. Was this the end of the explanation? "I'm sorry," I said, "I still don't quite see . . ."

Jenny's eyes focused on me once more. Some of the tension went out of her shoulders, as if she'd gotten past the worst part of her recital.

"We'd had a glass of wine with dinner," she said more quietly, "out of one of those big jugs. At least, Charlie only had half a glass, he hardly ever drank. But when I'd gone . . . Afterwards they . . . they said it looked like he'd drunk most of the rest of it. That's why he didn't wake up when the fire . . . it would have been like he was doped. And he wouldn't have done that, you know, drunk all that wine, unless he'd felt really hurt, really angry. Because of me. Because of what I said."

I had my mouth open to reply when she said, "Oh, I know. It wasn't really my fault. The doctors at the hospital made me understand that. But at the time . . . I wasn't just being hysterical, I did have a reason for feeling responsible. You do see that?"

"Yes, I do," I said. "It was a terrible ordeal. I'm very, very sorry."

Jenny nodded solemnly. Then, unexpectedly, she

smiled. "Thanks for listening," she said. "I feel better having told a real person. Not a doctor, I mean. It never seems like telling a doctor really counts, you know?"

A rather cavalier dismissal of the therapeutic community, I thought. But I simply smiled back and said, "I'm glad."

She walked over to the boudoir chair and plumped herself down. "I'll tell you something I haven't told *anybody*. But I think I'm ready now."

"Oh?"

"Everybody thinks that all Charlie's music—all his compositions—got burned up. But I have one. He wrote it specially for me, a song, and I kept it in a special place. A place the fire didn't get to."

"How wonderful," I said. "To have something like that. Something so much a part of Charlie."

"I have it with me," she went on. "I haven't been able to sing it since . . . but I think maybe I could one day soon."

The shrill of the telephone made us both jump, then both laugh at ourselves. It was Chris Fox. I pressed the button that would signal Anna in her studio. I waited to hear her rich voice say, "Chris! My darling, I am mostly glad to hear from you," before hanging up on my end.

Jenny did not revert to the subject of Charlie's song. Instead she rose and crossed back to the file drawer. As she passed the desk, she retrieved the picture of Rita's family. "Do you have children, Phoebe?"

"No," I said. Then, feeling that her flood of confidences deserved some return in kind: "We wanted to, but . . . I had a complicated miscarriage. And then we couldn't."

"That's too bad," Jenny said. "You would have been a terrific mother."

I stared at her unconscious back, bent over the file drawer. She was hardly the first well-meaning person to have made some similar remark. Why at that moment had those casual words homed with such painful accuracy in on my most secret memories? Very briefly, I glimpsed the answer, and as quickly pushed it away. This, I thought, scanning the office, the blank, waiting face of the computer, the piles of memos, the ever-burgeoning list lying on my desk, was not the time or place for epiphanies. Epiphanies I could deal with on my own time.

I turned on the PC, summoned up the perkily titled *Let's Publish!*, and picked up the phone to dial JERRY.

13

Here's the evidence you needed!

act 2, last scene

"Fascinatin'!" Theo Morse murmured.

He clicked on "Dutch," "36," and "OK," and suddenly the words *Così fan tutte* swelled on the screen to impressive size.

"Will y'look at that!" He leaned back in my swivel chair to admire his work. "An' I thought computers were s'posed to be complicated!" He brought his face close to the screen again. "Now s'posin' we put 'W. A. Mozart' in these Swiss eye-talics . . ." His long left-hand fingers poked happily at the keyboard while his right hand sent the mouse scurrying around its white pad.

It had been some fifteen minutes since I had ceded my place at the computer screen to an ever more closely hovering Theo. His delight in the discovery of this new toy, coupled with what appeared to be instant comprehension of the principles of *Let's Publish!* had been irresistible.

I should really, I thought, put him in touch with Jerry. I had spent an illuminating, if exhausting, hour on the phone with the computer tutor and could now, having made personal contact, lowercase him in my mind. Jerry, who sounded to be at the tail end of the voice-changing process, had much the same qualities of enthusiasm, quick-mindedness, and tunnel-vision absorption that Theo was now displaying.

The director sat hunched over the computer, the sleeves of his shirt (a pattern of yellow lightning streaks across a turquoise sky) rolled to the elbows, his eyes, bare of their horn-rims, inches from the screen. Occasionally he frowned and paged through the instruction book lying open on the desk. If he remembered that Larry Peterson and I were also in the room, he gave no indication.

How far, I wondered, did this ability to focus exclusively on the business of the moment extend? I remembered, at the barn, how Theo had been the first to respond to Amanda's wails of distress. One moment he'd been wrapped up in the finer points of Mozartian production. The next, all his energies had been shifted to dealing with a real-life drama.

Since then he had seemed, of all of us, the one least affected by Frank's death and its implications. As if, perhaps, it was not his nature to waste mental or emotional energy on a matter beyond his ability to control.

On the other hand, for all I knew he could be a monster of deviousness and subtlety. Looking now, though, at his rapt face, catching bits of the tune he hummed under his breath (from *Figaro*?), I didn't believe it.

At lunchtime (a subdued and speedy affair) Anna had announced that Christopher Fox would be arriving tomorrow to join the cast of *Così fan tutte*. And no, she had heard nothing further from the police. I, in turn, had put in my bid for bios for the program. Most of the cast said I could just use the one from last year. Theo and Larry had offered to help with the program's design (since this computer-generated product would be a Colony first) and had accompanied me back to the office.

Now Larry and I sat on metal folding chairs at a small table I'd cleared for the purpose, cutting and pasting samples of programs past. Small rectangles of paper littered the table's edges while in the middle the chosen samples of potted biographies lay in careful juxtaposition like a doll's black-and-white patchwork quilt.

"Rita Michaels . . . graduate of Stony Brook University . . . Rosina in *Barber of Seville*, Varovna Colony . . . studied in Milan . . . favorite roles include . . . currently teacher of voice at . . . married to director Theodore Morse . . . three children."

"Jason Lee Jones . . . born Kingston, Jamaica . . . NY H.S. of Performing Arts . . . appeared on Broadway in . . . tours . . . music degree, City Univ. of NY . . . vocal teacher and coach . . ."

"Amanda St. James . . ."

I did a double take. "Amanda was a finalist in the Met auditions?"

Larry had been engaged in the knotty problem of fitting six biographical rectangles into space for five. He stopped and looked at me with some amusement. "Oh yes. Ten or twelve years ago. Amanda's extraordinarily gifted. Well, you heard her singing the hell out of Fiordiligi the other day—not one of your easier roles."

"Yes, I thought her voice was very fine. But then why . . . ?"

"Why is she here for the summer, rather than off at Aspen or Glyndebourne? Simply put, it hasn't happened for Amanda. It still could, she's relatively young, she sings a lot, she's known. But there's a big difference between 'finalist' and 'winner.' No doubt winning that Met audition could have made all the difference. In our various ways you could probably say the same about most of us Colonyites. There's a lot of the crapshoot about chasing a career in music. Most of us are still waiting to roll that seven."

There was enough bitterness in this last observation to make me reluctant to press for particulars. I reverted to Amanda.

"But Amanda came close. To the Met, I mean."

Larry shrugged. "They picked eight that year. And I wasn't the only one who thought she could've won just as well as the two sopranos who did. But when I say 'crapshoot' . . . well, look. Suppose—and this is purely hypothetical, could be any competition—you have three young sopranos who've made it to the finals, so you can accept they have the basic equipment, training, and so forth. And say the judges have to pick one. Now suppose on The Day one of the finalists has a sniffle—just enough to take the edge off, make her overly careful. And suppose the second one has chosen an aria that one of the judges happens to loathe. And suppose soprano number three reminds another judge of his childhood sweetheart. And suppose a third judge just found out yesterday that her cancer is no longer in remission and she couldn't give a crap about who wins the damn thing. What do you want to bet that soprano number three gets the pick?"

I grimaced and nodded an acknowledgment. "I guess I knew that—subliminally. But it's much more comforting to believe that the best talent will win out in the end."

"Your problem, Phoebe, is that you've been associated too long with the minuscule top echelons of the music world. Unreality in a big way. The Varovna Colony, my dear, this is the real world. And not a bad world at all. Whatever our lack of renown, there's no one here who doesn't love the thing that we do."

My eye fell on one of the discarded rectangles pushed to the side of the table. "Frank Palermo . . . Manhattan School of Music . . . Opera Theater of St. Louis . . . Escamillo . . . Valentine . . . recipient of grant to study in Berlin in the coming year . . ."

Larry followed my gaze. "Even Frank," he said quietly. "Maybe especially Frank. When he found that he had this voice . . . he really wanted to be good, you know, and he had a lot of catching up to do. That first year, he practically camped out at Anna's place in the city. Lessons every day . . . God, how he worked at it!"

It was, I realized, his first mention to me of Frank since our dinner at the Old Mill. He picked up the piece of paper with Frank's bio on it and stared at it. I couldn't read his expression. "Jesus," he said, "I hope—"

"Phoebe? Oh, there you are!" It was Amanda the White Queen, momentarily disoriented at seeing Theo sitting at my desk. She swept over to our table.

"Good, you are working on the . . . let me just see. . . ." She put her hands on Larry's shoulders in a proprietorial sort of way as she peered down at his handiwork.

"But, Larry," she said, pointing to his bio, "you haven't put in that they're doing your *Larksongs* at Tanglewood in July."

Larry shrugged. "Not necessary. We're short of space."

"But you must! It could be important, you never know who's going to show up out here in the Hamptons." She turned to me. "Larry is quite a well-known composer, Phoebe," she explained kindly. " 'Larksongs' is his piece for chamber choir and strings. It's been performed several times this past year."

"Oh, really," I said.

Larry, usually so quick with a rejoinder, looked uncomfortable but said nothing.

Amanda patted his shoulder. "I'm sure you'll find the space. Speaking of which, I just want to make one change in my . . . yes, here it is." She leaned over and pointed at the relevant rectangle. "Here, right after Mostly Mozart. Add the Handel and Haydn Society *Creation* at—"

"Hold on," I said, grabbing up a pencil. "Run that by me again."

"Handel and Haydn," Amanda said, speaking with great distinctness. "H-a-n—oh here, I'll write it down for you." She relieved me of my pad and pencil and scribbled busily.

I saw Larry's mouth begin to open and shook my head.

"There," Amanda said, handing back the pad. "All clear? Thanks so much." She smiled graciously and swept out again.

"Provin' once more," Theo said, his gaze still fixed on the computer screen, "that that gal's vocal cords should be licensed purely for singin'. Now, Phoebe, how do I get this thang to print out?"

Theo had done yeoman's work. By the time he and Larry left, the program's format was largely set: front cover, notes on *Così* and synopsis of the plot, rundown of scenes, cast of characters, technical staff, biographical notes, write-up of Varovna and history of the Colony, list of Benefactors, Patrons, etc. On the back cover, notice of future productions and a handy coupon soliciting donations for the Varovna Scholarship Fund.

Most of the information I had at hand. Chris Fox would presumably supply his when he arrived. With the final dress rehearsal scheduled for a week from tomorrow, it seemed to me that the program was in at least as good shape as the rest of the production.

Calls had begun trickling in requesting ticket reservations for the six performances. Since seating was on a first-come, first-served basis, the record keeping was minimal. All I had to do was take the name, date, and number of tickets, or, if I was especially busy, let the answering machine do it. Tickets were held at the box office and paid for on the night of the performance. A system, Anna had explained, whose simplicity made up for the inconvenience of occasional no-shows.

Most of the calls I took were prefaced by a tentative, "You *are* going ahead with the opera?" I tried to keep my assurances neutral—neither too cheerful nor too sober. But in truth it bothered me terribly that the sudden removal of Frank Palermo from among the living seemed to have resulted in so little disruption. As it turned out, I couldn't have been more wrong, but that's how I felt at the time.

In between answering the phone, I typed information into Theo's neatly designed spaces and borders.

"Stefan Kowalski, a graduate of Stony Brook University . . ." Wait, hadn't I seen . . . yes, Rita had also gone to Stony Brook. So they had very possibly known each other before coming to the Colony. *Was* something going on there? And was Theo as unaware, or at least as unperturbed, as he seemed? And why did my conversation with Frank pop unbidden into my head? Was there a detail I should be remembering?

Larry and Amanda, I noted, were both on the faculty of Manhattan School of Music. Frank had graduated from Manhattan. And Larry had mentioned teaching composition to Charlie—Jenny's Charlie. Presumably that had been at Manhattan also. No surprise, really, but still . . . it was borne in on me how deep the connections ran between the various members of the Varovna Colony staff.

Larry had *not* added the upcoming performance of *Larksongs* to his program bio. Just as well. One more line would have thrown the page out of kilter. Demonstrating, I thought, that unlike Amanda, Larry was capable, for the greater good, of passing up one small item of self-promotion.

"Anna Varovna . . . long and illustrious career with the Metropolitan Opera . . . Aida . . . Gioconda . . . Lady Macbeth . . . San Francisco . . . Chicago . . . concerts . . . renowned teacher . . ."

Wait a minute. Where was the rest of it? Where was the stuff about her being a heroine of the Resistance that had always been a feature of the Met program bios? And where was La Scala, the Paris Opera, Vienna, Sadler's Wells? Surely the great Varovna had had an international career.

I searched the material Jenny had culled for me. No, it appeared that while Varovna's career may have been illustrious, it had also been, by modern standards, singularly constricted.

Now why, I mused, was that?

At shortly after four o'clock, Gerta Hofstetter appeared at the office door. "Ve must all go to the front room," she said. "Anna said to tell you. It iss the policeman from yesterday. And the vooman."

I translated this to mean the lieutenant and the Princess. My stomach did a quick flip. Were they here to make an arrest? Apply the third degree? Tell us that, after all, Frank's death had been an accident?

Gerta lingered while I logged off the computer, turned on the answering machine, and searched for my purse. If I had thought Anna looked strained, Gerta looked positively haggard, as if she had dropped ten pounds in the last forty-eight hours. She was wearing dark brown polyester pants with a rayon shirt of an unbecoming green tucked haphazardly into the elastic waistband. The protuberant eyes, pale green in the reflection of the green shirt, were darkly ringed, the iron-grey hair dull and lank.

She looked so miserable that I said, "Don't take it so hard, Gerta. Maybe they've come with good news."

Gerta caught my arm. "You think, Phoebe? But no, I do not believe good news iss possible. But you are a nice girl to try to cheer up old Gerta. I look bad, huh?"

She located the small mirror hanging on the back of the office door, took a comb out of her pants pocket, and pulled it through her thick bob. Then, surprisingly, she produced a lipstick from the same pocket and dabbed her mouth with it.

"There," she said. "That iss better?"

"Much better," I lied. On her flat white face the pink color stood out garishly, giving her the look of a badly made-up corpse. It occurred to me that I had read no biography of Gerta Hofstetter, though her name appeared on the program under "costumes" and "box office." What was her story? How long had she been with Anna, and where had she come from?

I located my bag hanging on the back of my chair under my jacket. As I slung the strap over my shoulder, I remembered Frank's mail. I had thought of it occasionally since yesterday but never at the right moment. This time I'd be sure to pass the letter on to the lieutenant and tell him about the one I'd lost. Or tell Anna, if by some miracle the lieutenant had simply come to say so sorry to have worried you and goodbye.

At the door to the open room, Gerta left my side and made a beeline for Anna, who was sitting on the sofa. I hesitated, then stepped inside and to the left, where I remained standing. From the window seat at the other end of the room, where she was sitting between Rita and Theo, Jenny caught my eye. She looked frightened. I thought she wanted me to join them, but the lieutenant was clearing his throat meaningfully. I stayed where I was.

Again Lieutenant Freed stood at the mantel. The Princess sat on the piano stool to his right, making a brave attempt, I thought, to be inconspicuous. She wore a dark blue pantsuit and had pulled her hair back into a low bun. On her lap was the inevitable notepad.

The lieutenant wore grey slacks, a brown tweed jacket, a white shirt, and a dun-colored tie. Not, I judged, an outfit to signal glad tidings. They were both situated to have the best possible view of the room's inhabitants and their reactions to whatever was about to be said.

So, I realized, was I. Furthermore, no one was watching me—every gaze was fixed on the lieutenant.

"I'm going to make this short," the lieutenant said. His voice was perhaps even a shade more mournful than yesterday. "Evidence collected at the scene of Mr. Palermo's death and elsewhere indicates that his death was not accidental. That penicillin in tablet form was deliberately introduced into one of Mr. Palermo's bottles of vitamins. Specifically, into a bottle of five-hundred-milligram vitamin C tablets. This is now, ladies and gentlemen, officially an investigation of homicide."

I saw:

Gerta Hofstetter's hand shoot out, at the words *not accidental*, to clamp down on Anna Varovna's arm with a grip that made Varovna wince.

Larry Peterson, sharing the wicker chaise with Jason Lee Jones, drop his head into his hands, and Jason Lee lean back against the cushions and close his eyes.

Stefan Kowalski bring both fists down on the arms of his chair with a harsh exclamation of "Christ!"

Jenny Allen shrink, white faced, against Rita, who hugged her close with one arm. Rita, with her other hand, wipe the tears that suddenly coursed down her cheeks.

Theo Morse pat his wife absently and repeatedly on the knee while slowly shaking his head and staring at his feet.

Amanda St. James slide slowly off the chintz cushion of her basket chair into an insensible heap on the floor.

What I did not catch was a look of serious annoyance on the face of the good lieutenant, but I assumed it. The element of shock, causing, as I understood from my reading of murder mysteries, the sudden blurting of significant facts or baring of interesting emotions, was effectively dissipated in the flurry occasioned by the White Queen's collapse. By the time cold water and brandy had been applied, respectively, to the outer and inner

Amanda and she had been ensconced on the wicker chaise, the initial impact of the lieutenant's statement was long gone.

To do Amanda credit, when she came to she appeared to be genuinely embarrassed. Also uncharacteristically subdued. She apologized to one and all, said she didn't know how she could have been so stupid. She was perfectly all right now. The fact that the lieutenant's announcement had more or less echoed her own accusations of the day before remained unspoken.

I had the feeling, when he finally had our attention again, that the lieutenant was still operating with gloves on. I did not have the feeling that this was necessarily a permanent condition. For now, however, he outlined politely enough the evidence of which he'd spoken.

What it boiled down to was that Frank's fingerprints, smudged and many times overlaid, were all over his jars of vitamins and supplements. Except for one. The jar of vitamin C had been recently wiped clean. Two sets only of Frank's prints had been found on its surface. And no, it wasn't a new jar; there were only a few tablets remaining.

Analysis of the contents of the jar had revealed traces of penicillin, such as could have flaked off of a penicillin tablet. Analysis of the contents of Frank revealed that he had ingested close to 250 milligrams of the stuff. The conclusion clearly was that some person had placed a penicillin tablet in the bottle of vitamin C, wiped the bottle clean of prints, and replaced it on Frank's bureau.

Stefan Kowalski burst out, "But why wouldn't Frank have noticed? The smell, the look. The damn pills wouldn't have been identical!"

"No," the lieutenant said, "but close. Close enough for a person who routinely swallowed several tablets at a time. Especially a person who had probably never seen a penicillin tablet. Even then he *might* have noticed it, yes. But he didn't."

Silence. I wondered how many were picturing, as I was, Frank's palm extended, the white tablets falling into it, the jaunty gesture as he brought the pills to his mouth, tossed them in, gulped down some water, reached for the next bottle. . . .

"Which brings us to the question," the lieutenant continued, "of where the penicillin came from. And we were fortunate there." He reached into his pocket and drew out a small amber cylinder. "This was found in one of the large trash cans outside this house by the kitchen door. It's an empty prescription bottle for penicillin, prescribed and filled locally. For a"—he squinted at the bottle—"Magda Davidovitch. Ring any bells?"

"Of course it does," Rita said abruptly. "Magda was here last summer for four weeks. Came down with strep. Stayed in one of the guest rooms upstairs. Most of which I bet you've already found out." She flung a scornful look in the lieutenant's direction. "Don't play games, Lieutenant. Things are fucked up enough without that."

"Fair enough," the lieutenant replied mildly. "Then let me just ask if anyone remembers seeing this bottle anywhere."

Jason Lee's eyes, which had been hovering at half-mast, shot open, then narrowed in thought. "Wait a minute," he said. "I think . . . yes, the upstairs bathroom." He pointed overhead. "When I was up there last week sometime. I opened the medicine cabinet looking for aspirin and I saw a prescription bottle. *Not* what I was looking for, so I didn't pick it up. Could have been that one."

The lieutenant nodded thoughtfully. "Notice the name? Notice any pills in the bottle?"

Jason Lee shook his head. "A name, no. There might have been a couple of pills. I thought, if anything, it might have been Gerta's or Anna's, none of the rest of us has been here long enough this year to get sick. I didn't think of it being left over from last year."

"It vass *not* mine, *not* Anna's!" Gerta said loudly. She turned around on the sofa to glare at Jason. "How can you say this? Ve haff neffer here had the penicillin, neffer!"

Jason Lee rolled his eyes. Anna put her hand gently on Gerta's arm. "Is nobody thinking that, my darling." To the lieutenant she said, "Magda, yes, she came for month's study. Unfortunately, she became ill, so I move her from cabins into this house. Is quieter, you understand, warmer. Is very unfortunate, hardly can she sing at all."

(Did she get her money back? I wondered. I bet not.)

"And yes, she have the doctor, she have prescription. Is very possible she leaves this bottle here. Always doctor says, 'Finish all of pills,' and always patient feels better and thinks, 'I do not any longer need this.' I do not know. I have not before seen this bottle."

In a small voice, Jenny said, "I think I saw it—the bottle. Last week when I was cleaning the upstairs bath. I remember thinking, Oh, you're supposed to throw out old prescription medicine. But then I thought I'd ask Anna first, maybe she wanted it, and then . . . I just forgot. Oh God, maybe if I hadn't . . ."

Rita groaned. "For God's sake, Jenny, don't start blaming yourself for that. Besides," to the lieutenant, "how can you be sure that bottle's where the penicillin came from? Maybe it *was* empty and someone just finally threw it out."

"If anyone here can tell me precisely that, I'd be happy to hear it," the lieutenant said. "Perhaps they could also explain why the bottle was wiped clean and wrapped in a piece of Kleenex."

There was another silence.

"What about Sarah Kirk?" Stefan said.

"Ah yes," Jason Lee said, "the delectable—and absent—Sarah. Do let's blame her, by all means."

"I'm not *blaming* her, Jase. I'm just saying she could have thrown the thing out."

"Oh sure," Rita said. "Like our Sarah would lift a finger outside the kitchen. Hell, she won't even sweep the dining room, Gerta has to do it."

The lieutenant had been attending to the foregoing with his head cocked slightly to one side. Now he said, "As soon as Sarah Kirk is . . . well, to be blunt, as soon as she stops throwing up, we'll be asking her about the bottle. In the meantime, tell me, is that upstairs bathroom used a lot?"

"Yes," Stefan said impatiently. "We all use it. Whenever the downstairs one's not available. We could all have seen the bottle, if it was there, any of us could have taken it. Hell, any of us could have walked into Frank's cabin and put penicillin into his vitamin C. That's what we're talking about, right, Lieutenant? Opportunity?"

The lieutenant regarded Stefan speculatively but didn't answer directly. "What I'd like," he said, making his gaze general again, "is for anyone who remembers or thinks he remembers seeing that bottle to come talk to me. Shortly. Starting with Mr. Jones and Ms. Allen. Detective Delgado and I will be upstairs. Madame Varovna has given us a room there, so as not to tie up the office." For the first time that afternoon he acknowledged me with a look.

"But first I have one more question. Does the word *Amadeus* signify anything—uh—relevant to anyone here? It seems that Mr. Palermo may have tried to use that word as a signal of some sort. To the identity, perhaps, of his killer."

Amanda, coming to life and true to form, snorted, "Amadeus, Lieutenant, is Wolfgang Mozart's middle name."

"Actually, Ms. St. James," the lieutenant said, "I was

aware of that." In spite of himself, I thought, some asperity had crept into the level voice. "What I'm hoping for is some reference, some allusion, that would be known by you people here, that wouldn't be available to us outsiders."

"Oh," said Amanda. "Well."

The lieutenant waited a beat. When there were no takers, he sighed. "Think about it, please," he said.

He raised his eyebrows at the Princess. She rose, folded up her notepad, and followed him to the hall doorway. He stepped aside to let her pass through and turned once more to the room. When he spoke, there was a new edge to his voice.

"We're going to find out who killed your friend," he said. "We count on your cooperation.

"I'll be upstairs."

14

This is really a case that makes you wonder!

act 2, scene 8

"MY DARLINGS!" ANNA VAROVNA SAID. "IS SOMETHING WE must discuss."

No shit, I thought, and then, Good luck. I'd never met a group of people more determined *not* to discuss an increasingly bald reality.

But I had again underestimated the Varovna pragmatism. What Anna had in mind was not a question of soul-searching but one of logistics. Frank's body had been released by the coroner's office. There was to be a wake tomorrow evening in Queens. Everyone at the Colony had been invited and "naturally, my darlings," everyone would attend. It was now a question of divvying up the attendees among the available vehicles for the trip to the city. One of the available vehicles, it turned out, was mine.

After some mild wrangling, passengers were assigned and departure time set for midmorning, most people being in favor (once it became clear that the day would be shot anyway) of a few extra hours in the city. I was not one of those people, but I'd been saddled with Amanda, who'd suddenly discovered a pressing need to visit both Schirmer's and someone in the hairdressing line named Ralph. My other passenger was to be Jenny Allen.

I wondered whether the blanket invitation to Frank's wake had been issued before or after Frank's parents had been told that their son had been murdered. I wondered this even more when Anna announced that Frank's mama had asked members of the Colony to provide some music.

Since this part of the discussion didn't involve me, I caught Anna's eye, received her nod, and went quietly out. I could learn tomorrow what selections had been deemed appropriate to be sung by his colleagues at the wake of a man who had almost certainly been killed by one of them.

I headed up the stairs. This time I would not be the last to be interviewed. I would get in first, give the lieutenant Frank's letter, and get out.

At the top of the stairs a corridor led off toward the back of the house, paralleling the one below. To the left of the landing a door standing ajar revealed the bathroom. When I turned around, doors to either side of the landing led, presumably, to two rooms at the front of the house. One was ajar and I knocked on it. It was pulled open by the Princess, who grinned broadly on seeing me. "Hey, Loot, it's Phoebe!" she said.

The room was a sizable one with double windows on two sides, curtained with blue-and-white-flowered chintz. The walls were papered in a creamy, rose-sprinkled pattern, not new and showing here and there the ravages of mildew. The floor was painted white. Twin beds, counterpaned with blue chenille, had been shoved to opposite sides of the room and a small mahogany table pulled out into the cleared space. Lieutenant Freed sat at the table in a matching straight chair. In front of the table was the boudoir chair from my office, returned, I assumed, to its natural habitat.

It seemed an unlikely setting for police work but the

lieutenant appeared unfazed. He'd been sitting with both elbows on the table, chin propped in hands. As I came in he straightened, and would have stood, I thought, except that I preempted him by dropping quickly into the little armchair.

"I really don't have anything new to tell you," I said, speaking with rather more nervousness than I'd expected. "It's just something I forgot to tell you yesterday. Or rather, to give you."

I took the *Prevention* magazine and the letter out of my purse and put them on the table. "They're Frank's," I said, and explained about my picking up and distributing the mail yesterday morning.

The Princess, who had again stationed herself at a discreet distance, jumped up and came to bend over the table. *"Prevention,"* she breathed. "Jeez, talk about your irony!"

The lieutenant picked up the letter and examined it soberly. "From the postmark," he said, "and the return address, I'd say this is from his mother. Would you like me to see she gets it back?"

I caught the polite puzzlement in his tone, and flushed. "No, that's not . . . Well sure, give it to her. But the thing is there was another letter, one with a French stamp on it, that I lost. On the way, I guess, from the theater to Frank's cabin. It must have fallen out of my bag. Because when I looked for it later, at Anna's House, it was gone. And I wondered whether one of your—uh—men might have found it somewhere on the grounds."

The lieutenant and the Princess exchanged glances and the lieutenant shook his head.

"It's probably not important," I said. I started to rise. "I just thought I should . . ."

"Please," the lieutenant said.

I sat.

"When you say you looked for the letter 'later,' how much later?"

"Fifteen, twenty minutes? We were sitting in the room downstairs. I suddenly thought of Frank's mail and looked in my bag. The magazine was there, but not the letters. Then I spotted this one on the floor."

"The floor?" Where, exactly, he wanted to know. And then, who had been sitting near me, and had there been a lot of movement in the room?

I described the scene as best I could. Jenny on the window seat, Jason Lee in the chaise nearby. Gerta handing around coffee. Yes, there could have been other people getting up and down, but that was all I could remember. Why? Surely I must have dropped the letter in the confusion of that run up the hill to Amanda?

"Odd, then, that it hasn't been found," the lieutenant observed. "Ah well, we'll keep an eye out. The fact that it *hasn't* been found, of course, makes it interesting."

"The curious friggin' incident of the dog in the nighttime!" exclaimed the Princess from her corner.

I looked over at her, startled. The woman had an infinite capacity to surprise.

The lieutenant frowned. "Detective Delgado has an unfortunate taste for mystery fiction," he said.

Huh! "But the dog did nothing in the nighttime," I said to the Princess.

"That was the curious friggin' incident!" she crowed. "And you don't hafta frown, Loot. Phoebe knows I wouldn't carry on like this except I really like her . . . you know, trust her. You should see me most times, Phoebe. Little miss fly-on-the-wall by-the-book."

I wondered. It occurred to me that Detective Claire Delgado's value to the lieutenant might lie in this very ability to size people up and play them accordingly. I could imagine her, for instance, with Stefan Kowalski discreetly seductive, with Amanda St. James humble and somewhat dim. With Phoebe Mullins open and engaging? And wasn't it working?

I directed my attention firmly back to the lieutenant. "Anyway, that's what I wanted to tell you. There really isn't anything else."

"You're sure," the lieutenant said.

I thought briefly through the welter of confidences, impressions, and bits of information I'd received since yesterday. Had any of it suggested a motive, let alone a temperament, for murder? Sure, I had some questions, but...

I shook my head.

"Because to be honest, Phoebe"—was he doing it too?—"what we've got so far is a whole lot of opportunity and damn-all for a motive. Plus a bunch of people who aren't talking. And most of them acting like they're guilty of *something*. So if all but one of 'em would just come in here and own up to whatever it is so we could eliminate 'em ... well," he raised his hands in a gesture of defeat, "then I guess we'd be living in Mr. Palermo's Land of Truth or whatever. Instead of in the real world."

It was still raining as I walked to my car. Not hard, but straight, with a kind of surly persistence. Beyond the silvered green of the lawn the bay was the color of slate, dimpled with the raindrops but otherwise calm.

There were no voices raised on the saturated air. The Princess had followed me downstairs to catch the group just before they broke up and relay the lieutenant's request for any information on the whereabouts of Frank's letter. I'd ducked out the kitchen door. I had no expectation of information being volunteered from this lot. If anyone *had* found the letter and not mentioned it, presumably the person thought he/she had good reason.

Besides, I badly needed some thinking space. I had not, after all, been wholly candid with the lieutenant. It wasn't so much that I had learned nothing as that I'd had no time to put what I'd learned into coherent form.

I drove by Frank's cabin, its encircling yellow tape

now mud spattered and beginning to sag. Then right at the road, through the woods, left onto Mile Hill. There was no other traffic. I drove slowly and forced myself to start thinking in an organized fashion.

The first surprise was that I had to convince myself all over again that Frank had indeed been murdered, and by one of the group I had just left in the front room of Anna's House. Not a mistake, not an accident, but a deliberate planting among his vitamins of what, to Frank, was poison.

All right. Accepted.

Then why?

Because Frank Palermo, alive, was a threat to someone's . . . what? Well-being? Livelihood? Reputation? These were *singers*, for God's sake, *artists,* people whose life stories were routinely documented in program notes, in newspaper reviews, in publicity releases. What sort of dark secret—dark enough to murder for—could we be talking about?

Money? The lieutenant was certainly in a better position than I to know if anyone benefited financially from Frank's death. Wouldn't he have mentioned it to me? Maybe not. I was still smarting from the suspicion of having been manipulated. Him with his sad looks and his "to be honest, Phoebe"s.

All right, what else? Love? A woman—or man— scorned? Hatred? I considered the man I'd known so briefly. Sweet, I'd thought. Earnest, not intellectual, with quite a lot of charm. Somewhat humorless, perhaps. Possessed of a beautiful voice. No more egocentric than most performance artists. Certainly well-meaning. What was it Jenny had said—"one of those types who's everybody's friend." Hard to believe that the Frank Palermo I'd met could have inspired either a crime of passion or a murderous hatred. But then who did I think I—

A horn blast shattered the air directly to the rear of my left earlobe, causing me to leap toward the Toyota's ceiling. A silver Porsche was riding my tail. I was about to make the kind of rude gesture I was sure to regret seconds later when I noticed my speedometer needle pointing to twenty. Okay, perhaps that was a mite slow for a public highway, even a backwoods one. I scrunched over onto the narrow, grassy shoulder and let the Porsche pass, which it did with what seemed to me an unnecessary amount of engine noise.

I pulled onto the road again, determined to prove to myself that I could drive and think at the same time. Now, where was I?

Ah, yes: Frank had been killed. For motive(s) unknown. Not, so far, conclusions you could call revelatory.

As for opportunity . . . Frank had arrived, I understood, last Thursday. The rest of the staff had been in residence since the previous weekend, Anna Varovna and Gerta a week or so before that. Any of them could have made a quick, unobserved visit to Frank's cabin.

And what about the Mouse? From a quick perusal of the payroll ledger, I'd gathered she was on a fairly flexible part-time arrangement. Presumably, when the students arrived that would change. But even so she'd been on the premises almost every day for the past week and a half. She'd had the same opportunity as the rest of the staff. Was the Mouse a suspect? Had the lieutenant interviewed her at all? Was there perhaps something too opportune about her sudden illness? I would have described the Mouse as congenitally sour rather than murderous, but what did I really know about her?

For that matter, what did I really know about any of them?

The White Queen—Amanda St. James. Found the body (always a suspicious circumstance, according to popular literature). Would she have put herself through that degree of trauma (I had no doubt that the trauma, at least, had been real) on purpose? I couldn't believe it.

Had she been in love with Frank? Even if true, an un-likely motive. The two of them had appeared friendly enough. Why, though, had she been so quick to cry "murder" and so equally quick to shut up?

The Red Queen—Rita Michaels. She'd made no se-cret of being seriously annoyed at Frank. Suppose she and Stefan the Tenor *had* been having an affair (remem-bering that they'd known each other since college) and Frank had known about it. I racked my brains to remem-ber Stefan's words at Frank's cabin. Something about "staying out of my business" and "you've gotten it all wrong." But surely in this day and age you didn't murder someone because they'd stumbled on a bit of extramari-tal hanky-panky?

And in any case, would Rita, or for that matter Ste-fan (a weight lifter, I reminded myself), be so much in terror of the lanky, laid-back Director Morse? Was it pos-sible that Theo's remarkable ability to focus his energies could translate into the kind of implacable morality that would, say, destroy a family? Wrest a mother from her children? Or, on the other hand, kill the messenger?

Jenny Allen I almost dismissed out of hand, then, to be fair, set about considering. Just how unstable *was* "the little Jenny," as Anna had called her. Was it credible that, having suffered through the horror of one violent death, she could actually plot to bring about another? And what could she possibly have to hide, she whose story and most private emotions were common knowledge to all these people?

Jason Lee Jones, on the other hand, was, to me at least, a complete mystery. Gay, I assumed, but as a per-son totally hidden, all manner, all surface. Amanda had said she'd seen him quarreling with Frank. I'd never seen him anything but self-possessed—No, wait. In the office this morning, hadn't he seemed concerned about having his "personal space" searched? Well, who wouldn't? No, I could make no case either for or against Jason Lee.

Nor Larry Peterson. Gay, perhaps. Or bi. He and Jason were sharing the house called The Octagon for the summer. It was inconceivable to me that in this setting, among these people, sexual orientation could figure in a motive for murder. So what did I know, or might I deduce, about the Piano Man? That he was ambitious? No longer young, perhaps a touch embittered? Hardly damning qualities. His modesty in regard to the program bio hadn't been the mark of a person hell-bent to get ahead.

I'd come out of the woods now and was heading down Cedar Street, coming up on the fire house, into the village of East Hampton. Almost home . . .

Anna Varovna and Gerta Hofstetter. Last because, to me, the most unthinkable. At least Anna was. And yet there'd been that shocked reaction to Frank's mention of a meeting in Paris, a name . . . LeClair? Yes, "An old friend from Resistance days." And then the letter with the French postmark. A letter interesting, as the lieutenant had pointed out, because of its disappearance. Logically the connection, if any, must be with Anna. And, of course, Gerta, about whom I knew so little but who had been, ever since the discovery of Frank's body, acting scared to death.

And yet I could have sworn that Anna's appeal to me—to find out "who has murdered poor Frank"—had been genuine. And I could have also sworn that if Gerta were indeed the culprit Anna would know.

A sudden unwelcome thought came: Did Anna know, or think she knew, Frank's murderer, but prefer the discovery to be made by a convenient outsider? I'd had firsthand demonstration over the last few days of the force of the Varovna will and of her efficiency. But really! I thought, that would be going too far! I must be paranoid. I was *not* being used by all and sundry.

Or else I was.

My attempt at organized thinking had obviously reached its limit.

I pulled into Mrs. Schmitter's short, graveled driveway. At least, I observed as I got out of the car, the rain was stopping. What I needed now was a solid evening of forgetting about the Varovna Colony. And about murder, and motives, and . . .

"Oh, Phoebe!" cried Mrs. Schmitter's eager voice as I stepped through the door.

It was some hour and a half later when I finally reached the sanctuary of Mrs. Schmitter's upstairs back bedroom. Doris (as she'd insisted I call her, being in her evening, postdrinkie mode) had been irresistibly agog, as well as startingly well informed. I wondered whether the lieutenant was aware of the fount of information represented by "my friend Edith's grandson."

While I put together, and then consumed, a salad and a mushroom omelet, Doris sat at the kitchen table, teacup in hand, tiny feet dangling, chatting knowledgeably of fingerprints and autopsies. I was able, without betraying any information that might be considered privileged, to make her happy by describing the principal players and by passing on the news of Frank's wake, which had not yet hit the local grapevine.

I was also able, this time, to put my gin in a glass, consign it for a few minutes to the freezer, and garnish it with an olive. Doris observed this procedure with interest and said she really must try that sometime.

Alone in my room at last, I kicked off my shoes and walked barefoot across the big braided rug to the window overlooking Mrs. Schmitter's backyard. I'd closed it that morning because of the rain, and the air in the room was stuffy. Now I hoisted the bottom sash all the way up. Immediately, a breeze stirred the flimsy nylon curtains framing the window opening. I leaned my hands on the broad, low sill and let the same breeze cool my face. To my left, above the trees the western sky had

cleared enough for a red sun, dangling still several feet
over the horizon, to be visible through streaky clouds.

In Mrs. Schmitter's backyard, individual shadows
had merged into a uniform dusky blanket across the
lawn. The yard was a narrow rectangle, perhaps a hundred feet deep. It was bordered on the right by gnarled
and ancient lilac bushes, at the back by a neighbor's
stockade fence, on the left by a combination of bushes
and chain-link fencing. The grass was neatly mowed,
but several flower beds had long since reverted to weedy
tangles with here and there a few blossoms struggling
through. Presumably Robert Schmitter the Third was
willing to go only so far. Or rather to pay someone else
to do so—I didn't flatter him by presuming that he himself might be the lawn mower.

Amid the scents of grass and wet earth, another,
sweeter and more insistent, drifted up to my window.
Suddenly I was transported to my grandmother's house
in western Massachusetts. Fragrant, subtle, not cloying,
but . . . Honeysuckle! Honeysuckle had festooned my
grandmother's back porch, swarming up trellises
propped against the screens, where we'd sat in the
evenings to count fireflies and listen to the chirruping of
the cicadas.

This was my New England grandmother, my
mother's mother, and by the time I was seven or eight
we no longer visited. There'd been a "falling out," I was
told. Whether between my grandmother and my mother
or between my grandmother and my father, or whether
it had to do with all three, I never learned. By the time
my mother died when I was seventeen, her mother had
been dead three years. There was a sister too, my aunt,
who'd run away from home at an early age. I had no idea
whether she was alive or dead.

I had loved the house. I think I had loved my grandmother, though my memory of her was much less viv-
id. Someone large and abrupt was my impression, but

with time for things like counting fireflies and smell-
ing honeysuckle. Not, to this child at least, frightening.
What kind of terror, I wondered, could she have been to
her two daughters to cause such alienation?

And now there was only me.

Do you have children, Phoebe?

No. We wanted to, but . . . And then we couldn't.

The baby was a girl. Correction: the five-month fe-
tus was female. One of the many idiocies people will
spout in the name of "comfort." I'd tried to give them
credit for meaning well.

If she had lived, she would now be twenty-three.
The same age as Jenny Allen. No doubt the reason why
those words tossed carelessly over an unconscious
young shoulder had possessed such clarifying power:
That's too bad. You would have been a terrific mother.

*Maybe it's for the best, Fee. My poor darling, you already
have your hands full with me. How would you ever have managed with two of us?*

Poor Mick! I'd thought. Trying so hard to keep me
from feeling like the failed woman I obviously was. Hiding his grief—the wrenching grief any man would feel—
at the knowledge he would never have a child of his
own. Thinking only of me . . .

Now I said to the air above Mrs. Schmitter's backyard, "The bastard meant it!"

We wanted to, but . . . No. *I* wanted to. Mick didn't
want to. Mick was relieved. How *would* I ever have managed with two of them? How continue to pamper, nurse,
protect, cater to, support the husband in the style he'd
come to rely on, with the added demands of a child?

It really worked out very well. The bastard had
proved his virility—he'd gotten me pregnant. What happened after that was no fault of his. Only mine. Which
the bastard's mother had been ever so careful never to
actually come out and say. And leaving the bastard in the
enviable position of being able to feel relief with no guilt.

Had I known all along? Had *not* knowing been a necessary condition for the preservation of the marriage? Because I had, after all, loved the bastard.

I straightened up and turned from the window.

Did I love him still? Yes, I thought, in many ways.

But at the same time there was a distancing. A letting go. Even a forgiving. For him and for me.

What was it I'd said to myself that morning in the office . . . that that was not the time or place for epiphanies. And was an epiphany what I'd just had?

Yes, I believed it was.

15

Heaven protect them on their perilous journey!

act 1, scene 6

THURSDAY, JUNE 21

WHEN I ARRIVED AT THE COLONY THE FOLLOWING MORNING the first person I saw was the Mouse.

She wasn't the first I heard. That would've been Jason Lee Jones, from the direction of The Octagon hidden in the woods behind the boys' cabins. He was vocalizing, his rather dry bass-baritone rumbling from below the staff to unexpected heights and down again. As I made the turn toward Anna's House, a floaty and female sound, involving, I thought, at least three voices, drifted from the direction of the barn. From Stefan the Tenor's cabin, at the opposite end of the string from Frank's, came repeated phrases, separated by honkings and throat clearings, of "Panis Angelicus."

The Varovna Colony was warming up for the wake.

I parked behind Anna's House. A back door that looked as if it might provide a shortcut to my office turned out to be locked. Through its upper panel of thick glass I could see into a vinyl-tiled room containing twin corrugated sinks, tiers of unpainted wooden shelving, and two no-nonsense white laundry machines. Piles of crumpled bedsheets and towels overflowed plastic laundry baskets or were simply heaped on the floor. An opposite door no doubt opened into the kitchen. Not, in any case, I decided, a good route to follow. I passed on around the corner of the house. There a flagstone path skirted a roofed and latticed affair sheltering three large green trash bins and ended at the side entrance. To the left of this door a narrow window gave onto the kitchen. I thought I saw movement behind it, so on my way down the corridor I paused at the kitchen door.

Sure enough, there was Sarah Kirk, looking, thanks to an overall greyness of skin tone, mousier than ever. She was loading breakfast dishes into the ancient dishwasher and muttering as she worked.

"Hi!" I said. "Should you be back? Couldn't they give you some help?"

She turned to me and propped her hands on her hips. "Well, they're all singing, aren't they?" She made it sound like an accusation. "Course, nobody told me they'd be takin' off for the day." She sniffed. "Just as well. Give me a chance to clean up the mess they been makin' outta my kitchen." She turned back to the dishwasher.

Hmm, "they," I thought as I made my way to the office. At least that evidenced a degree of solidarity. Us working stiffs as opposed to, for God's sake, *singers*. I knew from the office records that Sarah Kirk had been cooking for the Colony for some years. Was the disdain a pose, and if not, why did she keep coming back?

On my desk the answering machine showed thirteen messages, all of which had come in yesterday after I'd left: eight orders for tickets and five media requests for statements on Frank's murder. I dealt with the media calls, and three more that came in within the next fifteen minutes, along the lines that Anna and I had arrived at: shock, full cooperation with the investigating authorities, carrying on the summer artistic program in the face of deep sorrow, all other questions referred to Suffolk County Homicide. ("Is after all, my darling, their job.")

I was hanging up from the last call when the Mouse

appeared carrying a mug of coffee—milk, no sugar. I was touched that she'd remembered.

"No point lettin' it go to waste," she explained graciously.

She didn't leave at once but remained standing in front of the desk, wrapping and unwrapping her arms in the outsized blue-and-white-checked apron. I guessed that there was something she wanted to say.

"You're not going to Frank's wake?" I asked, to help her along.

"Huh? No! you don't get me into that city in the middle of summer. You c'n fry eggs on the sidewalks!"

It was not the middle of summer, and though the day was clear and bright the forecast was for a high temperature of seventy-two. I waited to hear what was really on the Mouse's mind.

"That cop," she said suddenly, "the Suffolk County one. He going to be here today?"

"I'm not sure. I believe there'll be a couple of uniformed men keeping an eye on the place while we're gone. But if you mean Lieutenant Freed, I know he wanted to talk to you."

"I already talked to him," the Mouse said uneasily. "Tuesday night. He came to the house. Jeez, I was so sick I could hardly hold my head up. I told him I didn't know anything."

"I guess he wants to ask you about the pill bottle."

The Mouse turned a paler shade of grey. Her voice narrowed to a squeak. "What pill bottle?"

"The one they found . . . Hold on."

I took another phone request for tickets, recording the information carefully in a notebook labeled BOX OFFICE. When I turned back, the Mouse was gone. A minute later I heard the boiler-room sound of the dishwasher starting up.

Was it possible she did know something about how

the penicillin bottle had gotten into the trash bin? Should I go talk to her, try to find out?

On the other hand, the lieutenant was sure to be questioning her shortly.

Another ring of the telephone reminded me that, after all, being the Colony secretary was my real job and one I was having a hard enough time making space for. I put the Mouse and what she might or might not know out of my mind.

"My, Phoebe, you look *really* nice!" Amanda said as she got into the front seat of the Toyota.

And why not? I thought. I might have joined the ranks of the genteel poor but I still had a hell of a wardrobe. For today I'd chosen a Donna Karan sheath-with-jacket number in navy picked out with white. A blue and rose silk Benetton scarf, matching ceramic ear clips, Italian leather navy pumps. Coordinating Gucci bag. If, in putting the ensemble together, the thought had crossed my mind that it would be one in the eye for Amanda, well . . . I am an imperfect being.

Amanda was wearing a black-and-white-checked silk dress with a shawl collar and carrying a white blazer. Her carefully made-up face was topped by a green turban affair that completely covered her hair, presumably awaiting Mr. Ralph's attentions. She seemed uncomfortable, clearing her throat once or twice and glancing at me and then away as we waited by the girls' cabins for Jenny.

A screen door slammed and Jenny came running along the narrow boardwalk laid in the sand in front of the cabins. She was wearing a dark blue shirtwaist dress and sandals over bare feet. One hand grasped a largish straw bag. Her face was shiny and bare of makeup, her hair still damp from the shower.

"Sorry," she said as she wrenched open the back door of the car and climbed in. "I couldn't decide what to wear.

Is this all right? I've got pantyhose in the bag and makeup,
I can put those on later. Oh, and heels. Actually," with a
shaky laugh, "I've never been to a wake before."

"You look just fine," I said firmly. "Now are we all
ready? Okay then."

I did my passengers the favor of not telling them that
this was only my second time on the Long Island—or
any other—Expressway. I figured I was nervous enough
for all three of us.

As we drove up the slope, a lone uniform sitting in a
police car parked by the theater gave us a cursory glance
and a wave.

Not long after we'd started, Amanda turned to me
and said archly, "Really, Phoebe, you might have told us
you were married to Michael Mullins!"

So that was what had been giving her the fidgets! I
wondered who had broken the news.

"Oh?" I said. "It didn't seem significant. I'm not a
musician, after all."

Jenny said, "Who's Michael Mullins?"

Amanda began to sputter. I laughed. "Very refresh-
ing, Jenny! Actually, he was a conductor. Quite well
known. But he died a year ago."

"Oh," Jenny said. "I'm sorry."

Amanda flushed and raised her chin, giving me the
benefit of her remarkable profile. Shortly she began talking of other things.

In the backseat, Jenny closed her eyes.

I concentrated on my driving.

Traffic proved to be relatively light on the Suffolk
County portion of the LIE. We were approaching the
border with Nassau County and things were beginning
to pick up congestion-wise when Amanda, who had
fallen silent several miles back, turned around to check
on Jenny in the backseat.

"You asleep, Jenny?" she inquired. Evidently satisfied, she turned back. "I didn't want to talk about it in front of Jenny," she said in a confidential tone, "because—well, I'm sure you know her story. But you must think we're all behaving *very* oddly about . . . what happened to Frank."

I began to appreciate Jenny's irritation with this universal determination to treat her like an incipient basket case. For my part, I was fed up with euphemisms.

"You mean Frank's murder," I said.

Amanda winced. "That's just it, Phoebe. It's impossible for me—any of us—to believe that one of us would actually . . . *do* that to Frank."

My, my, I thought. We *have* come a long way from—what was it?—*Somebody did it on purpose.* And, *They've killed him!*

A dozen or so building-high wheels loomed up on my left. I wrestled the Toyota out of the semi's draft, grimly gripping the wheel as the monster vehicle roared by and barreled down the highway ahead. Then I returned my attention to Amanda.

"Nevertheless," I said, "the fact is that the police are convinced Frank was killed deliberately and that it had to be one of the people who knew him well. Who knew about the allergy and where he kept his pills and so on. There doesn't seem to be any alternative."

"What about Sarah Kirk? She's been at the Colony forever. She knew Frank."

"I'm sure the police are considering her. But from what I understand, Sarah's domain was the kitchen, period. Everyone says she never set foot anywhere else. And no one's suggested the hint of a motive for Sarah. Whereas, as I recall, you at one point seemed to believe there were several candidates."

Amanda made an impatient and dismissive gesture. "Oh, I know what I *said*. But let's face it, Phoebe, I was *hysterical*. I wasn't thinking clearly. I'd just come from . . . You have no idea." She covered her face with her hand

and drew a deep breath, then let the hand drop. "It was just horrible," she said, with a sincerity so genuine that I was startled into sympathy.

"Yes, it must have been awful for you," I murmured, at the same time maneuvering around a station wagon that was observing the speed limit, thereby creating a traffic hazard.

"But then when I'd had a chance to think, I couldn't really believe . . . and I began to realize what it would mean if the police started prying into all of our lives. I mean, people may have . . . painful things in their past that have *nothing* to do with Frank. But the police don't care, they just want to dig up whatever they can find. And the newspapers are the same. It just wouldn't be fair!"

"What happened to Frank wasn't fair," I said.

"Don't you think I know that?" she snapped. "And you needn't be so holier-than-thou, Phoebe. You hardly knew Frank, we've all known him for years. And yes, he'd been annoying people lately. But not like that, not to . . . to *kill* for. It's just incredible."

The "holier-than-thou" remark struck home. Something in Amanda did indeed seem to bring out the prig in me. And wasn't I having the very problem she described? "To tell the truth," I said, "it's incredible to me too. But the evidence—"

"If he had died any other way," Amanda said, "it would have been terrible and sad but at least we could have grieved normally. This way . . . well," her voice took on a plaintive note, "this is one the etiquette books don't cover."

Poor Amanda! Failed by Miss Manners! The remark opened up for me a new understanding of the White Queen's approach to life's problems. I found myself harboring an unexpected feeling of empathy.

"If only," she went on, "it *would* turn out to be that dreary Sarah Kirk and not one of us. Nobody would care half so much about *her*."

The feeling of empathy took wing.

However, here we were, stuck with each other for another hour. I might as well do a little discreet probing.

"What do *you* think 'Amadeus' might mean?" I said.

Amanda bridled. "*I* think it means nothing at all! Of course, the police, being so literal-minded, have no doubt decided that because the first three letters are the same as mine . . . well, naturally, it's *too* ridiculous. Frank must have been in a terrible state, he probably just fell on the score and it got marked by accident."

I mentally pictured the cover of Frank's copy of *Così fan tutte*. No, that *X* had not been a random scratching. For Frank, I was convinced, it had had meaning. Amanda, I presumed, hadn't actually seen it. But wasn't she perhaps protesting a bit too much? And she wasn't finished.

"And even if he *was* trying to leave a message, who's to say he'd gotten it right? Frank wasn't always . . . I was terribly, terribly fond of Frank, but—"

"Yes, I could see that. It must have been all that much more of a shock to you when he died."

Amanda shot me a look of extreme hauteur. "If you are suggesting, Phoebe, that there was anything *sexual* in my feeling for Frank, you're entirely mistaken. I loved him like a *brother*. And I had enormous respect for his *talent*. Sometimes I think I was the *only* one who truly appreciated Frank's gift. Who wasn't distracted into making fun of his little enthusiasms."

Gosh, Amanda, I thought, hasn't it sunk in that this last "little enthusiasm" may be the reason Frank's dead now? I decided I'd had about enough conversation with the White Queen.

"I didn't mean to suggest anything of the kind," I said quietly. "Goodness! Look at this traffic!" And indeed the combination of speed and congestion as we approached nearer to the city was becoming truly hairy. Amanda fell silent. I drove.

◆　◆　◆

We dropped Amanda off near Washington Square after a harrowing trip from the Manhattan mouth of the Midtown Tunnel. I headed for the nearest parking garage, where I gladly allowed my car to be held for ransom by the resident pirate. Until the evil hour when I would have to drive to the funeral parlor in Queens, Jenny and I would take public transportation.

We were walking up West Fourth Street looking for a luncheonette Jenny remembered, when she touched my arm. "Could we go down Perry for just a minute?" she said, pointing.

We turned, and shortly she stopped in front of a narrow apartment building five or six stories high.

"This is where we lived," she said. "Charlie and I. I haven't been back since and I just wanted . . ."

She stood looking up at the building's flat brick face for some moments. There were geraniums in two first-floor window boxes and other flowers—marigolds, I thought—in one on the third floor. Greenery just visible rising over the top parapet suggested a roof garden. Any evidence of fire damage was long gone.

I couldn't read her face, and in any case no comment from me seemed called for or even possible. I waited quietly until she turned, glanced at me, and started walking back toward West Fourth.

"Thanks," she said. "You really are terrific, Phoebe. And you know what? I'm feeling a lot better." She took my arm. "Let's get lunch and then—where did you say we should go? The Frick? I've never been, but it sounds—"

"Hold on," I said. "Isn't that Larry up ahead?"

But the Piano Man, if it was he, had turned West on Eleventh before Jenny could give an opinion. By the time we reached the corner no one resembling Larry Peterson was to be seen.

16

The way they're acting exceeds my expectations.

act 1, scene 4

"YOU KNEW MY SON?" FRANK'S MOTHER SAID TO ME.

"Yes, only briefly, I'm afraid. We talked. I thought he was . . . charming and . . . a very, very good person. I'm really so awfully sorry."

Mrs. Palermo's lips formed a tremulous smile. She ducked her head. "Yes, he was," she said, her breath catching. "Very good."

What, I asked myself, am I *doing* here, intruding on the grief of strangers? Where was it stated in my contract (leaving aside the detail that I didn't have a contract) that my duties included limousine service? I promised myself a stern talk with La Varovna: In the event of any more sudden deaths among the Colony staff, students, or friends, my car was no longer available for funeral duty. I was still suffering from the trauma of having made a wrong turn off the Queensboro Bridge. And now here I was facing a woman who undoubtedly also wondered why I was here. A woman who, I reminded myself guiltily, had just suffered a genuine trauma of the worst kind.

Mrs. Palermo was about my height, plump but not heavy, with silver-grey hair cut short and styled to frame a handsome face—large eyes, strong nose, soft mouth and chin. Unself-conscious tears had made damp pathways down her cheeks. A recurrent fleeting expression of bewilderment suggested some variety of sedation.

With one hand she gripped the arm of her husband, a distinguished-looking, balding version of Frank. He was a professor, I'd been told, of medieval history at Queens College—a big man whose black suit would have made him seem even more formidable except for the defeated slump of his shoulders.

On Mrs. Palermo's other side stood Anna Varovna. When I'd approached them, Anna had been talking quietly to Mrs. Palermo, holding her hand and stroking it. Mrs. Palermo didn't seem to mind. Whatever the police might have told her, she obviously felt no ill will toward the Colony's doyenne.

Next to Anna, so close as to appear joined at the hip, stood Gerta Hofstetter, looking dazed. When I moved over to her and asked an innocuous question about the trip from East Hampton, she frowned at me in puzzlement and made no answer. Feeling awkward and out of place, I moved to the shelter of a mammoth construction of yellow and white roses and occupied myself with the surroundings.

The room was large, dimly lit (although outside it was still full daylight), and oppressive as only a good old-fashioned funeral parlor can be. Green velvet curtains shrouded the windows, mouse-grey wall-to-wall carpeting deep enough to bounce on covered the floor. The woodwork was mahogany, the walls blanketed with flocked, dark crimson paper. Huge floral arrangements stood at intervals of a few feet around the room, smaller offerings in vases crowded every available surface. The smell of lilies and carnations was overpowering. Despite the air-conditioning evidenced by a pervasive humming sound, I felt the need to move slowly and take deep breaths. At least, thank God, *I* didn't have to sing.

At one end of the room on a raised platform, also carpeted, stood a bier holding Frank's coffin, banked by yet more flowers. The lid of the coffin, I noted with relief, was closed. Next to the bier was a cushioned kneeling stool. On the wall behind it, framed by yet more drapery, hung a two-foot-long crucifix carved of some dark wood.

To one side of the platform (stage left) was a rosewood-finished electronic organ. At the other was a wooden lectern. A couple of rows of red plush and gilt folding chairs were arranged to face the platform. At the end of one row, a priest bent over two elderly women dressed in unrelieved black. Both of the women were clutching rosaries and weeping unrestrainedly.

A stream of arrivals first paused to kneel at the coffin, then moved to speak to Frank's parents.

They then passed on to a further receiving line of a dozen or so people, many of them bearing such a strong resemblance to Frank as to almost render moot the decision to close the casket. It was a strikingly handsome family. Over and over, male and female, I saw repeated the brown, expressive eyes, the curling dark hair, straight nose, large white teeth, even the characteristic gestures of arm and shoulder. Had I been Frank's murderer, I mused, I would by now be having a severe case of the willies.

At the thought, I remembered Gerta Hofstetter's ghost-ridden expression. I looked for her and spotted her going through the receiving line at Anna's side. She appeared to have somewhat recovered. At least she was making conversation. Her abrupt handshakes, the quick little nods that punctuated her remarks, made an odd contrast to Anna's sympathetic warmth, complete with tears and embraces. I wondered again what was the bond that held these two together. Those little nods . . . I remembered Gerta as she had appeared at my car window on my arrival at the Colony that first day. Gerta, who had come *down the steps of Frank's cabin* to greet me. How could I have forgotten and—oh damn!—did I have to tell the lieutenant? When it was more than likely that she'd simply been supplying toilet paper or counting lightbulbs?

Well, I couldn't tell him now, could I? I pulled my mind back to the scene before me.

Jenny and I had arrived at the Bertolini Brothers' Funeral Home ahead of the rest of the Colony contingent with the exception of Anna and Gerta. Jenny had immediately disappeared into the ladies' to change her shoes and fix her face. Stefan, Jason Lee, Larry, Amanda, Theo, and Rita must have turned up soon after, because they were now entering the room together with Jenny. I watched them cross to where the Palermo parents were standing. Had they arrived at the Bertolini doorstep en masse by accident, I wondered, or had they waited to make a group entrance as a gesture of solidarity?

I thought I detected—or perhaps I imagined it—a shrinking away as the Colony staff made their way through the gathering that now filled the center of the room. There was an unmistakable ebb in the ongoing tide of conversation. Heads turned toward Mr. and Mrs. Palermo as if searching for a cue as to what their own behavior should be.

As Rita reached her, Mrs. Palermo held out both her hands. "Oh, Rita," she said, "thank you for coming!" and the two women embraced.

Something like a collective sigh swept the assembly. The level of discreet babble rose again. The newspapers must have gotten it wrong. In any case, an official posture had been established. Miss Manners, as it were, had spoken.

Spoken, that is, in terms of etiquette, not of what people were actually thinking.

"Chi è quella donna?" I heard one woman say sotto

voce to another as they stood at the end of the receiving line.

The second woman glanced in my direction and
turned back to her partner. *"Solamente la nuova segretaria."*

"Bene. Almeno siamo sicuri che non è l'assassino."

I supposed that being dismissed as "only the secretary" was probably a small price to pay for elimination as
a suspect. Still, I had to restrain myself from strolling
over to the two women, striking up a conversation in
Italian, and watching their faces.

I turned my attention to the receiving line. Frank's
two brothers and four sisters stood together with, I
guessed, their respective husbands and wives and a
number of older people who might be aunts and uncles.
Two of the sisters were visibly pregnant. At least one of
the brothers did not share his mother's attitude toward
the Varovna Colony contingent. I caught him in a look of
barely contained outrage and saw the woman beside
him whisper and place a hand on his arm.

As the members of the Colony passed along the line,
coming face to face with successive members of Frank's
family, the depth of the dilemma on both sides became
more and more clear to me. Because, as their body language made plain, these were people who knew one another well. Frank, I remembered, had been spending
summers at the Colony for some six or seven years.
How many times had his parents, grandparents, brothers and sisters and cousins made the trip to East Hampton to see the youngest Palermo son, the opera singer,
the flower of the family, perform? How many cast parties, beach parties, cookouts had they attended, how
many confidences had been exchanged? Even the angry
brother, I observed, was having a hard time maintaining
his stance in the face of these familiar individuals who
had been, for God's sake, Frank's *friends.* As for Anna
herself, it was plain that the family regarded her in the

light of mentor and benefactor, almost a surrogate
mother. She was greeted in every case with unstinting
warmth.

I watched Larry Peterson take the hand of one of the
aunts in both of his. He murmured to her, his mobile
mouth downturned in an expression of sorrow that had
to be—didn't it?—genuine. Theo Morse, unnaturally attired in a sober dark suit, bent his long neck to listen to
one of the sisters, then gave her a brief, enveloping hug
before moving on.

What on earth could they be *saying*? Anything, I
imagined, but what must have been uppermost in every
mind: By whose hand had Frank died, and why?

Rita stood facing one of the pregnant sisters. Except
for the significantly protruding stomach of the one, by
their attitudes the two women might have been mirror
images: the swelling bosom, palm of one hand planted at
the base of a gently swayed back, feet firmly apart. Then
Rita moved on, but not before I'd had my second revelation of the afternoon: Rita Michaels was pregnant! The
mother of three unplanned (by her own description)
children was working on a fourth. No wonder she was
cranky!

Hard on this insight came a memory. Frank's voice,
giving his example: *You're a married woman who's been
having an affair and now you find you're pregnant.* Somehow, Frank had known, or guessed, where others had
not—no doubt the result of growing up with all those
sisters. And had assumed that Theo was not the father.
But had he been right? And if so, how far would Rita go,
or Stefan, for that matter (assuming the baby was his), to
keep the secret?

Stop making yourself crazy, Phoebe. You're here to
attend a wake, to mourn and remember a human life,
not to play detective.

Besides, unless I missed my guess, there was a genuine detective on the premises—a stocky man with large

hands and feet, broad shoulders, and a small, neat head. He appeared to be on his own and attempting to be inconspicuous. Except for a few sidelong glances, people were going along by pretending the attempt was successful.

I had picked out as a second uninvited and probably equally unwelcome guest a young woman with a Brenda Starr cascade of red hair, wearing pink-framed glasses and an alert expression. One hand was tucked casually into the pocket of her navy blazer. Occasionally she cocked her head and murmured in the direction of her lapel but she didn't attempt to speak directly to anyone. She too was being studiously ignored. The Palermo family, I thought, should count themselves fortunate that only one reporter had shown up. Perhaps the speediness with which the wake had been arranged had caught the press off guard. Perhaps the speed had been calculated.

The room was by now quite full. Arrivals had tapered off. A few people had come and gone, but most lingered.

The receiving line had dissolved. Frank's father escorted his wife to the first row of seats, where she joined the priest and the two elderly women in black. Other family members filled in the remaining chairs. The rest of us remained standing or sought one of the two sofas and several occasional chairs placed against the red-flocked walls. Frank's father stood quietly below his son's coffin, looking out over the room, waiting for the murmurs of conversation to subside. Larry Peterson, I noted, had taken his place at the organ, with the five Varovna Colony singers seated nearby.

It was at this point that three new arrivals—a man and two women—appeared and paused in the wide doorway.

The man, perhaps in his thirties, was immensely fat. His beige seersucker suit strained at every button, and the collar of his yellow shirt and the knot of his dark brown tie were lost in folds of flesh.

One of the women was tall with large, strong features and a coronet of thick, grey braids. A sort of caftan affair, exotically patterned in magenta and blue, flowed to her ankles.

The second woman was petite with a snub nose and bright little eyes. She was dressed in a black peasant outfit, flouncy and full skirted, and tiny black stiletto-heeled pumps, as if, supposing that attendance at a wake called for black clothes, she had put on the only ones she had. At her throat was a string of jet beads; more dangled from her ears. She looked like a really depressed gypsy.

All three were regarding the room and the people in it with expressions of determined—even implacable—goodwill. It didn't take a great leap of intuition to guess who they might be.

I happened to be standing nearest the doorway. Frank's father was looking flustered. Several of the family were staring with undisguised displeasure. The three, whoever they were, had clearly not been on the invitation list. Nevertheless, there they stood, and given the effort that had been expended so far to avoid anything like a scene, here at last, I thought, was something I could do to be helpful. I approached the man, who had stepped somewhat ahead of the others, and offered my hand.

He shook it vigorously. "This is the wake for Frank Palermo?" His voice was carrying, and unexpectedly high.

I nodded.

"We just wanted . . . We're from the Children of Truth, you know."

Bingo.

The tall woman said, "We wanted to offer our condolences. To his parents. Could you point out . . ."

"I believe we're about to have some music," I murmured. "Do come in, and then you can speak to the Palermos afterwards." I put my hand on the man's arm and guided the three of them to the back of the room.

Frank's father shot me a glance both grateful and puzzled, having no recollection, I'm sure, of who I was.

Brenda Starr, who had been wandering the fringes of the crowd looking more and more bored, perked up and sidled over. I planted myself between her and the Fat Child. Across the room I noted the stocky detective giving the new arrivals a considering stare.

Mr. Palermo cleared his throat.

"My son Frank," he said, faltered, then started again. "Music was our son's life. My wife and I have asked some of those with whom our son made music, those who were his colleagues and friends, to remember him by . . . to sing some of the music that Frank loved."

He stopped, seemed about to say more, then shook his head, gestured toward Larry Peterson, and sat down heavily beside his wife.

Jenny, Amanda, and Rita moved to stand beside the organ. All three looked pale. The color Jenny had put on her cheeks stood out clownlike on her white face. Amanda's blond frizz had been plastered into a marcel with spit curls that sat on her head like a bad wig. Only Rita, in a simple black dress and with her thick braid wound into a low coil, looked relatively together and composed.

Larry gave them a single triad and they began to sing, a cappella. It was Mendelssohn, "Lift Thine Eyes" from *Elijah*. Their three voices rose on the cloying, insufficient air—Jenny's pure, floating soprano, Amanda's richer tone taking the second, Rita anchoring with her dark mezzo.

"Lift thine eyes, O lift thine eyes to the mountains . . ." They were taking a lot of breaths, I thought, but, professionals that they were, the sound didn't falter. Neither did it soar. The notes rose in delicate close harmony of thirds and sixths, hovered, and then disappeared into the smothering maw of heavy curtains and thick carpeting. "Thy Keeper will never slumber, never, will never slumber, never slumber. Lift thine eyes . . ."

The final tones were duly absorbed into the drapery. There was a perfunctory murmur of appreciation. Jenny and Rita sat down, their posture expressing their relief.

No such reprieve for Amanda. She was joined by Stefan Kowalski, Larry played an introduction, and they launched into a soprano-tenor arrangement of "Panis Angelicus." Stefan appeared solemn but at ease. His light-colored summer suit, well cut and straining only slightly over the muscles of his upper arms, gave him a look of dignified solidity. But Amanda's high forehead was beaded with perspiration, and the flared skirt of her silk dress hugged her thighs like an illustration for the horrors of static cling. As she sang, a single droplet of sweat slid down the length of her nose and poised at the tip.

"*O res mirabilis,*" Amanda soldiered on. "*O res mirabilis,*" Stefan echoed. Now he'd caught sight of the drop. For an instant his solemnity was breached. He pulled himself together and directed his eyes determinedly to the far wall.

For God's sake, Amanda, wipe it off! I muttered behind clenched teeth. Leave it there and you might as well be singing "The Man on the Flying Trapeze" for all anybody'll notice.

Although come to that, what did "Panis angelicus" mean, anyway? And being in Latin, who, presumably, cared? Syrupy, vaguely liturgical, suitable alike for weddings, wakes, and funerals . . .

The drop at the end of Amanda's nose let go and fell to the spongy carpeting below. From somewhere in the room a nervous titter was quickly turned into a cough.

"*Servus, servus et humilis,*" sang Stefan and Amanda, and "Panis Angelicus" came to a merciful end.

Another one down. The Varovna Colony, I was thinking, should've stayed home.

There was some movement of the "Is that it?" variety, especially among those of us who had been standing, by now, for an hour or more. But no, Jason Lee Jones had risen and was standing by the electronic organ. He nodded at Larry Peterson, who played a few simple chords of introduction.

"Deep river," Jason Lee sang, "my home is over Jordan."

From the first notes, a stillness spread across the room. The air-conditioner had been turned off, probably before the singing began, but I hadn't noticed until now. Jason Lee's eyes were fixed on the middle distance. His voice poured out, round, rich, refusing to be swallowed by the killer room. It homed straight in on each ear and heart, reminding us of why we were there.

"Deep river, Lord, I want to cross over into campground."

He stood easily, one hand resting lightly on a corner of the organ, the other hanging at his side. He didn't move or gesture, but sang with utter simplicity, the faint island accent giving even deeper universality to the familiar words.

"O don't you want to go to that gospel feast,
To that promised land, where all is peace . . ."

Tears were running down my face. I dug for a Kleenex. The sound of sobbing filled the room.

"Lord, I want to cross over into campground."

When Jason Lee stopped singing, no one moved or spoke for several moments. A number of people were crying helplessly on one another's shoulders or into their own cupped hands. Jason Lee walked over to Frank's parents, bent down, and embraced them both.

Sounds of sobbing gradually gave way to sounds of noses being blown. The priest rose, walked to the lectern, and looked out over the gathering.

Moved as I was by what Jason Lee had accomplished, I had forgotten all about the Children of Truth, who were still standing close to me. I was about to be reminded of them in a big way.

The Fat Child touched my arm and spoke in a tone that was probably meant to be confidential. Unfortunately, his voice carried easily halfway across the room, which had again quieted in anticipation of the reverend's remarks.

"So," he said, "I gather the cops still haven't figured out which one of 'em killed Frank."

17

Never dare to show your faces anymore!

act 1, scene 16

EVERY HEAD WITHIN THE SOUND OF THE FAT CHILD'S VOICE—
a radius of about fifteen feet—swiveled in our direction.
The faces expressed a mixture of outrage and titillation
that no doubt in other circumstances I would have found
amusing.

The stocky detective, who had drifted across to our
side of the room during the singing and had been leaning
with studied casualness against the door frame, jerked
upright.

Brenda Starr looked as if she'd died and gone straight
to heaven with no assist from the Bertolini Brothers. She
began an ecstatic communing with her lapel.

As far as I could tell, neither the priest nor the immediate family, situated as they were at the far end of the
room, had heard the contribution of the Child of Truth.
Directly on its heels the priest had begun what I took to
be a brief homily followed by a prayer.

I was uncertain as to the details because I was preoccupied at the moment with being included in the hostile
interest directed at the three Children. What comes, I
thought bitterly, of trying to be helpful. Well, my instinct
had proved correct, in for a penny, etc. I turned directly

to the Fat Child, uncomfortably aware of Brenda Starr breathing on my shoulder blades.

"I *don't* think," I said, with all the emphasis I could manage and still speak in an undertone, "that that is an appropriate subject to bring up here. Especially to Frank's family. They're having a hard enough time with the situation as it is." I looked sternly across his yard or so of yellow shirting to make sure the other two Children were paying attention.

The Fat Child smiled and nodded. All three looked at me with the sort of indulgence reserved for the terminally unenlightened. The Tall Child spoke.

"Of course," she said kindly, "we understand."

"Who're you?" said the Gypsy Child.

It was a fair question. I gave my name and explained my connection with the Varovna Colony.

"Oh," said the Gypsy Child, "then you're not one of the susp— Oops, sorry!" Her little eyes twinkled up at me.

We had been speaking in near whispers, but now it appeared that the priest had completed his prayer. There was hesitant movement on the part of the guests, as if, while knowing it was time to go, they suspected (rightly, as it turned out) that the real drama was yet to come.

The Fat Child started off in the direction of the Palermo family. I would have followed, but the Tall Child forestalled me. Her pale, exophthalmic eyes under her grey circlet of braids fixed me with an eager light. "Which one is the composer?" she said. "Mr. Peterson."

"And Madame Varovna," chimed in the Gypsy, "where's she? I've never met a real opera singer. Except for Frank, of course, but I heard she used to be really famous. I sing myself, you know, I—"

"Just how long have you all known Frank?" I said. "I understood he'd only recently gotten back from Europe and that's where he became interested in the, um, Children."

I was keeping an eye on the progress of the Fat Child. At the moment he was talking to one of Frank's brothers. The conversation, so far, appeared unexceptionable. Brenda Starr, I observed, was close on his tail.

"Frank came to us as soon as he got back," the Tall Child said. "A month or so ago. Our people in Germany put him in touch. Such a nice boy, so eager. Is that Mr. Peterson? The interesting-looking man who was playing the organ?"

I pointed out the members of the Colony, noting privately that the two women seemed remarkably well informed about a group of people they'd never met.

"Oh!" cried the Gypsy when I identified Anna, "what a ducky old woman!" and she took off after her quarry, tilted forward on her high-rise heels, black skirts and earrings swinging.

The detective, after appearing torn, had elected to follow the Fat Child. A thought occurred to me.

"Have you—any of you—talked to the police?"

The Tall Child looked askance. "No, why would we? We don't know any of those people. Only Frank."

"Well, obviously he talked to you about the Colony. Told you about his friends. Isn't it possible—"

"No, no, Phoebe. You don't understand." Again the kindly forebearance. "It's a common mistake. You see, at our meetings we only share the truth about ourselves, we don't tell other people's secrets. If Frank knew anything . . . anything, say, that someone else didn't want to admit, he'd never break a confidence. He'd just encourage that person to tell the truth himself. Or herself." She looked at me consideringly. "Perhaps you'd like to come to a meeting?"

I demurred but she produced a business card "just in case." Before I slipped it into my pocket I noted that the Tall Child's business was interior decoration. Not, I would have thought, a good line of work for the compulsively frank.

When I looked up, it was to see the Tall Child studying my face with a frown. "You look strained, Phoebe,"
she said. "Those dark patches under your eyes. I've always found proper elimination to solve so many problems. Ask your doctor to recommend a laxative." She
gave my shoulder a friendly pat and walked away in
Larry Peterson's direction with a swirl of the magenta
and blue caftan.

I suppressed a desire to giggle. If the candor remained at that level I was probably worrying for nothing. After all, despite their name, these Children of Truth
were adults with, one supposed, a certain amount of discretion, if not a sense of occasion. Then I thought of the
Fat Child's casual bombshell. Ah well, perhaps my word
of caution had sufficed.

Nevertheless, I kept watching the Children, more
out of a sense of curiosity than of a feeling that there was
anything more I could do. A good deal of emotional
leave-taking was going on now, as well as words of appreciation to the singers. I began to make my way to
where the Varovna contingent was gathered. Surely we
could be starting home soon.

The Gypsy Child was chattering away at Anna,
who stood stiffly, looking uncharacteristically discom-
posed. I caught several "Frank always said's" and "When
Frank was in Paris," and "Your husband, Mr. Dmitri,"
and "I've always sung Country myself, but people have
told me . . ." Next to Anna, Gerta Hofstetter was staring
at the Gypsy Child as a rabbit might stare at a snake.

Larry Peterson, backed against the organ, appeared
to be on the receiving end of a lecture on contemporary
music by the Tall Child. "Atonality" . . . "twelve-tone" . . .
"as Schönberg said" . . . "Frank told us that you" . . .
"everybody following the fashion" . . . "slavish imitation,
even outright stealing . . ." I had the impression that
(A) the Tall Child had boned up for the occasion from a
source at least thirty years out of date and (B) that what

she was actually doing was flirting. I wondered what Frank had told her about Larry.

Larry was mostly saying, "Ah," and dabbing his forehead and upper lip with a handkerchief. He caught my eye, said something to the Tall Child that cut her off in midflight, squeezed past her, came to me, and grabbed my arm.

"Good God," he muttered, "save me! Isn't it time to leave?"

Over his shoulder the Tall Child threw me a really dirty look before she bore down on Jason Lee, who was sitting on the organ bench, looking tired. Perhaps she'd have some pithy medical advice for him too.

"I suppose we should say goodbye to someone," I said to Larry. "And then I have to gather my riders."

The crowd had thinned a good deal. Over by the Palermo parents, the Fat Child had finally achieved his goal and was offering condolences in his high, carrying tones.

"Such a wonderful person, your son. So warm, so understanding. We all loved him, you know. We in the Children."

"Children?" Mrs. Palermo looked puzzled. Her husband murmured to her. "Oh yes, he did mention . . ." She looked ready to drop, and I willed the Fat Child to have a heart and say a quick farewell.

It didn't work.

"And Frank would have appreciated all this so much." The Fat Child gestured at the coffin, the singers, the room. His face shone with earnest benevolence. "All this outpouring of love and ceremony. Even though, of course, being a Child of Truth he'd given up Catholicism."

"Given up . . . ?" Mrs. Palermo faltered.

"The organized Church, hierarchy, that sort of thing."

"That sort of . . ."

"Well, you know. Ritual, popery, stuff like that," the Fat Child explained patiently.

"Potpourri?" Mrs. Palermo's voice was becoming thready. She turned in desperation to her husband. "Potpourri?" she repeated. "What does he mean? Frank was leaving the Church because of . . . *incense*?"

Mr. Palermo had been growing progressively more red faced with inarticulate outrage. Now he managed to mouth at the Fat Child: "Out! Get out!" One arm stretched straight, finger pointing to the door. With the other he encircled his wife's shoulders and pulled her to him. "No, no, *cara*, he doesn't mean anything. He's a stupid man."

At the same moment, Frank's two brothers converged on the Fat Child and effectively frog-marched him away.

Behind me, Brenda Starr queried excitedly, "Did she say 'incest'?"

I turned, lowered my head, and barked directly into her lapel pin, "No, *incense*. You know, the smelly stuff."

Brenda Starr jumped back. Her face under the improbable red hair creased with confusion. "Incense? But what does that . . ."

"Oh, say!" cried the Gypsy Child. She had either missed the Fat Child's sudden forced exit or it was, to her, an unremarkable occurrence. "You're Jenny Allen! Hey, I just love your voice!"

Jenny, who with Rita and Amanda had been making her way toward Larry and me, was brought up short in the middle of the room. She looked uncertainly at her accoster and murmured a tentative, "Uh . . . thanks." Behind her, Rita rolled her eyes.

"And oh!" the Gypsy Child persisted, "you're the one who had that terrible thing happen. When your boyfriend died in that fire. God, it must have been awful, coming home and finding him all burned and dead and everything. When Frank told us I just couldn't . . . Frank felt so awful, you know, about the whole . . ."

Jenny, who had been staring openmouthed at the Gypsy Child, gave a little sigh, her eyes rolled up, and she dropped down onto the mouse-grey carpet.

The Gypsy Child's hand flew to her mouth. "Oh, my goodness!" she said.

Rita exploded forward. "You *idiot!*" She dropped to her knees beside Jenny. "Somebody get some water!"

Apparently from nowhere, Stefan Kowalski appeared with a glass. He kneeled down, dipped his fingers in the glass, and sprinkled water on Jenny's face and lips. "Move away, for God's sake!" he commanded the onlookers who had instinctively gathered around.

Rita got to her feet and advanced on the Gypsy Child, who, to do her credit, was looking shamefaced and not a little frightened.

"What the f—" Rita glanced in the direction of the Palermo parents and lowered her decibel level. "What is it with you people? Do you have to check your friggin' brains before you can join that loony outfit?"

The Tall Child swirled to her cohort's defense. "Well, really!" she began.

"And you!" Rita's tip-tilted eyes, now narrowed almost to disappearing, sent palpable sparks over her cheekbones. "You certainly look old enough to have some common sense. For chrissake, try using it!"

The Tall Child fought to assume her expression of universal charity. "You just don't understand. The Truth . . ."

"The truth!" Rita said scornfully. "The truth is that you're a bunch of arrogant, fatheaded, insensitive . . ." she scrambled for a word, *"jerks!"*

"Well, really!" the Tall Child said again. She swiveled her head left and right as if searching for signs of sympathy. Finding none, she gave her braided coronet an aggrieved toss, took the Gypsy Child's arm, gathered her caftan around her, and stalked out of the room, dragging the bewildered Gypsy in her wake.

18

Damnation! When will there be an end to this?

act 1, scene 1

WE WERE ON MILE HILL ROAD, STILL HALF A MILE FROM THE turnoff to the Varovna Colony, when I got the first inkling that something was wrong.

Both of my passengers were asleep: Jenny curled up in the back, Amanda tilted almost prone in the seat beside me. There had been little conversation on the trip home. Back at the Bertolini Brothers, Jenny had recovered quickly, apologizing all around for being "such a wimp." Once everyone was assured that she was indeed all right, leave-taking and departure followed with a speed that bordered on the unseemly. We had, after all, a long ride ahead.

Going out the door I nearly collided with the stocky detective, who had pulled up short at the sound of his beeper going off. He mumbled an apology and went back inside, presumably to find a telephone.

As soon as we cleared the Queens–Nassau line I picked up a Public Radio station out of Connecticut and for the next hour or so listened to the Pittsburgh Symphony romp through *Till Eulenspiegel* and then settle into some serious Russian angst with the Shostakovich *Fifth*.

Somewhere between Riverhead and Southampton the station petered out. I turned off the radio and spent the rest of the ride home still trying, with mixed results, to keep my mind clear of everything to do with Frank's wake. Instead, I concentrated on the days to come, and my role in them. From what I understood, the schedule for the next week was a killing one. For starters, with the arrival of Chris Fox, the new baritone, rehearsals for *Così fan tutte* would shift into high gear. I wondered what this Chris Fox would be like and how he would compare with Frank. Anna must have a good deal of faith in him to ask him to . . .

Despite denials, wasn't it possible that Frank had told one or more of the Children something significant, and shouldn't the police talk to them? I could at least give Lieutenant Freed the Tall Child's card. . . .

Right.

On Saturday and Sunday the first contingent of students would be checking in, about fifteen strong. On Monday they would start lessons and coaching sessions, besides rehearsing the minimal appearances of the chorus in *Così*. However brief these might be, they still involved costuming. According to past programs, costumes were mainly Gerta's responsibility, along with whomever else she could rope into helping. (Anticipating which, I'd lied through my teeth and firmly denied acquaintance with anything involving thread or having a sharp point.)

Could Gerta Hofstetter possibly go around looking as consistently guilt-ridden as she had at the wake if she weren't, in fact, guilty? Or was it Anna that she . . .

Oops!

Thursday night would be the dress rehearsal, opening on Friday, with additional performances Saturday and Sunday. The same schedule would repeat the following weekend.

Meanwhile I would be finishing up the program, printing and assembling it, organizing a box office, typing up lesson and coaching schedules, answering the phone and the mail, keeping the books, checking the publicity . . . all those things about which Anna was "not worried whatsoever."

And speaking of Anna, did she . . . could she possibly . . . was she still expecting me "to discover who has murdered poor Frank"? No, surely that had been an aberration of the moment. I remembered suspecting that her main purpose at the time had been her second commission—being a friend to Jenny. That one at least, I thought, I'd been fulfilling pretty well.

How, after all, could anyone have anticipated the idiocy of the Gypsy Child? Or, for that matter, Jenny's reaction to it? I'd believed her when she'd said "I really am okay." Just how frail was she? And why . . .

Whatever. Enough was enough. I could see already that Anna's promise of "at least one whole day off every week, my darling," would likely turn out to have been a gentle pleasantry. The lieutenant would do his job, I mine, the singers theirs. Pulling off the production of *Così fan tutte*, under the circumstances, seemed to me enough of a major challenge for everyone involved, let alone trying to do someone else's—

What on earth was that odd light in the trees up ahead?

For a moment I flashed on the nameless heroine of *Rebecca* traveling in the darkness toward a Manderley in flames. Good God, was the Colony on fire?

But no, this light came and went with too much regularity. Like the revolving beam of a lighthouse. If there had been a lighthouse in the vicinity, which I was sure there wasn't.

At a curve in the road combined with a thickening of the branches arching overhead, I momentarily lost sight of the light. Then there it was again, definitely pulsating,

circling, now white, now pinkish, glancing off the leaves
and trunks of trees and the road sign that said HIDDEN
DRIVE. Like a . . . like a . . .

Like a police cruiser parked next to the VAROVNA
COLONY sign, its bubble light whirling merrily.

I slowed and stopped as a uniformed cop materialized from the darkness, holding up his hand. I rolled
down the window and squinched my eyes against the
intense beam of a flashlight directed at my face. In the
backseat, Jenny sat up abruptly. Beside me, Amanda
woke with a snort. "What on *earth* . . ."

Who were we? the cop wanted to know. I told him.
He consulted a list, nodded, and indicated that we could
proceed.

"Wait!" I said as he stepped away. "Why are you
here, what's going on?"

The cop hesitated, then shrugged. "There's been a
murder."

"We *know* that," Amanda said with predictable con-
descension. "We've just come from his *wake*."

But it was not Frank the cop meant.

It was the Mouse, whose body had been discovered
under a pile of dirty sheets in the laundry room off the
kitchen. The discovery had been made at just about the
time that the staff of the Varovna Colony was driving
away from the Bertolini Brothers' Funeral Home. From
preliminary appearances, she had been hit over the head
with an iron skillet some ten to twelve hours previously.

"Mrs. Mullins? There's, um, someone on the
telephone."

I was sitting at Mrs. Schmitter's kitchen table, my
eyes still at half-mast against the cheery morning sunshine streaking past the red-and-white-checked curtains
over the sink. I was wearing my comfortable old faded
blue chenille bathrobe and scuffs and had been counting
on a quiet quarter hour of communion with a mug of

very black coffee. The calico-faced electric clock on the
wall read three minutes past seven. Whoever was calling, it wasn't likely to be with good news. I toyed with
the idea of telling Mrs. Schmitter to say I wasn't at home,
but decided that at this time of day she might find the
concept too disorienting.

I hoisted myself up and trailed my landlady down
the hall, where she turned, not to the left and the front
parlor, but to the right, toward the back of the house and
her bedroom. I had followed without thinking and was
about to apologize, when through the bedroom door I
caught sight of the phone ensconced on Mrs. Schmitter's
night table. Its receiver lay on the patchwork quilt covering an immense canopied four-poster. It was only by
luck that I hadn't tripped on the yards of wire emerging
from the parlor door and snaking along the hallway. Did
she move it in here every night? I wondered. Oh Lord, I
was really going to have to do *something* even if it meant
paying for a separate line. In the meantime . . .

"Phoebe, my darling. I am so sorry to have to
ask . . ."

The police, it appeared, were still declaring the
Colony kitchen off limits. Would I please bring from the
grocery store orange juice, bagels, cream cheese, butter,
pastries, milk, instant coffee, "all things like that. I leave
to you, Phoebe. And would be wonderful to have as
soon as possible."

I hung up the phone and groaned aloud.

Mrs. Schmitter gave a start and her eyes widened.

I assumed a reassuring smile. "Nothing to worry
about, Mrs. Schmitter. Just that I have to go grocery
shopping right away. The, uh, the police aren't letting
them use the kitchen yet at the Colony. That is . . . did
you hear about . . . ?"

Mrs. Schmitter nodded. Her little hands clasped together, hugging her midriff. Overriding her air of vague-

ness and timidity was something solemn in her expression, even accusatory. It echoed the impression I'd gotten from my contacts with the police last night: the parameters of the Varovna Colony affair had changed significantly. It was one thing for outsiders, summer people, to go around bumping one another off, quite different when they started in on the locals. Sarah Kirk was not only East Hampton born and bred but had a vast network of family and community connections. What had started off as a regrettable but nonetheless diverting summer event had become a local tragedy.

Somewhat to my own surprise, I was experiencing a similar reaction to the death of the Mouse, an anger beyond what I'd felt at Frank's death. Because it seemed certain to me that Sarah Kirk had been killed—almost literally swept out of the way—not because of who she was or what she had done but only because of something she knew or had inadvertently seen. Something she might have told me about if I had pressed her yesterday morning when she brought me coffee. If I had paid attention instead of assuming that someone else would get around to questioning her, listening to her.

And someone had. Someone the Mouse trusted, else why would she have turned her back on the killer? Hit from behind, they said, probably as she stooped to retrieve a dishtowel from a low drawer.

Someone who had then traveled to Queens to take part in the wake of victim number one. Incredible! How *could* anyone—anyone who wasn't a monster!

So now, to find the monster, police efforts would redouble—a classic case of shutting the barn door. Already last night there had been two plainclothes officers besides Lieutenant Freed and the Princess divvying up the preliminary questioning. I had drawn one of the new pair—a square and unsmiling woman who had sat silently while a pair of jeans, a sweatshirt, and some blue

Keds two sizes too large had been rounded up for me to replace the dress, jacket, and shoes I'd put on that morning and was now handing over to the law's representative. That the same procedure was being followed with everyone didn't lessen the feeling of unreality, almost of shame. The purpose, of course, was to search for bloodstains.

Indications were that the Mouse had been killed sometime before the collective departures of the Colony staff that morning. The autopsy was expected to narrow the significant period. In any case, I had been on the premises with, God knew, more opportunity than most to whip 'round the corner to the kitchen, pick up a frying pan, and strike Sarah Kirk (once? twice? many times? they hadn't said) over the head.

"But I didn't do it!" I'd wanted to cry. In fact I'd wanted to cry, period, and probably would have if my interrogator had been the lieutenant or the Princess. Surely *they* didn't suspect me!

Where *was* the lieutenant, anyway? Why hadn't he questioned me himself? Having just reached a firm decision to butt out and let the professionals get on with it, I now felt a sense of injury. Was I not, in fact, in a better position than anyone to observe, to be objective? Hadn't Mr. Detective Saul Freed asked me himself to do exactly that? So why was I being turned over to some stone-faced minion who acted as though I might actually be a murderer!

I had caught only a glimpse of the Princess as she was starting up the staircase (I myself had been questioned downstairs in the office). She had rolled her eyes and thrown up her hands in a gesture expressive at once of helplessness, sympathy, and a general state of running her tail off, and then she was gone.

So, shortly afterward, was I, and without the chance to express what I so desperately needed to (but not to Ms. Rockface): the terrible sense of guilt I felt for not having paid attention to the Mouse. The more I dwelled on her appearance in my office that morning, the more plain it became that she had had something on her mind and that I might have persuaded it out of her. But I hadn't, and the Mouse had died.

And if *I* was feeling responsible, what must the lieutenant have been feeling? How had he missed asking Sarah Kirk the right question at the right time?

And why had it taken so long to realize she was missing and then to find her body?

Well, I mused now, with some grim satisfaction, alive the Mouse might have slipped through the cracks, been taken for granted, been almost invisible. Dead, her absence would be suffered more keenly than most. Baritones by the gross might be waiting eagerly in the wings, but a good cook on short notice would be hard to find.

With which thought I left Mrs. Schmitter's bedroom to get dressed and make a shopping list.

19

It's true, I admit it.

act 2, scene 6

FRIDAY, JUNE 22

At eleven o'clock, Anna Varovna leaned back in her chair, passed both hands over her face, and let her arms fall limply to her sides.

"I think, my darling, we should take a break. Some coffee, yes? No, no, you sit. I will get."

She got up from her chair on the opposite side of my desk and went quickly out the door before I had time to make more than a token protest.

And what the hell anyway, I thought wearily. We were both equally tired and Anna Varovna owed me one. More than one. After everything I'd . . .

My conscience kicked in. What, in reality, were my pains compared to Anna's? Some lack of sleep. Some feelings of being overpressured. A dodgy moment or two on the LIE. As opposed to the murders of two long-time associates; the knowledge that another longtime associate must be responsible; the demoralized exhaustion of a staff faced with a one-week deadline for the full-scale public performance of a very demanding opera; policemen traipsing through the buildings and grounds; the imminent arrival of twenty eager students expecting to be adequately housed and fed, instructed, entertained, cosseted, all those things for which they were paying through the nose. A massive threat, in sum, to the reputation, even the continuation of her beloved Colony.

Considering which, it was amazing that she looked as good as she did. When I'd arrived with my bundles she was presiding over the removal to the dining porch of the giant coffeemaker from the kitchen (special dispensation by the lieutenant). She wore a simple but elegantly tailored floral-print dress, hose, and her usual platform sandals. Earrings, necklace, bangle bracelets on her small wrists, all were in place. The neat chignon of silvered hair obediently hugged the back of her neck. Only a deepening of the depressions under her dark eyes and of the lines at either side of her mouth gave evidence that this was a woman of seventy who, in just five days, had lost to violent death a baritone, a cook, and possibly her livelihood.

It was a subdued crew that gathered over the fruits of my early-morning foray into the A&P: bottled orange juice, bagels warmed in a toaster oven (contributed by Stefan Kowalski from the utility room at the boys' cabins), some prune danishes. Wan faces and a conspicuous lack of comradely chitchat spoke of insufficient sleep and a general state of trauma overload. And in one case (I had to keep reminding myself) the knowledge of having twice committed murder—surely enough to discourage the most ardent conversationlist.

Among them all, Theo Morse appeared the least affected. His round face was as smooth as ever, and the pink of his scalp under its wispy covering was echoed in his cheeks. But I read a certain defiance of the whistling-in-the-dark kind in his choice of cherry-red slacks topped by a flowered Hawaiian shirt gaudy even by Island standards. He had the score of *Così* propped in front of him, and a clipboard on which he was making notes. His announcement of the day's rehearsal schedule—individuals in the morning, ensembles in the afternoon when the new baritone, Chris Fox, would presumably have arrived—was met with little more than resigned nods.

Promptly at nine o'clock Anna bundled herself and me off to the office, leaving behind strict instructions that she was to be interrupted during the next two hours only for the direst emergency. Given the recent Colony track record for dire emergencies, this seemed to me an unnecessary tempting of fate. I averted my eyes from the yellow tape blocking off the kitchen area and my ears from the evidences of activity inside the forbidden precinct. But not before the words *missed another goddamn blood spot* had penetrated my defenses.

And for the next two hours we actually accomplished a good deal. Anna dictated a number of letters, which I then typed up while she went over the books and bills. Together we double-checked the living assignments for the incoming students. So far only one, an eighteen-year-old coloratura, had withdrawn, or rather been withdrawn by her parents. The poor girl had called in tears to say that she would defy her parents in a moment and come anyway but that, of course, they'd never pay for her. Anna had been soothing and sympathetic and said the Colony would really miss her. ("I suppose," she mused to me, "I must return their deposit." Well, yeah, Anna.)

We worked out the lesson schedules and Anna explained to me about the sign-up sheets for the three practice cabins in the woods beyond the theater. We went over the program, inserting a dedication of the production to "the memory of our dear friend and gifted colleague." The choice of a suitable memorial to Sarah Kirk was put on temporary hold. (More than one murder victim per program, I couldn't help thinking, might indeed be straining the limits of good taste.)

We discussed the management of tickets and seating on performance nights, Anna shrewdly suspecting a larger than usual turnout for this comic opera where all the traditional operatic mayhem seemed to be occurring offstage. "Is not a big opera community, this East Hampton," she observed. "Is mostly people from New York who go already to the Met, for them this is small turnips. But maybe this time—who knows?"

Judging by the growing list of requests for all performances, I wondered if the casual first-come-first-served-but-don't-worry-you-can-always-get-a-seat system might not backfire this time. But, "Do not worry, my darling, will be plenty of room. Only we will, perhaps, rent some chairs."

Responses to media queries, Anna decreed, were to be a polite but blanket "no comment" with referral to the Suffolk County Homicide Division.

Anna now returned from her foray into the dining room with a coffee tray, including a couple of leftover prune danishes (not, it had turned out, the best choice for a bunch of people in varying states of shock) and the welcome news that by dinnertime the kitchen would again be available. Which left only the problem of finding someone to cook in it. Stefan, Anna said, would make a lunchtime deli run and Gerta had offered to pull together an evening meal.

"But the poor Gerta, she is exhausted, she cannot do this forever. Besides, she is terrible cook. Ah well, I have made many calls. Someone will rescue us."

She blew on her coffee, took a sip, sighed, and leaned back in her chair. Her small, beringed hands enfolded the mug as if for warmth, though the room, like the day outside, was bright with sun and verging on sultry.

"So, Phoebe," she said, "you cannot yet tell me who has done these wicked things?"

I choked on a bit of soggy prune and took a hasty gulp of coffee.

Anna smiled pleasantly. "I make little joke, my darling. Of course, you have not had time. And now this second terrible killing . . ." Her expression turned somber and a muscle twitched in her jaw. "The poor Sarah. She has done nothing, nothing to deserve this. About the poor Sarah I am very angry."

"I don't really know exactly what happened," I said. "Except that she was hit over the head. With a frying pan?"

Anna nodded, but she was evidently thinking along other lines. "You must understand, my darling, for seven years Sarah Kirk has been cooking for me here. She is brusque, yes? She does not often smile. In opera she has no interest. Even it seems she has no interest in the people who come, like her, year after year."

"That was pretty much the impression I got."

"Ah, but you see, is wrong impression, my darling. To me Sarah Kirk is mostly devoted, mostly loyal. And to my singers also, though they would not perhaps believe it. Suppose she knows something or sees something that is strange, she will think, 'But this person, this friend of Anna's, could not do a bad thing, there must be mistake.' And before she tells anyone else she will go to that person and say, 'Explain to me thus-and-so.' "

"And you think that's what happened?"

"I am sure of it. She has been placated and she has been betrayed. Ah yes, I am mostly very angry. So you see, Phoebe, you must find out the truth."

"Aw, Anna, come on . . ." I gestured at the piles of paperwork covering my desk and two auxiliary tables.

"No, no, my darling, do not worry about all this, for this I get you help. Is much more important that you discover for me the bad apple who is upsetting the cart. Already, I am sure, you have seen much, you begin to have some ideas, yes?"

"If you mean about who has done these . . . who the murderer is, no, I haven't a clue. There do seem to be a number of undercurrents here, but—"

"Ah, you see! Undercurrents! You will put together these undercurrents, you will begin to see a picture. You will talk to people." She gave me a straightforward look that contained a hint of challenge. "Even, you will ask me whatever you want to know."

Did she mean it? Suppose I came back with, *Okay, Anna, what happened in France? Why did Frank mentioning this Monsieur LeClair leave you looking like you'd just had a close encounter with a Gorgon? Or more plainly, did you murder Frank Palermo?* But in that case, why this elaborate charade of asking for my help? Did I believe for a minute that Anna Varovna had committed murder? No.

I returned the steady gaze of those dark-circled eyes and voiced the second thought that had come into my head: "I don't understand Amanda's behavior. One minute she's shouting 'murder' and virtually accusing all her friends. And the next she's backpedaling as fast as she can and blaming it all on hysteria."

"Oh, Amanda." There was relief in the tone. "Sure, I tell you about Amanda. In confidence, you understand . . . Yes, my darling, what is it?"

It was Rita, poking her head in the door. "Foxy-Loxy is here." Her expression indicated little joy in the announcement. "He seemed to think you'd want to know."

"Ah!" Anna rose. "I will go see him, yes. And, Rita, my darling, you will tell Phoebe, please, what is Amanda's story. I have just been going to do it, but now . . ."

Rita's eyebrows rose and she shot me a curious glance. But she shrugged and nodded as she stood aside for Anna to leave. "Sure, why not. As long as I can sit down while I'm doing it."

She dropped heavily into the chair Anna had vacated, draped one leg over the other, and crossed her arms under her considerable bosom. She was wearing jeans and an oversized navy tank top. Her long hair was unbraided and pulled tightly away from her face into a ponytail, seeming to stretch the wide-set green eyes even farther apart. The eyes were mossy with fatigue.

"Christ!" she observed. "What a mess! What a bloody, awful . . . sad mess! D'you know there are cops going through our stuff right now—the closets, the dirty laundry. Looking for bloodstains, I suppose. Not exactly what you were expecting, huh, Phoebe?"

I shook my head.

She gave a heavy sigh. "So why do you want to know about Amanda?"

"I just mentioned to Anna that I didn't understand her reaction to . . . all this. The inconsistency, I mean. Anna's asked me . . ." well, she hadn't said not to tell, had she? I might as well lay it on the line, "she seems to think I might be able to figure things out about the murders. Don't ask me why."

Rita threw back her head with a hoot of not-unfriendly laughter. "That's so Anna! She's wonderful, I love her to death, but talk about your Great Manipulator! So she's got you playing detective. Bet *that* wasn't in your job description."

"Actually, there wasn't any job description. There still isn't, but I have to say it hasn't been dull."

Rita laughed again. "You're a good sport, Phoebe, if nothing else. Okay. Amanda. I'll give you the short version. When Amanda was a kid—really young, about five or six—her parents were both bludgeoned to death in their home by a couple of thugs who were burgling the house. It was a mistake, the family was supposed to be away but plans had changed at the last minute. Well, these two morons panicked when they went into the bedroom and came face to face with these people who weren't supposed to be there, and they killed them.

"Amanda slept through the whole thing. But she was the one who found her parents' bodies in the morning."

"Good God!"

"Indeed. She was adopted by her mother's sister and her husband. They changed her name so people wouldn't always be connecting her with the murders—they made a pretty big splash, her father was a district attorney or something. The guys were caught, they'd been really stupid, left all sorts of evidence. Anyway, for two years Amanda didn't speak, didn't say a word. Then she came out of it and grew up to be the woman we all know and love. She never talks about what happened, I'm not even sure we're supposed to know, but you know how it is . . . a story like that is bound to get around. And I suppose when she went into that cabin and saw Frank it triggered a sort of flashback."

"Of course. And then later she just wanted to remove herself as far as possible from the whole mess in case someone started digging up her own past."

"Yeah. Amanda would hate the idea of people—her public—connecting her with that kind of sordid stuff. That's why we all pretend we don't know."

I nodded abstractedly. I was experiencing the unbecoming feeling you get when someone you really rather enjoy not liking turns out to be a survivor of major suffering: that the fun is forever undermined. Beyond that, it seemed that I could pretty safely scratch Amanda from the suspects' list. That she would have deliberately inflicted on herself the discovery of Frank's body was unthinkable.

I brought myself back to the job at hand. "Have any thoughts about 'Amadeus'?" I said.

Rita looked skeptical. "They're taking that business seriously? Well, okay, Nancy Drew." She leaned back in the chair, legs extended, feet crossed at the ankles, and frowned at the opposite wall. "Amadeus, Amadeus. Beloved of God. *A* for Amanda? Hey, doesn't Amanda mean 'beloved'? There you go! Solved! Oh, all right. *A* for Anna? Well, Phoebe, you asked. What else leaps to mind? Let's see . . . Peter Shaffer wrote the play. What about the movie? F. Murray Abraham? Tom Hulce? Salieri . . . Sally . . . Sarah, Sarah Kirk. Doesn't this all strike you as pretty silly?"

She straightened up and brought her gaze back to

me. "Shit, Phoebe, my problem is that I'm looking at the facts and I can't believe any of it. That Frank and Sarah are dead, or that any one of us killed them. Because I can't think of a *reason*. Oh, I know, Frank was being a pest, but still, there wasn't anything. . . . Now if Charlie Judd had been here . . ."

"Jenny's Charlie?"

"Yeah. Now *there* was a catalyst for mayhem. Except in that case I wouldn't have expected Frank to be the victim. Frank, I'm pretty sure, was one of the few people who wasn't in love with Charlie."

"Oh?"

Rita's lips twisted with a sort of grim amusement. "Sexy little bastard. Cut quite a swath that summer he was here."

"But ended up with Jenny."

"Yeah. Another odd couple, you'd have thought, but hey, who am I to say? They seemed happy."

She gave a large sigh, then pointed to the tray on my desk. "Anyone belong to that danish?"

"Help yourself," I said. Then, subtle as a battle-ax, but what the hell: "No problems with morning sickness?"

She paused in midbite, grimaced, put down the pastry, and said without rancor, "Son of a bitch. Guess it's time I broke the good news to Theo."

"He really hasn't noticed?"

"Theo is directing an opera. I *think* he's aware that two murders have been committed in his vicinity. At least he noticed at the time. Beyond that I couldn't say."

"But Frank knew."

"Oh yeah, Frank was amazingly tuned in to that sort of thing. Unfortunately, he only got it half right."

"You mean he thought the baby's wasn't Theo's. Sorry, it was just something Frank said to me. I didn't understand it at the time."

"Jesus, Phoebe, you don't beat around the bush!"

She glanced over her shoulder, got up, and closed the door to the hall. She came back to the desk and placed her knuckles on it, leaning slightly forward. "Not that it's any of your goddamn business, but just to set the record straight, the baby is Theo's. Anyone else who . . . might or might not have been involved is . . . shit, he's had a vasectomy. *One* little piece of information that slipped by our nosy friend. And furthermore, again not that it's your business, whatever might or might not have been happening with this other person is . . . not happening anymore."

She dropped back down into the chair, gave me one last glare, and burst into tears.

I stared at her, appalled. From now on, I told myself angrily, Anna could do her own dirty work. "Rita, please, I'm sorry. It *wasn't* any of my business. Really, I'm . . . here." I pushed a box of Kleenex across the desk.

She grabbed a handful, mopped her eyes, and blew her nose. "Hell, it's all right. I probably needed that."

I scrambled for a positive note. "You said 'break the good news.' Theo will be pleased?"

"Theo will be, as one of his oh-so-colorful brothers back in South Carolina would put it, happy as a pig in shit." She wadded up the Kleenex and tossed it with accuracy into a wastebasket several feet distant. "That's the main reason I've put off telling him. He just doesn't *get* it, what this means to me. How torn it makes me. Not to brag, Phoebe, but I could have had a big career, I had an offer from La Scala. I was in Italy on a grant when I met Theo. He was on a summer trip, studying the opera houses. It was heaven. He was going to be the big director, I'd be the world-renowned mezzo. Who knew I'd turn into a goddamn baby machine? No morning sickness, no varicose veins. Theo gets a gleam, and bingo, I'm pregnant. Nine months later, out it pops. The nurses all tell me how lucky I am. And I love 'em, I love my kids! But it's not as if I can wait till they're all in college and then take up singing again at fifty." She shrugged. "That's why I haven't been in a big hurry to give Theo the glad tidings. I don't know how much joyful reaction I can take without slugging him." Her eyes wandered to the middle distance. "And it's also, I suppose, why I did something so stupid as to have an affair." She brought her gaze back to frown at me. "Which God knows why I'm telling you, Phoebe. But people do talk to you, don't they? Maybe the Great Manipulator knows what she's doing after all."

"Would Frank have told Theo? About the baby and . . . so on?"

"Nah. Frank wasn't sneaky like that. But God, he wouldn't let it alone, he was driving me nuts. He saw us in New York, you see, Stefan and me—oops! well, no surprise to you, I'm sure. We were coming out of a hotel. My one pathetic attempt at adultery and I get caught first time out. Well, almost. Anyway, Frank started in on me as soon as he arrived at the Colony. How the truth would set me free, how Honesty was the Only Way. I was so mad I wouldn't even tell him about Stefan's vasectomy. The whole thing was none of his fucking business! And anyway, it was over by then. I was just trying to come to terms with being pregnant and here was this idiot buzzing around telling me how to run my life. I could have killed him!"

She stopped abruptly, then gave a short laugh. "But I didn't. And neither did Stefan." She shuddered. "What was done to Frank . . . that was awful. I still can't imagine what he could have done or threatened to do to make anyone kill him that way."

"Have you told this to the police?"

"The lieutenant, you mean? And the Latin Bombshell? Hardly! Why should I?"

"Clear away irrelevancies. He's got to be wondering what all the hostility was about. I bet he'd believe you. *I* do."

"Huh! Thanks, I suppose. I'll think about it." She paused and looked briefly down at herself, folding her hands across her abdomen. "That obvious, is it? I thought I at least had another fuckin' month."

She'd been forthcoming in a big way to someone who was, after all, virtually a stranger. It wouldn't hurt to reciprocate.

"At one time in my life," I said, "I became an expert on other women's pregnancies. I could practically spot 'em before the sheets were dry. My guess would be that most of your friends here are too distracted to be paying that kind of attention."

"You wanted kids, huh?"

"Yup."

"Have any?"

"Nope."

Rita shook her head. "Life's a bitch."

"Phoebe, my darling," Anna said, sailing through the door with a tallish, sandy-haired person in her wake. "Is lunchtime. And here is Chris Fox, who wants to meet you."

Chris Fox appeared to be in his middle thirties. He had bright blue eyes set close together, a sharp nose, and the grin of someone who's been called "impish" once too often. He swanned over to the desk, grasped the hand that I'd held out, and gazed deeply into my eyes. "Phoebe!" he intoned. "A name for a goddess, and very rightly too! Say I may sit by you at lunch!"

He raised my hand to his lips and gave me the benefit of a second impish grin, combined this time with an exaggerated wink. The reek of manly cologne almost made my eyes water.

"Come, Chris," Anna said. "Everyone is hungry."

As he followed Anna out the door with what could only be described as a swagger it occurred to me that here might be a very satisfactory alternative to Amanda in the not-to-like sweepstakes.

20

Don't be afraid to say what's on your mind.

act 2, scene 4

AS IT TURNED OUT, I ESCAPED THE PLEASURE OF CHRIS FOX AS A luncheon companion. He was commandeered by the White Queen, who wanted to talk about the dubious career moves of several mutual acquaintances, and Theo Morse, who wanted to talk about *Così fan tutte*. From what I could hear at the neighboring table, Theo, by doggedly ignoring Amanda's presence, came out ahead by a nose.

At our table too the opera, and how much still remained to be done, was the topic of choice. Larry Peterson reminded me to double-check with the piano tuner, who was also a freelance bartender and prone to overbooking during the summer months; Gerta moaned about the condition of the costume closet; Jason Lee Jones and Stefan the Tenor discussed a problem with the light board. Jenny said she was afraid she might be coming down with a cold, which produced a barrage of advice, culminating in Stefan's admonition to "load up on vitamin C."

At the sudden silence that fell on the table he at first looked around, puzzled, and then came to with an "Ah, Christ!" and spent the remainder of the meal staring glumly in the direction of his place mat.

Stefan and the Red Queen had arrived in the dining

room late, though separately. Rita had taken a seat by her husband, and Stefan had joined our table. I thought he was glancing my way rather often. Had Rita told him what I'd said? At least the glance seemed speculative rather than angry.

Following Stefan's unfortunate remark, conversation at our table returned to the production problems of *Così* with what seemed to me a kind of hectic determination. The atmosphere was getting me down and I decided to skip dessert in favor of some outside air. I excused myself, pleading the pressures of the office, and went out through the french doors to the front room.

My hand was on the latch of the screen door when my eye was caught by the Colony group picture I had noticed that first day—the one with the slippery-eyed boy who looked like a faun. I had been meaning in any case to take another look because I was now certain that that was Charlie Judd—Jenny's Charlie. It was somehow hard to believe that the boy in the photo, with his look of being from another world, had been after all only mortal and was now dead. I studied the picture for a long minute before pushing open the screen door.

Outside Anna's House I stood and stared across the sloping lawn at the scene I'd barely had time to appreciate in my five days at the Varovna Colony. Again the sun was shining (during the week I'd been on the East End it had rained once) and the air had that special transparency that had purportedly motivated Pollock, the de Koonings, and several hundred lesser lights and wannabes to relocate to the Hamptons. Today that crystalline quality seemed especially intense. Beyond the bay waters, each rock on a spit of land that curved from the right like a protecting arm was as definitively etched as if seen through a magnifying glass. To my left I could pick out individual trees on Barcelona Neck. A sailing-school fleet of Sunfish, their single sails colored red, yellow, and blue, skittered back and forth across the burnished water. The air was acrid-sweet with the smell of blossoming privet from the surrounding hedges.

Something orangey red flickered past me, pulling my focus back to my immediate area. I followed the something's direction to a maple tree. A small black bird perched on a low branch, wings half-spread and tail fanned, showing the bright orange patches that had caught my eye. As I watched, it took off again, darting, fluttering, swooping across the lawn, turning back on itself, then disappearing into the higher reaches of the maple.

"In Cuba, they call it *la candelita*," Jason Lee Jones said from just behind my left shoulder. " 'The little flame.' The bird winters there. Sorry, did I startle you?"

"No," I said, "I always jump like that when people talk to me. And I thought you were from Jamaica."

"I am indeed. Was. My family moved here when I was nine. But I had a Cuban friend. A dear friend. Gone now, like so many. Would you care for a walk down to the beach?"

I would, and we did. At the small drop from the lawn's edge onto the sand, Jason Lee jumped neatly down, then turned to offer me a hand. When I'd accepted it and landed on the sand beside him he said, "Are you a dancer, Phoebe?"

"No," I said. "Well, yes. Well, no, not anymore. But I love it that you asked."

"Ah, I thought so. It's in the walk. And the way you're put together. What happened?"

I knew what he meant. If I could have been a dancer, why wasn't I? "My mother died and my father needed me. I was a senior in high school and I'd been accepted at the School of American Ballet for after graduation. But I didn't have the guts to insist on staying in New York when my father asked me to tour with him. Well, assumed, really, that I would. I still took class whenever I could, but . . . and then I got married."

We had been strolling, as I spoke, to the end of the

dock, where we sat down side by side, feet dangling just above the water. Jason Lee shook his head. "Ah, Phoebe, Phoebe, you should have followed your heart."

"My heart was in a good deal of demand at the time," I said with some asperity. "I followed it in the direction that pulled the hardest."

"With no regrets?"

"Of course I had regrets. Still have, sometimes. But who's to say I didn't gain more than I lost? My life hasn't been dull."

Jason Lee cocked his head and gave me an appraising look. "Still take class?"

I laughed, partly at his insistence, partly at my defensiveness. "Yes, when I can. Even though I'm usually old enough to be everybody else's grandmother."

"Ah, good, I thought so," he said. "And I apologize, Phoebe, for my nosy questions. I have been thinking a good deal lately about how one lives a life and how quickly it may end." He hesitated, then added, "Because of Frank, naturally." His hands with their papery veins lifted to sweep back over the close-cropped, greying hair, then dropped again to grip the edge of the dock.

"I meant to tell you," I said, "how moved I was by your singing yesterday."

"Thank you," he said. "Poor Frank. I am really terribly sorry that he is gone."

"You'd known him a long time?"

"Since he began coming to the Colony, four years ago. Not as long as some of the others. He was a sweet boy, Frank. A beautiful voice. And so young. As the great Will put it, 'He should have died hereafter.' "

"Like Charlie," I said, surprising myself. The photo by the door had moved me more deeply than I'd known.

"Ah! You know about Charlie?"

I nodded. "Not much, of course, mostly just about what happened to him. But I noticed his picture in the Colony photo from two years ago—at least, I assumed it was Charlie. Slender, curly haired, looks like the pictures of Nijinsky in 'Afternoon of a Faun.' "

Jason Lee said, "Oh yes, that's Charlie all right." Then, to my amazement, he made a movement very much like a shudder.

"You didn't like him?" I said. "I got the impression he was a big favorite around here."

He gave a short laugh. "Oh, everybody loved Charlie. To begin with, he was a genius, which is always fascinating, don't you think? As well as being enormously attractive. A dangerous man."

The characteristic bantering tone had disappeared from Jason Lee's voice. I stared at him. "Dangerous?"

"Not by intention, you understand. But there was something missing in Charlie, a sort of emotional void. Your faun analogy is apt. I used to think Charlie studied people to learn how human beings behaved with each other, that otherwise he simply didn't know. That's what made him a danger." He cocked his head at me. "And yes, my dear Phoebe, as you, being a noticing person, have doubtless concluded, I was not immune to the general peril. That summer is not one of my happier memories."

There was a finality in his voice that let me know the subject was, for him, closed. In any case, my mind had made another leap.

"In a way," I said, "there was something missing in Frank too. Nothing so basic as what you've described, of course, but . . . a sort of blind spot. A lack of judgment."

Jason Lee smiled. "What you are trying to say, Phoebe, in your very nice way, is that for all his golden qualities, Frank was not a clever man. He could be, yes, incredibly blind, incredibly exasperating. Even to his old friends—perhaps especially to them."

I hesitated to ask the question that immediately came to mind, but Jason Lee forestalled me.

"Ah yes, the famous kitchen confrontation described so vividly by dear Amanda." (Was my face that transparent? Some investigator I made!) "I will only say that the truth of that . . . conversation, considering what followed, is a huge irony and that it had nothing to do— but nothing—with Frank's death."

I waited a beat, but again Jason Lee appeared to have said all he intended to. I tried another tack: "Do you have any thoughts about what 'Amadeus' may have meant to Frank?"

"The mysterious final message?" He shrugged. "One thinks of the play, of course, the movie. Mozart and Salieri. Genius, jealousy, revenge . . . who knows? Given that Frank's thought processes were not notably subtle, I'd lean toward a literal meaning of some sort. But what it could be? I have no idea."

He stared across the bay for a moment, then turned back to me. "About Frank and me. Perhaps, after all, Phoebe—"

"Hello there," a voice called out from the beach behind us. It was Stefan the Tenor, strolling with elaborate casualness across the sand and up to the dock. He was wearing light-colored jeans, a white shirt, and a straw hat with a wide brim and chin strap, giving him the look of an albino mariachi player. "Is this a private affair, or can anyone join?"

Jason Lee peered at his watch and rose fluidly to his feet. "I was just going. My *Così* score is back at The Octagon and I'll need it for rehearsal. The delectable Phoebe, dear Stefan, is all yours."

He grinned at me, gave a sort of salute, and walked away, passing Stefan at the end of the dock.

I could have kicked Stefan Kowalski in his not-inconsiderable rear. Jason Lee, I was sure, had been about to tell me the cause of his quarrel with Frank.

Nevertheless, I smiled more cordially than I felt and moved over to accommodate Stefan, who took up a good deal more room than Jason Lee had. He dropped down beside me with that unexpected grace possessed by some large people that I'd observed in him before.

"Pretty, isn't it?" he remarked, squinting across the water from under the brim of his hat. "I don't spend a lot of time at the beach because I burn like a bastard. The lieutenant's here."

"Oh?" For some reason I found myself feeling pleased at this news. Would he want to talk to me? I wondered.

"He was asking for you. Rita's with him now." The mariachi hat swiveled in my direction. "She's doing what you advised, coming clean about what was going on with us and Frank. It's what I've been telling her we should do, but she's not listening to me much these days. Glad you were more successful."

"Oh, well..."

"Because anybody'd be a fool to think that either of us would kill Frank over ... well, something that was over and done with." He propped one foot on the floor of the dock and leaned back against the pier, causing the brim of the straw hat to tilt upward. His round, white face with its snub nose glistened in the heated air. "And Frank never would have blabbed, we knew that. He wasn't mean, you know."

"Excuse me, but what I don't understand is why you simply didn't tell him that the baby couldn't possibly be yours."

"Oh, I would have. Even though it's not exactly something I broadcast. But Rita can be incredibly stubborn when she's pissed off. She was damned if she was going to explain anything to Frank." He hesitated, then said, "You're probably wondering why I had a vasectomy in the first place."

Actually, I'd filed this under the category of things I didn't really need to know. Stefan, however, plunged on. Maybe he just needed to talk.

"I was married. Much too soon, right out of college. Well, I'd gotten the girl pregnant, I thought I loved her, it seemed like the right thing to do. But God, all I really wanted to do was be an opera singer—go to New York, find a good coach, you know," he waved a mocking hand, "become a star. And I thought, Well, okay, that's over. So I got a job teaching music at a high school on Long Island. And then when the baby came, it was stillborn."

He shifted position, leaning toward me, eyes wide open and solemn. "I swear to you, Phoebe, it was the worst moment of my life. And at the same time I had this overwhelming feeling of having been set free. Talk about guilt! But a year later I was divorced, living in New York, and I'd made sure nothing would ever again come between me and my brilliant career." His voice took on a self-mocking tone. "I was going to be the most famous Polish tenor since Jan Kiepura. That's why I didn't change my name. Unlike Jenny."

"Jenny Allen isn't her real name?"

"Uh-uh. Tessie Zgrodski. Comes from somewhere in western Mass." He grinned. "To be fair, if my name had been Zgrodski I probably would have changed it too."

"How many others here have changed their names—taken stage names, I mean?"

"Well, Rita had changed hers by the time she went to college. I never knew what it was originally, something Slavic, I think, and pretty much unpronounceable. After she married Theo she went by 'Michaels-Morse' for a while, but that was awkward so she went back to Michaels. And there's Amanda." He gave me a questioning look. "Do you know about . . . ?"

"Her family and the murders? Yes."

"Her real father's name was Gottfried. I know because it happened not far from where I grew up on Long Island and I heard my parents talking. Later on I made the connection. But the aunt that adopted her, she had married a man who really was named St. James. Lucky break for Amanda, huh?"

I nodded. That was, after all, one way of looking at it.

Stefan grimaced and again leaned back against the pier. "Anyway, Kiepura's reputation was safe, my brilliant career never materialized. I went back to teaching and started coming to the Colony in the summers. With me, Anna gets a passable tenor along with a damn good handyman." He allowed himself a deprecatory smile. "A bargain she couldn't pass up."

"I see," I said. Inadequate, but what *do* you say when a relative stranger turns a sunny boat dock in the Hamptons into a confessional booth and a well-meaning secretary into a mother confessor?

"Yeah, I think you do," he said. "Rita was right, you are easy to talk to. No wonder Anna elected you private sleuth."

"Okay," I said, "as long as you've brought it up. What do *you* think Frank meant by 'Amadeus'? If anything."

Stefan frowned. "The police think that means something, huh? Actually I hadn't taken it that seriously. Let's see . . . Amadeus—'Beloved of God.' " He paused, face puckered in concentration. Finally he said slowly, "Oddly enough, the person who comes to my mind is Frank himself. I mean, I'd always envied him, he seemed to have everything—looks, a gorgeous voice, a career that was really taking off, women all over him, scads of friends. And even more than Frank, there was someone else—a guy who was here two summers ago—"

"Charlie Judd."

"Yeah, Charlie. Now there was a guy you'd have said was touched by God . . . nature, genius, whatever." He shook his head wonderingly. "And now they're both dead."

21

Either fight with me or apologize . . .

act 1, scene 1

THE LIEUTENANT WAS DRESSED EVEN MORE SOMBERLY THAN the last time I'd seen him—his tie a particularly grim affair in thick black and grey stripes—and his face matched his clothes. As I entered the room on the second floor of Anna's House, the Princess, who'd been leaning over the lieutenant's shoulder as he sat at the makeshift desk, straightened. When she saw it was I, she raised her eyebrows significantly, jerked her head at the lieutenant, and rolled her eyes before moving to her customary position at the side of the room. I assumed she was trying to tell me something.

"You wanted to see me?" I said.

The lieutenant nodded shortly and indicated that I should sit. What, I wondered, had happened to the courtly manners, the collegial atmosphere?

He shuffled through some papers on the table, picked up a set of stapled sheets, turned over a couple of pages. He looked up at me. "Didn't I understand you to say, Ms. Mullins, that you had never met any of these people before this week?"

"Yes," I said. What was going on?

"Then how do you explain this statement of Mr. Peterson's?" Referring to the paper: " 'Phoebe Mullins's husband was a well-known conductor. I met them both once, ten or so years ago.' "

And to think that I'd actually come to this interview with a certain pleasurable anticipation! I felt like someone who'd graciously offered her hand to be kissed and had it smacked instead.

"What Mr. Peterson is referring to," I said, furiously aware of burning cheeks, "amounted to a handshake and a 'So nice to meet you.' Until he reminded me, I had no idea where I might have seen him before. Because of my husband's career, I met hundreds of people every year. The world of classical musicians is relatively small, it's not surprising. . . ." I broke off abruptly, my bruised sense of dignity telling me that I was beginning to babble.

"Exactly," the lieutenant said. "So do you now remember any other occasions when you may have met any of the Varovna Colony staff?"

"No," I said.

He glanced again at the paper in his hand. "This time that Mr. Peterson refers to . . . he was involved in a competition for composers?"

"Yes."

"But he didn't win it?"

"No."

"Was your husband on the judging panel for the competition?"

"No, he was not."

"Ms. Mullins, would you say that Mr. Peterson is a successful composer?"

"I really have no idea."

Lieutenant Freed sighed. With thumb and forefinger he rubbed the bridge of his nose. "Look, Ms. Mullins . . . Phoebe . . . I'm groping here. But let me run this scenario by you."

Oh, it's "Phoebe" again, is it? You're not sucking me

in with that again, buster. I shrugged. "If you like." At the side of the room the Princess, who had been uncharacteristically silent, flipped over a page of her notepad. I thought she was trying to catch my eye, but I refused to look.

"Here you have," said the lieutenant, "a fifty-year-old guy—Mr. Peterson—who's been trying all his life to make a name for himself in the music world. And then you have a young guy—Mr. Palermo—maybe not as smart, maybe not as well educated. But everything seems to fall into his lap—the good looks, the voice, the connections. If there's one thing everyone here seems to agree on it's that Frank Palermo was headed for a major career. Now suppose . . ."

I could see where this was going and I couldn't help myself. "You mean like Salieri and Mozart in *Amadeus*? That's ridiculous! In the first place, if you're looking for a precedent, Salieri didn't really kill Mozart—that's total fiction. And in the second place Larry Peterson wouldn't . . . I mean, what would he possibly get out of Frank's death? They weren't even in the same field. He'd have to be crazy!"

The lieutenant observed me, I thought, with interest but without offense during this little speech. Then he said, "Okay. Speaking of crazy, why did it take me so long to discover that one member of the staff here came out of a mental hospital not long ago?"

Was this the man I'd actually felt rapport with? "Oh, really!" I said icily. "I thought that kind of Neanderthal thinking went out with calling them 'insane asylums.' Even in police departments."

His eyes narrowed and I detected a slight flushing of his flat cheeks. Goody for me!

His voice didn't rise, but it did take on a bit of an edge. "The diagnosis for Jennifer Allen—whose real name, by the way, is Tesia Zgrodski—"

"I knew that," I put in, with as much umbrage as if I

hadn't come by the information a scant fifteen minutes earlier. "She took a stage name, for God's sake, is there supposed to be something sinister in that?"

"The diagnosis was post-traumatic stress syndrome. According to her doctors—"

"You've talked to her *doctors*? What about confidentiality?"

"With Miss Allen's express permission," he said evenly. "According to her doctors, Tesia Zgrodski left their care fully recovered and of no conceivable danger to anyone. I find, however, in the literature—and I do read, Ms. Mullins—that post-traumatic stress can be triggered long after the original event."

"So what," I said hotly, "is supposed to have triggered Jenny Allen to kill Frank Palermo? You have absolutely no basis—"

"That's what I was hoping you could tell me," the lieutenant interrupted. "And I sure hope that if you can, you will. Two people, Ms. Mullins, have been murdered—"

"Oh please, spare me!"

"And if there's anything—"

There was a knock at the door. The lieutenant said something short under his breath. The Princess went to the door. She spoke briefly to the person on the other side, then looked back at the lieutenant. "You'd better hear this, sir."

The lieutenant got up and strode out into the hall, closing the door sharply behind him.

I slumped in my chair.

The Princess came over and propped one perfect buttock on a corner of the desk. The limpid eyes peered gravely down at me. "He's really pissed," she said. "At himself, y'know? Because of Sarah Kirk. He thinks it's his fault."

I winced. "He should join the club," I said, and then I

told her the terrible guilt I'd been feeling about the Mouse's death. "If only I'd pressed her—just a little—I'm sure she'd have told me what was on her mind."

"Aw, Phoebe, that's tough," the Princess said. "Tell the loot when he comes back. Maybe it'll make him feel better."

I was about to remark that at this point I didn't really feel like telling the "loot" his coat was on fire, when he reappeared. He was frowning, but there was an animation in his face that hinted the news he'd just been given hadn't been entirely bad. He started to say something to the Princess, then, seeming to realize all at once that I was still on the premises, checked himself. He went behind the desk, sat, picked up a pencil, tossed it once or twice, then gave me a direct look. "Can we start again?" he said.

I was torn between maintaining my (as far as I was concerned) quite justified anger, and the knowledge that if I took the high road I'd miss being in on the latest development. I compromised with a semimollified nod.

"Frank Palermo's apartment in New York was broken into sometime yesterday," the lieutenant said. "The guys in New York say it doesn't seem that anything much was taken, but it looks like his papers were messed around—his desk and music scores and so on. They're waiting for the family to get back from the funeral so one of them can go over it, see if they can spot anything missing."

"Oh, wow!" the Princess said. "Time to round up the usual suspects, huh?"

"Yup. A whole new set of statements." I thought there was a certain satisfaction in his tone. "I gather most of 'em are at the theater, rehearsing. I've sent Simpson and Wright over there to get started."

Oh boy, Theo was going to love that. I thought of something else. "I can tell you one thing, Lieutenant.

Jenny Allen and I were together from the time we left the Colony to the time we got back. Unless, of course, you think we're in it together."

The lieutenant registered a small smile. "No, Phoebe, I don't think you're in it together. But for the record we'll need a statement of your movements yesterday. So as long as you're here . . ."

While I recited the facts—the drive to the city, the dropping off of Amanda, Jenny's and my visit to the Frick—I was trying to account for the lightening feeling that had come over me on hearing about the burglary, as if a weight I hadn't known I'd been carrying had been lifted. It was because of Jenny, I suddenly realized. The fact that I knew for a certainty that Jenny could not possibly be connected to the break-in. And since it was almost inconceivable that the burglary and the murders were unconnected . . . My high horse took a sudden stumble. The lieutenant wasn't the only one who'd had misgivings about Jenny's emotional stability. I remembered her intensity as she'd told me about the quarrel with Charlie. Then I remembered her horror on the path outside Frank's cabin, the way she'd clung to me. That, I knew, had not been acting. And now the last niggling doubt was snuffed. Yesterday, Jenny had been with me all day. I found myself a lot closer to forgiving the lieutenant.

"I understand," the lieutenant said when I had finished my recital, "that it was you who persuaded Rita Michaels to level with us."

"Yes, I suppose it was. Did you believe her?"

He nodded thoughtfully. "Sounded reasonable. Not that she couldn't have some other motive we don't know about, but yes, her story held up—cleared away some of the murk. Anything else you'd like to tell me?"

He spoke mildly. The olive branch, it appeared, was being proffered. Did he know, I ventured, about Amanda St. James, about the murders of her parents?

Yes, it turned out, he did. Of course, I thought. All sorts of probing and information gathering was going on that we at the Colony knew nothing about. In which case, why was I going out of my way to dig up this stuff?

I said as much to the lieutenant.

"No, no, Phoebe, what you're doing *is* helpful, believe me."

"Like with the Rita woman," the Princess chimed in. "What a mouth! But she never woulda come in. Said she didn't know why the eff she had, it was nobody's effin' business, but you talked her into it."

The lieutenant leaned back in his chair, ankle on knee. His right hand massaged his face. "Motive, that's what we still haven't got. And opportunity's what we've got too much of. Also, this person has been incredibly lucky. Got in and out of Frank's room without being seen. Ditto for the kitchen to kill Sarah Kirk at a time when everyone in the place was on their own for at least a part of the morning. Would you believe not one person has a checkable alibi for the couple of hours before everyone left for the city?" He waved a disgusted hand at the pile of papers on his desk. 'In my room getting dressed.' 'Taking a shower.' 'Went for a walk to collect my thoughts.' 'In the barn going over some music.' "

" 'In the office typing and answering the phone,' " I said. "Nobody came in the whole time. Except for Sarah Kirk, of course." Suddenly my eyes were hot. "If only I'd . . ."

The lieutenant held up his hand. "My fault entirely. I talked to her Tuesday evening, the day before we found the pill bottle. Said she didn't know anything and she was sick as a dog so I didn't press her."

"Barfing up a storm," the Princess put in helpfully.

"Wednesday I sent a man over but the husband told him she'd just gotten to sleep for the first time in twenty hours. By the time we got around to her on Thursday nobody was home. We got hold of a daughter who said she'd given her mother a ride to the Colony. When we didn't find her here, we assumed she'd gone to New York with the rest of you. It wasn't until her husband got home late from work, wanting to know where she was and telling us she wouldn't have gone to the city on a bet, that we began looking for her in earnest." He glared at a spot on the far wall. "We found her under a pile of dirty sheets in a corner of the laundry room. Whoever did it was very neat—mopped the floor and put the skillet to soak in the kitchen sink. Missed a few blood spots, though, on the cupboard. There wouldn't have been a lot of blood in any case and the skillet got most of it. No blood found on anyone's clothes."

If he'd meant to enlist my whole support, he'd done a good job. "I saw Gerta Hofstetter," I said. "Monday, when I drove into the Colony for the first time. She was coming out of Frank's cabin. But I suppose she's already told you that."

"Gerta Hofstetter," the lieutenant said wearily, "has told us nothing. Except to say many times that she knows nothing, has done nothing, seen nothing, and that we are persecuting her darling Anna, who is a saint on earth. Anyway, thanks for the information. Unfortunately, she had every right to be in Frank's cabin or anyone else's, it seems, it being more or less her job. Still . . ."

"You're forgetting the letter, Loot," the Princess said.

I perked up. "Letter? The one with the French postmark? You found it?"

"The Kraut found it," the Princess said. "At least, that's what *she* says."

The lieutenant frowned briefly in the Princess's direction, then turned back to me. "Handed it over sweet as you please. Said she'd found it under a bush near the barn. Nonsense, of course, we'd combed the whole area. Besides which, the envelope had been steamed open and resealed."

"What was in it?"

"A mash note of sorts. From a young woman in Paris who seems to have met Palermo briefly. But memorably, at least on her side."

"Anyway," the Princess said, "not what the . . . uh . . . German lady was in a tizz about. A course, if it *hadda* been what she was in a tizz about we never woulda seen it."

"Then you think she picked it up in the front room at Anna's House—that morning after we found Frank?"

"Most likely," the lieutenant said. He hesitated. "I don't suppose you've been able to find out anything more about this . . . French connection?"

I shook my head. I didn't think he'd want to hear about how close I'd come or understand the feelings that had prevented me from asking Anna that one question. Especially since I didn't quite understand them myself. Something to do, I thought, with awe, respect, admiration—and a conviction that had solidified into a faith that Anna Varovna was incapable either of murder or of shielding a murderer. The "French connection," if there was one, had to be far in the past. And if the secret was important enough to Anna that she would stonewall the law to keep it, that, I had decided, was good enough for me.

The lieutenant brought his foot down from his knee. "Maybe we'll get some useful information out of this break-in. Assuming it's connected, of course. Although," he went on gloomily, "it'll probably turn out that everyone went their separate ways as soon as they hit town. Except, of course, for you and Jennifer Allen."

"Like it wouldn' be connected!" the Princess crowed. "Cheer up, Loot, I got a good feelin' about this."

"Yeah, sure," the lieutenant said. He stood up and offered me his hand across the little table. When I took it, his grasp was warm, and lingered, I thought, a fraction

longer than Miss Manners might have approved in a
purely friendly handshake. Evidently the forgiveness
process on my side was complete, because I didn't mind.

When our hands parted, I felt a fleeting moment of
awkwardness. Had something just happened, or had I
imagined it? I turned to say goodbye to the Princess. She
was gazing at the ceiling. There was a self-satisfied little
smirk on her face and I thought I heard the sound of
humming.

I had almost reached the door when another
thought struck me and I turned around. "Where is
Frank's apartment in the city?"

The lieutenant checked his notes. "Bank Street. In
the Village."

I sighed. I really hated this. "When Jenny and I were
walking up West Fourth, near Perry Street, I thought—
thought, you understand—that I saw Larry Peterson up
ahead. But then whoever it was turned off and I didn't
see him again."

The lieutenant nodded thoughtfully and scribbled
on his notepad. "Point taken," he said.

Shortly before six o'clock, I was draping the computer in its vinyl nightwear when Lieutenant Freed appeared at my office door, unaccompanied. He stood
there a moment in an irresolute sort of way.

"Yes?" I said.

He cleared his throat. "I know . . . um . . . where they
make the best pizza in the Hamptons. If you'd care to
join me."

———— ✦ ————

22

By far the best cure for lonely hearts . . .

act 1, scene 8

UNTIL LIEUTENANT FREED AND I STEPPED FROM THE SIDEWALK onto the path leading to Mrs. Schmitter's front porch, I'd thought I was home free. In fact, I had just turned to offer a final handshake and a "Thanks so much for the pizza." But then he reached out and touched my face and I knew I hadn't quite made it.

Married at twenty-two, I had been that anomaly of the 1960s (if you believed the propaganda), a virgin bride. Sex with Mick had been a revelation and a joy. Twenty-five years of marriage had occasionally mitigated the joy but never permanently, and for the year since Mick had died it had been as if the sexual side of me had clicked off and disappeared with him. In my more sentimental moods I had wondered if I were like the swan who mates for life and dies soon after the death of the partner. Not that I had any intention of dying, but a life of cheerful (and not unattractive) celibacy had, I thought, a certain cachet.

However, the past two hours had blown the faithful swan theory all to hell.

We had sat opposite each other in a booth at a dim and crowded restaurant/bar in Amagansett, sharing pizza and a pitcher of beer. Actually, I had drunk most of the beer, since I'd dropped my car off at home and the lieutenant was driving. We had chatted first about the latest developments on the break-in at Frank's and then about ourselves. The lieutenant was divorced, he told me, with two grown children. He lived in Yaphank, the home of the Suffolk County Police, but was camping out for the duration of the case with his sister and her family in the Springs section of East Hampton. He told me funny stories about his sister's kids. I told him about Mrs. Schmitter and the telephone and the gin. We laughed a lot. When the lieutenant laughed, the downward slant at the corners of his eyes disappeared in a starburst of tiny wrinkles, and parenthetic curves bracketed his mouth. I discovered that I was finding this extremely attractive. In fact, I was finding all of the lieutenant extremely attractive. In fact, the sexual me that I had thought frozen for good was undergoing a thaw of massive proportions. I was thunderstruck. I was grateful.

I was also glad, even as I savored various warm and fluttering sensations, that having reached years of discretion, I would be able to handle this abrupt revelation without loss of dignity. The lieutenant was evidently enjoying my company—God knew he needed an hour or so of relaxation—but had not so much as offered to hold my hand. I didn't think the energy flowing across the empty pizza pan was entirely one-sided, but we were, after all, both middle-aged people. We left the restaurant and drove back to East Hampton, the lieutenant on his side of the stick shift, I on mine.

And then, on Mrs. Schmitter's front walk, he touched my face and my insides plummeted to my knees, my thighs began to bask in the glow of their own personal heat lamp. Under the demure baby blue of my cotton pullover, my nipples were damn near saluting. When he kissed me, his hands gently cupping my face, I found myself grabbing his lapels to steady myself. And when he wrapped his arms around me and kissed me again, I gave myself up entirely to rekindled pleasures: the taste of lips and tongue—beery and sweet—the silky brush of the mustache, the prickle of cheeks in need of a shave, the mixed scents of sweat and aftershave. I began to picture, vividly, me and the lieutenant entangled and naked on the fourposter up in Mrs. Schmitter's upstairs back bedroom . . . upstairs . . . the back bedroom . . . Mrs. Schmitter. . . .

I wrenched my lips away from the lieutenant's and swiveled my head toward the house, half-expecting to see a curtain twitch, or Doris herself appear on the porch. All was quiet. Around us, the twilight was only just deepening. I had been passionately embracing, practically in broad daylight and in public, a man I barely knew. Somehow I felt that Doris, in her postdrinkie incarnation, would probably be more intrigued than otherwise, but still. . . .

I looked up at the lieutenant. "Oh dear," I said. "I really think I should . . . um . . . go in."

He raised his eyebrows. "Sure?"

I nodded.

To my relief (mostly), he gave me an answering nod. "Yeah, you're probably right."

He smiled gently and seemed to be waiting for something. It dawned on me that I was still clutching the lapels of his jacket. I loosed my grip. The fabric was pretty crumpled, and I gave the lapels a smooth or two before stepping away. "You'll need to press those," I said.

He glanced down. "Yes," he said gravely.

"Well then," I said. "Thanks for the pizza, and . . . thanks."

He stood and watched me climb the porch steps, open the door, and go in. When I turned to look through the lace-curtained glass on the upper half of the door, he was walking slowly back to his car.

My estimate of the likelihood of a day off anytime in the near future (zero) had proved accurate. "Just this weekend, my darling, when students are coming. Is mostly important that all is going smoothly," and a vague reference to the weekend after. When, of course, the Colony would be deep into public performances of *Così fan tutte* with its attendant calls on the box office staff, which, as far as I could determine, consisted entirely of me.

Anna had allowed, however, that I could be spared until after lunch today (Saturday), when the students would begin arriving, and I was taking advantage of this largesse by doing my laundry. A washer and dryer were squeezed into a pantry alcove off Mrs. Schmitter's kitchen. There I sorted my whites and coloreds, humming the "Habanera" and throwing in a flamenco step or two on my way back and forth between the alcove and the kitchen table. The air was rich with the smells of coffee and soapsuds. I leaned my elbows on the table, clutching the warm coffee mug (why hadn't I noticed before how pretty it was, all blue and white and flowery?), and watched bemusedly the dancing dust motes that sequinned a broad shaft of sunlight pooling warmly on the yellow and white linoleum at my feet. When Mrs. Schmitter put her head around the kitchen door, I gave her a smile so broad that it appeared to propel her several steps backward and leave her temporarily speechless. On recovering, she announced that Little Bobby was coming to drive her to a doctor appointment. "And you will ... um ... remember to ... the water, you know ..."

I assured my landlady that I would follow her laundry instructions (which were also listed in forbidding block capitals and taped up prominently above the machines) to the letter. Another dazzling smile sent her scurrying back along the passageway. I was, as you may gather, in an awfully good mood.

So good that any niggling questions about whether I had made a fool of myself last evening and what the lieutenant might think and how we would behave the next time we met were pretty much beside the point. The fact was, I didn't really care. Did I actually want to jump into bed with the lieutenant? No. (Well, yes, but you know what I mean.) Did I regret what had happened? Not for a minute. Did I feel a pang, even a sense of betrayal toward that marriage of twenty-five years? Oh, yes. But the clichés, it seemed, were true. In that horrible phrase of modern psychotherapy, the "grief process" had been following its inexorable course. Life was full of surprises.

If I *had* been inclined to brood on the subject of Lieutenant Freed, once I'd arrived at the Colony that afternoon I wouldn't have had the time. The three-car parking area behind Anna's House was full and I had passed another vehicle parked in front of the boys' cabins, its open trunk spilling duffles and laundry bags. The yellow tape, I noticed, had been removed from the front of Frank's cabin, though a large padlock still secured the door. I pulled onto the grass verge beside the hedges and took the back pathway to the house.

From the front room came a babble of voices and laughter. I recognized Anna's and, I thought, Larry Peterson's, but the rest were unfamiliar. By snatches of conversation emanating from the kitchen—a French-accented basso rumbling punctuated by Gerta Hofstetter's Germanic staccato—I gathered that a cook had been located and installed. In my office, I encountered a tall youth wearing cowboy boots who smiled shyly and, by God, addressed me as "ma'am." Anna, he explained, had allowed as how a lady named Phoebe would let him know which bunk had been assigned him. The Varovna Colony had suddenly come to new and vigorous life.

Over the rest of that day and much of the ensuing week I occasionally had to remind myself of the horrendous events of the one just past. It was as if the Colony had undergone a reincarnation in which violence and pain, guilt and suspicion were once again relegated to the operatic stage, where they belonged. Not a police-man was to be seen. The lieutenant neither called nor came. Among the newcomers, an initial flurry of in-quiries, headshakings, and solemn looks quickly gave way to a lively interest in who would be cast in the sum-mer's second production, *La Bohème,* whether their coaching sessions were scheduled for morning or after-noon, and what the water temperature was in the bay.

And to singing. By Monday the woods, the shore, the pathways, and virtually every building on the place resounded with coloraturas, lyrics, spintos, mezzos, contraltos, tenors, baritones, and basses. In vocalises, arias, and songs, in French, German, Italian, Russian, En-glish, and in at least one warm-up technique that sounded like hog calling, the singers did with gusto what they had come to do. There were thirteen woman stu-dents and seven men; on a still afternoon with no fog you'd have sworn there were fifty.

As for myself, I was kept incredibly busy. In addition to running the office I was shanghaied, despite my best efforts, to the costume room, a dank and claustrophobic closet behind the stage. There I joined Gerta in draping, and in some cases stuffing, singers of various shapes into generic peasant-type garments for their appearances as the chorus in *Così fan tutte.* Jenny, near tears, appealed to me to dissuade Theo from insisting that she wear a wig as Despina that made her look, she moaned, like Pippi Longstocking on a bad hair day. I sorted that one out in Jenny's favor, then hurried back to the office phone to deal with a company that had sworn to provide us with a hundred folding chairs that, it now appeared, had already been promised to someone else. I was having a wonderful time. At night I amused Mrs. Schmitter with stories of a life in the arts, before falling, exhausted, into bed.

Along about Tuesday, though, I did begin to wonder where the law was keeping itself. Presumably the police

were still following up on the burglary at Frank's apartment. And, I supposed, still digging into the past histories of the Colony staff. Nonetheless, I found the sudden
drop-off in police presence strange, even unsettling. At
least I was unsettled and yes, in the case of the lieutenant, considerably miffed.

He'd told me, that evening in the Amagansett bar,
the basic facts about the break-in on Bank Street. The
apartment—a first-floor-through of a brick townhouse—
had been entered by jimmying a door to a small deck at
the back of the house. Ridiculously easy to do, the lieutenant had said, but not entirely Frank's fault; the apartment hadn't actually been his. It had been on loan from
one of those patrons of the arts without whom the entire
cultural life of the U.S. would collapse. The owner was
in Europe. Neither the basement nor the upstairs tenants
had been at home. A canvass was ongoing of all the tenants of the surrounding buildings whose apartments
overlooked the patio.

As for the members of the Colony, apart from Jenny
and me, only Theo and the Red Queen claimed to have
been together for the entire day. The others had scattered on various errands and appointments. Larry Peterson freely admitted to being in the Greenwich Village
area that day. So did Jason Lee and, of course, Amanda.
They had all come up with plausible agendas, none of
which could be entirely corroborated. Anna had visited
her apartment in the Ansonia, had lunch with Gerta at a
restaurant, and then gone by herself to do some shopping at Macy's. She'd bought a wedding present for a
former pupil's daughter and a summer dress on sale for
herself. Gerta did not enjoy shopping. After lunch she
had gone for a walk in Central Park. Again the field of
suspects was wide open.

The Palermos had at that point not yet been heard
from as to what might have been stolen. The impression
of the New York cops, as relayed through the lieutenant,

was that Frank's books and papers had been the primary object—"Sheet music, notebooks, scores, letters, stuff like that. Impossible to say whether any of it was missing." Television, VCR, disk player were untouched. The implication was clear: It was information (read "incriminating evidence") the burglar had sought, not a source of quick cash. Implication number two: If a member of the Colony staff had *not* been involved it sure was a mind-boggling coincidence.

Toward the end of Wednesday afternoon, I was mulling over some of the foregoing as I walked past the boys' cabins on my way to the theater. My excuse was to assure myself that the promised box-office table actually existed, and to check on its placement. Basically I was taking a break. The air was deliciously warm, the sun just beginning its westward slide. That morning had seen the raucous invasion of three men on giant mowing machines, and the scent of fresh-cut grass mingled on an offshore breeze with the salt tang of the bay. From the direction of the beach came sounds of splashing and laughter. From somewhere to my right, a tenor voice proclaimed triumphantly and repeatedly, *"Dein ist mein Herz!"* Somewhat farther along, deeper tones, the melody seductive and French, informed someone named Psyche that he was jealous of *"toute la nature."* The sun's rays, the wind, the very air she breathed, it seemed, *"avec trop de plaisir"* caressed his beloved. As I neared the theater, an ethereal soprano breathed in Italian, *"Tu lo sai . . .* ("You know, cruel one, how much I love you . . ."). I began to feel a little dizzy. No wonder, in this atmosphere, that Jenny had fallen in love. How could anyone not?

Why hadn't the lieutenant at least called me? Not that I hadn't been relieved . . . in a way . . . but still. Had he, possibly, been even more relieved? I felt myself grow warm. The important thing, I'd told myself, was the revelation itself, the breakthrough. The lieutenant had simply been a catalyst. Now I found myself very much wanting to encounter the catalyst, if only to give him a piece of my mind. . . .

A figure emerged from the woods behind the barn, on the path that led to the practice cabins. For a wild moment I thought it was the lieutenant and God knew, in my heightened state, what idiocy I might have committed. A second glance told me it was the Piano Man, Larry Peterson, walking quickly toward me, but without seeming to see me. I stood where I was and as he got closer I could see that his face was white and set in an expression of such pain that I almost cried out. In another moment, though, he'd registered my presence. Color flooded his cheeks and he greeted me with a kind of forced heartiness. We exchanged a few banalities and he passed on, turning up the road away from the theater.

Ye gods, what had that been about?

Somewhere in the woods a rich contralto voice rose and fell in scales mounting successively by half-step intervals. From deeper amid the trees drifted a lighter, soprano sound. It occurred to me that I'd never seen the practice cabins. Surely I could snatch another five minutes to do so now.

About twenty yards into the trees, where the path made a sudden turn, the first cabin appeared on my right. It was made of logs and only somewhat larger than a child's playhouse. A recently renewed three-step unit of pale boards led to a doorless opening. The owner of the contralto voice was in residence, so I passed quietly by.

The path itself—dirt and barely a yard wide— became even more rudimentary as it wound its way among the trees and through the undergrowth. After tripping heavily on a tree root, I kept my eyes down and almost missed the second cabin. At first I thought it was unoccupied. I was about to take a look inside, when a soft feminine giggle followed by a bass murmur alerted me to the fact that at least something was being practiced there. I trudged on.

Ahead of me, the soprano voice became clearer, singing a melody I'd never heard before—a poignant tune, simple but compelling. I stopped on the path to listen. It was Jenny's voice, I was almost certain, pure, sweet, almost vibratoless. I waited until the song came to an end, then continued to the third cabin. Just before I reached it, Jenny herself appeared in the doorway. She stood there for a moment without noticing me, head lifted and slightly cocked, lips parted. I thought her cheeks were damp.

When she saw me, she started, then broke into a welcoming smile. "Hey, Phoebe! What a nice surprise! You've never been here, have you?"

I admitted my ignorance regarding the cabins and my curiosity to see them.

"Well come on in, I'll give you a tour of the facilities." She giggled. "Such as they are."

The inside of the cabin was perhaps ten feet square, with a plywood floor and one square window cut into the wall opposite the door opening. Cobwebs draped the beam at the center of the peaked ceiling and the uncovered walls showed spreading areas of damp. A spinet piano with flaking blond finish and missing several ivories stood against one wall. "Totally out of tune, of course," Jenny said. She perched on the rickety piano stool and plunked out a sample. "They put them inside someplace over the winter, but even so. . . . Still, you can use them to pick out a tune if you need to, and anyway we all carry pitch pipes." She produced hers from her jeans pocket. I noticed she was carrying nothing else.

"What were you singing?" I said. "It sounded lovely."

She looked up at me, her face serious. "It was Charlie's song. The one he wrote for me. It's the first time I've sung it since . . . well, you know."

Somehow I had known that. "What are the lyrics?"

I said. I thought they sounded familiar but I couldn't quite . . ."

"It's Shelley. You know, 'Hail to thee, blithe spirit.' Just the first three verses. It's about a bird, of course, but Charlie said . . . Charlie said it reminded him of me." She hesitated, pressing her lips together hard, before going on. "And I've been thinking . . . that last line, 'Like an unbodied joy whose race is just begun.' I've been thinking that the best thing I could do to remember Charlie is to go on with, you know, the race. I mean, you . . . you've done it, haven't you?"

"Yes," I said. "Yes, I have." I hesitated in my turn. "I hope I get to hear you sing the song again soon."

"I don't know. Maybe. I don't mind that you heard it, but . . ." She stood up and slipped her arm through mine, smiling again. "Anyway, I'm glad you came along just now. Were you going on any farther, or can I walk back with you?"

"*Is* there any farther?" I said.

"The path goes on for a ways but then it sort of peters out. This is the last cabin. It's okay if you're up for a real hike in the woods."

Since I wasn't, we made our way back along the path together. Cabins number two and one now stood deserted. At the theater we parted, Jenny to her living quarters on the beach, I to my office. It was getting late, I could check on the box-office table tomorrow, and I was preoccupied with a new puzzle. Who or what had Larry Peterson encountered on that path to make him look as if he'd been stabbed to the heart?

23

Very soon we'll raise the curtain . . .

act 2, scene 15

THURSDAY, JUNE 28

ON THURSDAY JUST AFTER LUNCH, THE LIEUTENANT KNOCKED on the jamb of my open office door. I was on the phone talking to the still-delinquent purveyor of folding chairs, a conversation involving on my part (tomorrow being opening night) plain language and a louder tone of voice than I usually employ. I saw the lieutenant's eyebrows shoot up as he came into the room in response to my nod. I made my own grimace, concluded my business, and replaced the receiver more heavily than I'd meant to.

I thought the lieutenant flinched. Quickly and without preamble, he said, "I've been out of town. Out of East Hampton, I mean."

"Oh?" I said pleasantly.

"I thought of calling, but . . . I don't really like telephones. I seem to need to, uh, see people when I'm talking to them."

"Ah!" I said.

He rubbed his hand over his face, sighed, and appeared to study something beyond the window at my back. "And basically I wasn't really sure what to say. Whether, I mean, you'd want to talk to me at all."

I couldn't help it, I laughed. "Gee, and here I thought I was throwing myself at you."

His expression brightened and he brought his eyes back to my face. "You ran into the house so fast. I was afraid maybe . . ."

"Why don't you sit down?" I said. "Unless of course you're in a hurry."

"Well, there is someone I need to see, but I wanted to see you first." He pulled up the only available chair (the others were all down at the theater) and parked himself on the far side of the desk. "Then you're not, um, mad at me?"

Good lord! It seemed that fragile egos were not the monopoly of performing artists. "Certainly not," I said. "I like you a lot. I thought I'd made that pretty clear." Oh dear, how much to explain without sounding like a neurotic prude? I plunged ahead. "It's just that . . . well, look, I'm just not ready to go as fast as . . . as it seemed we might be going. Or maybe ready at all. I just don't know. You see . . . without going into a lot of detail . . . the whole thing really took me by surprise."

The lieutenant nodded once or twice solemnly. "Understood," he said. His face broke into its rare eye-crinkling smile. "How about a movie?"

My hormones clanged, my mind groaned. I was really going to have to watch it. "Sure," I said. "After we've gotten through the performances of *Così*." His other statement suddenly registered. "Who is the someone you said you needed to see?"

"Madame Varovna."

"Why?" I felt an uncomfortable flicker of something. Maybe fear. Were the police zeroing in? Had they found some fresh evidence?

"Because I'm hoping she can be persuaded to be more helpful than she's been so far."

My stomach unclenched. "Then you haven't gotten

any further with the investigation? What about New York? The burglary?"

He shook his head. "That's where I've been, partly. There and in Yaphank. There's nothing so far from the New York end. Otherwise we've turned up one or two things but nothing necessarily significant."

One or two things? I waited, but the lieutenant was not forthcoming. Well, I wasn't going to beg.

He leaned back in his chair. "How about you?" he said a shade too casually. "Anything happened or . . . occurred to you?"

I almost wished something had so I could *not* tell him. But in fact there was nothing to report. There had been that strange encounter with the Piano Man, but I hadn't the slightest reason to think it might relate to the murders. I had checked the sign-up sheet for the practice cabins for Wednesday at four o'clock. Cabin one had indeed been claimed by the student I'd glimpsed in passing— a first timer from Canada. Two and three had not been signed for. Jenny of course had been in three, but who had been the duo in the second cabin, I had no idea. I had tried, without success, to conjure up a romantic triangle involving Larry Peterson, and then given up. In any case, it didn't amount to anything worth passing on.

"No, not a thing," I said. "In fact, I've been so busy, there've been stretches when I've managed to forget about murder."

The lieutenant sighed heavily and rose. "Not me. I'm getting a lot of pressure from people who aren't at all happy about how long this is taking. So if there's anything . . ."

"Of course," I said.

After work, I stayed on at the Colony for supper and the dress rehearsal. Anna joined me as I set out to walk to the theater. As always, she was impeccably put together and showed no outward signs of having under-

gone a police grilling, except that I thought she was quieter than usual.

"Have you seen any of the rehearsals?" I asked.

"No, no, my darling. Rehearsals I leave to Theo and
Larry, they know what to do. Will be wonderful, I know.
The folding chairs, now, they have come?"

Yes they had, and when we entered the theater
there they lay, neatly bundled and stacked against the
walls instead of set up in rows as I'd been promised.
Well, we still had tomorrow. On the other hand, here
was a gaggle of students in servant costumes standing
around, escapees from a backstage area roughly the size
of a memo pad. I got them organized into a work gang
while Anna looked on approvingly.

Gerta Hofstetter appeared from behind the stage, saw
what was going on, and barreled up the aisle, arms waving. "Ach, no! The costumes! You will get them dirty!"

"Is all right, Gerta," Anna said. "They are being
mostly careful. You must not worry so."

To my surprise, Gerta shot at Anna what could only
be described as a dirty look. She made no reply, but
turned away and began fussing with the first costumed
singer who came to hand, straightening an already sym-
metrical neck cloth, brushing away nonexistent shoulder
lint. She looked as if she'd lost even more weight, her
green polyester pants drooping low on her hips so that
the cuffs almost swept the floor. But there was a brisk-
ness to her movements and a square set to her shoulders that spoke of a newly found resolve. I wondered
whether the evident rift with her darling Anna had anything to do with the afternoon's interview.

"All right, people," Theo called out. "Let's get this
thang movin'."

Due to loss of rehearsal time and the integration of a
new cast member, tonight's run-through was not only a
dress but a tech, and it was pretty much a mess. The fili-
greed set pieces (some still awaiting a coat of white

paint), designed to be shifted about to suggest changes of scene, threatened to, and occasionally did, fall over in transit. Lights blazed and dimmed at inappropriate times. The ten-member chorus barely managed to squeeze onto the stage before their first brief number was over. Then they took even longer to get off, causing Theo to smooth his bald spot repeatedly while instructing, "Y'all in front, y'have to go *all the way* off. Don't *stop* just 'cause you know you're outta sight. There are people behind you who *aren't*. So keep going! Off, off, off, off, off!" It was the closest I'd heard him come to losing his temper.

In the face of the general chaos, I would have expected the principal singers to improve the occasion with their own displays of temperament. But whether because of long experience or from simple emotional and physical exhaustion, the cast of *Così fan tutte* appeared laid-back almost to a fault. Arias and ensembles, frequently interrupted for either technical glitches or refinements in the staging, were tossed off at half-voice; comedy degenerated into horseplay; more than once, a fit of helpless laughter brought proceedings to a standstill.

As act one came to an end, some three hours into the rehearsal, I stole a look at Anna sitting in the plum-colored plush movie seat beside me, to see how she was taking it. She caught my expression, laughed her deep chuckle, and patted my arm.

"Do not worry, Phoebe. Tomorrow night all will be fine, will be smooth like satin. Tonight the singers, they let off some nerves, they allow these others to play with their props, with their machines. But tomorrow, my darling, tomorrow will be only Mozart, will be only music."

I nodded doubtfully. What about opera as a collaborative art?

"Is all about singing," Anna went on, as if reading my thoughts. "Is technique and is feeling. We feel in here" (placing her hand on her heart), "we express here" (a sweeping gesture up and out). "How many times I have gone onstage with one rehearsal only, or not even one. Today is too much carrying on, you see, about deep psychology, about what composer is really meaning. Mozart, my darling, he knows exactly what he is meaning. Is all there, in the music, waiting to be sung."

She beamed at me, got up, and started down the aisle, presumably to have a word with her director and her pianist.

Well, I mused, it certainly was a point of view. No wonder she'd been so cavalier in consigning the rehearsals to Theo and Larry. I was also certain that she had a well-founded faith in their abilities. The Anna Varovna I knew and loved would have an extremely shrewd idea of the importance to her audience of set, costume, and clever direction.

I thought back, though, to a moment in tonight's first act, the Fiordiligi/Dorabella/Don Alfonso trio. There, in a rare, uninterrupted moment, the music had indeed spoken for itself. Grouped under a pool of clear light, with only the simplest of movement and gesture, Amanda, Rita, and Jason Lee had delivered one of Mozart's most beautiful creations with heart-stopping purity. Over a gently undulating accompaniment, they wished the departing soldiers and lovers a fair voyage, gentle wind, and fortune's protection. No matter that the two women were foolish and deluded, or that the Don was perpetrating a somewhat ill-natured hoax. Listen, the music said, who among us has not been foolish, deluded, ill natured? But who among us is not also capable of genuine feeling, of love, even of beauty? *"Mozart, my darling, he knows exactly what he is meaning."* All right, Anna.

The rehearsal resumed.

It had been a long time since I'd seen an entire production of *Così fan tutte*. Now, as the plot came back to me, I was struck by its reiterated themes of deception and disguise. Don Alfonso makes a bet with his two young friends, Ferrando and Guglielmo, that he will prove within twenty-four hours that their two fiancées are as fickle as all other women. To this end, he has the men pretend to march off to war, then disguise themselves as "Albanians" and each woo the other's girlfriend. The Don enlists the pragmatic ladies' maid, Despina, to encourage the wooing, without letting her in on the new guys' real identities. Despina herself dresses up as a doctor to cure the "Albanians" when they pretend to take poison in despair over being rejected. Later she turns up disguised as a notary to marry the two newly constituted couples. At the last minute, of course, the soldiers "return," all is discovered, all (more or less) is forgiven, Don Alfonso has made his point, and the opera ends in heartfelt, if somewhat chastened, rejoicing.

To accept all of this undetected masquerading requires, needless to say, a huge suspension of disbelief. But in the case of one of these people, I thought, an even more successful masquerade was taking place. One of the people on the stage or in support of it was a killer disguised as a friend; a person living in fear but displaying none, laboring under a terrible burden but feigning a light heart. How long could such a person, could any normal human being, maintain such an act? For how long could the self-preservation instinct overbalance the weight of guilt and repulsion this person must be feeling? Assuming, of course, that this person was not some kind of monster, and I did assume that. Both killings, I reasoned, had been murders of opportunity: the first made possible by a chance discovery of a bottle of penicillin, the second by an even more spur-of-the-moment impulse. But who? And in Frank's case, why?

I began again to go down the list, starting with the singers.

The White Queen and the Red Queen, Amanda and

Rita as the fickle sisters, were in the midst of their second-act duet. Sitting side by side on a lacy white garden bench, they cheerfully divvied up the new guys ("I'll take the brunette"; "Okay, I like the blond anyway"), their voices twining together in pitch-perfect good humor. In fact it occurred to me that the Colony staff was displaying more togetherness on this occasion, more evidence of the deep bonds of friendship I'd heard so much about, than I had yet seen for myself. Both sisters were dressed in approximations of eighteenth-century gowns, low necked, full skirted, laced and flounced, Amanda in pale green, Rita in yellow.

I studied Amanda's face, the overlarge eyes, the long nose. The features that up close came perilously near to caricature translated onstage to definition and authority. What had happened to Amanda? Why wasn't she at Glyndebourne or Aspen, enjoying a major career? Was she, perhaps, bitterly disappointed? Still hopeful? Reasonably content? Dangerously warped? If the last, I'd seen no sign of it. Annoying, dislikable, yes, but homicidal? And finally, I couldn't get beyond the conviction that Amanda would never have been the one to discover Frank's body if she'd had the remotest idea of what awaited her on that cabin floor.

Nor did I any longer seriously consider Rita a suspect. Especially since she and Theo had alibied each other for the break-in at Frank's apartment. That the two of them were involved together was even more unbelievable than that either had committed murder separately. I wondered if she'd told Theo the baby news. Judging by the way she was poured into her costume, or rather threatening to pour out of it, it was fortunate that the run of *Così* was to be a short one.

Now came Ferrando and Guglielmo, Stefan Kowalski and Chris Fox, in their pantaloons and fezzes and huge, pasted-on mustaches. Chris, more than living up to the promise of our first meeting, had gotten a good deal of mileage out of going around declaring that he, above everyone else, had had the best motive for getting rid of Frank. Which made him, of course, guilty of nothing more than really bad taste. His voice and his acting were just serviceable enough to make me realize, even from short observation, how much better Frank would have been. The thought gave me considerable satisfaction.

Stefan was having trouble with his mustache, which finally dropped off altogether, causing merriment and yet another halt in the proceedings. I thought back to my conversation with Stefan on the dock. Now *there* was a case to be made for bitterness. And for jealousy of the younger, handsomer, more gifted man who had seemed destined to achieve all the success that Stefan had craved in vain. But do people kill out of jealousy, especially with no discernible benefit to themselves? Chris Fox, now . . . what a pity he *hadn't* been on the spot. Chris Fox was, after all— Uh-oh. I was beginning to sound like Amanda. "Not one of us," was, I acknowledged, the gist of where my thoughts had been leading. I directed my attention back to the rehearsal.

The chorus, in their second brief appearance, finished singing their twelve or so measures and beat it into the wings with exemplary dispatch. Then Don Alfonso and Despina joined in urging the two couples to pair off and get on with it.

Jenny had been taking this rehearsal, I thought, rather more seriously than the others. I remembered her telling me that this was her first big role and how important it was to her. Although at times she'd seemed to be saving her voice, at others she'd let fly, and after both her major arias she'd gotten applause from the cast. Ever since the trip to New York and my certain knowledge that she couldn't have burgled Frank's place, I had put to rest any doubts I might have had about Jenny. And even if that hadn't been the case, there was the insurmountable question of motive. What could Jenny possibly have to hide?

I watched as she and Jason Lee put their heads together in a fast, self-congratulatory sotto voce commentary and exited in their turn. What had Jason Lee been about to tell me, down there by the water? Once again, I cursed Stefan Kowalski's inopportune interruption. Had I learned *anything* from my tête-à-tête with Jason? Mostly, of course, I'd been disarmed (and, face it, flattered in a big way) by his recognition of me as a fellow dancer. But beyond that . . . Oh yes, we'd talked about Charlie, Jenny's Charlie. What was it he'd said? "A dangerous man." Followed by Stefan's assessment: "Touched by God." A potent personality, that Charlie. No one who had mentioned him had done so with indifference. Was it perhaps there, in the past, that the motive would be found? Did the lieutenant even know about Charlie?

Dorabella (Rita Michaels) was now being wooed by Guglielmo (Chris Fox), not recognizing him as her sister's boyfriend. (Well, it's a silly story.) By the end of the duet, Guglielmo, a fast worker by anybody's standards, had worn down Dorabella's admittedly paper-thin defenses. They exited arm in arm.

I looked toward what I could see of Theo Morse—a tuft of blond hair cresting the front-row seat in which he slouched. Did he know now, I wondered, about Rita and Stefan? If he had, and if he'd wanted to kill anyone, wouldn't it have been Stefan? Anyway, hadn't I eliminated both Theo and Rita from my list? What list? Shit, why was I doing this to myself?

Larry Peterson flipped over another page of the score without, as far as I could tell, missing a note. I studied his profile as he sat, eyes riveted to the music, fingers racing over the keys like independent entities, obeying the lightning messages that flashed from printed page to brain cells to digits. I had played the piano just enough to be in almost superstitious awe of this process with its combination of gift, instinct, and countless hours of practice. What did it feel like to sit there, more of a musician, perhaps, than any of those receiving the kudos onstage, perpetually undervalued, overlooked, taken for granted? Did his life as a composer make up for it? I wondered. *I'd* never heard of composer Larry Peterson, but then, true disciple of my husband, I knew virtually nothing of contemporary serious music. I thought of his face as I'd seen it on the path from the woods. What encounter could he have had, what could he have seen or heard that had produced that look of pain? I had been quite sincere in not bothering the lieutenant with that bit of irrelevant information, but now I wasn't so sure.

Anna Varovna was smiling as Chris Fox delivered Guglielmo's lively complaint directed at women—the gist being that ladies, while delightful, are never to be trusted. Well, okay, he was doing it pretty well. The second act had been proceeding a good deal more smoothly than the first, Anna had a right to feel pleased. I wondered what had happened during her afternoon interview with the lieutenant, and felt a sudden and fierce sense of solidarity with the woman seated beside me. The lieutenant might have awakened my dormant sexuality, but Anna Varovna had inspired in me a rare admiration and loyalty. In a standoff, there would be no contest. I believed in her, in her integrity, in her moral center. And by extension in that of her companion, the enigmatic Gerta Hofstetter. It would take a direct statement to the contrary by one or the other to shake my conviction.

Therefore, it came as a stunning blow to learn on Saturday morning that directly after the curtain came down on the Friday-night opening of *Così fan tutte* (a smashing success), Gerta Hofstetter had driven herself to the East Hampton Town Police Station, demanded to see the officer in charge, and confessed forthwith to the murders of Frank Palermo and Sarah Kirk.

24

So the sudden hand of Fate
will take away the joy of living.

act 1, scene 6

SATURDAY, JUNE 30

"BUT DOES ANYBODY KNOW *WHY*?" I SAID.

Stefan the Tenor shook his head. From the rest of the group gathered in the front room of Anna's House came a chorus of negative murmurs.

"All Anna told us," Jenny said from the window seat, "was that Gerta had confessed. She didn't say anything about a reason."

"Where is Anna now?"

"Back at her place, I think," one of the students offered. "Still trying to get in touch with her lawyer."

"Who is no doubt floating about somewhere on his yacht," said Jason Lee. He waved a languorous arm.

"Oh, yes," Amanda said with enthusiasm, "Anna's lawyer has the *most* beautiful—"

"Christ, Amanda, that's hardly the point!" Rita broke in. "Which, in case you missed it, is that Gerta is in really deep shit and needs help."

Amanda sniffed. "Well of course we all *know* that Anna will do everything possible for her. And excuse *me*, but isn't the point actually that Gerta has turned out to be the murderer?"

There was an uncomfortable silence.

Theo looked up from the clipboard he'd been studying. "Phoebe, could y'all give us a hand backstage tonight?"

Why? I was about to ask, then remembered and nodded. The costumer, dresser, props mistress, and for all intents and purposes stage manager might be in jail for murder, but the performance of *Così fan tutte* would go on. "Sure," I said, "as long as the box office can carry on without me." The two women students who'd been delegated as box-office assistants assured me, with a kind of impressed solemnity, of their ability to handle the job.

Theo stood up. "Okay, then. Cast, I want to see y'all at the theater in half an hour. Just a few notes." He walked past me and out the front door.

Rita rolled her eyes, rose, and followed after him. "First things first," she murmured as she went by.

"Phoebe, you have heard what has happened?" said Anna's voice on my office phone ten minutes later.

"Yes. I—"

"Is of course ridiculous. Gerta has done nothing. And now that foolish woman will not speak to me or let me see her. Is *quite* ridiculous, my darling."

She certainly sounded more put out than worried, I thought. I started to make some appropriate noises of sympathy, but Anna was not finished.

"So she stays for now in their not so comfortable jail, yes? Meanwhile I have found finally my lawyer, who says to me, Do nothing until I arrive. Is pointless, I know what I must do. But is, you see, what I pay him for. Anyhow, my darling, I have asked for the lieutenant to come at two o'clock and I would like for you also to be here. At my studio, please."

"Well, sure," I said. "But what—"

There was only a buzz in my ear. Anna was no longer on the line.

◆　◆　◆

I had not yet had occasion to visit Anna's studio home. I set out promptly at five minutes to two on the path leading into the woods directly behind Anna's House. The ground rose slightly before me as I walked, and in less than a minute I had reached the studio.

It stood among sheltering oaks and pines, a rectangular, two-story building sided in rough-cut boards weathered to a soft grey. A narrow redwood deck supported by slender columns ran the length of the second floor in front of an entire wall of sliding glass doors. I went through the barn-red front door into a small, tiled foyer, up a curved, wrought-iron staircase, and found myself facing the glass doors and beyond them a panorama of treetops, bay, and sky.

"Ah, Phoebe," said Anna's voice from behind me, "is mostly good of you to come. Over here, my darling."

I turned around. Anna was standing by a fieldstone fireplace to my left in an area framed by a cozy arrangement of chairs and sofas. On a long, low driftwood table was a laden tea tray as well as a sherry decanter surrounded by squat little amber glasses. On two of the chairs sat the lieutenant and the Princess. Both were balancing teacups on their knees. The lieutenant looked bemused, the Princess delighted. She was dressed in a sky-blue suit with a creamy shirtwaist blouse. Around her throat was a single strand of pearls. Her feet, in matching sky-blue pumps, were crossed demurely at the ankle and she wielded her teacup with practiced ease. The Princess, I reflected, had a keenly developed sense of occasion.

On one of the sofas sat a man I didn't know, a substantial person wearing a three-piece grey suit and, on his tanned and fleshy face, an expression of disapproval. I assumed he was the lawyer.

I walked over to join them, taking in as I did so the other main features of the room. In the right-hand wall, tall casement windows threw dappled light onto an ebony grand piano. A fringed Spanish silk shawl was draped over its curved end. Beyond the piano, floor-to-ceiling shelves were crammed with books and scores. Oriental carpets of various sizes decorated the polished light oak floor. Scattered about on occasional tables were a few photographs in frames; white plaster walls were hung with a number of oil paintings, still lifes and seascapes. I had been expecting, I realized, something more on the order of old-world clutter, foreign bric-a-brac, mementos, wall-to-wall photos of Varovna or of famous colleagues inscribed with fulsome sentiments in large, dramatic hands. Instead, the room was light, airy, almost spartan. The leafy branches visible from every window gave one the feeling of being high up and hidden, as if in a nest. Once again, Varovna had confounded my expectations.

Anna, I saw, held a glass of sherry, while the lawyer had evidently refused any refreshment. I took sherry. I had a feeling Anna Varovna was about to make a difficult statement and I wanted to make clear whose side I was on.

I was introduced to the lawyer, a John Billington, and exchanged nods with the representatives of Suffolk County Homicide. I had the impression that the Princess was restrained from a display of significant eye-rollings only by her determination to maintain tea-party manners.

The amenities concluded, Anna sat down in a wooden captain's chair to one side of the fireplace. She placed her sherry glass carefully on a small table at her right, folded her hands in her lap, and lowered her head briefly, as if to gather her thoughts.

Before she could begin, John Billington harrumphed and turned to Lieutenant Freed. "I want to go on record as objecting to my client making any sort of statement to the police at this time and to note that she makes this statement against my advice," he said sternly.

"And so, my dear John," Anna said, "your good conscience may now be at rest." She reached over to pat the plump and carefully manicured hand resting on the arm of the sofa beside her. "But you see," shifting her focus to include all of us, "the poor Gerta has made this meeting necessary. Also, I believe," eyeing Saul Freed with a kindly twinkle, "that the lieutenant feels is more than time that Madame Varovna should be, like they say, clearing away some of the forest so we may see more plainly the trees. Is right, my darling?"

If the lieutenant was at all thrown by having a suspect call him "my darling," he covered it well. Or perhaps he was too occupied in figuring out her reference to trees and forests to notice.

"What you must understand,"Anna continued, "is that the poor Gerta, she has made this ridiculous confession for one reason only. She has convinced herself that I have done these murders, and for me she makes this foolish sacrifice." She sighed, took a sip from the little amber glass, and continued absently to hold it in her hand. "Why she does not think further that if this is true, she will by trying to take the blame compel me to confess all, I do not know. But I cannot confess because of course I have not killed Frank or the poor Sarah Kirk. So now I explain to you why Gerta is so frightened that she can imagine I have done these terrible things."

She replaced her glass on the table, straightened her already erect back, and regarded us with an expression that for the first time had something in it of the struggle that must have preceded this decision. None of us said a word or exchanged a glance. We sat, each one, motionless, gazing at the small woman in the captain's chair.

"I am not, you see, my darlings," Anna Varovna said, "in spite of what you may read in these biographies, a heroine of maquis, of French Resistance. Is rather to the contrary. And Gerta," she shook her head slowly and with something like a wry smile on her lips, "Gerta, you see, is not even Gerta. Her name is Frederica and she is daughter of my German lover."

My God, the woman knew how to tell a story! If her audience had been attentive before, we were now mesmerized.

"I am in 1942 eighteen years old," she went on. "I do not excuse, I only tell how it was. In 1942, the Nazis have been occupying Paris for two years. And in 1942 for first time I fall in love, with a man who is fifteen years older than me, and who is also enemy of my adopted country."

In short, a German officer; a man of culture and education (and, it was clear, vast attractiveness), who attended a concert at which the young Anna was one of the soloists. Bad enough that she should tumble into an affair with a member of the detested German occupation forces, but even worse because her family was indeed deeply involved in the Resistance, serving as a kind of clandestine post office for the passing of information. "They are of course Russian, but they are passionately on side of fighters against the Germans. From their experience they have mostly deep sympathy for anyone who suffers, you see, from misuse of power."

But to the young Anna, "head over toes" in love with her Karl, the danger, the secrecy, the romance of brief encounters and stolen moments, had been heady, their passion worth any risk. Karl had managed to bring his eight-year-old daughter to Paris to live with him, his wife having died some years before. The child, Frederica, became greatly attached to her father's pretty young friend, and Anna to her.

Amazingly, Anna and Karl managed to keep their liaison secret for almost a year before the inevitable discovery, which came about in a particularly cruel way.

Anna overheard her parents and older brother discussing a Resistance operation that, she realized, would directly threaten her adored Karl. She warned him, swearing him to secrecy. But Karl was, after all, an officer in the German army. In the ensuing debacle, Karl was fatally wounded and three Resistance soldiers killed outright. One of them was Anna's brother.

Hysterical with grief and guilt, Anna confessed everything to her parents. To their credit, they protected their daughter insofar as they could, "but there were those, my darlings, who suspected, even who knew. After the war . . . things were done, you see, to women, even to young girls, who had loved German men . . . things I will not speak of. But by then my parents are dead and I am living in tiny room, alone, far from our old quarter and I think I am forgotten, am safe."

Also after the war there was Gregory Dmitri, who'd happened on the club in Montmartre where Anna was singing her Russian folksongs to audiences of big, healthy American boys and their skinny French girlfriends. Dmitri had plucked her from the Left Bank, paid for teachers and coaches, guided her onto the operatic stage, married her, and eventually arranged her American debut.

And there was another faithful friend: Frederica, Karl's daughter, orphaned and abandoned in the maelstrom of Germany's defeat. At fifteen, she had seen Anna's name in a newspaper, run away to find her, and never left her since.

Unfortunately, Frederica arrived at Anna and Dmitri's doorstep without passport or papers of any kind. She had been living with distant relatives, she said, who abused her but who would also try to get her back. Please, please, would her darling Anna protect her?

Dmitri, from what Anna both said and did not say, appeared to have been a somewhat shadowy, perhaps even shady individual. "Dmitri, you see, was man with many acquaintances, many contacts," she explained rather too carelessly. But he must also have been a man with heart, or at least a heart for whatever Anna wanted. Frederica was accepted into the household as Anna's personal secretary, dresser, and companion, and shortly thereafter was mysteriously possessed of identity papers and passport in the name of Gerta Hofstetter. When the Dmitris sailed for New York in 1952, Gerta went with them.

It was a year later when the blackmail began.

"Who is this man, this Georges LeClair, I do not know, not even that Georges LeClair is truly his name. Only I know that he is sadist. Is not much money he wants, only to punish, only to cause misery."

LeClair's demands were two: that a small amount of money be sent monthly to an accommodation address; and that Anna Varovna never again set foot in France or anywhere else outside of the United States. Otherwise he would publish the true story of Anna's wartime "activities" and also alert the authorities that Gerta Hofstetter was an illegal, and possibly criminal, immigrant. "He has names, he has dates. We are furious and we are helpless. We do as he says. We go abroad nowhere, and we send the money, every month, year upon year upon year."

Until two months ago, when the envelope containing the blackmail money came back marked DECEASED. "My God, how we cried, Gerta and I! At last to have the dagger, you see, snatched away from over our heads! And then comes Frank, with his story of meeting this Georges LeClair, and there is dagger again swinging. And then Frank is killed. Gerta, you see, she knows *she* did not kill him, and though I assure her many times I have not done it, she does not believe me. And when Lieutenant Freed, on Thursday afternoon, again comes to see me, she is certain that the police are, like you say, burrowing in on Anna Varovna as murderer, and she makes up her mind to this foolish confession. And that is truth, my darlings. Gerta is not murderer. I am not murderer."

Anna stopped speaking. Her voice, with its unexpectedly deep alto timbre, had not faltered until those last few words, but over the course of her narration the dark patches under her eyes had seemed to deepen. Now, with slightly raised, questioning eyebrows, she gazed at each of us in turn, ending with the lieutenant. He gave himself a small shake, as if emerging from a trance. I thought I knew how he felt. I, for one, was as emotionally drained as if I'd just sat through an intermissionless double bill of *Cav* and *Pag*.

"It would have saved a good deal of trouble," he said mildly, "if you'd told me all this on Thursday."

"Ah, yes, but I still hope then, my darling, that real murderer will be discovered before I am having to tell this mostly painful story."

Her eyes flickered momentarily to mine. I felt first a huge sense of failure, then an equally lively umbrage. Hey, I'd done my best.

The Princess spoke up. "Frank Palermo. Did he actually come and tell you he knew all this stuff?"

No, Anna said. There had been nothing beyond his dropping of the name at the lunch table. And the loaded phrase, "an old friend from Resistance days." "So what we think, of course, is that this LeClair must have sought Frank out, must have heard somehow that Frank is pupil of Varovna. Maybe he tells the whole story, maybe he drops only hints. Maybe he knows he is dying, maybe he wants one last time to torture us—'tell Anna Varovna that I remember her'—like that, you see. We do not know. Frank does not come to me the rest of that day and next morning he is dead."

The thought immediately leaped: But if they didn't even know for sure that Frank knew the story, there goes the motive for both Gerta and Anna! I looked across at the lieutenant, sure he must be thinking the same. But he was already rising, taking his leave, stopping to exchange a few words with Lawyer Billington.

I lingered outside the front door of the studio and as soon as the lieutenant and the Princess emerged, I asked, "What happens to Gerta now?"

"She'll be released," the lieutenant said. "Could be charged with obstruction, but I don't know . . . hasn't been an entire waste."

"Shit, we didn't think she'd really done it," the Princess remarked. "Too many whatchacallems . . . discrepancies in her story."

I turned on the lieutenant, who was looking distinctly annoyed with his partner. "You mean you put Anna through that for nothing?" I demanded. "You were going to let Gerta go anyway? And now it turns out their big motive is no motive at all because they didn't even know whether Frank knew!"

The lieutenant looked straight back at me. "All we know," he said, "is that Madame Varovna *says* she didn't talk to Frank."

A chill rippled through me. I felt suddenly sick, with anger at him and disgust at my own stupidity. What the hell had I thought I was doing, playing Nancy Drew while people's lives and dignity were being ripped apart? Well, no more! I wasn't the police, I wasn't a private eye, and I sure as shit was no longer pretending to be objective. I turned, refusing to be diverted by the Princess's obvious distress at having so royally stuck her foot in it, and walked quickly away down the path.

25

My, what a nice, convenient type of conscience!

act 2, scene 2

SATURDAY AND SUNDAY, JUNE 30 AND JULY 1

I SPENT A LOT OF WHAT WAS LEFT OF THE AFTERNOON AN-
swering the phone. Many of the calls were requests for
tickets; word of mouth on *Così* had been favorable and
swift. I refused to speculate on the ratio of opera lovers
to scandal groupies.

The grapevine—or perhaps the police blotter—also
produced a raft of press inquiries as to the Gerta (or Berta
or Erda) Hofstetter (Hapsenpfeffer, Hoofstoffer) said to
be in police custody. I repeated my litany of ignorance
and referral to Suffolk County Homicide, and it occurred
to me that in this case I was almost telling the truth. I
didn't know what was going on. The gathering at the studio, Anna's dramatic revelations, and the lieutenant's response had left me with as many questions as answers.
Did he really suspect Anna of murder? What were the
"discrepancies" the Princess had mentioned, those details that the police had obviously been keeping to themselves? Would Gerta be charged with obstruction? Far
worse, would her illegal status be disclosed?

As far as Anna's personal history went, I was confident her story would not travel out of that room. Angry

as I was at Saul Freed, I didn't believe he would be gratu-
itously cruel. Unless, of course, he actually came to the
point of making a case against Anna as the murderer.

I pushed the thought from my mind. How strong,
after all, was her motive? Who would care now? Forty
years ago, yes. I remembered hearing about the great
Norwegian soprano Kirsten Flagstad and how her post-
war career had suffered from accusations that her husband had been a Nazi collaborator. But Anna—what
would she suffer now if the story came out? Was her
pride such that she would murder to save it? I didn't believe it.

But Gerta, the illegal immigrant, Anna's companion,
friend, protégé—Gerta's peril, I had to admit, was far
more real. But was it? Again, who would care enough to
start the cumbersome machinery of deportation for a
woman in her sixties who was guilty of nothing much
more than being on the losing side of an old war?

Anna was no fool. In telling her story to the lieutenant she had in effect thrown herself, not to mention
Gerta, on his mercy, but I was pretty sure she felt as I
did—that he would not consider it his business to rat on
Gerta. Homicide, not immigration, was his concern. I
wondered what he and John Billington had been discussing.

My eye fell on the program for *Così fan tutte* propped
on my desk against the bowling trophy. (Okay, I was
proud of that program.) It reminded me of my surprise at
Varovna's lack of an international career, now explained
in spades. How, I wondered, had she explained it at the
time? Limited ambition? Fear of flying?

The combination of mental turmoil, phone calls,
and a steady stream of droppers-in among the Colony
staff and students soon made it clear that workwise the
afternoon might as well be written off. After a few
abortive stabs at some truly delinquent bookkeeping, I
wiped the spreadsheet program off my computer screen

and wondered at what point, if ever, I would actually be free to do the job I'd been hired for.

It hadn't been until I was halfway back to Anna's House and my office that I'd realized I'd been given no instructions, no scenario to deal with the inevitable questions that would be coming my way. The arrivals of Mr. Billington and the police would not have gone unnoticed. Anna had only thanked me gravely for coming and held my hand in both of hers for a moment before turning back to her lawyer. Now I was overwhelmed by the trust she had shown in my discretion. On the other hand, I would have welcomed a practical suggestion or two.

I had recruited Jenny to man the office in my absence, so hers was the first inquiry.

"What was it?" she said as soon as I came in. "Is Gerta okay? Are they going to let her out?" Her eyes, wide and anxious, searched my face.

"Gerta's fine. And yes, I believe they're going to release her soon." I fumbled through my thoughts for how much I could safely tell. "The police are . . . um . . . not sure . . . that is, they don't really think she did it."

"But why would she confess if she didn't do it!"

Ah! a sticky point indeed. Damn, why hadn't Anna given me a clue?

"I don't know," I said. "They think the stress . . ."

Jenny's shoulders had slumped in a gesture that might have been either relief or disappointment. She gave me a look of apology. "Of course I'm glad that it's not Gerta," she said, "that she's going to be okay. But at least, you know, we thought it was . . . over. And now . . ." She frowned. "But if Gerta isn't the murderer she must have thought she was protecting someone else." Her head jerked up. "My God, she must have thought it was Anna! Is that what the police think too?"

"No, no." I skirted the desk and put my arm around Jenny's shoulders. "I'm sure not."

But indeed the implication was inescapable. Gerta had done more damage than she knew.

My conversations for the remainder of the afternoon followed pretty much the same pattern as the one with Jenny. Time after time, I searched the questioner's face for signs of . . . *something*: guilt, satisfaction, fear. One of these people (assuming I was right and both Gerta and Anna were innocent) had committed the murders for which the two women now appeared to be prime suspects. Why didn't it show? Instead I was met universally with surprise, indignation, sympathy, solidarity. I finally resorted to reminding myself that all of them, all the staff—Rita, Amanda, Jenny, Jason Lee, Stefan, even Larry and Theo—were experts in a field in which feigning emotions was a basic skill. One of them, at least, was a master.

Gerta did not, as I'd half-hoped, turn up at the theater that night. She was at home, Anna told me, penitent, exhausted, in bed, and under doctor's orders not to exert herself in any way for at least a week. "So we are mostly grateful, my darling, that you are here to pick up the slump."

Despite my initial nervousness, the amount of slump to be picked up turned out to be manageable. The rousing success of opening night had taken the edge off the singers' nerves (and, inevitably, off the performance as well; I had learned never to attend the second night of any production) and they coached me cheerfully through my duties. I buttoned and zipped and safety-pinned; I called "half hour," "fifteen minutes," "five," and "places" with increasing aplomb; I made sure that the props—among them banners and bouquets for the chorus, the flasks from which Ferrando and Guglielmo pretended to drink poison, Jenny's various disguises—were conveniently at hand.

And when it was over, virtuously turning down several invitations to join an impromptu beer bust down on the beach, I went home to bed.

On Sunday at one o'clock I arrived back at Anna's House determined to do some serious catching up in the office. Tomorrow I was taking (hallelujah!) the whole day off and I didn't want to spend it thinking about the work piling ever higher in my absence.

Unwarily, I went in through the front door and was immediately accosted by Amanda, who stood in the middle of the room holding aloft a small boxy object. She appeared to have just made an announcement to a postlunch contingent that included several students and most of the staff.

"Phoebe!" she cried gaily, grabbing my arm with her free hand, "you're just in time! We're going to listen to a tape of Larry's 'Larksongs.' A friend sent it to me from a performance at Michigan State. She says it's *really* excellent."

The Piano Man, standing next to Amanda, looked anything but pleased. "For God's sake, Amanda," he said tightly, "put that thing away. Nobody wants to listen to it now. They want to go to the beach."

"Now, Larry, you're entirely *too* modest; of *course* we want to hear it," Amanda insisted. "Don't we?" she added to the room at large.

There was a general murmur of assent and encouragement. Theo Morse said, "Sure thang, Larry, I've been wantin' a chance to hear the piece."

"Besides," Amanda went on, "everyone who was planning to drive over to the ocean has already gone."

Larry glanced around the room and shrugged. "Oh, all right," he said. He threw himself into a nearby chair, crossed his legs, and proceeded to stare at the ceiling. If this was modesty, I thought, it bore an uncomfortable resemblance to sulking.

However, it made it easier for me to say, "I'd love to

stay and listen, Larry, but I've come to work and I really have to get on with it."

Larry brought his eyes down from the ceiling long enough to give me a strained smile and a nod. Amanda sniffed. I left.

But I didn't close the office door. I was curious to hear Larry's music and there was no rule saying I couldn't listen and compute at the same time.

"Larksongs" turned out to be settings for chorus and string ensemble of poems about or incorporating (surprise) larks. The music, I thought, was attractive, more lyrical, more tonal than I'd expected, with intricate choral harmonies and a nice clarity in the setting of the words. Even from a distance I recognized "Hark, hark, the lark," followed by Browning's lines about the lark being on the wing, the snail on the thorn, and so on. Then an unfamiliar verse . . . something about "out of the clouds" . . . ? I became at that point absorbed in the nitty-gritty of payroll deductions. Good Lord, was *that* the salary of the large French person taking Sarah Kirk's place in the kitchen? Anna must have been truly over a barrel; I certainly hadn't noticed any dramatic change in the quality of the meals. The discrepancy, I mused, must be in the difference between a "cook" and a "chef": in this case, about ten dollars an hour.

"Larksongs" receded pleasantly to the edges of my consciousness.

At what moment the music began again to insinuate itself into the forefront of my attention, I was unaware. One instant, it seemed, I was engrossed in the intricacies of FICA and workmen's comp, the next I was staring blankly at the computer screen, my hands frozen over the keyboard, my body rigid with shock. That haunting, compelling melody, those words:

Higher still and higher
From the earth thou springest:
Like a cloud of fire . . .

Shelley, "To a Skylark" ... soprano voices in unison ... the song Jenny had been singing in the woods ... Charlie's song!

Oh, Larry! No wonder you were so reluctant to have "Larksongs" played for your colleagues!

Jenny! Was Jenny among those in the front room? I didn't remember seeing her.

Movement came back to my limbs in a rush. I jumped up, blundered around the desk, and sprinted down the corridor to the doorway of the big room. A glance told me that Jenny was not there. I looked at Larry. He was leaning back in his chair, eyes closed, on his face an expression very much like the one that had so shaken me that day on the path to the practice cabins.

Ethereal voices spun the song's final, plangent phrases: "... Thou dost float and run, Like an embodied joy whose race is just begun." Oh, Larry!

As the section ended and a new one began—full chorus, quickened tempo—Larry opened his eyes and saw me in the doorway. My face must have been as much of a giveaway as his own, because he flushed painfully, then looked away.

On the tape the chorus ebbed and swelled, voices and strings circling one another, twining, breaking free, recomposing. Accomplished music, technically even brilliant, *good* music. But next to Charlie's song, pedestrian, forgettable. Amadeus, I thought, oh my God, yes. Salieri and Mozart; Larry and Charlie. The lieutenant hadn't been so far off, he'd just picked the wrong combination.

Frank must have discovered, must have known that Larry Peterson was a plagiarist, must have wrestled with that knowledge: "... a grey area ... I'm having a bit of a problem. ..." And Larry had responded by ...

I turned and fled back to the office. Shutting the door behind me, I sat down at my computer and tried desperately to focus on numbers—percentages and bottom lines, things of order and logic, things with no grey areas.

It wasn't fair! Had I asked for any of this? No, I'd been cajoled and manipulated and . . . okay, *flattered* into probing where I had no business to probe. Into hearing confidences I didn't need to hear. And look where it had gotten me! Into holding another person's reputation, career, even his life, virtually in my hands. Because if anyone had a motive for murder, Larry Peterson did.

To be revealed as a plagiarist! And a plagiarist, to boot, of a dead man, a former pupil. Surely that was enough to put paid to any composer's career. Even supposing that this was the only time Larry had ever stolen someone else's work, the suspicion would linger: Wasn't that passage, this phrase, reminiscent of so-and-so? Well, of course he did it before . . .

I found that I was trembling. What would I say to Larry, how would I act? What did I plan to *do* with this unwanted and unwelcome knowledge?

The first thing, I decided, was to get the hell away from here right now, to give myself time to think. Yes, that was the thing. . . .

There was a brief rap on the door, it opened, and Larry Peterson walked in.

As he came toward me, I shrank away involuntarily. He stopped, retreated, and leaned his thin shoulders wearily against the doorframe. The lines on his long, asymmetrical face looked as if they'd been drawn in ink. "You think I killed Frank," he said flatly. "And Sarah too, I suppose."

I stared but made no reply.

"Well, I didn't." His lips twisted sideways in a sour smile. "I'm a thief, yes, but I'm not a killer."

Sure, I thought, I bet that's what you told Sarah just before you bashed her head in. Tongue-tied, I faced him across the desk, glad for its bulk between us.

Larry raised his long, bony hands, fingers spread in a gesture of helplessness. "Jesus, Phoebe, don't look like that. What I've done is bad enough, but I haven't murdered anybody, I swear. Look." He reached for the one rickety straight chair, plunked it down against the shelves lining the far wall, and sat. "Here, I'm as far away as I can get. Now can we talk?"

I nodded, still not trusting my voice, not believing how frightened I'd been. Still was, actually, although less so. Larry didn't look like a killer, *said* he wasn't a killer. But then he would say that, wouldn't he? I strained for sounds of movement, of voices from the front room, but could hear nothing.

From the open window behind me, someone said my name, and I whirled around. It was Rita, passing by on the path with an armload of beach towels. "I'm just going to get into my suit," she called. "Take a break in a while, why don't you, and come for a swim." She shaded her eyes, peering in. "You too, Larry."

"I just might," I said. "Thanks."

When she had disappeared beyond the hedge, Larry said bitterly, "There, you can relax. I can't kill you now, can I? Because then I'd have to kill Rita too. And of course Jenny."

Jenny. "Where is Jenny?" I said.

"She drove over to the ocean beach with the others. If she hadn't, you can be sure I'd have gotten that tape away from Amanda if I'd had to—" He broke off, shooting me a glance both angry and defensive. "No, I wouldn't have hurt dear Amanda. But I would have gotten the bloody tape."

"Jenny doesn't know?"

Larry shook his head. "I'm sure I would have heard about it," he said grimly. "Just as I'm sure the much-lamented Charlie told her he was giving the song to her and her alone. Seeing as how that's what he told me. The poem made him think of me, he said. Evidently it made him think of Frank as well, since he gave him a copy too." The corners of his mouth sagged in a bitter grimace. "Not that it's any kind of excuse for what I did, there isn't any. But Charlie Judd was a real little shit."

That, at least, I was beginning to believe.

My heartbeat had slowed, making possible the return of rational thought. Something, I realized, had been puzzling me. "When did Frank get a chance to hear 'Larksongs'? I thought he'd been in Europe for the past year."

"Same way as Amanda. A friend sent him a tape of a performance. University of Chicago, I think. I'd sent the thing around to a number of college music departments where I knew people. The tape was waiting for Frank when he got back to New York. As soon as he got to the Colony he told me he knew what I'd done."

"What was he going to do about it?"

"Nothing. No, really, Phoebe. For one thing, I'd already started to call the piece in, make excuses, tell the people I'd shown it to that I wanted to rewrite it. It was getting to be a nightmare. Everyone who heard it had the same reaction as the one review I saw." He closed his eyes and quoted, " 'It is in the fourth section of the piece that composer Peterson truly comes into his own.' " His shoulders slumped and he reached up to massage his lower lids with thumb and middle finger. "Christ, if I'd wanted to prove to myself that I was a second-rate composer I couldn't have chosen a better way."

I wasn't ready to feel sorry for Larry Peterson. "You mean to tell me that Frank wasn't going to say anything?"

Larry gave a short, humorless laugh. "Oh, he gave me the whole song and dance about announcing my sin to the world, freeing myself from the shackles of deceit, and so on. Frank, as you must have gathered by now, could be incredibly obtuse. But I told him I was withdrawing the piece from the Tanglewood performance. And I did. Showed him the letter I'd written that night, as a matter of fact, the night before he died. He made some more noises about how much better I'd feel if I made a clean breast, et cetera, but I think that in spite of himself he felt I'd done penance enough. Also, Frank wasn't completely unaware of Charlie's tendency to use people. I mean, thinking back, it was typical of Charlie to make this wonderful, unique gift to three different people. Who were each, of course, suitably touched and grateful."

"You're sure it was only three?"

He shuddered. "Jesus, I hope so."

I couldn't help myself. "Why did you do it?" I said. "Why did you run the risk?"

"Ah! The very question I've been asking myself." He took a deep breath and blew it out, puffing the full lips. "When Charlie brought me his piece I was working on 'Larksongs.' It seemed serendipitous. And then when he died, I thought, Well, it was a gift, wasn't it? Hell, maybe I was trying to prove to myself that crazy little Charlie wasn't that much more gifted than I, that no one would notice. . . . Well, I've told you how that worked out. I've paid, Phoebe, believe me. Groveling to Frank was just the last installment." He raised his hooded eyes to meet mine directly with a kind of weary defiance. "Although telling you about it is almost worse."

"You broke into Frank's apartment," I said, a statement, not a question.

"Yes. He'd told me that's where his copy of the song was, and I found it there and took it and later on I burned it. For a while I thought I was relatively safe."

"Until you heard Jenny in the practice cabin."

"God, what a shock. And there you were, walking towards the woods. Later I saw the two of you coming out together, so I assumed she'd told you it was Charlie's song."

I nodded.

"Today I could only hope that your musical memory wasn't all that good. You'd only heard the song once, after all."

"It's a memorable piece of music," I said.

Larry's chin jerked up as if I'd struck him, but after a moment all he said was, "Indeed."

"What are you going to do now?" I said.

"Isn't the question rather," he replied dryly, "what *you* are going to do, dear Phoebe? It hasn't escaped my attention that you've been pretty cozy with that homicide cop, what's his name . . . Freed. Are you going to tell him?"

"No," I said. "You are."

Larry's eyebrows rose, the mobile upper lip curled slightly. "Or?"

Suddenly, I'd had it. I stood up and leaned forward, hands braced on the edge of the desk. "Or of course I'll tell him myself!" I said. "I'll tell him you were the one who burgled the apartment and that you had a damn good motive for shutting Frank up. You say you didn't kill him. Okay. Frankly, I don't much give a shit *who* did it anymore. But I am getting seriously pissed at being constantly put in the middle of this mess, which God knows I didn't ask for. *Somebody* did it. So goddamn right you're going to tell the lieutenant what you told me and let *him* figure it out!"

Larry stared, his eyes open wider than I'd yet seen them. My knees buckled and I sat down again. "The only reason I hope it wasn't you," I said more quietly, "is because then Jenny would have to find out about Charlie, and I think it would break her heart."

Larry rose. "I'll see the lieutenant first thing in the morning," he said grimly. "Will that do? We do have a show tonight."

I nodded.

After he'd gone, I wondered if I'd been a fool. So sue me! Larry'd been right about one thing: If he was determined to safeguard his secret against all possible leaks, he'd have to wipe out who knew how many more people, starting with me and Jenny. I didn't think he'd run, either. After all, as he'd said, he had a show to do.

26

You must have courage,
be prepared for a shock.

act 1, scene 3

SUNDAY, JULY 1

IN WHAT NOW SEEMED TO ME A SERIOUSLY MISGUIDED MO-
ment, I had invited Mrs. Schmitter to the Sunday-night
performance of *Così fan tutte*. So at six o'clock, having
made what I considered under the circumstances to be
heroic inroads on the Colony bookkeeping, I begged a
sandwich from the French Chef and ate it in the car as I
drove back to the village to pick up my landlady.

The scene with Larry Peterson had left me drained
and sad. The sandwich went down dry and proceeded to
turn my stomach into a miniature acid factory. I longed to
crawl into bed, cover my head, and sleep for a week. Instead, besides having to return to the Colony and face
Larry and my performance duties, I had saddled myself
with responsibility for a dotty old lady. Since there was
no one else to be sorry for me, I managed a creditable effort on my own behalf.

Mrs. Schmitter was waiting for me in the hallway,
her small round body swathed in a black lace creation
that a vintage clothing store would have killed for. The
wispy hair had been freshly permed into tight little
ringlets and from her tiny wrist hung a black-beaded
drawstring evening bag.

I felt an immediate surge of guilt for having begrudged for a moment a gesture that had cost me so relatively little and was obviously worth so much. I exclaimed over her appearance, and she flushed with pleasure. "I haven't mentioned it, my dear," she'd said to me when I made my offer, "because I didn't want to worry you. But on Monday I'm going into the hospital. Oh, nothing major, just for overnight, and I'm not really concerned at all. Still, it will be grand to have something else to think about the night before."

At the time, once convinced that the surgery was indeed minor, I had felt relief at the thought of having the house to myself for a whole twenty-four hours. Now, ashamed, I was determined to make my landlady's outing as gala as possible. Due to my commitment backstage, we had to be at the theater an hour before curtain, and I only hoped that Mrs. Schmitter's gin-induced alertness would last the evening.

She excused herself gaily to fetch a last-minute article from the kitchen and reappeared tucking a stoppered perfume bottle filled with clear liquid into the beaded bag. I felt considerably relieved. Mrs. Schmitter was evidently well primed for her introduction to the world of opera.

I got my guest settled in an aisle seat and went to drop the word that the small lady in black was to be given the royal treatment. In the half hour before the doors were opened to the general public, one by one the cast members good-naturedly stopped by her seat to introduce themselves and write their names in the autograph book she delightedly offered them. I heard Jason Lee's rich chuckle, caught sight of Rita demonstrating her technique with a fan, Jenny smiling and nodding as she bent her head over the autograph book. Theo Morse sat with my landlady for several minutes, apparently engaged in a lively description of the action of *Così fan tutte*.

Even Amanda took a moment to graciously scribble her name and admire the black lace dress.

I felt my heart warming at these demonstrations of kindness and goodwill. After the traumas of the past two days—Gerta's confession, Anna's painful story, the revelation of Larry's plagiarism—I found this evidence of simple human decency extremely soothing to a mind (not to mention a digestive system) in turmoil. *This*, I told myself, was the Varovna Colony at its best, this was the true expression of lives lived for the glory of Art, a demonstration of the ennobling influences of Music, of Beauty. . . . My euphoria grew, fueled by a counter-reaction to my former gloom as well as light-headedness caused by insufficient nourishment.

By the time the curtain opened on the first act of *Così fan tutte* I was close to tears of maudlin joy from the wonder of it all.

I had discovered a corner of the downstage left wing from which I could see the action onstage without being seen by the audience, getting in the way of singers' exits and entrances, or knocking something over. There I tucked myself in and watched happily as the third-night performance unfolded with just that extra edge of sparkle and energy that had been missing the night before. The three men—Jason Lee, Stefan, and Chris Fox—tossed off the first scene with style and precision. Fiordiligi and Dorabella then took the stage and sang meltingly their opening duet. Don Alfonso rushed back on: "How I hate to break the news!" and the plot was off and running.

Shortly thereafter I was flagged with frantic gestures by one of the choristers and hauled off to deal with a back zipper that had suddenly given way. I administered safety pins and rooted out a shawl to cover the less than aesthetic result. At another time I might have had sour thoughts about people who insisted on wearing everything two sizes too small; now I smiled and reassured and got back to my niche in plenty of time to hear my favorite trio.

The first act flew on with unabated zest: Dorabella's big aria, then Despina's. A lively and comic sextet. Fiordiligi's rip-snorting paean to the strength of "love that only death can end."

I wondered how Mrs. Schmitter was reacting and wished I could see her face. From my vantage point I could just spy half of Larry at the piano. Whatever inner turmoil he might be experiencing, it certainly wasn't affecting his playing. Beyond a brief nod, we had managed to avoid each other—easy enough in the preperformance hubbub. Now I felt myself softening: Had Larry after all done anything so terrible, and wasn't he making amends as best he could?

In fact, did any of the motives dredged up so far stand in the face of scrutiny? I, for one, didn't think so. No, there had to be something else, something in all that welter of information that I had missed, Anna had missed, the lieutenant had missed. Or something entirely new, hidden, unknown . . . Why was I doing this to myself?

Directly across from me, in the stage-right wing, Theo Morse stood at the lightboard, the student who'd been handling the lighting having been a sunburn casualty of that afternoon's trip to the ocean beach. Theo appeared to be enjoying himself with a practical task to occupy him, as opposed to prowling the perimeter of the theater feeling useless as only a director can once the curtain is up.

Stefan delivered Ferrando's silken tenor aria with more warmth than I'd yet heard from him, and we arrived at the wonderful first-act finale.

The two sisters started it off, wallowing happily, in thirds, in the drama of their loss. The two disguised lovers burst on the scene: "A double dose of poison, that is the one solution!" and proceeded to drink the fatal brew from their flasks. Don Alfonso whipped up the melodrama with dire predictions; the sisters shrieked and hovered. Despina, in the center right wing, stood poised for her entrance. In the shadows behind her, Anna Varovna, her face illuminated by the spill from one of the stage-left lekos, her hands clasped below her breast, looked on. I hadn't known she was backstage, she must have just arrived. Theo's head swiveled on its long neck back and forth from his cue sheet to the action onstage.

Suddenly I flashed on the rehearsal I'd watched on my first day at the Colony. Instead of Chris Fox staggering comically about the stage I saw Frank and heard his robust, honey-smooth baritone. I remembered his handsome, good-humored face, the dark hair falling over his forehead, the way he'd clutched his score and tried so hard to follow the blocking. Poor Frank! Frank, who had been murdered. My euphoria suffered a sudden chill.

The two lovers collapsed onto the ground . . . and again it was only Chris Fox, flailing and mugging, milking the audience with an excess of grimacing and gagging. The two sisters wrung their hands and cried out for Despina. Jenny entered, and stared in amazement from one to the other of the prone lovers. "How did they come to lie here in such a helpless state?"

And in that moment, like a stop-frame, I saw a mask slip. One face among those directed at the supposedly dying lovers wore for an instant a look of undisguised grief and horror . . . and guilt. It was the face of Anna Varovna.

The moment passed. I sank onto my haunches and ducked my swimming head between my knees, forcing back nausea. Sounds became dim and garbled. Only an anguished voice inside my skull rang loud and clear. *Why?* it said. *Why?* And what do I do now?

I forced my head up, forced my eyes to focus on the stage. Had anyone else seen what I had seen? Had Anna perhaps intercepted my look of recognition and shock?

It seemed not. Her attitude as she stood between the first and second right-stage teasers was unchanged. Her face again wore its customary look of calm command. On the brightly lit platform between us the first-act finale was romping merrily along as if there were no such thing in the world as murder or guilt or deceit. Or a heartsick woman crouching miserably in the wings.

Incredibly, less than a minute had passed since my moment of revelation. A few seconds more and Despina would be coming offstage to put on her doctor disguise. I should be there to help her. I found, however, that I still couldn't trust myself to stand up. Perhaps Jason Lee, exiting at the same time, could do it, I thought. And had I made sure the giant magnet was in its proper place on the prop table?

Good God, what was I thinking! Costume changes and props! I clapped both hands over my mouth against a wave of hysteria. Giant magnets, wigs, burst zippers, late entrances—all trivial and meaningless beside the stark fact that I, and apparently only I, knew who had killed Frank Palermo and Sarah Kirk. Of that I was certain, with the kind of dazed, icy certainty that I imagined would be felt by someone vouchsafed a vision of the Dark Angel. And with about as much chance of being believed.

What the *hell* was I going to do?

Despina was back onstage now in her doctor persona, using the magnet to revive the suicides. Ferrando and Guglielmo, coming to, made passionate declarations to the sisters, who began to show the first signs of wavering. Don Alfonso, with oily encouragement, stirred the emotional stew he had created. As the finale swept into the closing allegro, Theo bumped the lights up to full.

But for me the joy, the brilliance, the lighthearted-ness were long gone. What, after all, was the reality of the story unfolding on the stage: three characters pre-tending to be what they were not; lies, manipulation, foolishness, inconstancy—I saw it all through a sour veil of shock and sorrow.

I had managed by then to get back on my feet. There was just time before the curtain came down on the first act to make it outside via the backstage exit. Unobtru-sive as I tried to be, I had to wave off several solicitous approaches from chorus members as I passed. I assumed I must have looked like hell.

In the darkness behind the barn I drew deep breaths, lifting my face to catch any slight movement of the salty, brackeny air. The night was clear and very warm. I stood for a few moments, willing my limbs to stop trembling, my heartbeat to slow. The shrilling of crickets from the surrounding undergrowth overrode the last breakneck phrases of the first-act finale drifting, muted, from be-hind me. Then came the drumming of applause fol-lowed by the babble of an emerging audience. And again, like a dim-witted litany: What do I do now? How do I behave? How can I talk to anyone here, knowing what I know? Anyone except . . .

Mrs. Schmitter! Thank God for Mrs. Schmitter! I skirted the theater, searching faces as I went, and finally found my landlady on the front stone terrace. She was in the act of putting the stopper back into her little bottle and greeted me with joy.

"Oh, Phoebe! Oh, my dear! Those voices! I never knew . . . so beautiful! And the dresses!" She chattered on, clinging to my arm, while I smiled and nodded and made answering murmurs.

How could I have been so blind, so wrong! Phoebe Mullins, who had actually begun to pride herself on her insight! What had Anna said about Frank . . ." One of those people who thinks he knows human psychology . . .

whereas truly about people he is very stupid." She might as well have been talking about me! Had she seen that, and had that been what she was counting on? Stupid, stupid Phoebe! I had failed the lieutenant, I had failed Sarah Kirk, I had failed myself.

I looked down at Mrs. Schmitter's hand resting more heavily now on my arm, and then at her face, pink and lightly perspiring. Had I done the right thing, bringing my landlady there? Should I have consulted her doctor? Was I perhaps guilty of encouraging alcohol dependence in the old and frail? My self-confidence, never robust, was careening to a new low.

And I still didn't know what to do.

27

Wait! An idea!

act 2, scene 11

MONDAY, JULY 2

WHEN I WOKE THE NEXT MORNING IT WAS AFTER NINE o'clock and Mrs. Schmitter had already left—presumably picked up by Robert the Third for her trip to the hospital in Southampton. In the kitchen Mr. Coffee sat on his shelf silent and empty. No carefully rinsed juice glass, coffee cup, and cereal bowl drained in the wire rack by the sink. My landlady might not be at her most acute in the mornings but she was an early riser with regular habits. I missed her presence and hoped she'd be okay.

I filled the coffee machine and while it belched quietly at my elbow I stood at the sink, looking out at the narrow side yard. A desultory rain made streaks down the windowpanes before falling onto the scraggly rhododendrons below. So much for my beachgoing plans. I had even, in happier times (three days ago!), had thoughts of spending a part of my precious day off with Lieutenant Freed. Now that I had everything—and nothing—to tell him, I was grateful that we were not speaking.

I had endured the second act of *Così fan tutte* by dint of massive denial and pleas of indigestion to explain my lack of cheer. Afterward, Mrs. Schmitter, who by that time was glassy-eyed and visibly flagging, was my excuse for immediate departure. After seeing her safely into bed, I had gone upstairs sure I would be incapable of sleep. On the contrary, I had passed out almost immediately and not only slept but slept late. Now as I contemplated the day ahead I wished it had been even later. However . . . I sat down with my coffee cup to do some serious thinking.

For starters, in the wake of a solid night's rest, last evening's orgy of self-flagellation began to seem excessive. Anna Varovna a murderer! How could I have known, or even guessed? Come to that, what *did* I know? Certainly nothing that could be conveyed, for instance, to a police officer. "Ah . . . an *expression*, you say. On her face." I cringed at the thought.

But I knew what I had seen: the staring, haunted eyes, ashen skin, mouth open and grimacing. And something beyond those—an almost tangible projection of pain and regret. I had been sure then; I was sure now. Remembering, a pang shot through me almost equivalent to what I had experienced last night, and my eyes grew hot. How could it be! I had believed her, trusted her, admired her! Now my sense of personal betrayal brought home to me the extent to which I'd relegated Anna Varovna to a place apart. How I'd discounted or ignored any inconvenient facts that might have pointed in her direction. Well, I would make that mistake no longer.

I lugged a second week's worth of dirty clothes, sheets, and towels down to the laundry room and set the washing machine to work. I poured juice, made toast, refilled my coffee cup, and started over from the beginning, trying to clear my mind of all preconceptions. What had the various members of the Varovna Colony staff actually said to me about themselves and others, what had they actually done, how had they behaved?

My memory, while not photographic, is pretty good. I was able to close my eyes and run a mental tape of the past two weeks starting with my arrival at the

Colony and ending with last night's painful moment of revelation: the rehearsal, lunch at Anna's House, the visit to Frank's cabin, dinner with Larry, Frank's death, waiting in the big room at Anna's House, the wake and the Children, the death of the Mouse . . . and through it all, conversations—with Anna, with Jenny, with Frank himself, Rita and Amanda, Sarah Kirk, Gerta, Stefan, Larry, and Jason Lee.

I was searching for something new, something overlooked. Anna's motive, I was now convinced, would have nothing to do with Paris and Gerta and the mysterious Monsieur LeClair. That whole elaborate "confession" now seemed to me a brilliant and audacious bluff. What a performer the woman was, what a consummate actress! What reserves of nerve and will to be able to pull off such a masterpiece of fakery! How could I have forgotten the Varovna reputation for the realism of her portrayals? How could I not have seen that she alone, an artist head and shoulders above the rest of the Colony staff, was the one with the resources—not to mention the guts—to pull off such an impersonation?

And, I reasoned, it must be a secret far more damning than a piece of regrettable but long-gone history that had carried Anna Varovna to such lengths. A dark corner of her life into which neither I, nor the lieutenant, nor the Princess had thought to probe.

I propped my elbows on the table, took a sip of lukewarm coffee, and again closed my eyes against outside distraction. What could it be? What possible aspect of Anna's history had we not— My eyes flew open. Her husband, Gregory Dmitri! The well-connected Mr. Dmitri, never, in my hearing, referred to by Anna until the afternoon she told her story to the lieutenant. And then what had she called him? "A man with many acquaintances, many contacts." As well as being Anna's rescuer, patron, manager, lover, and husband. Wasn't it peculiar that she should mention him so seldom? What was the truth of that long relationship? And, come to think of it, the truth of the relationship among Anna, Gregory, and Gerta?

My brain leaped into overdrive. Was Gerta, perhaps, in love with Gregory Dmitri? Or with Anna? What were the circumstances of Dmitri's death? Eight years ago, Jenny had said. And Larry—hadn't he spoken of Frank practically "camping out" at Anna's place when he first started singing? I did the math. Yes, Frank could have been around when Dmitri died. Could either Anna or Gerta have hastened Dmitri's death, and Frank have somehow known? At the wake, what had the Gypsy Child been saying to Anna about Dmitri that had even Anna looking uncomfortable and Gerta downright frightened? Or alternatively . . . what about the Russian mafia? Was it possible that Dmitri—?

I brought myself up short. What was I doing except indulging in sheer speculation and fantasy? *Not* productive, Phoebe. Nevertheless, I could not rid myself of a niggling and intensely irritating sense of something I should be seeing and was not—or perhaps not seeing from the right angle.

The thing to do, I decided, was to give my conscious mind a break and let the subconscious take over. I put the laundry into the dryer, found an aged but intact umbrella in Mrs. Schmitter's hall closet along with a crumpled plastic raincoat, and, to distract myself, went out into the rain.

I walked in the direction of the village, trying to blank out the Colony and murder, concentrating instead on the picture-perfect brown-shingled windmill, the very old graveyard across from the Methodist church, the cropped lawns, rose-draped fences, clumps of orange lilies silvered with raindrops. Also on crossing streets without being mowed down by a brisk parade of Mercedeses and MGs; folks who summer in the Hamptons haven't gotten there by being laid-back.

Under an intermittent drizzle, downtown East Hampton was vibrating with the waspish murmur of swarming vacationers who had been counting on going to the beach and instead had just spent half an hour circling a parking lot in the wet. I dodged my way along the broad sidewalk, feeling like an alien among the chic in my plastic mac, clutching the old umbrella. Feeling, actually, alien from the whole world under the grim burden of my secret knowledge.

Because of course it had been ridiculous to suppose I could make myself stop thinking about . . . I gritted my teeth. Yes, but I could damn well try.

On I plowed, past the antique stores and galleries, past the real-estate offices offering million-dollar-plus homes, past Scoop du Jour and Cashmere Hampton.

"You have to stop *trying* to see," said a voice on my right. "Just relax and it'll jump right out at you."

I stopped so abruptly that a man walking behind me trod on my heel. He swore, gave me a dirty look, and circled on by.

"I don't care what you say," complained a second voice. "Some people can see these things and some people can't."

The voices, I was relieved to discover, belonged to two women standing under the front awning of a gift shop, staring at a large 3D illusion print displayed in the window. Still, it had been spooky. I shivered and trudged on.

The row of shops came to an end. From there on, the sidewalks were virtually deserted and I made good time past the Ladies' Village Improvement Society, the Historical Society, a museum, the East Hampton Free Library.

The library. At least I could check one fact. Even if he had died in New York, I was certain that a prominent summer resident like Gregory Dmitri must have rated a local obituary in the *East Hampton Star*. Besides which, I could dry out for a bit.

The library was warm, carpeted, and wood paneled, with a less self-conscious charm than much of East Hampton, and I was not the only sodden soul who had sought its comfort. I added my umbrella to the collection by the doorway and went to consult the librarian.

Shortly, I was seated in front of a microfilm machine, perusing the eight-year-old obit of Gregory Dmitri, "famed impresario and husband of Metropolitan Opera star," etc., etc. Mr. Dmitri, it seemed, had died at home, in his apartment in the Ansonia Hotel, of heart failure "after a brief illness."

My shoulders slumped with disappointment. "Brief illness" indeed! What kind of illness? How brief? Had questions been asked? Ah well, unlike its tabloid namesake, I could hardly have expected gossip and innuendo from this *Star*—a paper that, I had once been told with glee, in announcing the marriage of Linda Eastman and Paul McCartney, had referred to the groom as "a member of the Beatles, a British musical group."

In any case, I was still left with myriad possibilities and not one smidgen of evidence.

As I passed from the cubicle that housed the microfilm machine into the library's reference room, a woman sitting at a nearby table gave a grunt of exasperation and shoved away the book she'd been consulting so that it just missed falling onto the floor. She rose with some difficulty from her chair and struggled into a raincoat. As she brushed by me on her way to the door I saw that she was a good eight months pregnant.

Curious, I glanced down to see what sort of reading matter had so frustrated her. On the table in front of the empty chair were several books with some variety of "Naming the Baby" in their titles. Not so long ago, I would have averted my eyes. Now I was glad to find that I could smile in amused sympathy. What a responsibility indeed, this choosing of a name for an unknown incipient person! A name that would inescapably become a defining element in how that person appeared to the world. Except, of course, if you were in the performing arts, then you could . . .

Seized by a sudden thought, I plopped down in the empty chair, opened the first book that came to hand, and started leafing through it. Hadn't Larry cited the meaning of names as one of Frank's short-lived hobbies? Perhaps that final desperate attempt to communicate his killer's name had been more specific than anyone had guessed. I quickly became engrossed, searching one book, then pulling up the next.

It was about fifteen minutes later when I found myself staring down at a page, immobile with shock and bewilderment. But if that was right . . . if that was what Frank thought . . . No, it couldn't be! But if it *were* true . . . My God, how could I have gone so far wrong? Or had it been Frank who was wrong?

I slammed the book shut, causing several faces to turn with disapproving expressions in my direction. I needed to get out of there, go where I could be alone and think. I stood too quickly, my head swam, and I had to lean on the back of the chair until it cleared. As soon as I was sure I could walk a reasonably straight line, I made for the front door, grabbed my umbrella, and left the library.

The rain had intensified into a downpour. In my miserable state, it seemed completely appropriate. I trudged stolidly back the way I'd come while impressions careened through my head like errant pieces of a mosaic, forming first this picture, then that. If Frank had been right, if he'd really known . . . But why, what possible motive? And how could I find out?

By the time I regained the business district my feet were soaked, my jeans clinging to my calves, my back and arms clammy under the plastic raincoat. Sheer physical discomfort had distracted me to the point where all that occupied my mind were thoughts of home and dryness.

Therefore it was a particular jolt, as I peered out from under my umbrella preparatory to crossing the parking-lot exit, to see half a block ahead of me Gerta Hofstetter and Anna Varovna, huddled together under their own umbrella, coming in my direction. Oh God, not now! Not until I knew!

I lowered my umbrella like a shield and turned left into the lot, dodging narrowly between a shiny new Jeep and a vintage Thunderbird. Over the resulting horn blasts I thought I heard my name being called. At not quite a run, I zigzagged across the lot, emerged at the Newtown Lane access, went through another lot to North Main Street, then down the hill, right at the IGA, left . . . home.

The towels in the dryer were still warm. I shed my wet clothes onto the floor of the laundry room, draped myself in warm terrycloth, and went upstairs. There I lay down on the bed—just for long enough, I told myself, to give my pulse a chance to slow to normal and my breathing to regulate itself.

When I awoke, the digital clock on the bedside table read 7:36 P.M. Impossible! But through the back window I saw that the sky had cleared and late rays of a low-westering sun were just touching the tops of Mrs. Schmitter's lilac bushes. I had slept all afternoon and into the evening. My eyes were gritty, my head ached, and I was fiercely hungry.

In the kitchen I heated up tomato soup, tossed onion, peppers, and mushrooms into a three-egg omelet, and set a fat bagel to toasting. Not until I'd eaten enough to ease the throbbing in my temples did I venture into the complications of sequential thought.

Now that my initial stunned reaction to my discovery at the library had worn off, I was able to begin grappling in a logical way with the facts I possessed. And the first fact was that *if* Frank had been right about his killer's identity, then I had been (mentally) doing Anna Varovna a huge injustice. Yet I had been so sure! I pictured again the scene on the stage: Stefan Kowalski and Chris Fox downstage right and left, writhing in pretended agony; Amanda and Rita center stage, wringing their hands; Jason Lee and Jenny hovering in turn over the supposed suicides. And Anna Varovna in the wing, staring, staring.

Yes, I had seen what I had seen. I had not imagined the anguish in that gaze, the sorrow, the guilt. But was there conceivably an alternative interpretation?

I tilted back in the chrome-and-plastic kitchen chair and scowled at the acoustical-tile ceiling. Ugly stuff, slapped up no doubt to cover cracking plaster. It had the kind of geometric pattern that could be interpreted either as a projecting cube or as a square depression. I played with it, making the shapes shift . . . out . . . in . . . out. . . .

The chair's front legs hit the linoleum with a thump. What if Anna had been revealing, at that moment, not her own guilt but her knowledge of someone else's? And if so that would mean . . . that Anna suspected one of the people onstage of the murders of Frank and Sarah Kirk! That the grief, the pain, the regret were all for another, for the one of those longtime friends, students, protégés, who had betrayed her love and her trust. For the twentieth time I conjured up that gaze, followed its path.

And this time I saw it. Saw with disbelief and a sinking heart toward whom she had been looking.

Why hadn't she told me? Well, I hadn't given her a chance last night, had I? Or was it, as in my own case, a combination of uncertainty, unwillingness to believe, and a lack of tangible proof? Or was it because my first instinct had been right and Anna was indeed the guilty one?

My world tilted once more as I racked my memory. If Frank was right, if he'd known the truth . . . the truth . . . the Children of Truth . . . the wake. The Gypsy Child babbling at Jenny: "Frank felt so awful about . . ." and then being cut off by Jenny's collapse. What had the Gypsy Child been about to say? Felt awful about what?

Well, finally, there was one question for which I could find the answer. The Children would know. I had to get in touch with the Children—but how?

Of course! The Tall Child had given me her card. I had put it . . . in the pocket of my jacket. When I'd had to turn the jacket over to the police, the night of the Mouse's death, I'd felt the card there, taken it out, and put it . . . in the drawer of my desk at the Colony. Shit! Of all the places I did *not* want to be at that moment. I thought with dread of driving up to Anna's House, perhaps meeting on the way the person I now suspected of murdering Frank Palermo and Sarah Kirk.

At least I could phone the office number first, perhaps someone would still be downstairs at Anna's House and would answer. A request to look in the desk for the Tall Child's card would be innocent enough. And if the wrong person answered, I could simply hang up. It was worth a try.

I jumped up and ran down the hall to the living room. No phone was to be seen, but, an old hand by now, I looked for the cord, found it, and followed it down the back hall to where it disappeared under Mrs. Schmitter's bedroom door. With an indulgent grimace, I turned the doorknob. Rattled it, shook it. The door was locked. Moreover, closer inspection showed it to be a Yale lock, a serious lock, not the old-fashioned type of keyhole affair vulnerable even to an amateur like me. Mrs. Schmitter's daytime paranoia had overcome the fragile trust I thought we'd been building together. The specter of the Monster Phone Bill had won out. I couldn't decide whether to laugh or scream.

Instead of doing either, I went out to my car, heaved my reluctant self into the driver's seat, and started for the Colony.

28

How can you be so blind!

act 1, scene 1

DUSK WAS EDGING ACROSS THE LINE TO DARKNESS WHEN I made the turn at the Varovna Colony sign and entered the woods. The breeze that had finally blown the day's clouds away had died with the sunset. I drove with the windows down; the air on my face carried with it the scent of wet pine needles. From both sides of the dirt road, where the all-day rain had augmented swampy depressions into small temporary ponds, hundreds of little frog voices trilled in a high-pitched, tuneless chorus. The sound surrounded me, shrill and dissonant, causing, along with the sudden plunge into blackness, a sensation of panic and disorientation. Where was I, and why, and how long before I could get out?

Then through the trees to my left I saw lights from Rita and Theo's house. The frog voices began to recede. A few yards farther on, from deeper in the woods, came a glimmer that I figured must indicate The Octagon, where Larry and Jason Lee were staying. I realized I'd never been to either of those houses and wondered whether my tenure at the Colony would last long enough for that to happen.

I came out into the open and made the turn left by

the boys' cabins. My headlights swept a deserted vista of lawn, dark water, and the outlines of the far shores rising like black cutouts against a purpling sky. No human figures strolled the paths or stopped to wish on the first star just quivering into view in the east. Whatever was happening at the Varovna Colony tonight was evidently happening indoors.

And a good deal of it seemed to be happening in the boys' cabins. Once past the frog bacchanal, I'd become increasingly aware of another sound, thudding and insistent. The source, it now became clear, was the middle section of the cabins. The sound was a maximum-decibel rock recording featuring a singer whom even I recognized as Michael Jackson, reminding me that the Varovna Colony was after all part of the real world. Along with the throb of the music, voices and laughter drifted through open windows. Candlelight flickered on rhythmically moving bodies. I could almost taste the wine and the salt of the potato chips. I slowed the car to a crawl. If only, I thought, I were on my way to join the party, instead of pursuing yet another piece of information I would basically rather not have.

Michael Jackson was replaced by another voice, female, slightly breathy, unfamiliar to me. The sound traveled clearly on the still air, and I could even make out the words—a lament of betrayal, of misplaced trust, of the singer's blindness to reality.

I stiffened, momentarily transfixed. Was there some kind of ghostly conspiracy at work here? Or was I only the victim of an overtaxed psyche, reading significance where none existed?

Nonetheless, the voice dogged me as I drove on toward Anna's House.

"Blind," it taunted, "blind."

There was little chance, I thought, with a party going on, that I would run into anyone on my way to the office. The French Chef was resident in one of the upstairs bedrooms, but although an outside light partially illuminated the parking area in back, no lights shone from either the upstairs or downstairs windows. Perhaps Antoine was at the party, or pursuing interests further afield. As I turned off the car's motor and sat for a moment while my eyes adjusted to the darkness, I felt a small shiver of nervousness at the thought of walking alone into an unlit, empty house at night. Ah well, I would go in, make my call, and leave quickly.

Before heading down the path, I turned to look back toward the woods. I thought I had seen . . . yes; though in the daytime Anna's studio was virtually hidden among the trees, at night the glow of lamplight from the big upstairs room was visible from where I stood. Somehow the sight only intensified my feeling of vulnerability.

Another bulb shone dimly outside the kitchen entrance. Inside the screen door I felt for the wall switch, was rewarded with yet another low-wattage response from a ceiling fixture, and scurried along to my office. There at least the amperage was adequate; I'd had no intention of sacrificing my eyesight on the altar of Anna's notions of frugality. I turned on both the overhead light and the desk lamp, opened the desk drawer, and took out the Tall Child's card.

It was a Manhattan number, and when I dialed she answered so promptly that I surmised she'd been expecting a call. Not mine, though. It took her a moment or two to process just who I was, and when she finally did there was a distinct sniff from her end of the line. At the same time I heard another sound, the soft but unmistakable click of an extension phone being lifted from its cradle.

This was a complication I hadn't foreseen. Swiftly I ran through the possibilities in my mind: boys' cabins, girls' cabins, Rita and Theo's house, Anna's studio, The Octagon. Who had noticed the tiny red glow of the light indicating that the line was in use? Whose ear was now pressed to the receiver, whose hand clamped across the mouthpiece to smother the sound of breathing?

"Excuse me," I said in as authoritative a tone as I could muster, "but I'm using the phone right now."

"What? What did you say?" said the Tall Child irritably.

Supposing the listener had hung up, the Tall Child's voice would have effectively covered the sound. I had to make a decision and my decision was that the time for dithering had passed. I plunged ahead.

"I'm sorry," I began. "For bothering you, I mean. But something was said at the wake that I've been thinking about and I need to ask you a question. It's a matter," I added in a flash of inspiration, "of establishing the truth."

The Tall Child said something that sounded like "hmmph," followed by an elaborate sigh. "Well?"

I asked my question.

She answered.

I thanked her and hung up the phone.

So where, I thought, is the feeling of triumph? I had uncovered the motive for Frank's murder. I should at least be enjoying some sense of accomplishment, of self-satisfaction. Instead, I was truly experiencing for the first time the meaning of the term *heavyhearted*.

When my baby had died, and years later Mick, the sensation had been more of a tearing at the heart, of inner bleeding (clichés, after all, don't come out of nowhere). Now a weight of enormous density seemed to have invaded my chest cavity, anchoring me to the chair, making it impossible to take deep breaths. Along with this increase in gravity, my senses had become painfully acute. The skin on my forearms prickled unpleasantly where it made contact with the desk blotter. The distant throb of a bass guitar pounded at my eardrums. And why were these lights so unbearably bright?

I pushed myself up from my chair and walked

heavily across the room to switch off the ceiling fixture. From there I looked back at my desk, now an island of light among the shadows. The big, uncurtained window reflected the desk and the lamp, the computer, that ridiculous bowling trophy, and beyond them my pale face. It occurred to me that anyone could be observing me through that window and I moved so that I stood behind the desk but slightly to one side of the window frame.

Because I was waiting. In concert with my other heightened senses, a sixth one told me that someone was coming. Would it be the murderer? Or would it be another person, who, hearing my question and the Tall Child's answer, now knew what I knew? I waited, standing by the desk with its oasis of light, my eyes fixed on the door.

29

Feigning simplicity, lying, deceiving . . .

act 1, scene 8

WHEN SHE APPEARED, IT WAS SO SUDDENLY THAT I CAUGHT my breath. One moment the shadowy doorway was empty, the next she was standing there, a small figure dressed in white. Another second's observation told me I'd been wrong: she was wearing a white cotton nightgown, but the wrapper over it was pale blue. Her face, though, matched the nightgown. In the dim light the fair hair seemed almost colorless.

I said the first thing that came into my mind: "Why aren't you at the party?"

"My cold's worse," Jenny said. "I'm trying to take care of it so I'll be okay for the performances next weekend."

I looked at her feet, thrust into a pair of white canvas sneakers with no laces. "Your shoes are wet," I said, pushing away the thought that for Jenny there would be no performances next weekend.

She glanced down, then stooped to pull off the wet sneakers. Leaving them where they dropped, she moved to the straight wooden chair that Larry had occupied what now seemed aeons ago. She sat, pulling up her knees and tucking the white nightgown around her bare feet. "I came across the grass. I wanted . . . I was in the common room down at the cabins, making some tea. . . ."

"And you saw the light on the extension phone."

She nodded. I waited for her to continue, but she hesitated, looked at me irresolutely, looked away. It occurred to me that she had not had time to formulate a posture, that she was still assessing how much I really knew.

I thought of the conversation she had overheard:

"When your friend, the, uh, young woman in black, when she was talking to Jenny Allen just before Jenny fainted, talking about the fire and . . . the death and so forth . . .

"Yes?" impatiently.

"She said something like, 'Frank felt so awful about . . . and then Jenny fainted and she never finished. Do you know what it was Frank felt so awful about?"

"Oh, that!" dismissively. "Yes, I know about that. Frank had the silly idea he might be partly responsible for what happened. Something about giving a piece of advice to this young man, this Charlie person, that may have caused a quarrel or some such nonsense. We told him of course that he was absolutely blameless, if people can't deal with home truths and handle their own lives . . . well! But he obviously felt badly about it, so we encouraged him to tell Jenny, get it off his chest. Ask for forgiveness, you know, if it would clear his mind. But as I say, all a big fuss over nothing."

"I see. Thank you. You've been very helpful."

I went to the chair behind the desk and sank into it, no longer apprehensive about being seen from outside.

Across the room, Jenny spoke tremulously, her gaze focused on the corner. "I know what you're thinking, Phoebe, but it's not—" She turned her face to me.

I don't know what she saw, but I know what I was feeling: sorrow for two people who had so needlessly died; sorrow for a young life first dangerously damaged and now ruined. Sorrow—and anger too—for the young woman who could have been my daughter, who had lied to and manipulated me, who had wasted not a minute on our first meeting to impress on me how many people might have it in for Frank. The seemingly fragile young woman with nerves strong enough to go directly from disposing of victim number two to singing at the wake of victim number one—running to my car damp from the shower, carrying the panty hose and make-up she'd had no time to put on. The young woman I had been asked to protect and could protect no longer.

The young woman, I reminded myself, whom I knew beyond any doubt to be guilty and against whom I had exactly zero concrete evidence.

Jenny's face had become, if possible, even paler. She drew in a quick breath. Tears welled and began to run unchecked down her cheeks.

"He told me he was *sorry*," she said. The word was harsh with scorn. "It was in this room. I was sitting right there where you are, trying to type a letter for Anna. Frank came in to give me some vitamin C pills, he said I looked run-down. They were in a plastic baggie and he put the baggie on the desk. Then he said, 'Jenny, there's something I need to tell you.' "

The tears continued to stream. She brushed at them impatiently with the sleeve of the blue wrapper. "And then he said that he'd been the one to tell Charlie he should leave me alone to," she spat out the phrase: " 'get on with my life.' He wondered whether that had had anything to do with . . . what happened later." She gave a bitter laugh and repeated the mopping gesture. "I was so . . . I almost fainted. I should have known, you know, I should have known that Charlie wouldn't have said those things if someone hadn't told him. . . ."

"What did Frank do then?" I said.

"He was looking at me with this worried look and he started to come around the desk. I jumped up and told him not to touch me. I told him he'd murdered Charlie. I told him I hated him. I told him I wished he was dead."

The tears had stopped as suddenly as they'd started. Her voice was flat and a sour smile flickered on her lips as she said, "That's when he said he was sorry. God, how I wanted to hurt him!" Her eyes locked on mine, suddenly wide, full of sincerity. "That's all I meant to do, Phoebe, to hurt him. I didn't mean to kill him."

I gazed back at her. "You gave him poison," I said flatly.

"I didn't know, Phoebe, honestly I didn't!" She was sitting straight now, bare feet braced on the rung of the chair, her body tilted forward. "You know Frank! Well, maybe not—but he was such a hypochondriac, he was always talking about how he couldn't eat this before he sang or he couldn't do that because of his bad back or what the weather was doing to his sinuses. I thought the penicillin thing was just another exaggeration. You saw how I was when we found out he was dead! I couldn't believe it!"

"And Sarah Kirk, could she believe it?"

"That I'd killed Frank? No, of course not—" She broke off with a sudden awareness of what she was saying.

It came to me with force how fatally self-absorbed Jenny was. Now I watched her struggle to regroup.

"Sarah . . . that was . . . oh, Phoebe, it was so awful!" The knees had come up again. She hugged them close to her chest and her hunched shoulders. Her hair fell forward over her face, her body made little rocking movements. "She'd seen me. She saw me through the kitchen window on Sunday morning, putting the penicillin bottle into the trash. I didn't even notice she was there, I was in such a hurry to get back to the office. Everyone else had gone into town or somewhere and I was supposed to answer the phone. And I was sitting there by myself, thinking about how if it hadn't been for what Frank told Charlie . . . And then I remembered the bottle I'd seen in the upstairs bathroom. I went and got it.

There was one pill left and I could see it looked like the vitamin C ones Frank gave me. So I ran to his cabin and . . . and just after I got back the phone rang and it was you, and . . . oh, Phoebe, I just . . . all I meant to do was teach Frank a lesson!"

Her breathing had quickened now so that she sounded much as she had on the phone that day. Of course she didn't know, because I hadn't left a message on the tape, that I had called before. Called during the time when Jenny had been putting the pill into Frank's bottle of vitamin C, wiping the bottle clean, then doing the same to the penicillin bottle . . .

"What did Sarah Kirk say to you?"

"She said I was looking funny, pushing something way down into the bin, so after I'd gone she went and looked. She said she was worried that I might be taking drugs or sleeping pills or something, but when she saw it was just an empty penicillin bottle she put it back. But then when she heard they were asking about penicillin she knew she'd have to tell the police. Only she wanted to check with me first."

She had stopped rocking, the words now spilling out almost eagerly, as if she were narrating a story that had happened to someone else in another time and place. I watched silently, fascinated and repelled.

"So I told her the police knew all about it, that I'd found the bottle on the path and just thrown it away. She said she'd thought it must be something like that, she looked really relieved. But then I thought, She's going to tell them about seeing me and they'll know I lied, they'll know I did it. And . . . Oh, Phoebe, I just panicked, I just wanted to shut her up. She turned away and stooped down to the drawer and I picked up the skillet. . . . It was like I didn't know what I was doing until afterwards and she was lying there with her head caved in and I knew she was dead. I had to drag her into the laundry room without, you know, getting any blood on me or anything and then I had to wash the floor. And the skillet, of course. And all the time I was thinking, Someone's going to come along and see me. But no one did. So I went to the cabin and took a shower and got dressed to go to the city."

"How, Jenny? How could you do it? After you'd just killed another person, how could you behave so normally? How could you face Frank's family, for God's sake?"

Jenny shrugged. "I learned in the hospital," she said, "when I was feeling better enough so I just wanted to get out of there. If you say you're happy and you act like you're happy and like everything's okay, people believe you. I mean, they have to, don't they? Even the doctors. They're not, y'know, as smart as they think they are. And I'm a good actress," she added with a touch of pride.

The understatement of the decade, I thought.

She continued to gaze at my face, a hint of wariness creeping into her expression. "How did you know it was me?"

I had been staring, I realized, openmouthed during Jenny's recital. Now I pulled up my lower jaw and roused myself to answer.

"I saw Anna last night during the performance, looking at you. I could tell she suspected you, it was all there in her face. Pain, sorrow. Horror. I just couldn't think *why*. Until I thought about what happened at the wake."

The smooth brow wrinkled with incredulity. The big eyes narrowed. "Is *that* all? *That*'s what you're going to tell your cop friend? That you *saw* it in someone's *face*?"

"That and the motive," I said. "Once they start looking in the right direction, they're sure to find evidence, Jenny. And then, you see, Frank—"

"No, they won't!" She stood up abruptly, hugging the blue wrapper closer around her thin shoulders. "They won't find a damn thing! Because there isn't anything! And if you try to tell them about what I said I'll say you're lying!" She moved toward the door. I half-rose, thinking she was about to leave, but she whirled around and advanced toward the desk. Her face was flushed now, and not so pretty, distorted with accusatory anger. "You made me tell you all that stuff and you didn't even really know! I thought you were my friend, Phoebe. Do you want me to go to *jail*?"

I stood in turn, facing her across the desk. "That's not the point, Jenny. I am your friend, and I know you'll never be able to live with this. You talked to me just now because you couldn't stand not talking any longer. And if you go on not talking, you'll destroy yourself."

"I suppose you think I should 'expiate my sins,' " she said with a sneer. "Christ, you sound just like my mother! With her, everything was a sin, my dad too. Dancing, wearing nice clothes, being pretty—shit, being happy was a sin, 'cause it must mean you'd been doing something you shouldn't. The only reason music was okay was because they did it in church. Sex, forget it!"

She had begun to pace, restlessly touching objects as she passed—a book, a framed photo, the pencil holder on my desk—pausing every so often to glance at me as if to make sure I was listening.

"Do you know that I never in my life saw my mother and father touch each other? They were both of 'em cold, *cold* people! Hell, they never touched *me* if they could help it. When I found out about sex I couldn't believe my parents could ever have brought themselves to do that! And when they found out about Charlie! I went home once after I'd started living with Charlie. I wanted them to see how happy I was, to know that I'd gotten away from always being miserable and scared and full of hate for everyone that wasn't like them. I lasted for one day. 'He is an evil man, Tesia.' 'You are living in sin, Tesia.' 'You will go to hell, Tesia.' "

Her voice had altered uncannily to become pinched

and hard with self-righteousness. In spite of myself, I shivered. But she had reminded me of something else.

"When did you change your name?"

She pulled up short in her wanderings and blinked at me, momentarily disoriented. "Change my name? Oh . . . two years ago." Her face softened. "Charlie did it. I'd been planning to take a stage name but I couldn't decide, you know, what it should be. And then Charlie came up to me, the first day he was at the Colony, and asked me who I was. And I said, 'Tessie Zgrodski,' and he said, 'No, you're not Tessie Zgrodski, you're . . .' And he stood looking at me for a few seconds, this beautiful, beautiful boy. . . ." She was standing quite still now, her face lifted, eyes focused on memory. " 'You're Jennifer Allen,' he said. 'A lovely sound for a lovely girl.' I fell in love with him right there."

And why not? I thought. The magical Charlie, creator of this new identity, this awakened woman, this Jennifer Allen. Had he had any idea of what he was doing? Had he perhaps been looking for a summer dalliance and found himself instead on the receiving end of a lifetime of pent-up passion, of yearning to love and be loved? Had Frank's suggestion perhaps struck him as a plausible way out?

As if tuned in to my thought waves, Jenny brought her focus back to me. "And he loved me!" she said fiercely. "Charlie could have had anybody, but he loved me! He would never have left me, never! He was the only person who ever, ever loved me!"

Standing in the middle of the room, head bowed, hands hanging limply at her sides, she burst into racking sobs. I jumped up, went to her, and held her tight. Her body felt small and bony as a bird's.

She clung to me until the paroxysm ebbed, then pulled away, searching my face. "You can understand, can't you, Phoebe? How awful it was when Frank told me what he'd done? He killed Charlie, Phoebe, he did! If it hadn't been for Frank, Charlie would be alive, we'd be together! Please don't tell anybody! Frank's dead, we can't do anything about that. I'm sorry he died, I really am, but in a way he deserved it, don't you see?"

My momentary flight of empathy and pity suffered a nosedive. "Did Sarah Kirk deserve it too?"

Jenny took a step backward. "I *told* you I didn't mean to kill Sarah. She was an awful snoop, you know, she shouldn't have been snooping on me."

The flight crash-landed. My tolerance for adolescent self-delusion and self-pity went with it. I grabbed her by the shoulders. "My God, Jenny," I said, "listen to yourself! You sound like a child talking about swatting a couple of flies! Fucking *grow up*!"

Jenny's eyes widened in shock, her mouth dropped open. It took me a moment to recognize that she was reacting not to the message but to its delivery. The surrealism of the situation brought me close to hysterical laughter. Jenny might have killed two people, but mother-figure Phoebe, by God, had used the F word.

She wrenched away from me. "I hate you!" she spat. "If you try to tell, I'll say you lied because . . . because you made a pass at me and I rejected you."

My expression must have conveyed the chances of that one flying, because for the first time I saw the dawning of genuine fear. Her eyes shifted, darting around the room, and her breathing quickened.

Afterward I chose to believe that emotional overload was responsible for my ensuing spectacular lapse in judgment. What this girl needs to wake her up to reality, my suddenly idiot brain told me, is a truly significant shock.

"He wasn't worth it, Jenny," I said. "Charlie just wasn't worth it."

She stared. "What are you . . . How can you . . ."

"That song he gave you, the one he said was only for

you? He gave it to Larry too. He said the poem reminded him of Larry."

"You're crazy! Charlie would never—"

"And Frank. He gave Frank a copy too."

"It's a lie!"

"Ask Larry."

She moved with a speed I probably wouldn't have been prepared for even if I'd been thinking clearly. One moment she was standing in front of me, the next she had grabbed the bowling trophy off the desk and was swinging it, marble base first, at my head. I ducked too late, and it caught me on the temple. As I crumpled, I saw her arm rise again and heard a voice from the doorway say sharply, "Jenny, my darling! That is enough!"

Fortunately, Anna was moving as she spoke. Through the filter of blood that trickled over my left eye, I watched as she and Gerta wrestled the trophy out of Jenny's hands. Watched Gerta pinion Jenny's arms while Anna ran to the kitchen for wet towels.

Watched Jenny's face become slack and empty.

Saw as if it hung in the air before me in all its ironic clarity the entry in *The Ethnic Book of Baby Names*. Under Polish Female Names: "Tesia (from the Greek *Teofila*)— Beloved of God."

30

May all our sorrows and sadness
swiftly vanish far from our mem'ry . . .

act 2, scene 16

TUESDAY, JULY 3

"So Frank was right," I said to the lieutenant, "he did know who his killer was."

"Possibly. Unless he meant Mr. Peterson."

"You mean because of the Mozart-Salieri thing." I shook my head. "No, he knew. Out of all the people he'd talked to in those few days, he would've recognized the ones who were simply irritated with him and the one with the murderous anger. And Larry Peterson was telling the truth, I'm sure, when he said he'd convinced Frank he was pulling 'Larksongs' out of circulation and that he'd been punished enough. Did Larry come to see you yesterday, by the way?"

"Yes, he—"

"Good, I thought he would. I was sure—"

I stopped, suddenly aware that I was talking an awful lot and had been for the past half hour or so. It was eleven-thirty in the morning and the adrenaline, I supposed, was still pumping. Or maybe it was giddiness from lack of sleep due to being woken up every hour of the night by sadistic hospital personnel pretending concern about possible concussion.

I had agreed to go to the hospital only on the condition that one of the uniforms drive me there in my car. After being stitched up (six of 'em, just forward of my left ear) I'd been ready to leave. A very young, very serious intern, however, on learning that I would be alone, had sketched out a dire scenario involving coma and death. I thought of Mrs. Schmitter coming home to a dead body in her upstairs back bedroom, and agreed to stay.

In the morning I'd made my escape as soon as a doctor had been rounded up to pronounce me no longer a danger to myself or others, and headed for the East Hampton Town Police Station to make my official statement. I really, really wanted this to be over.

In a small, generic office room in the station off Montauk Highway, I had sat across yet another desk from the lieutenant as he himself took down my statement, then had me read and sign it. Now he sat quietly while I talked. And talked. Yesterday, action, the puzzling out of the truth, the determination to understand, had sustained me; today it was words.

"You see," I said, "Jason Lee had it right when he said to look for a literal meaning. Larry told me in our first conversation that one of Frank's hobby-horses had been the meanings of names. And given how thoroughly he'd jumped into the Children of Truth business, it was a good bet he did the same with his other enthusiasms— really studied up, I mean. The funny thing is that Jenny didn't pick up on it, I'm sure she didn't. The name thing must have happened the year before she first came to the Colony. You know, when I started looking through all those name books, it was amazing how many came close. Theodore means 'gift of God.' Michael (as in Rita Michaels) means 'who is like God?' Then there's Amanda's original name, Gottfried, which means 'God's peace,' and 'Amanda' itself means 'beloved,' which, put together, could seem pretty significant. But 'Tesia'— for someone who really knew their stuff, 'Tesia' and

'Amadeus' would be pure synonyms, only in different languages. Though why Frank thought anyone else would catch on . . . well, in the circumstances . . ." I shuddered and pushed aside the image of Frank Palermo's final moments. "And I didn't put it together until later, but Larry also told me that Frank had been close to both Jenny and Charlie."

I was running down. Exhaustion, sorrow, and shock were taking their inevitable toll. I came finally to the question I hadn't wanted to ask.

"What will happen to Jenny now?"

"Depends. Her parents are making arrangements for a lawyer. He or she will no doubt want a psychiatric examination, for starters."

"Temporary insanity? Three times?"

The lieutenant shrugged. "The young woman is admitting nothing. But for now she'll be charged at least with the assault on you."

"Where is she now?"

"She's here. Waiting to be arraigned."

I hadn't expected that. My head jerked around as if she might materialize at my side.

"Do you want to see her?"

I shook my head. "No. I think I just want to go home." It would take me, I knew, a long time to deal with my feelings about Jenny. I was too worn out to begin now.

The lieutenant nodded but didn't immediately rise. He really had very kind eyes, I thought. I wondered what sort of sorry spectacle I made. They'd had to shave my head where the marble base had bitten into my skull. I'd made an attempt to look less lopsided by pulling the remaining hair forward over the plastic strip covering my stitches, but the effect was still cockeyed. The cotton pants I'd pulled on for my drive to the Colony last night were wrinkled and sagging. The grey sweatshirt was stained with blood and perspiration, being much too warm for the day. My face felt as if most of it had sunk to the level of my upper lip.

"Claire Delgado asked me to say hi."

"Claire . . . oh, the Princess."

"Excuse me?"

I explained.

The lieutenant smiled. "I'll tell her. She'll love that." He hesitated, then said, "We'll be winding things up at this end in the next day or two. But Yaphank isn't the end of the world. Can I call you? Next week, say?"

"Sure," I said. I wondered if he would. Somewhat to my disappointment, I found I would be fine either way. Perhaps I was just terribly, terribly tired.

Terribly tired or not, when I got back to Mrs. Schmitter's house, I found myself wandering restlessly from room to room. I hadn't stopped to see her in the hospital but I'd inquired and heard that all was well and she'd be home later today. I had, however, before I left the hospital, dropped in on Jason Lee Jones, who, I learned, had checked in the day before.

"Pneumonia, my dear Phoebe. AIDS, you know. I've been HIV positive for three years."

"And Frank knew."

"Yes. Yes. And Larry, naturally, since we are sharing a house. And, as it happens, the good Lieutenant Freed. When the police searched our living spaces they naturally noticed the AZT prescription. I explained to him, by the way, what my small fracas with Frank had been all about—which you can imagine, I'm sure. Foolishly, perhaps, I preferred to keep my status private for as long as I could."

And the lieutenant hadn't told me. Quite rightly. It almost made up for what he'd done to Anna.

Jason Lee already knew the gist of last night's events. I briefly filled in the gaps for him, and, with characteristic delicacy, he didn't press for more.

"You'll be back at the Colony soon?" I said.

"Oh, yes. Surely. You and I, Phoebe, we will set up a barre and take class together."

"That will be wonderful!" I squeezed his hand and went to find my car.

Now, pacing from kitchen to hall to parlor and back, unable to light anywhere, let alone think of sleeping, I gave up. I got back into the Toyota and headed for the Colony.

As I waited for the signal at North Main and Cedar Streets I wondered why the traffic was even more dense than usual. It took a sputter of popping followed by a loud report from down the block to remind me that tomorrow was our country's birthday.

I found Anna in my office in the act of hanging up the phone. Remembering the sinister suspicions I'd been indulging only yesterday, I was feeling considerable embarrassment at now facing my employer. Her brisk normalcy, however, put me at ease. When she saw me, her face creased with concern.

"Phoebe, what are you thinking? You are looking terrible, my darling, you should not be here."

"I couldn't sleep. I guess I needed to come back just to be sure that . . . well, you know . . ."

"That here is still life that goes along? That through this window sun is shining? That even here is Anna Varovna who is making plans, who is being mostly practical?"

"Yes," I said. "That's it."

She pointed at the straight chair. "Sit down, Phoebe, before you are falling over. There." She leaned her elbows on the desk, chin propped on her clasped hands, and regarded me with immense sympathy. Her face, though still shadowed, had lost much of the accumulated tension of the past two weeks. "Is terrible experience you have suffered, my darling. And I am, you see, much blaming myself. I feel I have been mostly blind. I did not know. I fear, yes. I say to myself, of all these people I am knowing so well, who is the most damaged and also the most passionate? But I cannot believe. And I cannot see a reason."

I nodded. That about covered it, I thought. For all of us.

"How did you happen to be here last night?" I said. "And have I thanked you for saving my life?"

Anna dismissed that detail with a wave of her small hand. "I see from my house light shining. And I say to Gerta, Who is going there to office in the nighttime and what are they doing? So we come to find out."

"How much did you hear?"

"Plenty, my darling. I am only sorry we have waited almost too long. I have not expected that the little Jenny will attack you."

She rose, suddenly energetic. "And now, Phoebe, you must go home, you must sleep. Tomorrow will be much to do."

Wow! I thought. Almost getting killed earns me a whole day off! Wonder what would have to happen to get me two?

She took my arm to walk me outside, chatting as we went. With two of the six cast members of *Così fan tutte* now respectively in the hospital and in jail, a substitute performance was needed for the coming weekend. A concert, she thought; we would discuss the details tomorrow. A new program, of course . . . notices to all the papers . . . a special statement to be composed and circulated (to all Patrons, Benefactors, etc.) regarding the conclusion of the murder investigation . . . a clarification of the rules involving student use of the laundry facilities . . . appointment with the accountant . . . By the time we reached my car, some version of "I quit" was struggling to make it out of my brain and onto my lips.

Anna Varovna clasped my left hand in both of hers.

The dark eyes glowed warmly up at me. "You are re-markable woman, Phoebe. I am mostly lucky, mostly grateful that you are here. Thank you, my darling."

Oh, heck. How bad could it be?

By the time I reached Mrs. Schmitter's house, the amassed weariness of the past twenty-four hours had come crashing down on me with avalanche force. At least, I thought as I trudged up the porch steps, I'll have no problem sleeping now.

I opened the front door and started toward the staircase.

From the front parlor a familiar voice, slightly weaker than usual but still full of anticipation, exclaimed happily, "Oh! Phoebe!"

ABOUT THE AUTHOR

KAREN STURGES lives in Western Massachusetts
with her husband and a small dog.